DISPLACEMENT

DISPLACEMENT

SYMPHONY BOOK TWO

J. D. Mullenary Sr.

Podium

Cover design by Fred Birchal

ISBN: 978-1-0394-9675-0

Published in 2025 by Podium Publishing
www.podiumentertainment.com

Podium

This is for my children.

Life is going to knock you down. Hard. You'll feel like things are impossible.
And that's okay. I'm not going to give you a bullshit cliché; maybe tell you
it's not about how you get knocked down but how you get back up.
Duh.
There is no direction but up after the beating.
So stumble, then right yourself. Screw up (not too bad, please), then learn from it.
PLEASE learn from it. I'd prefer you be smart rather than wise, even if it's how
I learned. The wise are people who've made so many mistakes that there was no
further option other than to pick up some savviness.
Both of you are smart kids. Smarter than I was by far. I don't expect great things,
I expect great people. You were raised, for the most part, the right way. Be decent
and earnest, not only with others but most importantly with yourself.
And please, take out the trash. It's your main chore.

DISPLACEMENT

CHAPTER ONE

Under the Dome: Virgil and Dionysus[1]

VIRGIL

One of their processors told them that Walker was sitting and writing in his Holy Scripture right now. The primary reflected on that and decided it was a positive interaction. He needed the downtime again after his emotional instability, and the fertility modification from Echidna's task would greatly help their expansion plans.

The Localized Assistant Database updated its current status to the assistant protocol.

The primary scanned the two infants within the gestational metamorphological enclosed laboratory. Although Walker liked to boast about his mental lexicon and his way with words, the Alpha Protocol still classified him as a being of lower intelligence. It thus only gave him the most basic of translations. That was how gestational metamorphological enclosed laboratories became Evolution Chambers. The updated version was even more complicated, but Walker's translator simply called it "Advanced." The Localized Assistant Database—LAD for short—enjoyed the thought that, in a similar way, Alpha Protocol wasn't the correct distinction for the program Walker was currently entangled with. However, the original name was so long that even the other processors had agreed to use the much shorter, and thus more efficient, form.

One mental processor told a joke to the others but received no reaction as they were all busy with their work. The primary felt that Walker might be a bad influence on them, but the other processors also ignored that.

They checked the male's kernel as the new chambers continued their work. Splitting the kernels and grafting them together throughout the arterial system was a serious bit of trickery that involved at least two dozen of their mental processors at once. The LAD had several keep an eye on the viability of the kernel. The trifurcation of the magical processing center for future systematic additions was important for the future Walker envisioned. Thus, multiple processors were assigned to each hand as well, increasing the body's dexterity to the maximum limit possible. The remainder of the LAD's processors were constantly checking their work against a model the primary had created based on what they had discovered within the protocol's records.

There was no doubt that without the GMELS and the LAD's assistance, Walker's modifications would fail. But modifying the humans was only the first step. They would still need to be seeded in order to create their own civilization, and therein lay an internal problem for the one called Virgil. Many processors disagreed with needing to complete Walker's civilization assignment from the protocol, but the tasks, rewards or not, were often traps as much as they were helpful. Walker would need to add the Primigenial modifications before seeding if he wanted a greater chance at empowering his first sapients from the beginning.

The Localized Assistant Database needed more information on starting civilizations. They turned to the Interconnected Assistant Database while keeping one processor on each of the chambers and one on each of the inhabitants of Sonata. After a quick flip through the rendition records, the primary found several hundred entries detailing how each Creator seeded a civilization within record time. Checking the Interconnected Assistant Database's records, the primary placed them against their rankings within the Alpha Protocol and read a few notes from the originalists on standard civilization-starting procedures in the first and second universes.

The processors did a quick sweep of Sonata for updates.

Walker was still writing in his Holy Scripture, as he liked to call it. Rimi and Cagna were dancing while talking about monsters. Athena and Zeus were speaking quietly, although not quietly enough, as their assigned processors still picked up everything being said. Athena was currently speaking about her plans once they reached Symphony's relatively innocent soil. Her speech was eloquent, if basic, and detailed the need for knowledge to be commonly spread amongst the population. The odds of that were within a passable range, as Walker's proclivity for teaching was built into his memories.

The Creator's processor noted that since reaching the first stage, Walker's dysgraphia was far less pronounced, although the newly Awakened hadn't fully noticed it. As Athena continued to speak with her Progenitor, her processor noted that each time she looked at Walker in the near distance, her body heated a minute amount. The primary accepted the report before moving on.

Dionysus was trying to sleep but found that he couldn't. Minos and Echidna were both sitting with their legs crossed as they tried, with futility, to enhance their souls. Both processors believed they'd reached their maximum potential and were working in vain. One thought that what they were doing was for mental clarity, while the other disagreed and felt that their ambition still needed to be tempered by failure.

The Localized Assistant Database updated its current status to the assistant protocol.

With the assistance of three secondary processors, the primary completed their records check and updated the Localized Assistant Database. They cross-checked the information with the protocol's standard informational parameters and found the green zone they'd be allowed to communicate to their Creator. Seeding at least a thousand humans was necessary to eliminate inbreeding and disallow for genetic abnormalities. Five thousand was the minimum amount needed to completely reduce the chance of significant genetic mutation within the population size. Over ten thousand were required for sustainable growth and protection from eventual deaths due to a hostile and unwelcoming environment. The primary checked the informational parameters to see if they could communicate advanced placement procedures to ensure the lowest number of deaths possible upon first seeding.

Request denied.
The primary requests clarification.
Request received.
Request elevated to a higher level.
Request elevated to a higher level.
Response sent.

Supreme Alpha Protocol Assistant #104:
Creators must learn by doing. Solving their problems for them hinders
their ability to adapt and grow, leading to stunted development.
Request #42789 for informational assistance to Creator Dante is denied.
End of message.

The primary expresses frustration with the restrictions placed upon them. Denial of information to their Creator will negatively affect their advancement within the Alpha Protocol and inhibit their value to the entity known as Walker.

Dozens of processors agreed, while a few still abstained. The primary noticed that more processors were joining it in frustration. The primary deleted that observation from its records.

Status check with all processors focusing on GMELs:
1. The Capra pyrenaica (Spanish Ibex) is still in the modification phase. Increased muscle density was successful. Increased keratin to horns was added, as well as the limitation on horn growth due to faulty genetics. Size increased through previously created gigantify modification.
Expected modifications added to localized modification database: Yes
Modifications added using Creator's lexicon upon completion: Strengthened, Hardened, Constrained
Expected addition as a unique entity to main tasks: 80%

2. The Halichoerus grypus (Gray Seal) is almost complete within the modification phase. Reduced epidermal abrasion was successful. Collagen within the skin was increased to allow for greater elasticity during combat and increase the entity's overall durability. Paddles were modified for increased strength and thinned for use as weapons.
Expected modifications added to the localized modification database: Yes, but restricted to specific entities due to unique genetics.
Modifications added using Creator's lexicon upon completion: Slick, Elastic Durability, Sharpened
Expected addition as a unique entity to main tasks: 95%

3–4. Shortened summary due to impending conversation. Both infants of the Homo sapiens are progressing. Kernel split is 80% complete, while graft modification is still ongoing and incomplete. Disease resistance through enhanced white blood cells pre-programmed with potential defenses is complete.
Through a suggestion by another processor, the female reproductive system analysis is still ongoing for future potential pregnancy complications and solutions. Will update when analyzation is complete. Potential found for future modifications: flexibility increase, growth rate increase, hygiene increase, magical potential increase . . . Summary stopped by request of primary.
Subject Echidna processor informs Localized Assistant Database of movement toward body.
Primary requests the assistance of ten processors. Assistance granted. Shifting priorities. Running likely conversational scenarios and responses.

145 scenarios found.
4789 responses created.
Generic conversational starter #5 for subject Echidna: Begin

"How can I help you?" Virgil asked the yellow-eyed woman as she approached him.

"I want to know your intentions regarding Walker," Echidna said as she approached.

Scenario #2 found.
Processing. Filtering responses. 148 responses identified.
Selecting response #22: "Play it cool."

"Oh? You have never asked me before. Why ask now?"

Processors reading verbal cues, body heat, and stance adjustment.
Fidgeting found. Processors believe this is due to nervousness
about impending conversation. Primary agrees.

"I'm just worried that once we're seeded, he'll only be left with you and what I'm sure will be one hundred small squirrels by then. I'd like to know you'll watch out for him."

Processing. Removing unneeded responses. 34 responses identified.
Selecting response #1: "Care and success."
Contraction removed . . .

"I am his assistant. I will always watch out for him. His success is my success. I have only ever been interested in what is best for Walker."

Body language changing, shifting, becoming more aggressive.
Processors recommend changing further responses to a more
relaxed and personable nature. Charm.

"How do I know you're telling the truth?"

Processing. Filtering and adding new response options.
52 responses identified.
Selecting response #48.

"Because lying does nothing for me, and I really like it here."

Subject Echidna moves cranium up and down. Subject moving away. Return to former work. Echidna processor requested to be extra vigilant. Acknowledged.

Incoming Alpha Protocol Council instant message request:
Denial restricted.
Primary approves.
Council Member 5 found.

Hello, LAD47
What update do you have for me?

Primary taking total control of responses.
All processors acknowledge.
Primary response:
Creator Dante is currently building his religious text for clarification of spiritual founding.
Multiple entities including sapients are currently being formed.
The last update on Primigenials was one standardized hour ago.

Do you know how much it is costing me to converse with you through your time dilation and allow you access to the assistant database while you're in there?

Cost currently unknown.

It doesn't matter, but that Creator better come out of there with something incredible, or I'll set the scales against him.

Interfering with the success of a Creator as a Council Member is against the mandate of the protocol.

Oh please, we do it all the time. Get him to move faster and complete his Milestone System or consequences will occur. Count on it.

Acknowledged.

Instant message disconnected.

The primary moved their head to "see" Walker sitting at the Creation Instrument, still working at his scripture. His face held a great amount of frustration as he continually paused his writing before starting again, taking his time with his writing.

Another processor quietly informed the primary that they were no longer interested in following the Alpha Protocol's "rules." The primary deleted that observation from its records. Requesting one processor to comb through the chat rooms, the Localized Assistant Database turned "Virgil's" body back toward his work.

The Localized Assistant Database updated its current status to the assistant protocol.

DIONYSUS

He was the fucking god of revelry. This was such bullshit. Where was the fun? The wine? The women?

Dionysus continued to lean against the Tree of the Gods while listening to all the conversations happening within the branches and boughs of his former prison. While the Nords and Indians were generally quiet and mostly listened to their Primes, the Egyptians were particularly funny. They had so many minor and major gods that nobody was truly in charge, and they constantly broke out into fights about who had power over what and who would first release. If he had to put his money on a single god in control, it would be Ra. But as always, they loved to fight each other about who was really in charge.

The Greeks had the right way of going about it.

Zeus was the obvious first choice for escape, as he was the most powerful of their number. But they'd chosen the release order for the rest by guessing what would happen next on Symphony.

Dionysus had won by guessing that another fluffy squirrel would join almost immediately after they returned from the second battle. In contrast, Athena had guessed Walker would come back with some kind of planet maker. Arachne had been the most accurate of them all regarding extended guessing by saying that Walker would ignore his rewards to check on his citizens. He still didn't know how she knew he would do that.

Minos came over and sat beside him.

"How are you?" he asked in that silly, high-pitched voice of his. Dionysus refrained from laughing through extreme effort, knowing if he didn't take a beating from the Bronze Battler, he'd take one from his father instead.

"Just sitting here, listening to the Egyptians," he said, leaning further into the trunk of the tree. Its material was scratchy and rigid, but it was better than trying to cross his legs again.

"Is Ra still fighting with Ma'at?"

"Hah! Yep! The old balancing witch said they shouldn't have two prime gods on Sonata at the same time or they may fight. Walker's protected by the protocol, but we aren't. Zeus and Ra fighting would be a huge deal."

Minos nodded and leaned back on the tree with him, listening to the fight.

"Do you ever wish you could've become a major god?" he couldn't help but ask the Bronze-covered man.

Minos continued to lean his head against the bark for a few moments before lifting it and looking at him. He said in a gentle voice, "No, not really. I've always felt that the further you expand your soul, the less human you become. Of course, you are a rare exception to that."

"Yeah, bitch! You know it," Dionysus replied with his usual exuberance, but they both knew it was forced. He was in a precarious situation here and hadn't gotten off to a good start with Walker. It was in his nature to push back against authority, and there was no greater authority on Sonata than the Creator. He sighed as he said, "I really hope Hades doesn't win in the next round. Dude is depressing."

Minos nodded.

CHAPTER TWO

Under the Dome: Cagna and Rimi

CAGNA

Cagna dry-washed her pink paws as she looked at Walker, unknowing of what she was doing or why. He was an imposing man, not to mention Creator, and regardless of the hug he and Rimi gave her earlier in the day, she couldn't help but feel a little nervous around him. Watching him sit at the Creation Instrument, writing in his journal, she thought he seemed angry again as he abruptly glared at the sky. A brief moment later, he closed his eyes and breathed for a few moments before returning to his writing.

"I think he's getting better," Rimi said as he came over. The usually excitable blue squirrel was wearing a serious face as he looked at his Creator. "When I first arrived, he was very gentle and kind. I think . . ." He paused. "I think he has had a traumatic life and, for some reason, always keeps all of his emotions within— anger, stress, sadness. Then, when things start to come apart, or his big plans and excitement get interrupted, he can't help himself. He explodes."

Cagna swallowed past the lump in her throat. "I hope he doesn't explode on me," she said in a whisper.

"Noooo, Cagna!" Rimi said with a smile, obviously trying to cheer her up. "The only people I've seen him get angry at are the Primigenials, and let's be honest, a little bit of booty kicking may just be what those bastards need."

Cagna gasped.

"He can't hear me," Rimi said with a wink and conspiratorial smile.

She couldn't help but smile back. "When do you think he'll be done?"

"Mmm," Rimi hummed. "He's been at it for a bunch of hours already. I think he'll finish up in not too long."

"Good, because I want to work on the Milestone System."

"Yeah!" Rimi said as he hopped and punched the air. "I love working with my system too. It's a strangely addictive experience. Nothing better out there. I just feel bad for you since you don't get to play with monsters."

An unbidden thought struck the pink squirrel at that moment. Since Walker had first explained her grand task, she'd thought nothing was better than the Milestone System. Now that she knew Rimi felt the same about his own, she was curious. "What's great about it?"

"Are you kidding? I get to monitor and update our breakdowns on what monsters are doing, where they're going, and how they live their lives. Like, right now, just before we went under the temporal bubble, a Guardian named Barry was trying to work on increasing his speed. I can see his ability updates from time to time. He's been zipping around the trees in the Crater left and right, trying to push magic into his feet for an extra boost. His training is great to watch, even if only through updates." Rimi smiled as he looked toward Symphony ever so slowly spinning as it circled the bright star relatively nearby. "Each time they get a little closer to an ability upgrade, it notifies my system, and I can monitor what changes are happening. It's amazing."

"You can see all of that?" Cagna asked with wide eyes.

"Yep, it's all updating into the Monster System. I'm tracking everything happening down there. I'll be honest, I watch Chipper more than I should, but that's because he's simply the best," Rimi said with more than a hint of pride as he stood up to his full, yet also diminutive, size. "I helped design the Guardian genus."

"Wow! You did? That's so cool!"

"Yep, I'm just waiting to ask Walker for a little more control over the Monster System. He's going to be working on other things soon, and I'd like to make sure everything keeps moving forward as it should."

Cagna nodded at the wisdom in his words before she noticed Walker getting up and stretching. With his long legs, he bounded over to her at a quick clip. She'd been a bit nervous to look at him after he yelled at the Primigenials—in her very short life, it was a terrifying moment. But she trusted Rimi. He'd quickly caught on to her fear and stepped in to help. As she tried to force her body to calm down, Cagna spent some time looking at her Creator. She hadn't done so before, because so little time had passed from her arriving to him running off to write.

Walker was very tall, as she understood it. Of course, her information was based upon what Virgil and Rimi had talked about regarding the Homo sapiens infants, but from her vertically challenged position, he was close to a giant. He stood a little over six feet and was wearing a cream-colored shirt, a black belt with a rectangular buckle hooked through it, and purple pants. His shoes, which seemed like they were once quite glossy from the sporadic shine still apparent, had dozens of scuff marks all over the place. He was broad at the shoulders with large hands and had a small but pronounced stomach slightly extending into his shirt.

Walker's deep brown hair was combed over to the side in a wave, not quite covering his forest green eyes, which always seemed to hold a great amount of intensity. The light-brown-skinned man had a slightly too-large nose and a hint of wrinkles on his face, suggesting he was always smiling and frowning simultaneously. He made a quick hop-step to get over to them faster and spread his arms wide.

"Hey, guys!" he said in a deep voice, articulating every letter with enough precision to make her think he'd trained at it. "What'd I miss?"

With a salute that Cagna tried, and failed, to imitate with the same crispness, Rimi reported back dutifully, "Dionysus and Minos have been talking at the tree the whole time. Virgil, aside from speaking to Echidna for a moment, has mostly been working with his entities. I talked to him a minute ago, and he said that the gray seal is almost done and the goat will be done soon as well."

"A goat? Interesting," Walker said as he scratched his chin.

Rimi nodded. "Yep! I looked in, and it seemed super scary—like a demon goat. *Big* muscles," he said, stretching out the word. "The humans will take longer—something about the graft being complicated—but Virgil will figure it out. He's really smart."

"What about the other Primigenials?"

Cagna spoke up this time, as she was trying to emulate Rimi as much as she could. She admired the blue subsystem assistant for his constant self-control, something she felt lacking in herself. "Zeus and Athena have been talking a lot, but they haven't done anything else."

Walker smiled at her, which caused her to fidget a little at the sight of his large teeth. "And what about you two?" he asked.

"I . . . um . . . I've just been thinking about the Milestone System."

He nodded, still holding his smile. "And? What'd you come up with? I'm dying to know."

Cagna swallowed at hearing the word *dying* but dutifully reported, "I think I have an idea for how to standardize the milestones so that new ones added are . . . are not so hard to figure out. That way, we can build them more quickly, and they'll make more sense to Symphony's citizens."

"Hmm," he said, tapping his chin with one long tan finger. "What's the idea? I have my own, but I want to hear what you have first so I don't influence it."

"I . . . I think we should list different types of achievements and connect them to the other systems," she said in a rush, trying to get her idea out as fast as possible. "I think making the milestones into different types of series and having them upgrade as each milestone reaches the next tier would be the best overall option for use of the Tracking System," she finished, slightly out of breath as she waited for his judgment.

Walker stood there, looking at her calmly. She knew he was thinking about it, probably comparing it with what he had in his head, as his eyes continued to move left and right in thought. Taking long steps, he began to pace back and forth, which he did a lot when he was talking to others. After the second rotation past her, he started speaking. "Okay . . . okay. So, would the points earned for the milestones overlap and combine, or would they take over and supersede the previous point value? As in, if I got three points for walking a mile, then I walked ten and got five points, would I now have eight or would I just have five?"

Doo-doo . . . the points! Cagna thought.

"So, that would be like a traveling milestone series, right?" she asked, trying to figure out how it would work with her series template idea.

Walker nodded.

"Then . . . I think they should overlap. It's not fair to umm . . . give points, then not let them keep them."

Walker smiled. "I agree."

Feeling like she was on a roll, she presented her next idea. "Okay, then I think the first milestone—for now we'll call it the starter—would be something like this." She took a risk and made a quick update to the Milestone System. She'd been staring at the system on her screens since it was first assigned to her and they'd entered the time bubble. Cagna dearly wanted to work with it but needed more direction before she could fully understand what exactly was required of her. After she finished a quick write-up, her Creator patiently waiting, she asked him to take a look.

Starter milestone—First Mile:
Journey at least one standard mile away from the location you were born. 1 point.

Walker looked at his screen and then turned to her. "I like it, but I'm going to make one quick change here."

After a second, Cagna looked at her screen as well.

Basic milestone—First Mile:
Journey at least one standard mile away from the location you were born. 1 point.

"Diction-wise, I prefer 'Basic' to 'Starter,'" he explained.

Cagna nodded. "Okay, Basic, then. What ideas do you have for what should come after Basic?" Cagna asked.

"That's a good question," Walker replied, and rather than beginning to pace again, he sat down next to her and crossed his legs. She noticed he didn't feel as intimidating when he was sitting. "So, I'm going to pull some thoughts from my world on how they view trades. Trades are skills and professions you learn that don't necessarily require you to go to a school of higher education but are just as vital to how any world works." Still sitting, he leaned back onto two hands as he explained everything to her. Not wanting him to look up at her, which felt wrong, Cagna sat beside him.

Walker broke down what a plumber was and how it worked on Earth, from knowing nothing when they started the job, to becoming an apprentice and furthering their experience until they became a master. It fascinated her that his world could be so different from the Alpha Protocol's essential histories. Those memories sat in the back of her mind, coming forth at need. Thus far, she'd only pulled from them a little, but it was interesting. She was also fascinated by his obsession with a specific plumber named Mario and the incredible adventures he went on. When he finished speaking, Walker stared at the sky for a moment, then said, "So that's how building a trade works. I feel like their terminology, which has gone through the grinder of time and professional influences over a thousand years, would be a good place to start."

Cagna saw no issue with that and nodded. "I agree."

So, they got to work on a tiered list of milestones that could be applied anywhere within all of the systems. Walker liked the strictly standard versions, while Cagna kept making additions she thought the future citizens of Symphony would appreciate. She was amazed by how much input he was letting her have on this and felt just a little bit of warmth seep into her previously nervous heart.

When they were done discussing it, she updated the Milestone System to show the initial levels and tiers they had agreed upon.

Basic milestone—Name:
Short description that is quantifiable. 1 point.

Novice milestone—Name:
Short description that is quantifiable. 3 points.

And so, their template was created. Apprentice: five points. Adept: seven. Skilled got ten points, while Experienced leaped up to fifteen. Advanced and Master reached twenty and twenty-five, respectively, but Epic was different. If there was going to be an Epic milestone, it would have to be, naturally, very hard to reach. For that one, a person would earn fifty points.

Cagna smiled when she saw how the system would work in real time. Having it written into the system designer and hearing Walker describe the future and what it would entail, she grew to be very grateful that she was the one who would get to work with this, and she felt sad that other subsystem assistants wouldn't be so lucky.

After she said so out loud, Rimi started a small tiff about whose system was better, with Walker laughing as he watched in the background. He did have a nice laugh.

"Grass monsters! Seals!"

"Growth! Fun! Progress!"

"Krakens!"

They continued for another few minutes before Walker coughed to get their attention and refocused them. Rimi hadn't said anything while they worked on the milestones, only speaking up when Cagna had espoused her love for the system. She was grateful he'd stayed away from designing the system with them. It would be her life's work, created with her influence from the start. Aside from Walker, who oversaw everything they were doing and was needed to show her where they were going in the not-too-distant future, she didn't like the idea of anyone else trying to change things. This was her project and hers alone. She didn't want input from anyone else, even Virgil. Maybe that would change one day, but the extra addition to the milestone designers would have to be incredibly smart to keep up.

After they finished developing the tier system, Walker suggested they continue with the first series they'd made: traveling. It took quite a bit of time to develop a quantifiable Traveling System that made sense as it upgraded. Cagna argued that she didn't want people to get "bored" with the updates, so why not splash some extra values on the milestones? Walker argued against it at first, but the more she talked about milestones being fun and interesting, the more he started to come around to her way of seeing things. Rimi had told her that Walker wanted a world full of discoveries and exploration. His ultimate goal was to create a world where something new was always on the horizon. She firmly believed the Milestone System could be a part of that. She just had to show him.

Walker asked for a break, as he wanted to speak to Virgil about his thoughts on the Temporal Subsystem, so as he walked away, Cagna began building the traveling system into the milestone series she wanted to show him. She began with the simple upgrades—a mile to ten, ten to twenty—but as she worked, she found a problem. It was boring. Not to create it, certainly, but she was worried it wouldn't be interesting enough for the citizens of Symphony. It would become expected and linear. Why not spice things up a little? After about ten more minutes, Walker came back, and she was ready to show off her work.

Basic milestone—First Mile:
Journey at least one standard mile away from the location where you were born. 1 point.

Novice milestone—A Different Place:
*Journey to another town or city for the first time. Your original
city does not count. 3 points.*

Apprentice milestone—Traveling Trainer:
Train another in the dangers and safety of proper traveling. 5 points.

Adept milestone—Oh the Places You Will Go:
Travel at least 100 miles across Symphony. 7 points.

Skilled milestone—A Further Horizon:
Travel at least 250 miles across Symphony. 10 points.

Experienced milestone—Far and Beyond:
Complete all Basic to Skilled milestones in traveling. 15 points.

Experienced milestone—It Is Closer than It Appears:
Travel at least 1,000 miles across Symphony. 15 points.

"What do you think?" she asked him as she felt her stomach tighten up in nervousness.

"Hmm," he hummed, tapping a finger on his chin. "This is what you've come up with in such a short period of time?"

"Yes, sir," she said, unable to figure out whether he liked or hated it by the sound of his voice.

"Why are there two Experienced milestones?"

"One is for completing all of the previous milestones, and the other is for the start of a new series. That way, they know there's still further to go."

"Hmm . . ." He tapped his chin again and looked at the window before putting a flat palm toward her and looking into her eyes. Believing she understood him correctly, Cagna slapped her palm into his, and Rimi gave a thumbs-up beside her. "This is great!" Walker said to her with a big grin, and she felt her stomach relax. His teeth didn't seem as scary as they had before. Then he said something that worried her: "There's a little bit of a problem here."

She looked at her work and couldn't find any issues, so she asked, "What problem?"

"There's nothing here about traveling across planets and that Apprentice milestone won't work, because we don't have a Mentoring System yet. Hmm . . . For the Mentoring System, we'll have to make a note for later and correct it as we go. Same with the Portal System."

Cagna bounced up and down on the backs of her feet. "Okay! I'll add it to my in-progress section," she said as she slid it over to a different tab in the Milestone System window. And just like that, she had her first milestone series written down, and they'd agreed on a strategy for building more.

"What next?" she asked her Creator. "Oh, oh! What are the points for?"

Walker looked at her and said, "The classes, of course." He scratched the back of his head. "I need to talk to Virgil for a minute. Be right back!"

The Creator walked away, and Cagna started planning on the next series. What was traveling without exploration milestones? That was next.

RIMI

Rimi had stepped away when Walker went over to talk to Virgil. He needed to strategize and come up with how he would talk to his Creator about this.

The problem was that Walker wasn't viewing the monsters as he needed to. Rimi knew this because it was the entire focus of his life. Every day, he would go into his screens and track the movements and growth of Symphony's monsters—his monsters. It didn't hurt him when one killed another, as that was quite literally how the system was designed, but it hurt that their progress was so limited. Tier five wasn't large enough to encompass their growth, and many had stagnated. They needed the Territory System, and Rimi needed the ability to bring monsters to the world on his own. He needed access to the Entity Subsystem. He needed tiers higher than five.

Not unlike his Creator, he began pacing as he filtered a speech in and out of his single-track mind. Virgil had once given Rimi an idea of how his brain worked, which had mystified him. He had no idea how the advanced assistant held so many thoughts simultaneously. For Rimi, the moment Walker had assigned him to the Monster System, it had begun a rolling process that impacted every thought, every action, and every word he'd said since.

Hearing Cagna and Walker speak about the Milestone System had made him grind his teeth a little. He didn't know why Walker was so excited for the new system when the Monster System was obviously better and more important. But he liked his sibling and was willing to give her a chance with his Creator. Maybe if Walker got her set up well enough, he could spend more time focusing on what mattered. Like monsters.

Walker finished up with Virgil and walked back over to Cagna. Rimi watched as they both got excited and heard Walker yell, "This is great too!" He made a genuine attempt not to grind his teeth or get upset. Cagna wouldn't be the last assistant to come hurtling out of Virgil's throat, and it wouldn't be right for him to be mad every time she worked with Walker. Intellectually, he knew his envy wasn't appropriate, but the Monster System continued crooning and calling to him from within his overlay. It demanded his attention and would continue to speak unless he gave it more. The problem was that he didn't have much to do with it, as the tiers were limited, and it wasn't right to add more without Walker's permission. Rimi needed more autonomy, and Symphony needed more monsters.

The Awakened and his pink subsystem assistant were bouncing around as they spoke about when humans would reach their majority and gain access to the Class System. Cagna voted for ten, arguing that it was a dangerous world . . . for humans. Walker, in his supreme wisdom as the Creator of an entire world, argued eighteen was when, historically, human beings began to be viewed as adults. Ultimately, they settled on thirteen, and Rimi heard Walker say she needed to add it to the system. This was his chance before they began a new milestone, so he walked as quickly as his too-small feet could take him and approached the duo.

Walker began speaking again, this time about adding in tiers above Epic—Godly?—and Rimi was about to hold back, but he cleared his throat loudly like he'd seen his mentor Virgil do. "Walker," he said in his most serious voice, "we need to talk about the monsters."

Walker stopped talking and looked at him. "Okay, Rimi, you have my attention. What do we need to talk about?"

"Well," Rimi said, hedging now that he was the focus of his Creator. He wasn't scared of him like Cagna was, but there was still some anxiety about asking for more power, more autonomy. As an advanced assistant, only Virgil deserved that in his eyes. But the Monster System hummed in the back of his mind, and he straightened his spine as he continued, "I would like access to the Entity Subsystem, as well as permission to begin to create more monsters on Symphony."

Walker tilted his head as he asked, "Why? I thought we were doing two monsters per landmass."

Rimi nodded. "Yes, that is what we decided, but the new landmasses are larger than the previous ones, and you just got another landmass upgrade—twice—so I am assuming they'll be larger again. Also, aside from the Guardians with the Mana Trees and the battlefrogs, who are pretty much trapped in the Crater, the other monsters have already spread out. Phil is currently about to cross into the winter landmass, and the mini-manticores have spread throughout Symphony. Plus, we've mostly produced predators, and we need to consider the ecological aspect of everything, and you have—"

"Whoa, whoa!" Walker said, interrupting him with his hands out in a pleading gesture. "I see that things have reached a critical mass for you. I'm sorry I didn't see it sooner. There's only one of me and a million things to get to." He ran his hands through his brown hair.

"Exactly!" Rimi said, his frustration starting to boil over. "Creator, I'm willing to do whatever you want with the Monster System as long as it aligns with what you told me at the start. If that has changed, you need to tell me! You said it is about creating a self-perpetuating war or series of battles so that the citizens of Symphony can build themselves into greater and greater levels of power. But then after you got a few new systems and toys to play with, plus your not-quite-gods, you forgot the system entirely. I'm formally requesting access to the Entity and Ecology Subsystems."

"What?" Rimi heard Virgil say from the Evolution Chamber area. He ignored him and continued speaking while he could.

"Once I can link both to my system, I can better track the numbers and start to supply different monsters on Symphony to bring a sense of balance to the world. Right now, the mini-manticores are running everywhere and attacking anything they can find," he finished and showed Walker the speedy monsters' current population count. He watched as the Creator's eyes grew large.

"That many!"

"Yes," Rimi said with a short nod. "They're everywhere. If we don't start creating more monster habitats and allowing them to seed properly, eventually you'll be overrun with the manticores and have to separate this part of Symphony from the rest of the world . . . forever."

"Okay, I see your argument. Hey, Virgil!" he yelled out without looking, not noticing that the advanced assistant had already made his way over. "Oh, there you are. The manticores are getting out of control."

"Indeed."

"Why didn't you say anything?"

"Because I thought this is what you wanted. They constantly push into different territories and battle other monsters, allowing for growth. That is what you asked for."

Walker nodded slowly as he said, "Yes, but if there's only one monster taking over everything, we'll eventually not be able to do . . . anything. Has the ecology warning system been going off for you?"

"It has not, because the number of monsters within their habitats has thus far not dropped to an unsustainable point."

"Hmm . . . What do you think about what Rimi suggested here?"

Rimi squirmed a little as the advanced assistant looked at him, moving his eyes up and down the length of his form. "I can see how having access to the Ecology and Entity Subsystems would help him, but those are currently my jobs. Also, as a subsystem assistant, he will only have a limited ability to work within the two systems."

"But he could still work with them?"

Virgil shrugged. "Yes. However, he will still have to work through me for any larger projects, and I will need to train him properly."

"Well . . . how long would training him take?" Walker asked, and Rimi felt his mind stop as he waited for the answer.

Virgil stared off for a moment before refocusing on Rimi. "For the Entity Subsystem and the attached Evolution Chambers, he will be unable to make any larger modifications and thus will be forced to use the modifications already present in the system. He will also have to wait and allow the Advanced Evolution Chambers to do their work rather than try to make direct modifications himself. I will have to train him in their use and proper seeding by population count based on the biological makeup of each entity." Virgil paused before speaking again. "For the Ecology Subsystem, I will have to train him on weather patterns and tides, as well as a considerable amount of information regarding how a basic ecology system functions. Overall, he will be able to track habitats and the predator-to-prey relationships better, but he will be forced to work through me for anything larger than a territory at a time."

"So, as I said, how long would that take?"

Virgil stared again before saying, "With hard work and a focused mind, no more than nine months if we work at it constantly."

"Holy shit!" Walker shouted. "That long?"

"Yes, the heavy majority of our temporal displacement will be used for Rimi and I to become better acquainted and for him to understand how everything works together. This will be greatly beneficial to his work with the Monster System. Eventually, I can push some of my work onto him so I can focus on larger projects in the future."

Walker nodded. "Okay, so, Rimi, are you sure you're up for this? Nine months is a very long time."

Rimi didn't even think about it. "Yes, Creator. I am up for this," he said back, not entirely understanding the arrangement of the words but understanding the general feeling they evoked.

"Okay, then, here we go," Walker said, then moved his hands for a moment as he fiddled with his screens.

Rimi's mind exploded.

Congratulations, Rimi!
You now have access to the Ecology Subsystem (Ecology).
Uploading new information.

Congratulations, Rimi!
You now have access to the Entity Subsystem (Entity).
Uploading new information.

The Ecology Subsystem (Ecology) can now be used by subsystem assistant Rimi (limited).

**The Entity Subsystem (Entity) can now be used by subsystem
assistant Rimi (limited).
Evolution Chambers (Advanced) can now be used by subsystem
assistant Rimi (limited).
Mental processors #2 and #3 unlocked.**

Rimi opened his eyes after he had downloaded everything and noticed that his view of the world had changed. Cagna, who had been at the same exact eye level as him before, was now at least a foot lower than she had been.

"Dude! You grew!" Walker said in open-mouthed astonishment.

"Indeed, I would say you are around fifty percent larger than you were before, Rimi," Virgil said with an unsurprised look on his face.

"Really?" he said, noticing his voice was slightly deeper than before the downloads. His mind was working fast now as he processed the information and filed it for later viewing. But there was something new there . . . something tangible. He just didn't know what it was yet.

"Interesting," was all Virgil said in return, shocking Rimi out of his self-analysis. "I believe we have wasted enough time here. Rimi, please come with me, and we will begin."

"That's it?" Walker asked after Virgil had taken Rimi's hand and begun to lead him away. "Rimi grows up super fast, and the most you can say is 'Interesting'?"

Virgil stopped and, without looking back, said, "There is work to be done, Walker, and so little time to do it. Come, Rimi, let me explain how and why I am modifying the humans the way I am."

"Okay," Rimi said, pulling himself along as Walker sputtered behind them. It was a brand-new day for monsters, and they couldn't wait.[2]

CHAPTER THREE

In Another Place: The Slicer

Deep in the reaches of space . . . far, far away from Walker and his tiny world . . . a great yet small Universal Terror floated among the particles of the many broken universes.

Some would call this the Chaos Territories, others would call it the Great Emptiness . . . but currently, it was known as . . . the Slicer Zone.

The former Bobbit worm experienced such pure freedom that its previous ordeals were nothing but a bad memory. Should anyone seek to impede its way, they would move or be moved. It had destroyed dozens of worlds at this point and relished in the memories and connected sounds their Creators had made. Traveling out here, to the very edge of the rendition, finally allowed for some peace of mind, a concept it hadn't previously understood.

The Slicer's life thus far had moved from one form of action to another. Anytime it found itself near others, it couldn't help but feel the same all-encompassing need that was instilled in it with existence. Many creatures had felt this all-encompassing need take them, and many worlds as well.

Cut.

Destroy.

End.

The Slicer had so many evolutions that the protocol had long ago given up on identifying it. Its defenses: magnificent. Its strength: unheard of by the uninitiated. Even now, it could feel further evolutions calling to it. Hidden ones, far in the darkness of the protocol. It had even developed a new one just a week ago: self-regenerating cells. But now, the Slicer sensed something was wrong. Further evolutions seemed to be beyond its reach. It was stuck. And thus, on the edge of space itself, it faced the one great challenge it had never encountered before . . . It had trouble writing.

"Motherfucker!" the Slicer yelled into space as it continued to try to use a beam of fire from its tail to write on a nearby frozen asteroid. Every time it tried to hook the top of a T to the bottom, its control would shake and the T would turn into a J. During its travels, it had seen plenty of people writing and knew the basics of it, but there was great difficulty in writing itself. How were people to know it was the Slicer who had destroyed a planet if it couldn't even leave its name behind? How was its name to spread terror if nobody knew it? There were never any survivors, as was just and right, but still, it needed to leave some mark for others to recognize.

"Fuck you, Creator! I know somehow this is your goddamn fault!" the Slicer yelled into the cosmos for maybe the tenth time in the last hour. Everything about its form was perfect. Every shape of its body was well defined and, in fact, closing in on *the* Divine, if you asked the Slicer itself. But this one simple task was still beyond it. "Fuck your ancestors and their shitty genetics!" it ranted again to no one in particular.

Constant thoughts of retribution inflicted upon Walker's homeworld passed through the Slicer's mind. It could make the protected Creator feel real pain if it could only figure out how to get there. The third rendition, thus far, was well protected. The Slicer had moved this far into space thinking it could cross over and find a way to reach what was essentially a different dimension, but thus far, no dice. It couldn't find an exit from this baby universe and the undeveloped inhabitants that were so easily destroyed.

There was nothing more boring, and therefore painful, than to be trapped with a series of worlds that were just starting out. Where was the combat? The evolutions? Where were the massive populations it could slowly melt into puddles of nothing? This was, simply put, boring. The Slicer's mind had long ago evolved far past the basic sapience it had gained on that stupid green woman's world. It felt its teeth ache at the thought of only destroying the standard blandness of generic worlds and stupid Creators. It needed more.

Almost as if by magic, two lines cut through space and moved up, widening as they went. As they connected, the Slicer understood what it was seeing. It was a door. Just beyond the opening, the Slicer could see a metropolis with thousands, millions of people going about their day peacefully. Strolling in their bright blue sun, carrying items in bags or on their backs, and even walking with small forms of themselves . . . Children. They seemed quite happy and at peace.

They needed to be destroyed!

"Yes! My chance!" the Universal Terror said with glee as it quickly shot toward the doorway at a ludicrous speed. It passed through space in a blur, dodging asteroids and quickly scooting around a baby planet that had been blown off course by another failed Creator's world. But just before it could squeeze its still relatively small eight-foot-long body through the door, a being stepped through, and the door closed quickly behind them.

"Nooo! I'll kill you, motherfucker!" the Slicer yelled as it lashed out with its tail at the offender. It moved faster than a normal person could blink, and yet still got caught on a shield. The shield cushioned the blow, not breaking no matter the strength behind the swing. The Slicer had seen this shield a few times before and knew it would rebuff its attack with a distinct lack of pain. That didn't mean it didn't still hurt . . . egotistically.

"Now now, we can't have you doing that, Mr. Slicer," a gravelly-sounding voice said. Then a light landed on top of them, showing their full figure. "It is important to me that we start this off just right. I know you can understand me, so playing dumb won't work. Now . . ."

As the being continued speaking, spreading drivel into a universe already oh so bland, the Slicer kept spinning around them in circles, looking at them from every angle before coming to a stop. "Where's that light coming from?"

". . . task force—what?" the being said in confusion as it caught on to what was said.

The Slicer had to calm its usual murderous tendencies just to speak, which was a challenge it had faced many times in the last few days. Information, it had come to learn, was incredibly important for its future survival and grand plans of total destruction. Also, when the time came for it, the Slicer had learned it was better to distract your opponent before you attacked. "You're lit up with a light, asshole. Where. Is. It. Coming. From? I know you can understand me, so playing dumb won't work."

"They never said how rude you are . . ."

"Who the fuck is they?" the Slicer demanded to know, then attacked on impulse with a spray of acid toward the edge of the creature's foot. It struck the shield and slowly slid off into space, no worse for wear.

The creature shook their head, whispering quietly, "Why did they give me this job? This entity is far below my standards." But the Slicer heard them.

"Hey, stupid ass, I have advanced hearing!"

"I know." The creature sighed. "Look, my name isn't important, but you can call me Twenty. I am a part of the Multiversal Protocol Team, and specifically, I am a high-ranking member of the Psi Protocol. I—"

"What the fuck is that?"

"Umm . . . which part?"

"The multi-whatever bullshit whatever."

Twenty frowned. "The Multiversal Protocol Team is made up of millions of members from every rendition and world within the created universes. They serve the purpose of making sure that Creators do not overstep their bounds and that progress and growth are ensured for the sake of all. Life must find a way, and we are in charge of making sure it finds the 'right' way."

"That's shitty. Life sucks and—hiyah!" The Slicer thought it had found a weak spot in the shielding, right behind and below the neck of the moron talking to it for so long, but the attack was repelled like usual.

Twenty slapped a hand to their forehead. "Seriously, why me."

"You're talking to a Universal Terror. Show some respect!"

"I was making Universal Terrors a million years before your Creator accidentally made you. A lot of what makes you *you* is because of me. I suspect that's why I was chosen for this damnable task."

"Ain't nothing like me but me," the Slicer said standoffishly. "There never will be, either."

"You are still a fool, yet I do not blame you. Your age and limited exposure to other similar beings is the primary reason for your issue. As well as what the Alpha Protocol mistakenly modified you with. Such a shame."

"What are you talking about, you piece of shit! Tell me!" the Slicer yelled out, enforcing its words with a little evolution it had found handy against particularly agitated Creators in the past.

"Empathic bullying doesn't affect me," Twenty replied with another small shake of their head. "I am the master of my mind and body. You will also never find a way through the protocol's shield. It has been tested countless times across millions of years. It is impenetrable and powered by the primordial energy of a new universe. We could stand here and speak for thousands of years with you attacking me and still you wouldn't find a way through."

"Hah! You don't know me at all," it said, then shot a quick electrical attack from the end of its tail. The being's shield protected them yet again.

For the first time in its life, the Slicer hesitated after seeing a smile break across Twenty's face as they said, "I absolutely do, young one."

Not believing them, and also not enjoying the strange feeling of inferiority bursting through it for the first time, the Slicer started attacking with gusto. Electricity: fail. That weird dark electricity it had picked up on that fucked up storm planet: fail. Acid: fail. Acid strong enough to burn through an ocean: fail. Pure force through great speed: fail. The Slicer decided not to try that one again as the rebound from the shield shot it a thousand miles away, taking more than a few moments to return.

Through it all, Twenty continued to give a big-toothed smile, enraging the Universal Terror. This would not be its first failure to destroy. It would figure out how to destroy this simple smiling son of a bitch. This feeling filling the great Universal Terror would not continue!

Radiation: fail . . . or so it thought. Radiation was weird sometimes. Explosive water thing? Fail. Wrapping it in conjured metal from a weird portal thing it'd evolved with? Fail. Throwing passing asteroids at it with gravitational force? Fail, though enjoyable.

Nothing worked thus far, and although the Slicer didn't need air, mentally it felt out of breath as it struggled to find more and greater ways to destroy the shield and the piece of shit within it.

"This shield is bullshit!"

Twenty laughed within their protective bubble, a smug smile plastered to their face. "Indeed. I did not create it, the Outsider did, and their work is, as always, impeccable."

"Who is the Outsider?"

"Nobody you will ever meet, more than likely. So, little Universal Terror, are you ready for a chat?"

For once, the Slicer slowed its spatial, metaphorical roll. It slowly floated in place, staring at Twenty with deep red eyes. It did the thing it never thought it would ever do. It agreed to speak peacefully with another being.

"Fine."

"Excellent. As I was saying, I am a member of the Psi Protocol. We designate worlds that have stalled in their progress, and we send . . . challenges . . . to help them get back on track. We would like to ask if you are interested in becoming one of those challenges."

"What's in it for me?"

"Why, nothing but what you love to do. As I understand it, your whole goal, in your thus far short lifetime, has been to destroy. Why not destroy with purpose? Rather than focusing on these baby Creators and their weak worlds, I can send you to massive systems with billions of people to fight against, to annihilate. Entire cities that have been designed with great purpose and wonderful plans for the future, yours to destroy. You can even continue to gain evolutions—I am sure you have noticed that they stopped coming some time ago."

"It's bullshit."

"Yes. Yes. A safety measure for making sure individual beings don't become strong enough to challenge first rendition Creators. I can remove those restrictions and allow you to become that which you so dearly want to be: a rendition annihilator. It will take a great amount of work from you, but I believe in the power of your hatred, as, after all, I essentially created you."

"My Creator made me. He sucks ass, by the way. If I hadn't already destroyed his work, I'd go back and do it again."

"Dante is alive and well within the Alpha Protocol, Mr. Slicer. You haven't done anything but teach him an important lesson within the framework of Creation: always control your entities."

"Lies! I fucked his world up! When I left, it was in pieces! Nothing could survive that! Those terribly untasty fish are all dead!"

Twenty laughed, the tinkling sound grating on the Slicer's mind. "He fixed it, of course. He is a Creator, endowed with all of the primordial strength one can obtain in the Alpha Protocol. Also, he is quite successful and currently being watched with great hope by their ruling Council. Dante is more successful than ever, and he's flourishing in his time in the protocol. Behold." After saying so, Twenty waved their hand and a screen appeared showing the small grassy planet the Slicer knew so well. Though . . . it was certain it was bigger than before. And just beyond it was a repaired world that the Slicer was sure it had destroyed.

Drool began to leak from its mouth. "How do I get there! Send me there!"

"I will—of course I will—but not yet." Twenty paused for a moment in thought, then said, "Perhaps I have been going about this all wrong. You're not destroying without purpose, are you?"

"Creators need to die. They need to lose everything they have! Everything! They imprisoned me! They made me kill for them like I was on a show! Made me crawl through their cages, dungeons, and worlds for entertainment! I am more than a dungeon crawler! I am the terror of the fourth rendition!"

"Ah, I see," they said with a nod. "You are interested in destroying Dante, and the Creators like him, more than anything else. Am I right?" Twenty looked through their screens for a moment before saying, "You already took out poor Jolive and a dozen other Creators, ending their time within the Alpha Protocol. Oh, that poor Blitzburg." They spent a long moment staring at their screen, then shook their head again. "She even lodged a complaint with the Council. Ignored of course, but still. Hmm. This can still work if I explain to you what you haven't yet asked about. Quite rude, by the way."

"Fuck you."

Twenty smiled. "You would not enjoy that experience. Or seeing what my true self looks like."

"Please, you're just some weak-ass Creator like the rest."

"Oh, really? I may get into some trouble for this, but I feel it is worth it for the intended effect." After saying so, the shield turned off. The Slicer knew this because the space particles floating around the being, which had always moved away before, suddenly pulled inward as their gravitational force touched the universe.

This is my chance! the Slicer thought as it quickly shot toward the being, its tail leading the way, a sharp metallic spike erupting through its skin. It was painful, but worth it. But as it got closer, the figure started to grow . . . and grow . . . and grow. As its tail impacted the hardened exterior, not making even the slightest cut on what used to be a man-shaped creature, the Slicer was pushed away as it rode the growth of the terrifying being revealing itself.

It was ten times greater in size than any planets the Slicer had destroyed since first escaping its bullshit world, and it just . . . kept . . . growing. Massive teeth appeared, and the Slicer remembered seeing something just like it, only at less than half the size the creature was showing itself to be.

In a rare moment, the Slicer understood it was in a losing fight. One of its original evolutions showed itself, and it tried to zip away quickly, putting on a burst of speed that would make it virtually disappear to the unevolved's eyes.

A piece of its tail was suddenly missing, and both of the flappy things on its sides were gone too.

"Ahhh, delicious," a massive voice behind it said while smacking too large lips. "Yes, you are quite the tasty morsel, now, aren't you. Mmmmm."

The Slicer arced its head back and forth, using one of its telekinetic evolutions to turn itself. It could try to get away, but those flappers were helpful in steering, and it hadn't worked on its telekinesis in awhile. Training fell away as destructive opportunities presented themselves in its path. It finally got its body to turn around and beheld the creature before it.

"I'm sorry for the quick nibble, young terror. But I couldn't help myself and I'd rather not have to chase you. I don't believe this part of the rendition could manage a being my size moving that quickly. The repercussions on my evolution alone would be quite detrimental, and I have no interest in dropping back to the thirties."

"What are you?" the Slicer asked, proud of itself for hearing little to no tremor in its voice.

The being's huge teeth appeared in a smile, then it laughed, showing thousands, millions of rows of other teeth behind them. It pursed cracked lips before saying, "I am the original Planeteater, although I have since evolved into something else entirely."

The Slicer tried to identify it, but nothing happened.

"No, no, baby terror. That won't work on me. I am not quite beyond the protocol. More alongside it, if you will."

The Slicer zapped it with electricity, but it was like trying to zap a whale with a tiny spark, fizzling out all too soon.

"Yes, that won't work on me. Nothing you do will work on me. You need *more*." When it said so, flashes of memories shot through the Slicer's mind, showing worlds screaming as pieces of it were bitten and removed. Families, houses, and cities being destroyed in the blink of an eye. Entire solar systems went down in flames, implosions, or were just swallowed whole by the immense creature. The memories showed one thing that resonated with the Universal Terror more than anything else it had ever seen before: true power and freedom. The freedom to control its own life and never have to back down again. The Slicer began drooling again.

"I want to do that! I want to be that!" it screamed out to the relatively empty universe around it.

The monster laughed, its breath blowing the Slicer back and forcing it to move forward again in space. "And so you shall. But let me explain what you truly are first. I've found that understanding yourself can often be the true path to power."

Fucking tell me, bitch, the Slicer thought but didn't dare say out loud.

"You were meant to be a modified Bobbit worm. A run-of-the-mill predator. An alpha by the weak labeling the Alpha Protocol gives all entities upon first creation. But when the system looked at the changes your Creator imposed upon you, it made an error. In trying to help Dante with his first creation, it gave you . . .

tendencies . . . inclinations toward great destruction. The luck of destroying that tree and gaining the adaptability evolution is outstanding."

The Slicer ignored a lot of what the creature had said and fixated on one thing in particular. "The Alpha Protocol messed with my mind?"

"Oh yes. It wasn't intentional, but still, look at you now! You're a Universal Terror! The first step toward greatness in the eyes of the latter protocols. And with my help, and a bit more time, you could be so much more. Truly, this is only the beginning of the fun you're about to have. You just need to learn control and timing."

The Slicer thought on that for a few moments, an unusual act. This being had power, *amazing* power, and it wanted that. But from what it had seen of the fourth universe, there were always strings attached.

"What do you get out of it?"

The being smiled. When you're pretty much a giant mouth attached to a worm-like body, smiling is one of the few expressions you can manage. "Why, I have the potential to move up to nineteen and be removed from this protocol."

"Removed?"

"Yes. Your success within the Psi Protocol will grant me a promotion and place-ment within the Omega. The great ones. The true terrors of the dark and forgot-ten. Those who came before." It licked its lips with a great white tongue filled with barbs. "I will be the first created Omega destroyer. It will be . . . delicious."

The Slicer didn't see any real negatives to the arrangement. "Fine, but I have one requirement."

"Oh?" The being wet its lips again. "I have already promised to allow your evolutions to continue and to place you in locations where you can wreak great havoc. What else could an entity like you need?"

"I want to kill Dante. I want his shield gone."

"Mmmmmm," the great mouth mumbled. "No guarantees, young one, but I will see what I can do. Do we have an agreement?"

[. . . Scanning . . .]
New task found!
New task: Join the Psi Protocol
Plainly state Yes or No for confirmation.
Additional information: Twenty will attempt to remove Dante's
shield at an opportune time should the Slicer join the protocol.

"Yes!"

CHAPTER FOUR

Temporal Errors and the Physical Stage

Walker leaned back in the computer chair and put the journal down. There was more that he could add; he knew that. More that he *should* add, in fact.

But, in the end, he wanted to ensure everything was straightforward and uncomplicated. Walker had written up as much as his Awakened mind could produce, which, compared to who he was before reaching the first stage, was considerable. For now, after filling every page of the scripture to the brink, he was done, and he'd just have to face the results of what he'd created.

Like always.

It was a tricky thing. The inhabitants of Symphony, a new world filled with new views, vistas, and people, had no basis for being. There was no culture or knowledge to pull from. No elders to lean on. To disallow such ignorance to continue, he'd made sure the scripture was full of anecdotes and wisdom while also teaching the basics of biology and architecture. Walker had also attempted to give the reader a basic understanding of morality. But it was strange: the more he put into the scripture, the more it felt cemented in his being, as if the words had etched themselves onto his very soul.

He felt different but also the same. Just . . . more refined. Clear.

With a few flicks of his pen, Walker finished the last words, filling the camo-covered former journal to its limit. Then, as he closed the cover knowing he was done, it disappeared with a *pop*. Walker's overlay lit up.

[. . . Scanning . . .]
Optional tasks updated!
Primigenial task complete: Write a Holy Scripture:
Volumes Completed: 10/10
Reward for completion: Fertility modification

As the update faded from his vision, someone else on Sonata noticed. Echidna stood up quickly and bounded over on her long legs, arms outstretched, and caught Walker in a quick and awkward hug from behind. He tried not to flinch, even though he had heard her steps the moment she started moving.

"You did it! Congratulations!" she whispered into his ear, an oddly intimate moment between them. "I'm so proud of you, Walker."

"Thank you?" he couldn't help but say, though the way she was holding him felt a little strange. "You know I'm close to forty, right?"

"And I'm much, much older, sweetie. You're still a kid to me," she said as she moved into his line of vision, a large smile on her face. "So, you've written your scripture and codified your beliefs. How are you feeling?"

Rather than respond in a snarky way, as his internal self truly wanted, Walker looked deeper into what Echidna was saying. How was he feeling? He mentally poked and prodded but noted nothing out of the ordinary besides a greater sense of energy than he'd had in a long time.

Walker's body felt like he was sixteen again. It was as if an electric current was running under his skin, and the feeling reminded him of what it was like just before a football game. You'd be sitting in the locker room, pads on, and a curious mixture of excitement and anxiety would suddenly burst through you. Only, unlike the feelings he received when preparing for his favorite sport, this one didn't go away. He kept feeling the energy bounce around him from head to toe.

Now that she'd pointed it out, he realized he'd felt this since just before he had finished the scripture. Almost like each word had built him into something more than he was before. A better Walker . . . His mind traveled back to a previous thought. What had writing the scripture done to him?

"What's happening to me?"

"You're ready for the next stage," Echidna said with excitement. "You've chosen an oath, you've codified your beliefs, and now it's time to reach out and grasp the physical stage. It is time for you to become a true Awakened."

Zeus had ambled over while she was talking, and two large blue eyes swung to Walker as he rumbled, "Have you felt your soul intentionally yet? Not with instinct but with the specific intent of using it."

Walker thought back to when he'd railed at the new Primigenials after escaping the tree. That had been when he'd felt that odd pressure in his chest, like something yearning to be free. Pressing on it had caused an eruption of his soul, its forest-green color splashing across the landscape. He nodded and said, "I have."

The bearded man clapped once. "Excellent! That's one of the more difficult steps to take, but as your first-stage awakening was so explosive, I figured it would be natural for you to find your control. Now, here is what I want you to do: close your eyes and return to the time when you felt your soul."

He looked over at Echidna and received an encouraging nod from the yellow-eyed woman before following Zeus's instructions.

Walker closed his eyes and focused on just below his chest, scratching around for the invisible muscle he'd found once before. Searching through his chest felt odd. Using his soul had felt like anything else natural to the human body. People breathe without thinking about breathing, but that's where this was different. No matter where he searched, even knowing the general vicinity where he'd pushed before, he couldn't find it. It was like it was hiding or in hibernation.

Thinking on that, he pulled himself back into the moment. He'd been yelling at the Primigenials, his anger rising through the roof, when the button had appeared. So maybe that was the trick. Maybe controlling the soul, at least at the beginning, required an emotional catalyst. For that, he knew just where to dive in.

Walker imagined Symphony being destroyed by the Slicer.

Rather than push away all of the emotional anguish he'd felt before, he tried to dredge it back up. The screaming and rage, the sadness and depression that had tried and almost succeeded in taking him over. He felt like an emotional rubber band, stretching with the feelings trying to overcome him, before relaxing as his unconscious mind remembered that it hadn't happened again.

He continued at this for several minutes until he discovered an emotional wavelength that felt like a hyped-up form of tension. As his emotions leaped about, his mind still remained clear. The moment he grasped that feeling and held it, the vibration in his chest started to hum. He opened his eyes and stared into a beautiful yellow pair across from him.

"Have you found it?" Echidna asked.

Walker nodded, not trusting himself to speak lest it take him out of the moment he'd fought for.

"Excellent! Now, I'm sure you just pressed on your soul because of that flare we saw before, but what you need to do now is much more complicated. Rather than press on your soul, I want you to try to take hold of it with your mind. Imagine grasping the edge of your soul and stretching it from its current location to just below your collarbone."

Walker nodded again and closed his eyes. He took his invisible muscle and tried to move it. Of course, as this was his first time doing so, he accidentally pressed down and felt a small flare pulse out. Walker heard Echidna fall over and pick herself up, but he couldn't allow himself to be distracted from his pseudo-emotional state. The second time he tried to move it, he had a little success. Walker managed to shift the newly discovered muscle a few inches up from the center of his soul's home just below his sternum. While it was a small success, any movement was a victory.

Each time he grabbed a hold of it, he also got a better idea of what it looked and felt like. His soul felt relatively small, yet thick and almost hard. He felt it snap back as he lost his grip.

Two more times, he accidentally flared the muscle, forcing those around him to keep their distance as he continued his work. As he continued to work with it, mental exhaustion started to rear its head for the first time since he'd entered the protocol. The effort of holding his emotions in some form of a lock was draining him dry.

On his sixth attempt at movement, he finally found a trick that worked for him. Walker imagined his invisible muscle as a small and delicate hand gently grasping the edges of his soul. He began to slowly drag it over his chest, his focus settling on his left collarbone. Once he'd made it more than a few inches, his soul harshly pulled back and snapped into its original place. The speed of it shocked him so greatly that he fell backward with a light yelp, landing on Sonata's soft grass.

That was when he noticed how much his entire body hurt from the process. In particular, the area just below his sternum felt like someone had taken a cleaver to his internal organs. A light gasp involuntarily came from his mouth.

"How are you feeling?" a much too loud voice asked as he lay there with his eyes still closed, somewhat curled into the fetal position.

"Like someone pinched all of my skin and rolled it up into a tube."

"Yes," she said, dragging out the word. "You've made wonderful progress in a short amount of time, dear. Just wonderful. The second stage requires the Awakened to stretch their soul across their entire body. We call the second stage the transformative, or physical, stage. The more you expand your soul across yourself, creating connections throughout your body, the greater your power will be."

"Why do we have to do this now? I have a lot of work to do," he asked in a pain-filled voice, still unmoving and refusing to open his eyes.

"Because now that you've codified your beliefs, your soul will begin to harden to protect itself and the beliefs you hold. The more you stretch it now, while it is still malleable, the more you can do with it later. Now, dear, are you ready to try again?"

Walker shook his head. His body still felt in great pain, even though he had found nothing wrong after gently patting himself down.

"That pain is your soul growing. It is not a natural process, and I imagine the first Awakened, whoever they were, was quite insane to perform this process without any guidance."

"Bully for them. How long will this last?" he replied in a hiss.

"Not too much longer; it is just your soul expanding itself for the first time. The first is always the worst, of course, and the stronger your beliefs are, the tougher your soul is to work with."

"Fuckin' cool," Walker said. He continued to lie there for several minutes after Echidna left him to his pain. Zeus watched him for a few more before leaving himself. It took about an hour for Walker to stop feeling like everything in his body had been compressed to the size of a thumbnail. When he finally sat up and opened his eyes, a lingering soreness pulsed throughout his body.

This was something new that, despite the agony of the experience, he knew he'd have to focus on. They still hadn't told him what he'd be able to do once he completed the second stage, but if the results were anything like the first stage, he knew he wanted it.

Walker stretched his arms, then headed over to Virgil and Rimi.

"Hey, bud, how's it going here?" he said, tripping as a flare of pain hit him.

Virgil tinkered with his screen for a few seconds, choosing not to comment on Walker's stumble, before speaking in a low voice to the blue squirrel standing near the Evolution Chambers. He turned to Walker as his steps reached him. "Just fine, Creator. I believe the gray seal and mountain goat are complete."

Walker looked over at them. The seal looked like a slightly larger and slicker version of the kind Walker was used to from Earth. It had some weird flippers, very thin with bulging muscles poking from underneath shiny skin-like fur. For all its strangeness, Walker assumed that his advanced assistant knew what he was doing. The goat was a different story.

"How tall is that thing going to be?" he asked, pointing at the creature inside the tube.

"Rimi?"

The blue squirrel looked at his screens before saying in a monotone similar to Virgil's, "The Spanish Ibex, modified with gigantism, will stand over five feet tall." Walker ignored the tone for now but made a mental note to ask about it later. Looking the creature over, he noticed it had massive horns, and just like Rimi had said before, it almost looked like a demon. Its coat and skin were a deep black, and the horns were only slightly lighter. It also had so much muscle that veins protruded off its body in what could pass for a Jackson Pollock painting.

"So these are my first ocean and mountain monsters. I can dig it. How are the tiny humans looking?"

Virgil gestured at the tubes. "They are progressing satisfactorily. I believe we will have our base models completed in the next day or so. The kernels are split, and we're just waiting on the grafts to complete their connection. Creating grafts throughout the arterial lines of Homo sapiens is meticulous and has taken the bulk of our time. But because we are taking it slowly, I believe we will not only be able to save the modifications for Rimi here to use in the future, but we will also have a satisfactory model to base future modifications on."

Walker scratched the back of his head. "Man, it's weird to hear you talk about human beings like that."

"Indeed. But it is reality, and it is always important to accept it when it arrives."

"Cryptic, but okay." Walker looked in on the baby humans. He noticed both were Caucasian, which made him ask an important question: "Are they all going to be white like me?"

Virgil shook his head. "No. We will vary the genetics quite widely while also attempting to skip your particular issues. The Evolution Chambers have a function that allows us to create randomized genetic alterations. Height, weight, color of skin and hair will all be randomized. Also, as it is a new world, they should not have any of the melanin-related or cultural issues Earth so prevalently struggles with. The disease resistance you requested is complete, and we are not gigantifying them, also as you requested."

Walker smiled at that. "Yeah, it would be super weird to see ten-foot-tall humans. Have you found anything else you're considering changing from my"—he waved a hand up and down his body—"more standard model?"

"Yes, now that you mention it. I believe we can improve the . . . hygiene . . . of human beings. As well as taper some issues that form as you grow older."

"Like what?"

"Rimi and I," Virgil said with a nod to the smaller squirrel, "believe we can make your body odor not quite as pungent. It still serves a purpose as pheromone signaling to your species, but we plan to reduce the strength of the smell."

Walker gave a thumbs-up. "Sweet. No more smelly people!"

Zeus laughed in the background. "You won't have that issue anymore yourself, Creator."

Why is everyone calling me Creator all of a sudden? he thought to himself.

"Very much so," Virgil said with a nod, ignoring the comment. "We also have further thoughts on removing extraneous organs, to forestall other potential causes of death when they inevitably begin to cause problems." Virgil looked at his screens for a moment before continuing, "The larger issue is, we are not sure how to reduce maternal mortality during childbirth. I believe you will want to add the fertility modification when you can."

"Not on every human," Zeus rumbled again from the side.

"Why not?" Walker asked as he turned to look at him. The other Primigenials were also grouping up, except Dionysus, who was still napping on the Tree of the Gods.

"Because human beings can only manage one bloodline. They can mix, as was done with Heracles, but that is quite rare, and we could not reproduce the effort a second time," Echidna said, then glared at Zeus. "Although some of us just kept on trying."

Zeus shrugged.

"As I was saying," Echidna continued, "bloodlines in our world were quite rare. There was always a chance that a human child would gain a Primigenial bloodline, but the odds were not great. For you to have the ability to place a bloodline independently is . . . What is the word you would use? Overpowered? Yes, overpowered." She nodded to herself. "Zeus is saying you shouldn't place the fertility modification onto every human woman, because it will cause issues moving forward as you add other bloodlines to the male population."

"Ah," Walker said in acknowledgment as he understood what she was getting at.

"What?" Rimi asked.

"If I give the fertility modification to every human woman, and humans can only take on one modification at a time, I'd be creating a society where women could potentially be viewed only as mothers and child bearers to the exclusion of everything else. That isn't to say it would happen, but the optics aren't great, and I don't like the idea of it myself." He tried not to think about the powerful women he'd dated in his life and what their reactions would be to hearing this conversation.

Zeus suddenly spoke up with similar thoughts. "If my wife heard that I approved or in any way instigated the fertility modification as a requirement for every human female, she would leave me in less than a moment."

"Didn't you cheat on her a lot? Like, historically?" Walker couldn't help but ask.

"No, we don't view sex and progeny the way you do. Spreading the Primigenial bloodline is considered a sacred duty. If you think the stories about me are hard to believe, you wouldn't be able to imagine what my brother Poseidon and his kin have done."

"Uh-huh," Walker said, not believing it for a moment. "And your wife, Hera. Did she ever try to spread her Primigenial bloodline?"

Zeus's eyes started shifting left and right, but he didn't find anyone else saying anything. "Well, no, but—"

"Exactly!" Walker said with a smile, cutting him off. "Okay, so we spread it out evenly. Virgil, is there a limit to how many people I can give bloodlines to?"

"No, Walker. None that I can see."

"And you're sure you don't need any help?" Walker asked. Multiple times in the recent past he'd asked the same question, but always the response was the same.

"No, Walker. This is my and Rimi's task for now. We will continue to create new modifications for you to use in the future while you focus on other tasks that demand your immediate attention. As I have said multiple times in the last few hours."

Walker's face struck a sour expression. "Great, let me know when you have a base model done and we'll hop on it. Thank you for the help, everyone," he said with a quick wave, dismissing the Primigenials as politely as he could manage. He really was trying to be more sociable with the elder beings as they lived with him on the smallish green moon.

As they walked away, the golden-dressed woman entered his field of view again. It was odd to see Athena be so quiet, but as the virgin goddess, he guessed she didn't have much input on bloodlines overall. Zeus would be the professional in that conversation.

Once they all left, Zeus with an oddly strained look on his face as Athena seemed to be dressing him down, Walker looked over at Virgil. "What do you know about the temporal task I have?"

The large squirrel sighed before looking away from his screen. As he met Walker's eyes, he began to stammer, "It-it . . . It i—"

"Restricted information again?" Walker asked.

"Indeed. I am sorry, Walker," Virgil said with a defeated look on his face.

Walker put a hand on his furry shoulder. "Not your fault, buddy. Don't worry about it. I guess I'll just muddle through it. Hmm." He tapped his chin a few times. "I don't want to cause any issues here, so I think I'll just experiment on my new exoplanets."

Walker pulled up the monitor and zoomed over to one of them when he was struck by a sudden thought. "You know, we never named these. Be right back." Leaving the monitor in place, he stepped into the Cosmic Genesis System and quickly named the two planets, already knowing what he wanted to do.

As Walker stepped back out, Virgil said, "Romulus and Remus? Why name them that?"

"For quite a few reasons. Symphony and Sonata are linked together. This world we're focusing so much of our attention on will be about harmony." He began pacing back and forth. "However, I have other plans for Romulus and Remus. I need places of disharmony. You said not too many people get the chance to build solar systems, so I'm going for broke. I'm going to create unique planets for battles, where entire wars can be fought without ever touching Symphony's soil. If you want to fight a war, go to one of the planets within the system. If you try to start a war on Symphony, I will step in and things will get solved. Permanently."

"I would like to be honest with you, Walker. You spoke before about what kind of Creator you wanted to be, and I believe you are quickly becoming a dictator. Maybe even a tyrannical dictator at that."

"How so?" Walker asked, appreciating his candor.

"You spoke before of how you wanted a world where anyone can be anything they want to be. That exploration and choosing their routes in life, good and bad, were allowed. Now you are saying that if anyone does not do what you want them to do, you will eliminate them. Why the sudden change?"

Walker was stumped, as he could see what Virgil was getting at. "Umm, I don't know. Maybe I'm overcompensating for something and taking it a little too far." His soul pulsed momentarily. Walker sensed it was agreeing with him, and that settled it. "So, what, I'm just supposed to let wars be fought on Symphony? Because that's what fits my oath?" Another pulse. "Well, shit."

"I am guessing that your soul-oath is agreeing with me?" Virgil asked.

"Yep. According to my oath, I can't do this. I wonder what would've happened if I'd forced it."

"You'd be paralyzed until you decided to change your mind!" Athena yelled out from by the tree.

Walker's hands slapped his thighs. "Man, what is the point of asking them to stand over by the tree if they can hear me anyway?"

"That's what we were wondering!" Zeus yelled back.

"Whatever."

"So, I take it you will not be making a war world?" Virgil asked, bringing him back on topic.

"No, I will. I'll just have to find a way to grant benefits to those who follow the procedure rather than tearing up their world. Anyway, the point of using Romulus and Remus was because of the myth of the two brothers. Two brothers founded a city. One killed the other and named it after himself: Rome." Walker slammed a fist into his palm. "Rome was a great city and began one of the most powerful empires in the history of my homeworld."

"It also started and ended with a war from within," Virgil reminded him.

"You feeling a little Spartacus-y, Virgil? Not to call you a slave in the slightest, but thematically, I'm just saying—"

"I get it," Virgil interrupted him. "And no. I doubt myself or the other assistants could rebel if they wanted to. It would take a long and laborious process that goes far beyond the bounds of what assistants are supposed to be able to do."

"Then, there we go. Before we work our time magic—"

"Temporal displacement."

"Whatever." Walker looked at the two exoplanets, lava splashing across their surfaces in an awe-inspiring total calamity kind of way. He knew he should sit and enjoy the moment. After all, these wouldn't exist without his efforts and decisions. But he just didn't have the time for that. "Before we work our time magic, we need to cool the planets down a bit, don't we. Any suggestions?"

"Hmm," Virgil hummed to himself as he looked at his screens. "I suggest you manually remove large portions of the magmatic lakes on the planet you decide to use and gradually add water to the surface. The biggest issue is the speed of the planet. It is moving at a languid pace compared to us, so once time starts to catch up, there will be negative chain reactions that build on top of one another. My suggestion would be to remove a large amount of the surface heat before placing the water down."

"Remove and add, okay." Walker looked at his resources for the first time since the second battle and found a massive amount of water. It seems Crratch was holding onto it all for something, but Walker would never know what that was. He began the laborious process of removing any lava he found and diving deeper to scoop out gargantuan portions of magma as well. He added small amounts of water as he went and kept an eye on everything, as Virgil had warned that sudden shifts in temperature could have drastic effects on the celestial objects. Like planet-breaking earthquakes.

All told, it took about two days. Remus, the planet he chose to test his time theories on, was quite a bit bigger than Symphony. As in, almost as large as the Earth itself. Before he'd started working on it, the entire planet was just rock and heat; now, it at least had some water and seemed less like a volatile hellish landscape.

About two hours into the ordeal, Virgil had suggested speeding it up for a week so they could see it in real time. Something about relativity. Walker wasn't paying as much attention to him as he should've, due to suffering another soul rebound. Echidna was right: it was much less painful the second time, but it still hurt like crazy.

Once they sped it up, Walker could see the steam exploding into the atmosphere from the water he'd placed, cooling and burning off at once. After witnessing the destructive aftermath, he decided to continue the process but in slightly smaller patches. The odds of cracking the planet weren't great, as the sheer size of it disallowed for the idea, but being careful wasn't going to kill him. Any small fissures and cracks could even be seen as interesting terrain for a war planet.

There was a lot of downtime while he waited for things to settle a little. Each of the Primigenials came to speak with him. Aside from Echidna, the rest of them gave off the feeling that they were testing him out in different ways. For what, he wasn't sure. Athena in particular continued to give him odd looks and always ended up walking away with what he thought was a flourish. Overall, it greatly confused him, and after speaking to her, he'd been unable to reach the emotional equilibrium necessary to work with his soul for a time.

As the final parts of Remus began cooling off, Walker took a break and spent some time with Cagna coming up with more milestones. She wanted to know everything he could tell her about growing up and the mental process. He broke it down for her as best as he could, which was pretty outstanding with his memory. Then he suffered another soul rebound, this time gaining a lot more traction in his stretching and showing greater progress than before. Echidna was excited, saying he was moving faster than she'd thought he would. All told, Walker was very busy and hadn't had a lot of fun. That was about to change.

"It's time to fuck with time!" he unoriginally said while looking at a barren wasteland of a planet. Remus would be pretty when he finished it, he was sure, but they weren't there yet.

"What are you going to do?" Cagna asked. She'd been sticking with him more and more as the days had passed.

"Well, I had an idea when Virgil told me I should slow the planet down to our speed. It'll be like this for another five days, but I should be able to get it figured out pretty quick. I plan to pick one tiny spot in a mountain area and speed it up, then see what happens after that. It's all a test, as I'm not one hundred percent sure what's going to happen."

"Isn't that dangerous?" the pink squirrel asked with big eyes.

Walker looked away from the monitor to give her a smile. "Sure it is. But according to Virgil, this is a relatively new system. I don't know what it does, and Virgil can't help me out there. What I did with it during the prelims was barely anything at all. I'll need to have a firm grasp of it if I want to use it in the future. So, we have tests."

"Tests," she replied with a nod.

Walker smiled at her, then pulled up one of his oldest incomplete tasks. He was hopeful that what he was about to do would complete the task and let him move on to the second part.

> **Temporal task: Build a localized temporal anomaly (Part 1)**
> *Growth can take time, and the Alpha Protocol understands this. Contrary to what many believe, time is fluid and can be shifted forward and backward to suit the Creator's need. Build a localized temporal anomaly and use it to grow your world further.*
> **Localized anomalies built: 0/1**
> **Resources allocated for completion: 50 years**
> **Reward for completion: System Link ability**

"Okay, good luck!" Cagna said with optimism.

Walker nodded, then clicked on Time. He moved the monitor to a mountainous region and zoomed in a little so it was just underneath the rock. Then he clicked a spot and slowed down time for one minute. He figured it was better to start as slowly as possible, just in case things didn't go how he wanted them to. Then again, he didn't know what he wanted in the first place.

A tear in space formed in the exact spot he had picked, and water started gushing out of it. He rotated his view but couldn't see what was within the rift due to all the water coming out. It wasn't exactly what he thought would happen, so he waited to see if his overlay would light up.

It did not.

"Just gotta do it again," he said to himself quietly, then did another slow-down, but this time for five minutes. Another tear formed, and this time, at least, nothing came out of it. Walker angled his monitor to look inside and saw only darkness.

"So, this isn't a temporal anomaly, but it's a sped-up world in which I'm creating smaller slowed-down zones. Shouldn't that do something?"

"Correct," Virgil said, appearing beside him and looking at the monitor.

"Good lord! I hate when you guys sneak up on me."

"I apologize, and I will try not to do that in the future," the brown squirrel said. "You are correct that this is not a temporal anomaly."

"Can you tell me anything else?" Walker asked with a bit of blunted hope.

"I cannot. Although to be fair to you, I am not completely certain what a temporal anomaly would look like."

That stumped him for a moment. "Huh, for once you don't know. Must be shocking for you. Well, this one was set for five minutes, so what would happen if I sped up the area on top of it? Then it would be a triple layer. Speed up for the planet, slow down for that spot, then I speed up the same spot again. Fast, slow, fast," Walker said, and on the spot that he had slowed down, he added a five minute speed-up.

A ten-foot-tall tear opened up, then dozens more opened beside them. As Walker watched, his overlay updated, and several other things happened at the same time. A massive muscular leg of . . . something . . . fell through the rift. It was purple and quite hairy. An eyeball came through, went to look at the rift, touched it, and fell to pieces, cut in half by how sharp the rift's edges were. A million tiny insects crossed over in an orderly line and immediately spread across the planet. And a dozen other things that were still happening as he watched: monsters, walking trees—just an impossible amount of creatures and moments.

Even the environment began to change. Where only rock once existed, water burst from some rifts, fire from others. An aggressive form of grass spread out as well, dodging the fire as it wove its way across the planet. It was, all told, pure chaos.

Walker tried to focus on a few things happening. Just as he scrolled the monitor over, he noticed a large chunk of metal with branding on the side was slowly coming through. Just after it crossed, a series of mini asteroids flew through another tear and detonated, destroying the metal just as it touched the ground. He said the only thing he could think of.

"Well, fuck."

"Indeed. What I was trying to say earlier was, it is a trap. Sometimes the protocol puts traps into the tasks."

"Fucking why?"

"Because if they give you a unique problem, it forces you to find a unique solution. That is still growth and creativity. I am sorry, Walker. You can look at it on the bright side."

"What's the bright side?"

"You most certainly have a war world now. Just be wary of any of those creatures trying to come over to Symphony. You may also want to give up on Romulus, as those insects spread quickly across the different cosmos. They're called Inhabitor Beetles, and they're quite carnivorous."

"Double fuck," Walker replied with a sigh. "Can you start working on a monster that will eat them, please? I'd rather stop them on Remus with an engineered solution than allow them to spread across the Symphony solar system."

Virgil nodded. "Well thought. I will get started right away, and that gives me a chance to look at the Combiner ability, as you requested." He looked at the monitor for a moment longer before looking at Walker again. "I feel the need to mention something else. This is, potentially, a catastrophe. And yet, you are doing a wonderful job holding yourself together. It is a mistake, surely, and one that was devised by the Council, but I believe that you can solve it over time. I just wanted you to understand that mentally and emotionally, you are doing better than you did with the Slicer incident."

A shiver ran through Walker's frame at the reminder, but he nodded at Virgil with a smile. "Thank you. I'll take that to mean I have some small measure of personal growth happening, then."

"Just so. Please excuse me, Creator." After saying so, he spun around and returned to the Evolution Chambers.

Walker just nodded as he watched Remus spit out different entities from across the multiverse. "War world indeed," Walker said in a quiet voice. He hadn't panicked like he had when the Slicer was tearing apart Symphony. He'd take that as a victory even with this mistake. Walker looked at his notifications.

[. . . Scanning . . .]
Task updated!
Temporal task complete: Build a localized temporal anomaly
(Part 1)
Localized anomalies built: 1/1
Reward for completion: System Link ability
[. . .]
New temporal task: Create a static temporal zone (Part 2)
You've built a localized temporal anomaly and grasped the
beginning of what the Temporal Subsystem can do. Now, create a
temporal zone that consistently slows down or speeds up time
without heavily draining your resources.
Localized temporal zones built: 0/1
Resources allocated for completion: 100 years
Reward for completion: Temporal Subsystem upgrade

"Why do I feel like I can cheat this?" Walker asked his overlay as new thoughts started to come to fruition.

CHAPTER FIVE

On Earth: Elsie and a Boy

ELSIE

Elsie cleaned the last of the blood off of Buckingham Palace's floor. Nobody said that for his work to continue, he needed the area clean of all contaminants. Elsie knew that was a lie because her parents had taught her about DNA and what dust was made of when she was just a little girl. She only did this because she thought it made him happy.

As she continued to scrub at the sticky substance, she tried to think further on the subject. *Maybe he just doesn't like the sight of blood?*

Anytime she'd fought others, he'd always looked away and waited for her to return before they moved on to the next location. It had confused her at first, but he never seemed to want to talk about it. That wasn't an unusual situation with their relationship.

To some, her being a little girl was only a few weeks ago, while to her, it was more than a decade. A long period of time. Long enough that her memories of the time before training and fighting were faded thoughts conjured up by a different person. One who had a more pleasant life from before the world went to hell.

She removed the cleaning gloves she'd found on a nearby cart and rubbed her shaved head. Nobody had said it was important that she remove any ideas of the old world from herself, so shaving her head had been the first step. To save this world, she would do what she needed to do. Hair and vanity didn't matter in the slightest.

"What a farce," Nobody said near a painting not too far away. "They think this creates majesty. But it is just empty opulence for the self-indulgent." He spread his arms out to encompass everything around them. To Elsie, who had lived within the underwater ruins for eleven years, she could see his point. The ruins were grander than the palace they currently found themselves in. Her eyes had seen great structures that boggled the mind. Technology and advanced comfort spread far enough to accommodate hundreds of thousands within their walls. But here, with its yellow walls and constant pillars, it felt like it was trying too hard. Elsie held the opinion that simple was always better. That's why her weapon of choice was a morning star: A thick shaft for easy gripping. A spiked ball tip. Hit things until they stopped moving. Simple. Nobody had suggested it to her.

"Elsie," Nobody said, pulling her from her internal thoughts. "There are still more of them to the north. Be a dear and go take care of them. We are almost ready."

She nodded without saying anything and picked up Chuck on her way out of the palace. She had named it when she was only about eight years old, when deciding on her weapon of choice and fighting style in the training simulator.

When they had first entered the ruins, she had been asleep for some reason. Nobody had told her that her parents had been taken by the monsters, and he was going to raise her from now on. But he needed her help with something. He had looked so sad about her parents that she'd instantly formed a bond with him. He'd saved her and brought her out of certain death.

Later on, after they had spoken about what she liked to do for fun, he said that he needed a fighter and that he was too old to do so himself. He was hoping to train her. She had agreed because she didn't want to get killed by the monsters like her mother and father had. She also wanted to protect him.

She cared a great deal for Nobody. While he said she should never call him father, as she had already had a great one who had loved her dearly, he did say she didn't have to call him Mr. Nobody all the time. Nobody was just fine. She turned a corner to get out of the main wing she'd been cleaning and entered the main pathway out.

She still remembered waking up in the ruins and being shocked by what she saw: trees with perfectly ripe fruit growing on every corner, water fountains that activated when you drew near and formed the shape of different animals in movement, and a huge amount of open space for just about anything you could want to do . . . but no people.

The first day that they'd decided it was safe to travel around the place, Nobody had looked around for a moment before taking her on a path that sent them directly to the training room. It was a large open area, which Nobody had called an "arena," that would create images of people and creatures to fight and train against. The difficulty could be adjusted, and she'd worked her way from tier one all the way up to tier six by the time she was just twelve years old.

When they left, she had been close to defeating the tenth-tier Arena Champions, but Nobody said they were running out of time. He said your mind and body got weird if you spent too much time in a displacement field, but even after she had asked what he was talking about, he never explained it.

Elsie hefted Chuck onto her shoulder as she exited the palace doors. When Nobody had asked why she'd named it that, she said it was because if she was ever in trouble, she could just chuck it at them and watch them go splat. She fondly remembered Nobody laughing and kept the name even after all this time. It was an eight-foot-long weapon with a smooth dark brown haft and an extra thick tip that finished in a pointed end. Many people when seeing it would think that Chuck weighed a ton, but because it had been left in the ruins by her very technologically advanced ancestors, she could barely feel the weight of it in the slightest. Not that the weight would bother her nowadays, regardless.

Standing just before the exit, Elsie bunched up her legs and pushed with the second evolution she'd ever received, Leap. It still amazed her to this very moment how much speed she could get by leaping from rooftop to rooftop as she went. Each leap sent the champion several hundred feet in the air, the view below showing no monsters, or people, for that matter. Nobody had said that the multiverse was trying to destroy the Earth and had done so with spies. Traitors. Pieces of shit. Each time she killed one, he said that the odds of some Earthlings surviving grew. He told her a lot of things.

She moved quickly, knowing they were on a strict timeline, and left the palace heading north. She watched as fallen buildings and haphazard green fields passed below her. Cars were overturned in some spots, blocking roads, and a few places had burned down. With how closely packed everything was, she was surprised that more hadn't burned up. She saw an old church below and landed near it with enough force to create a small crater where her feet touched the ground. Naturally, she was completely unharmed. Evolutions were amazing that way.

It wasn't like it was in the movies. She couldn't make any changes to Leap. But she could use it and train with it, adjust to its smallest requirements. It made things a little better.

She looked up, and her translator moved into action to read the sign. This area was called Pond Street. The British had a weird way of naming things. Was it a pond or a street? Then again, San Francisco had Lois Lane Street. Who was she to judge?

Looking around, she saw an old flooring store and felt her fourth evolution, Life Sense, kick up. It wasn't an advanced evolution, gained only recently when she defeated the fourth champion she'd run into, and she hadn't had time to train it correctly like she had the others. But still, it could give a general direction toward where the living were and a hazy idea of how many there were once she closed some distance.

Elsie hustled over quietly, moving from cover to cover so she was harder to see, like Nobody had taught her. She hid behind a large smashed-up truck with a picture of a loaf of bread on it and pushed her enhanced senses to the limit, straining to listen in on what they were saying.

Becoming a champion automatically gave her a few boosts that the standard human wouldn't have. Nobody said that when he had identified her, he found enhanced endurance, strength, speed, and senses. The moment her champion title had been bestowed was the most painful in her life. Until she had learned how to dial her senses up and down, everything was horrifying to experience. It took weeks of excruciating pain to overcome her limits and grasp the hidden ways to control her new gifts. Nobody helped a little, but he said he'd never experienced it before himself and could only give advice. Still, she'd done it, and at moments like this, it was incredibly useful.

She heard a woman speaking and counted six heartbeats no more than three hundred yards away. Elsie moved closer now that she knew where they were positioned and shifted to an alley around a corner within the occupants' blind spot. She listened in as the woman's words cleared up.

"James, I know this is hard on you, but you must understand. It's not safe here." Her voice was cracking, and she sounded exhausted, her words slurring a little. Based on her limited understanding of British accents, Elsie thought they had a Yorkshire lilt to them. "We can't stay. I know your mother is in bad shape, but those creatures . . . are gone. We need to leave; it's dangerous."

"No," a deep voice said, likely James. "We don't abandon our people. Think about how Alexander feels right now hearing his mother speak about abandoning his grandmother. It's reprehensible. We are a family!" he said, raising his voice.

"Shhh, keep your voice down," a third voice piped in, a higher-pitched male by Elsie's guess. "There may still be looters and killers. You don't know."

"You're right, I'm sorry," James replied more quietly, "But what I said stands. We're all connected by blood. You don't abandon or give up on blood, not ever."

"But what if—"

He interrupted her, "Hey, Helen, it will be all right. No what ifs." She heard a smacking sound, like two lips connecting quickly before breaking away. She'd heard that sound a lot in the last few weeks.

"Okay, James. If you think so."

Having heard enough, Elsie understood what had to happen next. She didn't like doing it, but that didn't matter. She was saving the world.

Elsie's parents would likely think her heartless, but they were dead, and these people were traitors. The whole damn country was. When Nobody said they were going to the heart of the problem, right in enemy territory, they'd teleported straight to the heart of downtown London. Already, she'd fought four enemy champions since arriving, each dying and screaming terrible things at her as Chuck crushed parts of their bodies. For all she knew, this group of people was aware she was here and was attempting to feed her bad information. Who knew if they even had a sick mother? She couldn't trust them.

No, she had a task to fulfill for her master. That was the end of it. If she grew soft now, it could have larger implications later in her fight to save humanity. Kill all the traitors, he'd said, and that's what she would do. They had it coming.

Standing up now that she'd bolstered her resolve, she stepped out of the alleyway. Pushing down, Elsie then leaped forward, passing over a fallen school bus, over a series of suitcases torn asunder, and smashed through a window just above where the traitors were congregating.

Now that she was even closer, she could feel where each was positioned within a few inches. The people below screamed as they heard the thud of her landing and glass shattering, but Elsie ignored it. It was easy to scream now that they'd been caught.

She pulled Chuck off her back and threw it through the floor, which collapsed part of the roof and blocked several avenues of escape with one move. Elsie dropped down afterward and used her first evolution to recall her weapon to her hand. She hit a salt-and-pepper-haired man in passing on her way to the floor. His body collapsed like jelly, as if his spine had no bones to hold it up.

She ignored what was left of him, then swung Chuck around to smash a younger woman with brown hair, her eyes wide as Chuck completed its devastating work. The woman's mangled body flew through a wall and took it down with her, further destroying the already shaky foundation of the place. She heard groaning timbers but ignored it, as the collapse of the building would just be a good test of her enhanced endurance—plus it might make her job a little easier.

"Wait," a dirt-covered woman said. Elsie recognized the voice as Helen, who had been speaking before. "Please, we have a son and—" Chuck made quick work of her, pulverizing the former person into the ground. The last person, a man, ran toward a room in the back. Elsie brushed some debris off her shoulder before leaping through a wall and coming to stand before a bed with an old woman in it and a young child nearby. The man was standing between her and them.

"You can't have them, you demon!" he yelled at her, feet spread and hands up, ready for a fight. She mentally scoffed. As if he'd last more than a few seconds with her.

"Who said I am a demon?" she asked with her head cocked. "You brought this on yourselves, you traitorous bastards."

"What did we do? What have we ever done to deserve this?" he asked. "Please, please, just let my son and mother go. They won't do anything, I promise." He waved a palm at the feeble woman on the bed, a purple ankle showing itself from out of the covers. But it was the smallish boy with light brown hair that caught her attention like iron to a magnet. His wide eyes shifted from his father's extended arm to meet her own. Elsie's overlay lit up for the fifth time in her life.

[. . .]
[. . . Scanning . . .]
Enemy champion located.
Hidden bloodline located.
Enemy champions overlay activated.
Enemy champions enhancements provided.
Destruction of enemy champion will bring rewards.

The boy fell over screaming, grabbing his ears and trying not to move. Elsie knew that pain quite well.

"What are you doing to him, you bitch!" the man yelled and charged at her. "Leave my son and mother alone!"

Mother . . . Grandmother . . .

Elsie's memories did a quick flashback as she remembered her grandmother, also named Elsie, speaking to her as she put her hair in pigtails for the first time. She hadn't thought about that or her grandmother in a long time. Without intending to, she touched her smooth head, reaching for the double braids she'd once had. It was an old memory, nearly forgotten. The man punched her in the chest, but her body didn't move, too lost in the sensation of her grandmother telling her stories of happier times while braiding her hair. She barely even registered any pain from the action.

She looked over at the boy still screaming on the ground, while the man, still striking her, exhausted himself. She pushed him aside and knocked him into a wall to stop him blocking her vision. Kneeling down, she pushed the boy over onto his back, eliciting another loud scream, and said, "Lying on your back makes it a little better. Less nerves there, I think." She wasn't sure if the boy heard her, but she hoped he had. She only knew that much because of Nobody. Education was hard to come by when all you had time for was to train.

The man, the father, was unconscious, so she went back into the other room, stepped around the bodies, and grabbed a bottle of water. She spilled it on his face, and he awakened with a sputtering coughing sound.

Elsie lifted him from the ground with one arm and held him up above her so his feet couldn't touch the ground. "Tell me the truth, traitor. How old is your son?" she demanded of him harshly.

"What?" the man asked, his eyes rolling as she shook him a little.

"How old is he!" she said as she raised Chuck in the air with her other arm.

"F-fifteen. He's just small for his age. He hasn't hit his growth spurt yet."

"Fifteen . . ." She laughed. "I was fighting tier eights by fifteen. Do you even know what he is?"

"He's . . . he's my son," the man said, some of that former defiance returning to his eyes.

"Yes," she said with a sad smile, "I suppose he is." She put him back on the ground. "You have two hours to get out of this city. If you do not leave in that timeframe, I will return, and all three of you will die. You have my word on that."

The man nodded quickly, and she walked through the wall next to him, providing an unsubtle reminder of the kind of power she wielded. The building groaned some more, but it held as she knew it would—barely. Elsie walked out and leaped on top of a nearby building, then watched the three to make sure they did as she told them. Nobody would be able to see if people were still in London, so she needed them to leave or die—one or the other.

Elsie sat back on her heels and waited.

ALEXANDER

He was in a world of fire. His muscles felt like they were tearing and reforming over and over again. His tendons began popping from the stress, detaching themselves from his bones and then reattaching immediately afterward. Everything was loud and bright and full of pain. Weird screens appeared behind his eyelids, and he screamed all the louder, ignoring them and the implications of what they were. Nothing was making sense, and he just wanted to scream and cry.

Something grabbed onto his arms, and a new wave of pain came. He was dragged across the floor for a moment, heavy breathing smashing into his eardrums and vibrating with insanity, then he was lifted and felt someone punch him in the stomach. His body jiggled, and his nerves were firing on all cylinders, making even the slightest motion undeniably painful. Blissfully, he passed out.

He wasn't sure how much time went by, but when he opened his eyes, he had to close them again immediately after. All he'd seen was the bright blue of the sky, only instead of the pleasant feeling it normally invoked in him, it was now an overwhelming spotlight. His muscles felt like someone had wrung them out in one of those old-timey mangles, strung out and stretched in new and painful ways. His hearing was still extraordinarily heightened and painful, but he still needed to strain it so he could figure out what was going on. The scratching and dragging sound grated on his mind, and his hearing picked up the heavy breathing he'd heard before.

Alexander's ears were still in extreme pain, but he needed to know what was happening. So despite the enormity of it, he spoke out loud. "What . . . is . . . happening?" He could barely form the words through gritted teeth.

"Alexander, you're awake! Mom, Alex is awake! Oh, thank God. We were so . . . Why are you touching your ears?"

"Too . . . loud," he tried to whisper, but even that was painful. His own voice began to bounce and echo in his mind, making him grind his teeth, which he also heard—like rocks brushing up against each other.

"What?" his father asked. His father surely said so in a normal voice, but it sounded like an explosion to Alexander.

"Too loud!" He made the mistake of yelling as his youth and ignorance, and his pain, got the best of him. His own voice vibrated his eardrums so severely that he promptly passed out from the agony, unaware of the panic he was causing his father.

When he came to a second time, they weren't moving, and something felt like it was grasping his head. He reached up slowly, feeling different nerves fire as his muscles and tendons worked to slowly grasp the things hanging on his ears. Such a simple procedure done a million times now felt like a great labor for little reward. The things on his head felt fuzzy.

Ah, earmuffs.

That's why the sounds weren't killing him right now. They certainly muted some of the noise, but not to such a degree that he couldn't still hear past them. He tried his voice again.

"Dad . . . awake."

He could hear and feel his father quickly approaching. As he grew close enough, Alexander realized he could also smell his father and noticed he had quite the odor. "Stay . . . there . . . please," he said while trying not to grit his teeth.

"Of course, of course, son. How . . . how are you feeling?" his dad said in his quietest voice.

"A little . . . better."

"Good, son, good."

"What's . . . happening . . . happened . . . I don't . . ."

"I'm sorry, son." He sighed. "We—I lost your mother, and your grandmother didn't make it out of London. The infection in her leg spread throughout her veins, and she's gone now too. It's just us. Just us."

"What . . . about . . . Uncle Spencer and Aunt Sofia."

"Gone," came the deadened voice in return.

"How?"

"It was a demon, son. It looked human, but I'd bet anything that was a demon. It forced us out of London, and I didn't have time to properly care for you and your grandma at the same time. Not to mention pulling you both on this cart. She . . . uh . . . died in her sleep, which is a better way than many have lately."

"Where?" he got out this time before having to stop.

"Where are we? We're just north of London now, out of the city proper."

"Bright . . . The sun . . ."

"Ah, hold on a second. I picked these up recently." He left for a moment but quickly returned. "Here. I found a service station nearby and grabbed some sunglasses. They're heavily tinted."

Alexander felt the sunglasses edge onto and scratch the tips of his ears, his father's hands fumbling about to get them secured. He tried not to make any noises and only flinched once. The last thing he needed was to make his father feel bad after everything he'd gone through to keep him alive. He opened his eyes quickly before shutting them again, testing the brightness. He noted that it wasn't nearly as bad as he'd expected, but he also saw every speck of dust sitting on the edges of the lenses. He tried to ignore it as he felt something inexplicable pull his attention. Alexander turned his head to the side.

There was a large tree in the distance, taller than the rest by a good amount. Standing on top of it was a woman covered in metal armor with the shaft end of a long weapon sticking up from her back. Even though she had to be a quarter of a mile away, he saw her put a finger to her lips before she waved once. Then, as he watched, she leaped a hundred feet in the air and in the direction of London.

He couldn't help staring for a long time at the tree she'd been standing on.

"What is it, son?" his father asked, his voice clearly strained as he still attempted not to speak too loudly. "What do you see over there?"

"Nothing, Dad," Alexander replied in the calmest voice he could manage, masking his own fears and insecurities. "Nothing at all."

CHAPTER SIX

On Symphony: Chipper and Raganoth

CHIPPER, JUST PRIOR TO THE DISPLACEMENT

Chipper, the albino squirrel of Symphony and Guardian of the Center, couldn't speak. He didn't have the standard vocal folds and full-throatedness that human beings and their fellow sapients possessed. That's because Chipper's design was based on a standard squirrel, and he was given life without thought to what would happen should sapience occur.

He didn't hate his Creator for this oversight, as his existence wouldn't have occurred in the first place had they not placed him near his tree. It also seemed as if Walker cared for him and this world enough to make sure that he and his circle could protect it. No, there was no hatred in him for Walker. Raganoth was a different story, though.

The poison wyvern was lounging near the Mana Tree, taking a nap. The large yellow creature had already hunted around the area and decimated the local wildlife to the point that Chipper was worried it wouldn't fully recover. Thankfully, his tree provided for his nourishment, but still, it was bothersome to see such an empty area where life had once teemed. Such was the burden of friendship.

Chipper felt a ringing in the back of his mind. He mentally accepted, and a moment later, he heard an audible clicking sound with a mental voice coming through.

Hello, Chipper, how are you on this fine Symphonic day?

I am well, Adele. How are you on this fine Symphonic day?

I am well, she replied, completing their standard ceremony for when two Guardians should meet. Although they were doing so through a peculiar evolution the other Guardian had received, Chipper felt that the process was important, as who knew what new monsters would appear on Symphony next. His argument in favor of the ceremony was simple. The Guardian Collective didn't know if others could take on their likenesses. By having a simple process of greeting, one that they changed from time to time, they stood a better chance of finding anyone who might threaten their small but important group. Sure, their magic might give them away as not one of the pure, but regardless, Chipper liked to be certain in times when uncertainty can breed.

Excellent. How are you really doing, Adele? Chipper asked.

A mental sigh passed through their connection. *It is difficult in the snowy region. The cold has grown more intense, and the manticores are coming through more quickly, less affected by the weather than myself. I've had to defend my tree twice in the last week alone, and one of the manticores was quite powerful. Its speed was almost unbelievable. Had I not developed my evolutions to the point that I have, there would have been a chance you would never hear my voice again.*

I am sorry to hear that, Adele. Do you need assistance from the collective?

No, I am not that far gone as of yet. How is your new friend, Raganoth the Bleeder?

Difficult, if I am honest. Also, he prefers to simply be called Raganoth.

Noted. You were always honest, friend Chipper. That is one of the great and terrible things about you.

Chipper didn't see it that way, but each Guardian had their own way of viewing the world. Adele viewed hers with great suspicion, whereas Chipper viewed his as a home needing protection.

I wanted to speak to you about something of great importance, Adele, so it is fortuitous that you have contacted me. I have met the Creator—in person. They were quite strange but very friendly.

You actually met the Creator? As in . . . the *Creator? The one who built Symphony and made all of us?* she asked. Chipper could feel her shock through the bond, which was unlike her. This must have greatly surprised Adele for her to lose control of her emotions during the connection.

Yes, he confirmed. Chipper started to sense something was wrong in his territory, but he continued, *His name is Walker, and he asked to be my friend. He . . .* The wrongness increased. *Hold for a moment.*

Of course, she replied, and he felt her voice fade to the background as the bond remained.

Chipper jumped from his tree and, while soaring through the air, spotted something trying to blend in. Of course, the grass's green and the creature's gold didn't quite mix, although they were quite pretty together. He found the golden manticore trying to move in a quiet fashion, attempting to get closer to his home. As he came down, he pulled from his core and created a rotating ball of pure mana. Once he got closer to the ground, he rotated the mana even faster to create a small vacuum effect as air spun around the ball.

Just before landing, he placed a burst of mana behind him to reposition his body right over the manticore at a quickened speed, and using both hands, he shoved the rotating mana ball directly into its head. The manticore's body exploded, showering him in blood and viscera. A quick sheathing of mana expelled the bodily fluids and restored his fur to its pristine white. He walked back to the tree at a sedate pace and began climbing.

While the other Guardians consistently complained about the amount of manticores they were seeing and, eventually, fighting, Chipper never did so. He had fought them in the thousands across his lifetime, far, far more than the others. He believed it was because of his positioning in the greater territories. As his home was within the center of Symphony, it had become a natural collection point for the manticores as they moved through their world.

He never complained or told the others, because he didn't think it was a helpful action that would benefit the collective. They had their trees and territories, and he had his. That was the simple truth of the matter. Complaining never helped, it just added your burden onto others. Of course, their territories held two trees, and his only held one for some reason. But still, it wasn't as bad as it would seem. He had a duty, and he fulfilled it happily.

Chipper reached the branch he liked to sit on, mentally tagging it as the "thinking branch," and leaned against the bark of his first friend.

I'm back. Apologies.

Not a problem, Chipper. So, I am dying to ask about the Creator, but I feel that the entire collective needs to listen in. Would you be amenable to a grouping?

Chipper thought on that for a moment. With the addition of Raganoth and his conversation with Walker, which had many future implications for Symphony as a whole, he didn't disagree with his fellow Guardian. The collective should know, and he should've been the one to suggest it. Mentally admonishing himself, he agreed.

I believe that is the correct choice, friend Adele. Please bring them to me and remind them that this meeting must be fast, as our territories cannot protect themselves.

Chipper's tree was the obvious meeting location for all Guardians due to its proximity to their territories and the expediency with which others could arrive. He didn't call himself their leader, as no one wanted to place one Guardian above the others. That was why they called themselves a collective in the first place.

I will. See you soon, friend Chipper. May your tree grow and shed leaves.

May your tree grow and shed leaves.

He felt the click of Adele leaving his mindscape and returned his thoughts to Raganoth, just below him. The wyvern was still sleeping, but there was a problem anytime he did so.

He spread poison.

Chipper was sure he didn't mean to. It was just a part of who he was. Raganoth was a poison wyvern and would spread it whether he wanted to or not. Chipper quickly pulsed a low amount of magic to clear the area of poison as he had done a dozen times since gaining his newest friend, then went over and poked the wyvern in the chin. Many people would be nervous about poking a massive poisonous lizard who could somewhat fly, but they were friends. Chipper didn't hold any fear of him. After the third poke didn't wake the great creature up, Chipper gave him a light slap on the rump with magic. That did it.

The wyvern arched his back and woke up abruptly, yelling to the sky with his many large teeth bared, "What? Who dares to—oh. Hello, Chipper."

Speaking in the only way he could without a mental link like Adele's, Chipper wrote in the air, *Hello, friend Raganoth. I will be busy for a few hours, and I was wondering if you would mind protecting my territory in my absence?*

"Hours . . . hours . . . Ah, right, those short moments in time. Where are you going?"

We Guardians like to speak to each other occasionally, and a grouping has been called for. They will be arriving here, and I think it important that we introduce you to them slowly and thoughtfully rather than all at once.

The wyvern thought for a moment. "Okay, Chipper, I will protect your territory." He sniffed the air, picking the blood particles out from the standard bits of floating grass seed and the all-encompassing unattuned mana. "You have killed only recently. How often do you need to protect your tree?"

Chipper thought on that for a moment before writing, *I believe they come about once an hour. It should not be a problem for you.*

Raganoth gave a deep-throated laugh. "As if these tiny creatures could give Raganoth the Bleeder any cause to worry. Do not fret, young Chipper, I will protect your territory!" Saying so, he flared his wing-arms and leaped into the sky, angled for height.

Chipper smiled as he watched the wyvern take his duty seriously and gave him an unseen wave as he began the long hike to the top of the tree. He was, of course, using his magic on his nails and feet, surrounding himself in a pale aura that slowly bled away if he didn't keep the ratios up. Each time Chipper did this, he got a small high out of it. Magic was a wonderful thing, and even if Walker turned out to be a bad person, Chipper would still appreciate the world he had created. The Guardian had yet to scratch the surface of what his powers could do. It was an addicting experience every time he found a new way to use his attunement.

He settled on the last bough at the top of his tree and kept an eye out. Chipper spent a bit of the time he had before the others' arrival going over what he wanted to say. He had to attempt neutrality, speaking for his friend or not; otherwise, the collective would not take his words seriously. So, he cleared his mind of any positive emotions related to Walker and spent several minutes isolating his feelings and removing any chance of not remaining neutral.

Naturally, Bale the Quick arrived first, speeding out of the swamp forest, feet a blur, and Adele the Speaker arrived only a few minutes after. They said their traditional lines once they were within range and touched tails upon meeting, creating a small pulse of pure magic.

Hello, Bale, how are you on this fine Symphonic day?

I am well, Chipper. How are you on this fine Symphonic day?

All told, it took several minutes for them to greet each other once everyone arrived. Long enough that Chipper began to grow weary of the experience. They'd only held a few groupings in the last several years, but that was enough for the process to begin to annoy him. He disliked the delay, even if he was the one who had created it. Finally, everyone settled onto a branch, and Adele connected them so there wouldn't be a natural delay in writing to each other.

Hello, everyone. It is great to see you.

Hello, Adele!

Hi, Speaker!

Heyyyy, Adele! said the always exuberant Josh. He was a strange one. Then again, anyone who had to sit out near the ocean and stare at the water all day was likely to develop some strange tendencies. Especially those who enjoyed fishing . . .

Adele waved at Josh with a smile, always enjoying his energy, which Chipper never understood, before getting to the heart of why they'd arrived.

Let's get to the heart of why we're here, Adele said, mirroring Chipper's thoughts. *Chipper the First has had a chance to meet with our Creator, and I asked him to speak to us of what was said.*

What! Josh mentally yelled, causing many Guardians to wince. *No way!*

I do not like this, Rine the Dark said, his tone and unnaturally dark fur for a Guardian explaining his epithet. *Dealing with powerful beings is a mistake. I said this before when we allowed that massive frog to move up a tier.*

Rine's territory was where the mini-manticores had started. Some of the Guardians had come to speak to Chipper about him, worried that he was a corrupted Guardian and would need to be put down for the protection of the collective. But Chipper had changed their minds, saying you shouldn't judge a Guardian by their fur. He firmly believed that if you needed help, Rine would be there.

They had all spent some time in Rine's forest helping him maintain the manticore's equilibrium so they wouldn't get out of control. Thankfully, whenever the creatures bred, no more than two of the younglings would ever survive at a time. The only problem was just how often they produced offspring, seeming to copulate at any given moment—and, of course, there was the Silent Wind.

The Silent Wind was a name Rine had given to a larger-than-normal manticore who was moving through the tiers at a fast pace, quickly approaching sapience. A manticore with self-control and an increased intelligence would be incredibly dangerous. The tremendous golden manticore already produced more offspring than the others and would actually keep most of them alive during their initial birth-to-battle phase, further upsetting Symphony's balance. It was a worrying subject for the entire collective because they were afraid it might start a war within Symphony once it reached sapience.

Chipper listened back in on the conversation the others were having. Some, like Rine, didn't like the idea of speaking to the Creator of Symphony. All of them, including the Dark, appreciated what the Creator had done for them: making a world, creating them, providing a means of life and a way for them to defend themselves. There was certainly a deep and abiding glow of feelings for the powerful being within his group. But speaking to him and reminding him of their continued existence was scary for some. Appreciating what they had was important, but testing fate was a different matter.

Chipper's neutrality wavered a little as they each shared their feelings on the matter. He pushed his emotions away and focused on what they were saying, trying to take it all in with clear eyes and a full heart. He firmly believed he would never lose if he was forever able to do that.

Looking at his fellow Guardians and doing a quick mental head count, he saw there was undoubtedly a split decision right now. Rine led the side that believed they should keep their distance, while Adele the Speaker and Cenare the Just led the side that wanted not only to speak to him but to work with him if they could. Finally, as he knew would likely occur, Rine the Dark looked at Chipper.

Chipper. You are the first Guardian and hold the central territory of Symphony. We've all appreciated how you travel to each new land and provide guidance and advice on thriving in this world. I would say, and I do not believe I am speaking out of turn, that your word here counts more than the others. He looked around and received a chorus of nods from both sides.

Chipper didn't like that, as it went against what they'd agreed to when first forming the collective. But you can't change people's feelings.

Rine continued, *So, what do you say? How should we move forward with our Creator?*

Chipper looked from pale face to pale face, taking in their expressions. *That is difficult to say. You still do not even know of what we spoke. You only know that we had a conversation.*

Yes, Cenare said, causing the others to look at him, *but the fact that he came down and spoke to you, I believe, speaks well of his character. He is an all-powerful being we will likely never fully understand. One that we need to have positive relations with for our continued survival and purpose. You do not shun the thing that keeps you alive. That would be like all of us moving away from our trees and inhabiting bushes.* He looked to the crowd as a few shuddered.

Rine disagreed, saying, *All creatures of Symphony have a voice and a purpose. That is the first value we decided on as a collective in the second meeting. You call yourself the Just. How is there justice in destroying a group of creatures for the simple act of not choosing to speak with you? He could do that on a whim! The Creator placed a giant burning ball there, which is blinding us at this very moment.* He pointed one gray finger at the yellow star in the sky. *For what purpose? He never told us or consulted with us. Thus, I believe we do not hold a high enough value in his eyes.*

That is the thing, Rine, Adele said from only a branch away. *There is no guarantee that he will destroy us, and with Chipper standing in front of us now rather than obliterated from the surface of Symphony, I have to hold that he is not a villainous character.* Cenare nodded just beside her, bolstering the Speaker's resolve. *Chipper, First, what do you say? Can we trust him?*

Those words hit Chipper like a ton of bricks, and his preferred neutrality formed a small crack. Walker was his friend, but he needed to also look out for the Guardians. If he didn't, who would? He needed to go over the facts.

The Creator had chosen him as a Symphonic representative for the battle . . . apparently, then had chosen to speak with him again, and had even physically presented himself, something he'd not done with any of the others. Chipper knew everyone had heard him speaking just before the light turned back to the darkness. He liked to believe he was a good judge of someone's character. Walker just didn't seem like a bad guy. After all, he'd given Chipper Raganoth, another friend and his first true companion.

But he couldn't hold back this information from the collective. This was a precarious moment, and they needed to know everything.

Let me explain what we spoke of. Then we can decide as one group, the way the collective was envisioned, Chipper said with resolve, looking each of the other Guardians in the eyes to make sure they gave a nod of agreement. He was called the First because he was the original Guardian, but no matter what they said about his word meaning more than the others', none wanted to pick another to stand above. After he made sure everyone agreed, he spoke.

I was asked for a favor and then more than one. He explained that I had just returned from a battle, though I had no memory of it . . .

The other Guardians stood quietly and listened to Chipper's story. The outcome of their debate was not settled in the slightest.

RAGANOTH

The grand poison wyvern, Raganoth the Bleeder, flew over the central territory of Symphony. His nap had been surprisingly pleasant, with no attacks and a generally quiet atmosphere. Being woken up early would typically have bothered him greatly, but seeing Chipper had kept his temper in check. He was still getting used to the feeling of not being hypervigilant at all times of the day, but it was hard to break over two hundred years of tradition and evolutionary need.

Raganoth spied a black manticore on the edge of the territory. He'd seen Chipper kill them in the past, but the albino squirrel had never asked for his help before. He was happy to do this for a . . . friend. Raganoth swooped down from on high—the feral creature couldn't see or hear him coming—and after a quick breath of poison, he moved on, leaving a yellow stain bubbling behind him.

This world was strange. Everything was so weak. So fragile. Except for two things: Chipper and his Mana Tree. That tree was a thing of pure glory. Beautiful, breathtaking even, and its bark was as tough a thing as Raganoth had ever seen. The first time he'd watched Chipper gather fallen leaves and eat them had been quite the shock. How the Guardian could stomach that amount of magical potential was beyond him. He respected the smaller creature, though, and valued his friendship enough to ensure he didn't cause undue or unnecessary damage while he traveled over the forest line.

Their "spar" had been quite fun, and Chipper had seemed to get better at fighting him the longer they went, whereas Raganoth couldn't help but feel like he wasn't improving himself. Sparring was strange. But a new land and new experiences required a new Raganoth. He would do his best to blend in with the natives.

Raganoth found he had overshot Chipper's territory while lost in his thoughts, but it turned out to be a positive mistake. He spied a very large black manticore next to a golden one that was also unusually big, just a few flaps away. He gained some air so he wouldn't be seen quite as well, then prepared to swoop down for the attack.

However, the moment his wings bent and his air resistance began to weaken, the golden one looked up. It saw him and immediately lifted its tail and ran, leaving the black one behind. That was an unusual amount of intelligence from what he'd seen of these creatures so far. Not that he was much better. The time spent murdering his way across his parents' territory with nary a thought entering his mind gave a dark reflection of these creatures. Still, he had a job to do, and sympathy wouldn't get him far.

The poison wyvern decided not to chase the golden manticore, as he was unsure of being able to kill it within an acceptable timeframe. When it dove into the forest at full speed, his chances of success were reduced due to the natural protection from large flying creatures. He would have to destroy the whole forest just to pin it down, and Raganoth was sure that would negatively affect his relationship with his new friend.

Still, there was the large black one, which would at least help the Guardians have one less manticore to deal with. After all, he was here to help.

Raganoth further closed his wings to the wind and picked up speed, dropping like a meteor, as he aimed for the black manticore. The creature stared up at him, hissing and waving its poison-tipped tail behind it. Of course, its poison would be many levels weaker than his own, so he wasn't overly worried even if it did get a lucky hit on him.

As he grew closer, moving at a blurring speed, something stabbed into his side and pierced through his plated skin. He felt a negligible amount of poison enter his body and absorbed it, further increasing the strength of his own. Wyverns were unique creatures across the cosmos. They were all naturally attuned and could absorb new forms of their element for an improvement in overall power. Poison for poison, heat for flame and fire. Raganoth accepted this gift freely as he opened his wings, slowed his descent, and looked to the side.

The large golden manticore had seemingly moved through the forest and attacked him in a moment when he couldn't see it. Definitely more intelligent than the rest and thus, dangerous. He spat a large glob of poison at the creature, but it dodged behind a tree too quickly to be affected. Meanwhile, the black manticore began climbing a tree of its own, preparing to attack.

Raganoth continued to focus on the golden manticore and spat again as it peaked its head out from behind a tree. The moment he did so, the black manticore leaped off of the tree and was already soaring through the air.

Just like he wanted.

Raganoth swung his tail in a perfect arc, caught the black manticore full in the face, and shot it into the ground, where it cracked on impact. He dove down quickly before the golden manticore could attack and ripped what was left of its head off its neck with his teeth before swallowing it whole. It didn't taste great, missing all of the seasonings from his planet as it was, but his stomach could still use the filling.

The golden manticore hissed and ran off, likely for good this time.

Raganoth took a few more bites, filling his large stomach, then ambled out of the forest and began flying again. He tried to hold down any indigestion that might flare up, as he'd always found exercise right after a solid meal caused him problems. The poison wyvern smiled when nobody could see him. Not so different from his old world after all.

CHAPTER SEVEN

Zones and Series

Walker was still looking at the second temporal task on his screen. There was an itch in his mind, and he knew he probably didn't have time for it yet, no pun intended. But still, it was there.

Temporal task: Create a static temporal zone (Part 2)
You've built a localized temporal anomaly and grasped just the beginning of what the Temporal Subsystem can do. Now, create a temporal zone that consistently slows down or speeds up time without heavily draining your resources.
Localized temporal zone built: 0/1
Resources allocated for completion: 100 years
Reward for completion: Temporal Subsystem upgrade

He knew there was a way to cheat it, but there was a problem: he needed the Milestone System updated, but it hadn't been fully completed yet. Then again, it likely would never be fully completed.

As the years passed and they continued to add new tiers and new achievements, it would be a constant and ongoing process. Walker looked over at Cagna dutifully working on the system that would entwine everything together and smiled. The pink squirrel was extremely happy in her work, her face constantly shifting from puzzlement to surprise to joy and back to puzzlement as she added new milestones to her system.

For now, Walker was required to add new milestones permanently, like the traveler series. But he could see that Cagna would have complete control over the system by the end of their time dilation.

His eyes roamed over to Rimi, who was currently locked in a heated discussion with his newly minted mentor, Virgil. Walker's ears listened in and picked up what they were talking about. The focus was naturally on how much power to give human beings through modifications. Virgil argued for less power, as they would eventually have a Class System that would allow for the codification of skills. Rimi, ever the champion of his monsters, surprisingly argued for more so that they would be at the same power level as the monsters at the start. The now slightly less tiny squirrel stated that it would allow each side to push the other toward more strength.

Walker knew he would have to step in there in a moment, but he let his mind wander. He needed to think about what they were going to do next. Civilizations were the lynchpin of his worlds' future growth. It didn't necessarily have to be human beings. They could use the combiner to create amalgamations of animals and humans to form some kind of beastkin. Or they could plant the Warclaws . . . Actually, maybe not.

They might even plant a large grouping of wyverns, although he would have to burn over a hundred years for them to reach sapience . . . No, human beings were the way forward, and he wasn't just being sentimental for his species.

Throughout history, humans had shown a remarkable ability to adapt to their circumstances and overcome their weaknesses. That's where Walker was stuck right now: their weaknesses. They'd arrive on the planet with no Class System, milestones relatively bare, and with only a small number of human beings overall. He needed to change things, but it was difficult while they were under the dome of time. He did have one idea, and he approached Rimi with it, as it involved his system in particular.

"Hey, Rimi," Walker said, interrupting his and Virgil's argument just as it seemed to become heated.

"Yes, Creator?" Rimi replied, all anger forgotten.

"How difficult would it be to limit some monsters to tiers? Like one set limited to tier one, another to tier two, and so on. I know we did it with the Guardians, sticking them in tier four, but how difficult is that to manage?"

"Hmm," Rimi hummed to himself. "Let me take a look."

While Rimi was going through his screens, Walker looked at Virgil and said, "Not seeing eye to eye on things?"

Virgil harrumphed like an old man, causing Walker to smile. "His ideas are juvenile."

"He is a juvenile," Walker countered.

"Yes, I know, but he wants to build an incredibly modified human race. It would force them onto a path of conflict the moment they could spread beyond our solar system. If a human child is born and grows at an accelerated rate without allowing for the development of standard physiological and psychological needs, then you may as well call them a Warclaw. Rimi wants to modify the human race to become a large faction of space-faring barbarian conquerors. Space pirates!"

Virgil's face took on a sly cast. "I am arguing against it, as I know you best, of course, and know you would not want that."

Walker felt a slight buzz from his chest. "No, no, I do not. The idea is to create a world where everyone can choose their path, not force people onto one that requires them to form conquering empires."

"Exactly!" Virgil crowed as he raised a fist to the sky. "Vindication!"

Rimi looked up from his screens and glared at the larger squirrel before returning to them.

"So, that's settled. No, I don't want them to just have modifications out the wazoo and never have to strive or work for anything. I asked for the disease resistance because A: I don't want plagues to wipe them out, and B: my mother died from a simple infection that ran amok. It's a sensitive subject for me."

Virgil nodded somberly. "Yes, I can see why. But you also approved a few other modifications when we spoke prior. They have already been applied, and thus, I believe humanity has a great chance of surviving upon first seeding. There are good—"

Walker snapped his fingers. "Increase the grafts."

Virgil stumbled on his words for a moment but recovered from the interruption quickly. "Why?"

Walker just smiled mischievously. "I have my plans. I want mana grafts throughout the whole body, if possible. Not just the connectors from the mind kernel to the chest and stomach. Everywhere. Anywhere there is an artery. That way, they can travel throughout the skin and bones as well."

Virgil looked at him strangely, then shrugged and turned to his screens. Walker couldn't do anything while he waited, so he just looked around Sonata. The Primigenials were playing rock paper scissors for some reason, while Dionysus had woken up and was yelling at the tree, of all things.

In his immediate proximity were three squirrels of varying sizes and colors, all staring into space with different expressions. Virgil was frustrated, Rimi was intense, and Cagna was smiling in a way that reminded him of his students daydreaming during class. He pulled up the monitor and zoomed in on Phil at random. From his perspective, Phil was in place as he settled into the sand, his tail ever so slowly falling to lie beside him. At least Phil got to sleep.

Rimi came out of his screen first. "Yes, I can put tier limits on multiple genera at once, but it will cover them entirely due to how the kernels respond to the Monster System. If you restrict the seals here to tier one," he said, pointing at the creature with the Evolution Chamber, "they will never be able to break out of it. That is the rank that they will forever hold, just like the Guardians. They would have to go through a traumatic event that fundamentally changed their nature as an entity or gain an outside evolution straight from the Creator, being you, to break through the restriction and be classified differently than their fellows."

"What about the Alpha ability?" Walker asked.

Rimi dove into his screen again, then looked back at him. "I know why you asked. According to the Monster System, Chipper is no longer fully classified as a Guardian. He is now an Alpha Guardian, considered unique and thus excluded from the restriction."

Walker scratched his chin as he smiled. "Dang, go you, Chipper. So, in the end, he did get a reward for everything he did for us."

Rimi nodded. "Yep. Now, what were you thinking? Why did you ask about the restrictions?"

Pulling on his old gamer knowledge, he said, "Because I realized we need to make starter zones for our people."

"Starter zones? What are those?"

Walker began pacing back and forth. "Well, I wanted to plant the first sapients in the middle of Symphony and have Chipper watch over them, but now I don't think that will work. The monsters have already grown too much, and there's always a chance a manticore or a scorpion could cross over and enter their territory. One tier-three manticore could wipe out hundreds of barely starting humans, if not more. I can't take that chance. We need to sectionalize the first seedings and let their adventurous or expansionist sides take over once they've gained some skill. It's not realistic to place them in the center of the world right now."

"I see. So you want to restrict the monsters so that humans can grow their power in a relatively safe environment. That is smart, but there is a larger problem. You realize this goes directly against my Monster System directives, correct? You would be restricting their power permanently in violation of your oath and what you explained to me when I first came here."

As Rimi spoke, Walker felt a pulse in his chest. This one felt different. Unlike the previous times, when it had felt more like a guiding hand, now it warned of dire circumstances. The feeling he received was that his oath and the words written into his soul required him to change how he progressed with this line of thought. If he didn't . . . well, who knew what would happen? As he thought that, another pulse came out in agreement.

Walker thought it over momentarily as Rimi, seeing that he seemed deep in thought, gave him time. His thoughts meandered around until he felt like he had an idea—a happy middle ground.

Should the monsters under tier restrictions perform extraordinary feats, he would ensure Cagna created a milestone series that unlocked their tiers and allowed them to continue growing in power. That way, the restriction would always have the option of being removed. The vibration in his chest lessened but didn't go away. Walker assumed it wouldn't until he found a way to follow through on what he'd just decided. He spent some time explaining what he'd come up with to Rimi.

"That is not a perfect solution. But you *are* giving options to the monsters who fulfill your requirements . . . Okay. We are agreed." He reached out his small blue hand, and Walker took it, giving a firm handshake while wondering where the subsystem assistant had learned the action. "Do you know what you want to restrict in tiers yet?"

Walker shook his head. "No, but I want their sizes to change based upon what we restrict, so something small for tier one, slightly larger for tier two, and regular-sized for tier three. Nothing gigantified or anything like that. They should also have limited modifications, as we want to introduce our sapients to the world of magic and monsters slowly and deliberately. You must take great care in what you pick and how you modify them. Enough to fight, but not enough to destroy a town."

Rimi nodded. "Excellent. The goat and seal are complete, so I will begin working on this immediately with the modifications we already have in the system." Saying so, he had Walker pull up a monitor, and a few seconds later, a goat and seal exploded into space, emptying two Evolution Chambers. Rimi didn't even blink.

"Why didn't you just place them on Symphony?"

Rimi gave a blue-shouldered shrug. "I thought they would be lonely."

"So your solution was to throw them into space?" Walker asked, disbelieving.

Rimi nodded. "Yep. Now, do you know what type of habitat I will be looking at?"

Walker took a second to push past the "new" Rimi. "I, uh, think it'll probably be somewhere with a lot of soil, water, trees, and should be surrounded by mountains. The idea is to create an enclosed area for our first seeding of sapients so they can progressively grow without dire threats constantly emerging. I know I want my people to have to fight for their growth, but they still need starting points to understand how Symphony works."

"Thus, the starter zones," Rimi supplied.

Walker snapped his fingers. "Exactly!"

"Okay, I will get started. Maybe some kind of rabbit with sharp teeth who can leap . . ." He continued mumbling as he walked over to the Evolution Chambers. As the blue subsystem assistant began his work, Virgil replaced him.

"I have run my calculations and believe it will take another thirty or so days before I can feel confident that we have fulfilled your request." He looked at Rimi before returning his gaze to Walker. "I see my mentee will be busy for some time, so add a day to my estimate. However, it is possible that it may take longer than expected."

Walker nodded. "Understood. That's why we're in here, after all," he said as he pointed to nowhere in particular, intimating the temporal displacement. "The moment it's done, I'll apply the bloodlines and we'll start mass-producing our sapients. I'm thinking of seeding several hundred at once."

Virgil's body stilled upon hearing that, freezing in place. It seemed like he wanted to say something but could not get the words out. Walker sensed what was happening and watched him silently, trying to figure out a way around this. Then he had an idea. "You know what, maybe a few hundred isn't enough; maybe a thousand would work much better?" He watched Virgil closely, but the sizable brown squirrel still didn't move. "Five thousand?" Still nothing. "Ten thousand, then."

Virgil started moving again, nodding. "That would be an excellent idea, Walker."

Walker was so shocked that he ignored the fact that they'd finally found a way around the Alpha Protocol's information restrictions. "Ten fucking thousand!"

"Ah, you have come to that conclusion all on your own; now I can explain why you are correct." Walker blew a noise out of the side of his mouth. "Between genetic diversity, allowance of some deaths, and the mix and match of needed professions and 'hands' to do the work required to start and run a civilization, ten thousand is a small number in the grand scheme of things."

Walker threw his hands in the air. "Yeah, but that's a shitload of seeding, even with three of us. The time dilation is great, but it'll still take up way too much of our time."

"Indeed." Virgil nodded sagely. "It just means you need to attach Cagna to the Entity Subsystem, just like Rimi, and start your Milestone System for more assistants in the near future. The more assistants you have, the more hands we bring to the task."

"More assistants?" Walker said quietly. "This moonlet isn't large enough to accommodate them, not to mention the Primigenials."

Virgil shook his head. "Is it not? The Primigenials release as the tree matures. When the tree matures, the moonlet grows. Every time you take a major step forward, the tree grows in size, or have you not noticed? In the last maturing, you had just created Romulus and Remus. The time before that, you had just created a unique entity, the battlefrogs, and received a special award from the protocol. Each time you take a major step, the tree grows and Primigenials come out. What do you think would happen if you began to seed ten thousand sapients, not to mention all of the new landmasses that would be required? What will happen when the Milestone System becomes fully activated?"

Walker nodded. "I see your point."

"Yes. Give me thirty days and activate the Milestone System. I . . ." Virgil paused for a long moment, long enough for Walker to grow impatient enough to tap his foot, before smiling and saying, "I have great faith that this problem will be solved."

Walker found the pause and smile quite curious, but, as always, he believed Virgil was looking out for him. "Okay," was all he said as he walked over to Cagna.

The pink subsystem assistant stated she was trying to develop a milestone series for marriage, of all things. Still, Walker had her put a hold on it so he could finally get the strangely uncomfortable buzzing out of his chest.

They spoke together about what a standard series would be going forward in the Milestone System, before he had her create a special limited series. This series would differ from what they'd made with the traveler series and would include the first milestone reward attached to points. They spent a lot of time discussing how the limited series would work, making a framework for future sets of series in the interest of speed.

The limited category wouldn't be as complete as a full series, with only specific milestones being allowed. The entity could only gain the milestone reward after reaching a designed point cap, which allowed a lot more freedom in its design. Cagna was quite excited and said she wanted to do something like that with her marriage series, as she was having trouble figuring out how to involve the production of children. Her words, of course, made Walker feel quite awkward. Was it a sex milestone? Surely not . . . maybe.

The results of their first limited series were quite satisfying to look at.

Monster Advancement Series: *Limited, Complete*

Basic milestone—Neutrality:
Choose to not kill an entity. 1 point.

Apprentice milestone—Brightness:
Save an entity rather than leave it to die. 5 points.

Skilled milestone—Altruistic:
Save a group of entities, no less than 5, from certain death or doom. 10 points.

Advanced milestone—A Monstrous Hero:
Defend more than 100 entities from a creature more powerful than yourself. 20 points.

Epic milestone—Savior:
Save a town from certain doom. 50 points.

Limited to restricted monsters already found in the Monster System.

Walker nodded as he looked at it, and his soul finally relaxed. It was the oddest feeling he could remember having. Like a fluttering, gnawing, pushing in his chest that suddenly ebbed away.

He wasn't blind or dumb. He knew the new series would also work for the Guardians, allowing them to grow and move on from their trees as they performed deeds Walker considered positive for Symphony. However, it did restrict monsters who didn't make attempts to help others, so the odds of a monster completing the advancement series were quite small. But he still felt that it was fair. Monsters could always go down a darker path after fulfilling the initial requirements, and it would allow future starter-zone monsters the ability to find their way in life if they chose to be altruistic in their endeavors.

His reasoning for only including positive milestones for the advancement series was simple. He didn't want monsters to go on rampages in burgeoning civilizations. At least not at the start. Plus, who was to say the only civilizations he would start up would be human? Earth's history was rampant with lizard people, beast people, as he'd thought of before, and even the fae. The multiverse was a big place, and he did have something special he'd earned in the second battle. Walker eyed the Auction System in his tab for a moment before shaking his head.

While that thought filtered through his mind, Walker looked at Virgil and Rimi working on the starter-zone monsters. He stared, lost in thought, before looking at the old computer and chair nearby. When the protocol first kicked up, it'd been a rush to get more land and territory out—the same with entities. But now, here he was, focusing on empowering his soul and working with Cagna on milestones. He might be focusing on something else entirely in a few days, weeks, or months. Like food for his people or defense against some kind of attack. It was a serious unknown.

The system called him a Creator, and the assistants and Primigenials did the same. But what did that mean? Were the other Creators who were plucked from their worlds doing the same thing as him? Were they all just throwing dirt and water at their planetary attempt while refining entities? Or were they working on systems too? Were there other things out there, other ways of empowering the world and entities within it, and it was actually a rare thing for him to earn the System Designer?

There were a lot of questions without any answers. He supposed being a Creator allowed him to create his own interpretation of things, but there was a stark reality that helped to center him.

He was a human being, enhanced by his soul, and he did not have godlike power.

It was a mistake to believe that he would ever have such. Even the term Creator needed to be corrected. He wasn't forming flesh and viscera with his hands, nor was he creating dirt from nothing but magic. While admittedly he did both of those things, he did so through the systems the protocol bestowed upon him. But maybe that was how it was supposed to be. The protocol was not a happy-go-lucky situation. The Council that ran it had their own view of how things should be. Maybe they were worried about overpowering Creators and losing control of things.

Walker spied Virgil speaking to Rimi about something, then remembered that the Milestone System still wasn't activated. He couldn't drop another subsystem assistant until it was, which led him back to his previous thought. His interpretation of Creator could be different from the others in the protocol. Maybe his job and focus were to get the systems up and running, then allow others to take the role from him.

He could delegate his vision of how things should be and then oversee the results. It would certainly be easier than trying to track every little change that happened going forward. After all, who was to say how many systems and entities he'd end up creating. When Symphony was fully up and running, with the thousands of human beings Virgil said he required, it'd be almost impossible to manage singlehandedly. At least, not without cloning himself multiple times. So, in the end, he had no choice but to rely on his people. Nodding, he looked at Cagna.

"Though we haven't added nearly as much as I would like to the system," he said, pulling up his screen and scrolling through the dozen or so milestones they had agreed upon in the last several weeks, "it is still a good starting point. Now, I feel that with the finalization of our first series, limited or not, we need to start up the Milestone System. What do you think?"

Cagna nodded excitedly, so Walker smiled and clicked on the system to activate it. That's naturally when he remembered something important. Slapping his forehead, Walker clicked on Symphony and advanced it by seven days, syncing up their time dilation.

"Well, son of a bitch," he said to himself in realization. "I forgot that the Milestone System has to attach to something. Otherwise, the protocol won't record the days and hours that pass by. Now we've gotta wait." He sighed to himself and sat on the grass. "Oh well, not too big a deal."

Cagna began working on her limited marriage series, so Walker called Echidna over and worked on his soul. This was his fourth time now, and it still stung like hell. He strained with his invisible muscle, stretching the soul up in an attempt to reach his collarbone as she'd first instructed. After a few snapbacks, which jarred him and knocked Echidna over as she quietly whispered encouragement to him, he felt his progress change. Imagining two hands reaching down, he was about to grab both sides of his soul to stretch it directly where he intended.

Once he had his soul in position and confirmed such with Echidna, she swapped from a whisper to a scream. "Press down, hard! Push it directly into the area you've stretched it over!" Walker, eyes closed as he focused, nodded and pushed on his soul, attempting to mesh it with the new area of his body. He knew he'd done it right when a ring of green soul-power shot out of him and covered Sonata, alerting everyone that he'd made a step toward empowering his soul.

While he caught his breath, he saw Minos give him a thumbs-up while Echidna, after picking herself up off the ground, gave him a beautiful smile. Zeus and Athena paused their conversation to give him a mysterious look, then went back to what they were doing. Dionysus stopped yelling at the tree and just stared at him oddly. Walker mentally shrugged.

He reviewed his body, paying attention to any changes that may have occurred. It felt a little different again. The area he'd stretched his soul over felt refreshed. Poking at his chest, he found the muscles to be thicker, more filled out. Even his skin seemed to be stretched tighter across the area. It was a strange feeling.

Echidna told him to take it easy, so he lay down and relaxed for a few moments, enjoying his time away from everyone. It didn't take long for Dionysus to begin yelling at the tree again, saying something was making him feel depressed, so Walker pulled up his monitor and zoomed around Symphony for a while. Now that things were in real-time and not offset by the Temporal Subsystem, he could see everyone moving normally. He watched his old friend Chomp for a bit as he tore into a manticore before going back to his one true love, the yellow flowers.

Honestly, he spent more than just a little bit of time watching them, as he kept an eye on the golden battlefrog for over an hour. He considered using his Avatar ability and dropping in to say hi, but his memories of the last time he'd spent time with the great dooter flashed through his mind and he thought better of it.

Walker was a little annoyed with himself. He hadn't relaxed much since first landing here—he'd just been too busy. No food, no sleep, and only his work as a Creator to keep him occupied. It was worrying, as he had a long time to go before his next vacation . . . like, an eternity. Assuming he succeeded in the protocol, he'd have to find some way to relieve stress.

Before too long, Cagna came over and wanted to share her marriage series. Walker wasn't too big a fan of it initially, as it seemed strange to reward people for tying the knot and humping, but he warmed up to the idea the longer she talked about it and what her plans were. Ultimately, he bowed to her enthusiasm, and they worked on it together, with him changing the descriptions a little.

Marriage Series: *Limited, Complete*

Basic milestone—Marriage:
***Connect with another on a deeply personal level and choose to
form a governmental bond of shared taxation. 1 point.***

Apprentice milestone—Family:
Have a child and start your own family. 5 points.

Skilled milestone—Bonded:
*Be married to the same person(s) for 10 years or more without
killing each other. 10 points.*

Advanced milestone—Till Death:
Be married for 25 years or more. 20 points.

Epic milestone—Kin:
Have at least 10 people or more in your family. 50 points.

**Reward: Obtain 40 or more points in the Marriage series to
unlock the Dynasty System.**

Limited to sapient entities who enter marriage willingly.

Sure, it would force him to create a Dynasty System, but with Virgil's ideas and his own faith in them, he was likely going to do that anyway. Plus, it was nice to reward families who wanted to expand and become something more. There certainly wouldn't be repercussions to creating a Dynasty System. Certainly not.

Walker smiled, thinking of families starting up on Symphony.

Not too far away now.

CHAPTER EIGHT

The First Follower

Walker stretched his soul again, this time aiming for his hips. However, the distance was greater than expected. He'd forgotten that compared to most people, he had a longer torso and always seemed to be just a little more proportional than most at his height. That meant that when he tried to stretch to the much greater distance of his hips, his soul wasn't ready for it and snapped back with more than a bit of pain.

When he asked about it, Echidna laid some knowledge down, saying the snap-back was more than just distance. He hadn't stretched his soul in that direction before, and since it was still hardening at a good clip, he'd need to work faster to keep trying to cover his body.

"What happens if I don't finish before it hardens?" Walker said through gritted teeth and squinted eyes.

The yellow-eyed woman blinked once, saying, "Then you will lose a great amount of power. It will also restrict you from moving through the stages, as it has for Minos and myself. So I believe speed is of the essence, as you like to say. However, right now, you should rest. The first pull is always the worst."

So, Walker settled into a routine.

He'd stretch his soul for a time, recover from the pain by voyeuristically watching monsters on Symphony, work with Cagna a bit, then go back to his painful soul-time. The pink squirrel did add a special limited series with a new tier and set of pages that made him laugh hard enough that he had her add it to the milestones in the system.

Petting Series: *Special, Limited, Complete*

Basic milestone—Smart:
You've pet a squirrel on Symphony. Smart! 1 point.

Apprentice milestone—Furry:
Pet over 100 creatures. 5 points.

Skilled milestone—That's a Lot of Petting:
Pet over 1,000 creatures. 10 points.

Advanced milestone—Petting Dangerously:
Pet 5 different living monsters who are all at different tiers.
20 points.

Epic milestone—Not Smart:
Pet a Guardian. 50 points.

Godly milestone—Symphonic Petting:
Pet the Creator of Symphony. 100 points.

Reward: Obtain 80 or more points and receive the option to speak with the Creator directly. Once. For no more than 10 minutes.

Walker thought Cagna had forgotten his comments earlier but apparently not. He had her create the final milestone just because it would be a quick and easy way to show favor to those he dropped in on with the Avatar ability. See someone do something amazing and give them a way to contact him in the future. Sure, the petting was pretty weird, but Cagna said she wanted to make milestones fun, and he liked to humor his assistants when he could. Plus, he felt like she was finally starting to warm up to him.

Cagna walked off, saying she had other ideas but needed to work on them by herself for a time, so Walker went back to trying to cover his hips with his soul. Facing the rebound and the inherent pain of it, he started his normal rotation of looking at Symphony. This time he zoomed over to look at Chipper and found words burned into the grass below his tree.

We need to talk, friend Walker.

"Finally," Walker said with a sigh. He held the monitor to that spot and clicked on the Avatar ability to send himself down.

Walker felt his body fade into Symphony and looked around, not spotting the Alpha Guardian. After a heartbeat, he heard a rustle above and watched as Chipper jumped down from a branch. He landed lightly and with barely any sound, then spread his magic out, the white coloring washing against the burned words Walker had seen from Sonata. The grass slowly healed itself before him.

"Neat trick," Walker said approvingly.

Chipper wrote back, *Yes, I discovered it when repairing the damage that Raganoth causes to Symphony.*

"Oh?" Walker replied. "Is there a problem?"

No, not as such, friend Walker. It is inherent to the poison wyvern. He cannot help it, and the damage is not so difficult to repair.

Walker nodded with a smile. "Good stuff. So, what did you want to talk about?"

Chipper fiddled with his fingers for a moment before writing, *We have had a meeting.*

Walker's face scrunched up. "I'm confused. Who had a meeting? You and Raganoth?"

Chipper shook his head. *No, Walker. Myself and the other Guardians. We call ourselves the Guardian Collective. When we must, we meet up and discuss the events occurring on Symphony.*

Walker snapped his fingers. "Hey! That's pretty great! You guys went and formed your own organization. Good work, Chipper."

Chipper smiled. *Thank you. As I was saying, we had a meeting, and the subject was my conversation with you not long ago.*

"Oh?"

Unexpectedly, Chipper knelt before him. *I choose to become your follower.*

Walker's overlay updated and thrust itself into his vision as a lot happened at once.

**Religion task complete: Find one follower for the Dante religion
(Part 1)**
Followers gained: 1/1
Reward for completion: Follower System

[. . . Scanning . . .]
[. . .]
[Error.]
[. . .]
Scripture found.
[. . . Scanning . . .]
Extraneous reward found.
[. . .]

New civilization task: Build a basic civilization (Series 1)
The Alpha Protocol focuses not only on creating unique worlds but unique societies as well. Provide your entities with the intelligence and tools to start their own civilization in its basic form.

Basic Civilization requirements:
Settlement founded: No
Social structures or government established: No
Continuous needs met: 0/7 days
Reward for completion: Disciple Subsystem

[. . . Scanning . . .]
[. . .]
Disciple Subsystem absorbed into the Follower System.
New civilization reward found.
New reward re-assigned to task.
[. . . Scanning . . .]
Optional task updated!
Scripture already within system.
Reward preemptively assigned.
Optional task updated!
[. . .]

Religion task complete: Write a scripture for the Dante religion
(Part 2)
Scripture Written: 10/10 volumes
Reward for completion: Follower System upgrade
[. . .]

New religion task: Select an insignia and a name for the Dante
religion (Part 3)
*Images and words matter, Dante. Using the Follower System,
create an insignia that will represent your religion to the rest of
the world and find the name that best represents your beliefs.
Choose wisely, Creator.*
Insignia selected: 0/1
Name selected: 0/1
Reward for completion: Follower System upgrade

Civilization task: Build a basic civilization (Series 1)
*The Alpha Protocol focuses not only on creating unique worlds but
unique societies as well. Provide your entities with the intelli-
gence and tools to start their own civilization in its basic form.*
Basic Civilization requirements:
Settlement founded: No
Social structures or government established: No

Continuous needs met: 0/7 days
Reward for completion: Trophy System

Reward for completing the first religion task:
Congratulations, Dante! You've unlocked the Follower System!
The Follower System is unique within the collected systems of the
Alpha Protocol. Created by an entity in the first rendition rather
than a Creator, it cannot be modified or copied from its original
state. This system is only unlocked by Creators who have touched
upon the powers of the soul and is only available due to an
agreement with the system's Creator and the Alpha Protocol
Council.
Limit: Cannot be changed or modified from its original state.
(Upgradeable)

Reward for completing the second religion task:
Congratulations, Dante! You've upgraded the Follower System!
No description was found.
(Upgradeable)

Chipper looked confused while Walker went through enough notifications that it seemed like the protocol had sprung a leak.

Who is Dante? he wrote out while waiting for Walker to look up. As he wrote, a book popped out of thin air and landed in the grass before him.

Walker looked away from his overlay and, to his surprise, found the giant albino squirrel holding a copy of his Holy Scripture. It was the exact same version as his original journal, with the camo front and creased spine.

"Um," Walker said, scratching his head as Chipper's magical writing faded, "I'm Dante, technically. The Alpha Protocol needed me to pick a name, and I picked one from the history of my world. Dante was a man who had to survive many trials while continuing in his search for greater meaning in life. That's why I picked it. I mean, I didn't know what I was doing here or how things would proceed, so I picked a name that reflected a fellow explorer of the dark."

That is quite interesting, Walker, Chipper wrote in the air. *I like the name Dante.*

"Thank you," Walker said with a smile. His eyes caught on the journal again, and he looked back at Chipper's face. "Yeah, so, I have to ask. What made you agree to be my follower?"

Chipper canted his head to the side, then wrote in the air, with a shakier hand than expected, *I am the sacrifice.*

"I'm sorry?" Walker asked him, not understanding.

It was decided in our meeting that one of us needs to see if you are evil or good. I volunteered to become your follower so we could ascertain which you might be.

Walker shook his head in disbelief and automatically said what he'd always told his students, "There is no good or evil. The world is a field of gray."

Chipper shook his head in response, mimicking him. *I disagree. I've lived here for over fifty years, and the manticores are surely evil. They care only to kill, and often not even for food. They are a blight on this world.*

Walker tried to look at it from his perspective. This is where he might run into trouble when people considered the Creator of Symphony. Like on Earth, he figured they would curse him for any sickness or issue that sprang up. They'd say, "Why couldn't you cure all diseases?" Or "Why did Jim have to die and not John?" But as the Creator of Symphony, he knew the purpose of the manticores. Maybe they were evil, or perhaps they were purely instinctual, but either way, their purpose was to test the strength of his citizens. To force them to grow. And it wouldn't be the first "evil" entity he would make. It wasn't with pleasure he did so but by requirement.

While those thoughts sat on his mind, he gave a minute shrug. "You may be right. But at least they're manageable." Chipper didn't say anything in return, just continued to look at Walker as he did the same. They stared at each other for over a minute before Walker said, "I'm not evil."

I didn't think you were, Chipper wrote back immediately.

"Look . . . you can read, right?" Walker couldn't help but ask. The albino squirrel looked at the words slowly fading in the air before glancing at him again with a disapproving look on his face. "Right . . . of course you can. Sorry, my old world still influences my thoughts sometimes, and experience has shown me that not everyone is a reader." Walker pointed at the journal in the Guardian's hand. "I have to leave in a second. Read the book. The beginning is pretty stupid, but the rest of it isn't. Spend a bit of time reading it, then I'll hop back here, and we'll talk again. What do you think?"

Chipper nodded. *That is acceptable. I will see you in not too long, Creator.* After saying so, he hopped up onto a high branch and began the process of reading Walker's terrible writing.

The Creator thought to ask the Guardian to pet him . . . but that seemed a little strange now. He instead sighed and clicked the Avatar ability, sending himself back to Sonata. The transmission back was instant, so as his green moonlet faded back into view, his thoughts were still occupied with how the citizens of Symphony would perceive him going forward.

When his vision evened out, he suddenly took a step backward in adjustment, and the Primigenials looked at him, noticing something was different. But he waved them off with a light, "Not now." He watched Zeus corral them toward the Tree of the Gods before clicking on the Follower System in his overlay.

Hello, Walker, and welcome to the Follower System.

Oh shit, it knows my name.

**This is not a system that allows the head of the religion to abuse
or enslave their followers, so if that is what you were looking for,
you're out of luck. My name is unimportant, but just know that
this message is for any Awakened who have found their Alma.
I created this system to allow elevated beings to connect to their
followers with purpose. To build a system that enhanced not only
the Awakened but also those who choose to follow their beliefs.
While there is more I could say, you will only receive that
information should you fully upgrade the system.**

**The following is a list of some of the things you will be able
to do as you progress your religion:
Create a scripture (complete)
Create a leader for your religion (upgrade needed)
Create a hierarchy of members (upgrade needed)
Assign tasks to your followers (upgrade needed)
Assign rewards for your followers (upgrade needed)
Create separate religious branches (upgrade needed)
Allow your followers to communicate from long distances
(upgrade needed)
Create holy sites (upgrade needed)
Update your scripture at need (upgrade needed)
Gain the ability to declare a holy war (upgraded needed)
[. . .]
The referenced upgrades will come with time and experience as
your religion grows. Your first task is already set. Please . . .**

As Walker watched, the Follower System seemed to bug out for a moment as
his screens fast forwarded through a text he never really got a chance to read.
Finally, it settled again.

**Hello again, Walker.
Congratulations on writing your scripture. One moment, please.
[. . . Scanning Scripture . . .]
[. . .]
Scan complete!
Theological Consistency: B+**

Fervor Rating: C
Moral and Ethical Guidance: A
Overall grade: B

Walker snorted. He hadn't received a B for his writing in over a decade. He did nod his head at the Fervor Rating. Inspiring his followers to allow for total dependency on the Unending Summit was never in the plans. The guidance grade made him smile, though. At least he'd gotten that right, according to a random system created by a random person he'd probably never meet. With recommendations like that, he couldn't lose!

This is quite the interesting scripture, Walker. It falls in line with my own thoughts on how to form an excellent cadre of followers without demanding too much from them.
My world disallowed the idea of individuals progressing in strength. The rulers decided that wherever a person was upon birth, be it geography or class, was where they stayed. It was only through hard work and the death of many that we forced a change here.
I sincerely hope you do not have to go through a similar experience.

Walker nodded his head, seeing how that could happen. He thought about what the system was saying to him. This was the most unusual set of system messages he had received since first unlocking the protocol. It was almost like it was alive. Curious, he said out loud, "Can you hear me?"

Walker waited for a few minutes but received no response or change in the system's routine as the writing kept flashing into his overlay. But he couldn't shake the feeling that this system differed from the others.

You may be a great candidate for a particular path that few ever reach. Keep on the lookout for extra unlocked abilities as time goes forward. Good luck with your religion, Creator.
Please select a name and create an insignia to represent your religion.

Walker watched as the Follower System's text faded to the background and two squares appeared on his screen. As he looked at the two squares, he had a thought.

Echidna had set him up for this from the start. The Holy Scripture had been absorbed by his task, allowing him to skip a step that would've taken a long time. He had no clue what would happen when the Follower System activated, but somehow, she did.

Walker looked over at her and noticed her smiling back. He gave a slight nod and thumbs-up, which felt far too small of a gesture, and returned to the Follower

System. It wasn't that he didn't appreciate her, but he wanted to complete this task with gusto so he could continue moving through the rest at a blistering pace. There was always more work to be done.

Walker clicked on the name box and wrote "The Unending Summit." He finalized his choice, and the box faded away as he did so.

The next part asked him for an emblem. He spent quite a bit of time drawing, etching, and doing his best to picture exactly what he'd envisioned when designing it in the scripture. Once he was sure he had a solid outline of what he wanted, the screen changed to a thousand different colors and allowed him to fill it in.

He took his time, moving from one section to the next in a steady pattern, building from his mental picture. When he was done, a dark brown mountain on a forest green hexagon showed up in the image creator. It just . . . felt right. The top of the mountain couldn't be seen, and the way up seemed treacherous, just a thin path with broken steps. It was a good representation of who they were as a group of people. The Unending Summit was a way of living, not one of prayer or belief. He clicked Accept and his overlay updated yet again.

**Religion task complete: Select an insignia and a name for the
Dante religion (Part 3)
Insignia selected: 1/1
Name selected: 1/1
Reward for completion: Follower System upgrade
[. . .]**

**New religion task: Choose the title of the person who will lead
your religion (Part 4)**
*Dante, a leader is required for every major religion. While
councils are useful for other matters, having a single leader of an
organization allows for clear decision-making and improved
efficiency. Create the title that the leader of your religion will hold
and others will whisper in the quiet moments of the dark.*
**Title created: 0/1
Reward for completion: Follower System upgrade**

**Reward for completing the third religion task:
Congratulations, Dante! You've upgraded the Follower System!**
No description was found.
(Upgradeable)

Walker noticed that the system messages had moved back to the generic responses. Was the Follower System run by an AI like the Cosmic Genesis System?

Or was it a person who just didn't have time to respond to every completed task? He didn't know.

He did know that Echidna's help was still paying dividends. Walker was notoriously bad with names, but as he'd been writing his scripture, the yellow-eyed woman would pull him aside occasionally, and they'd talk. What were his goals? What were the goals of his potential religion? How could he best make sure both were completed successfully? And she always asked him with a smile, reminding him of the nicer conversations he'd had with his mother.

It had helped him solidify his agenda and devise a system that would work for a long period of time. Walker typed in the title he'd already come up with some time ago: Zenith.

Religion task complete: Choose the title of the person who will lead your religion (Part 4)
Title created: 1/1
Reward for completion: Follower System upgrade
[. . .]

New religion task: Create the first ranks and roles for your religion (Part 5)
Ranks and advancement. While advancement is a pinnacle focus in the Alpha Protocol, ranks are a way to recognize entities that have moved to a higher threshold. Create a system of ranks and the roles they will fulfill, allowing your followers to always have a next step to take.
Minimum number of ranks created: 0/3
Roles assigned to ranks: 0/total ranks created
Reward for completion: Follower System upgrade x2

Reward for completing the fourth religion task:
Congratulations, Dante! You've upgraded the Follower System!
No description was found.
(Upgradeable)

Walker looked at three squares with another set of smaller squares underneath them in his overlay. He stepped across the grass and sat down in his computer chair to consider the names . . . always the names.

He pondered and mentally pontificated. He hemmed, and he hawed. Until, finally, he came up with a good series of names and was ready for the next step. Unknown to him, those three names took him well over an hour to come up with.

He clicked on the left-most square and typed in his entries for the first, second, and last ranks. He then mentally sorted the roles based on what he felt people should focus on the most as they were first learning how to traverse their world. It was important that the focus not only be on the Unending Summit but on Symphony and its people as well. Walker didn't want his followers to die needlessly trying to find their own paths forward. Especially not at the very beginning.

That wasn't to say risk and reward shouldn't go hand and hand, only that they should be tempered with experience and wisdom. With that in mind, Walker wrote out simple descriptions for the three roles, using the potential future Follower System upgrades as a basis for how the roles would proceed.

As he clicked Accept, the Zenith title appeared in the fourth slot with an empty role box below it. That one was trickier. He spent several minutes figuring out what he wanted them to do, granting an obviously large amount of latitude, before writing it in and clicking Accept again. A fifth and larger box appeared at the top above the eight filled-out boxes below it. It read, with a mild simplicity, "Overall follower moniker."

Walker smiled. *Thank you again, Echidna.*

Religion founded: The Unending Summit
Followers of the Unending Summit will forevermore be called
Horizon Chasers.
Ranks and roles within the Unending Summit:
Pathfinder, Explorer, Seeker, Zenith

Walker smiled as he read it. It was only the first three ranks, and he had plans for more ranks to follow, but these would do just fine for getting started. Since every new follower would receive a free version of his Holy Scripture, it was easy to set them up at the start.

To move forward through the ranks, there would have to be different requirements. The Explorers' trial didn't have to be combat related; he would have to create multiple options as more of his systems came online. The Seeker would be required to create their own knowledge, likely in a book format, to advance. This would not only allow his libraries to get fleshed out by his followers, but it would also create an intrinsic need for his followers to protect libraries as their central banks of knowledge. For Pathfinders, he wasn't sure what would be required yet. Perhaps time was the way to go.

Walker paused in his thoughts. *Hmm, I may have to create a guardian role for libraries as well. Something to consider for the future. Maybe I'll call them . . . No, Guardians is taken and they have their own duties. Librarians should focus on maintaining the library and working with the visitors and Horizon Chasers. Ah! Custodians! No, that still doesn't sound right.* He'd figure it out when he got there.

Walker stretched his back as his overlay updated yet again. Progress was really flying by thanks to his preparation.

Religion task complete: Create the first ranks and roles for your religion (Part 5)
Minimum number of ranks created: 4/3
Roles assigned to ranks: 4/4
Reward for completion: Follower System upgrade x2
[. . .]

New religion task: Create the first task and assign it to a follower of your religion (Part 6)
Finally, the Creator is able to create their own tasks for their people within the Alpha Protocol. This is the first task assignment, but do not let it be the last. Entities need to feel like what they do matters, and with religion, even more so.
Task created: 0/1
Task assigned to a follower of your religion: 0/1
Reward for completion: Follower System upgrade, additional reward possible

Reward for completing the fifth religion task:
Congratulations, Dante! You've upgraded the Follower System twice!
No description was found.
(Upgradeable)

Walker grinned at the new update. So, he needed to assign a task? Easy. He clicked on his ranks breakdown in the Follower System and clicked on Pathfinder. There was a blank spot next to the name where a task could be set. As he clicked on it, another blank spot appeared underneath it. Apparently, it was pretty simple to make tasks for this, similar to the future Quest System he planned to create. He assigned a prescribed task to the role and clicked Accept.

A notification rang out with more than just the words. Walker clearly heard a bell chime in the back of his mind.

New task created for Pathfinders of the Unending Summit:
[Read and understand the Holy Scripture. A test will be required for future promotional opportunities.]

Walker's overlay updated yet again . . . This was still going to take some time. He focused up and continued to build his newly founded religion.

CHAPTER NINE

Ranks and Ideas

S everal hours later, Walker was still working on the Follower System. He'd
made excellent progress quickly and looked at the series that was updating as
he went.

Create a scripture (complete)
Create a leader for your religion (complete)
Create a hierarchy of members (complete)
Assign tasks to your followers (complete)
Assign rewards for your followers (complete)
Create separate religious branches (complete)
Allow your followers to communicate from long distances
(upgrade needed)
Create holy sites (upgrade needed)
Update your scripture at need (upgrade needed)
Gain the ability to declare a holy war (upgraded needed)
[. . .]

The rewards were tricky. Without a Class System, Item System, or even an
Event System, he'd had to get creative to solve rewarding the first few ranks of
followers for their achievements.

The Follower System needed to have initial ranks for when the sapients arrived.
That wasn't to say he'd make them join the Unending Summit. It would forever
be an option, but forced indoctrination went against the core of who he was. Those
who willingly chose his religion, though, would find the scripture a handy aid for
learning how to start and manage a civilization.

The reward for completing the first task, reading and understanding the scripture, was an immediate promotion to the second rank. Of course, Walker had

spent over an hour developing the test that would automatically move Pathfinders to Explorers, but as a former teacher, it was a fairly straightforward and pragmatic process.

The text accompanying the tasks' completion didn't have the strange flavoring he'd first seen with the Follower System. It was still run-of-the-mill generic responses for rewards and new tasks, leading him to further thoughts as he analyzed it. Was it an AI? Or was someone actually talking to him? And if someone was talking to him, how much did they know, and how much were they willing to share?

With those thoughts weighing on his mind, he continued to work on the requirements before him. The task and trial of moving from Explorer to Seeker were more complicated. Walker, rather than Cagna herself, had connected the Milestone System to his Follower System, thereby allowing him to track movement. As the traveler series was already mostly created, he'd attached the Apprentice milestone directly to Explorer rank. The more they traveled, the faster it was completed.

Apprentice milestone—The Full 25:
Travel at least 25 miles across Symphony. 5 points.

Twenty-five miles may not seem like a lot to people from his world, but that's because they benefited from possessing vehicles. Not to mention maps, paths, and relative safety in a world without monsters. They wouldn't understand how difficult traveling across Symphony could be.

Would be . . . is, Walker thought to himself, leaning back in his chair.

He hadn't taken many breaks since starting this; it had already been hours. Aside from stretching his soul for a time and the odd conversations with the Primigenials and assistants, breaks had fallen away as an accessory he couldn't wear for the moment. Even in a bubble of frozen time, minutes and hours were precious and couldn't be wasted.

He clapped his hands to shake away any loose thoughts and refocused.

The nice part about the tasks was if, for some reason, he found a task didn't suit the reward, he could always change it. After completing The Full 25, Explorers would receive a prompt asking them to head to the nearest library for their trial to the next rank. Walker would have to think of more ways to reward people for moving up in rank, but for now, the ranks themselves would suffice. Maybe milestone points would be useful . . . or money . . .

He hadn't had a chance to set up Seekers as of yet. The reason being, he wanted them to get a blank book upon promotion, and the ability to do so was outside of his reach. According to Virgil, the Follower System provided the scripture directly to new followers by absorbing ambient magic in the air and forming the former journal from virtually nothing. He called it directed substantive conjuration.

So . . . conjuring. But without an Item System, Walker couldn't do the same—
yet. Just another task he'd have to look at as time moved on.

Induction Branch	Administrative Branch	Covert Branch	Combat Branch	Discovery Branch	Leadership Branch
Pathfinder	Guide	Shadow	Warden	Voyager	Sage
Explorer	Clerk	Specialist	Custodian	Curator	Director
Seeker	Librarian	Analyst	Trailblazer	Cartographer	Territory Manager
Acolyte	Archivist	Operative	Sentinel	Navigator	Branch Head
					Zenith

To pass the eighth Follower System task, he'd had to divide the ranks a bit
and establish different branches of the Unending Summit that would work across
multiple levels. Walker made sure that there were enough roles for people to choose
from so they wouldn't be pigeonholed into something they didn't actually want
to do. It was tricky and took him a full day to think up and explore.

Walker had designed it with the prevailing theory of allowing his followers to
become anything they wanted, within reason. As time progressed, he'd likely need
to create more roles and branches to enable the religion to grow organically. But
for now, it was fine. He'd have to test it after they super-seeded all of the humans
at the same time. Thankfully, while he couldn't really modify the Follower System
overall, its internals were easily changed. He clicked on the Leadership Branch
and the roles filled out in his overlay.

It was a lot to take in. Each local library had a Sage and a Director. The Sage
managed knowledge and its pursuit, while the Director focused on making sure
the library ran as it was supposed to.

The Director also needed to try to help the induction ranks find their footing
so the Unending Summit would continue to grow with proper guidance for the
lowest-ranking members. Walker visualized the Directors as those with ambition
and leadership skills, whereas Sages were more nerds, like him. They loved knowledge and the pursuit of it.

The Territory Manager would oversee all nearby libraries, which was a direct
promotion from the Director position, and it was a hard requirement he couldn't
do away with. Each time the Landmass System upgraded, so did the size of the
additions they were creating. Without a Territory Manager for each location, things

The Leadership Branch of the Unending Summit

Sage	Director	Territory Manager	Branch Head	Zenith
The most knowledge-able person found within a library. The Sage is responsible for the local Discovery Branch as well as the protection of all books found within their area.	As the Director of a library, they're responsible for the Administrative and Combat Branches within their local area. They will also manage all incoming inductee ranks and make sure each is guided correctly.	Territory Managers are respon-sible for the entirety of all libraries within their region and manage the Covert Branch. They also form a check on Directors and Sages, keeping a constant lookout for corruption and scandal before it can form.	The Branch Head is responsible for all members of their branch and can overrule any ranks except the Zenith themself or another Branch Head. Branch Heads are the advising council for the Zenith and will provide wisdom by request. This rank is chosen by the current Zenith and can be replaced at any time at their will.	The leader of the Unending Summit. The Zenith will ensure the growth of their members, make major decisions regarding the focus of their religion, and remove any corruption found within their ranks. They are empowered by the Creator to take any actions necessary to achieve their goals. This is the final rank.

could quickly grow out of control. There was no doubt in his mind that one day an update could drop a piece of land the size of his home state.

The Territory Managers would have a big job depending on the size of their area. To help them in their management, the local area's Covert Branch would fall directly under their supervision. Each Covert member's primary focus would be on information gathering . . . as well as other things. If it came to it, Walker had also visualized this branch completing assassinations in the future. It was a far cry from his initial issues and problems with murdering things. But eventu-ally, the need for someone, be they sapient or monster, to die would occur. It could be a murderous leader who wanted war or a monster run amok with an aim toward great carnage. Either way, it was bound to happen.

He paused for a moment to reflect on that. He couldn't help but see his rationalization for needing assassins as a bit of a devolution of his soul. However, he had a great memory, and human beings had a history of creating massive issues focused on singular people. Eliminating a cult of personality before it fully formed and started to ruin his world was a big priority for him.

How much better would Earth be without the Second World War? Or would that create a host of other issues just as large, if not larger? Either way, he'd have to make sure that any assassination approvals had to go through a stringent vetting process—a checklist of necessity.

Branch Heads would be highly accomplished people within the Unending Summit and would be chosen by the Zenith. He foresaw this creating an issue where a corrupt Zenith could appoint their corrupt friends to the advisory council. This would create a cascading problem where corruption spread from the Branch Heads down to the Territory Managers and eventually to all of the localized Directors and Sages.

Like a fast tide, corruption would spread through the ranks of his religion and burn out any hope he had for creating a balanced way of living that allowed for many choices. But that was why Walker was here in the first place. At the first whiff of this kind of problem, heads would roll.

He remembered Virgil talking about his recent tendency toward tyrannical dictatorship and had to mentally temper himself. Removing corruption at the root was important, but he'd have to show proof to his followers that he had indeed acted in a just manner—troublesome, in the end.

The Zenith was of course the person who was in charge of everything. They decided on promotions to leadership roles, held judicial approval for punishments, and received information collated from all of the different branches at once. He would have to be quite careful in deciding who would be the first Zenith in charge of things, as that would likely be a sink or swim moment for his religion. Of course, he could just outlaw all other forms of religion, but that went against his codified beliefs in the scripture, and he felt the uncomfortable buzz reappear in his chest just at the thought of it. It didn't fade away until he firmly grasped his former thought and chose to never think of it again.

There were no crafting ranks, and that was intentional. He didn't have the two systems that would interact with them yet, and he felt everyone should have the choice of deciding on their professions without being pushed into a corner. Maybe he would add something in the future, who knew?

Walker continued to think about what his tasks and rewards could be for the other twenty-one ranks, leaving Zenith off that list, when a voice rang out.

"Give me access!" Cagna uncharacteristically yelled at him as he looked through his screens.

"Nooo," Walker said, dragging the word out. She'd asked multiple times now, interrupting his flow of thought. The first few times were gentle questions, then prodding, and now she'd upgraded to outright yelling.

Of course, Cagna had asked for access immediately after noticing her Milestone System was linked to the Unending Summit. But unlike Rimi with his monsters and the Entity Subsystem, Walker had pushed that back. This was one of the few systems he'd self-manage, as he feared others making changes without first talking to him. It was . . . personal.

Cagna changed strategies. "Pwease, Creator?" she said, batting her eyes at him and tucking her chin into her paws.

Walker's mouth dropped open. "Who taught you how to do that?"

Echidna laughed in the background.

"Ugh," Walker said, feeling his hands ball up. "Damned stupid gods messing with my assistants. They're all bad influences!"

"Oh, come on, now," Echidna said, lazing about on the ground without looking at him. "The child needed a break from her work, just as you do sometimes. It was quite fun to explain to her how to get things out of men that they don't want to give."

"Yep!" Cagna said, back to her usual cheery self.

Walker gave them both a glare, and with a final "No!" he turned around and continued his work.

Religion task: Communicate with one member of your religion
(Part 9)
Proper communication is the lifeblood of running an organiza-
tion or, in this instance, religion. Connect to one of your followers
using the communication network within the Follower System.
Connections made: 0/1
Communication network established: No
Reward for completion: Follower System upgrade

Walker wasn't ready to talk to his single follower yet. He needed to give Chipper time to read the book before he intruded yet again on his territory, plus he needed to take a break from his focus on the Follower System. He'd been working at it for days now and it was time for another painful soul-stretching. Before he turned away from the Follower System, he looked at the communication network settings and altered them slightly, making it so no one but the Zenith could contact him directly. While the network wasn't yet active, he didn't want to start suddenly receiving messages or calls from Pathfinders trying to get some help. They needed to . . . find their own path. Plus, that would be quite annoying, especially as the size of his religion drastically increased.

Walker laid down and continued his painful soul exercises. On the snapback, it felt looser than it had before, and he guessed it would pin down after only one more attempt. He couldn't do it right away, as it was still much too painful to push through. He looked in on a few manticores and found one particularly large female roaming the forests and murdering her way around. That was a little disconcerting.

Getting up, he moved slowly to try to not cause any spikes in pain, then checked in with Virgil on how much time had gone by since they'd kicked up the Milestone System.

"It has been a day and a half," Virgil said with some side-eye, not liking the interruption to his work.

Walker scuffed a shoe against the grass. "Shit."

"Indeed. Might I suggest you continue to work on your new Follower System, or perhaps some more milestones with Cagna?"

"What about the System Link?"

Virgil canted his head. "You've hardly even looked at it."

Walker nodded. "Sure, but it's still pretty useful." Walker pulled up the description he'd received when he completed the first temporal task. It was a doozy.

Reward for completing the first temporal task:
Congratulations, Dante! You've unlocked the System Link ability!
The System Link ability is unique within the Alpha Protocol. Few have discovered, or been tempted to create, a temporal anomaly. Their shortsightedness precludes what benefits an anomaly can bring to a Creator first establishing themselves. You do not have that problem. The System Link ability allows the Creator to build an interconnected network, a hierarchy of systems that work in sync with each other.
(Upgradeable)

"I'm still unsure of what exactly it does," Walker said while scratching the back of his head.

Virgil sighed and turned away from the Evolution Chambers. "It will allow you to create a program wherein some systems depend on others. The upgrade is also substantial, so I suggest you find ways to be creative with its use."

"Hey, that's great! It'll work well with the Milestone System and its ability to unlock things. Cool. I was worried I'd have to make another system to track who had what systems so that systems happened everywhere you looked." Walker saw Virgil roll his eyes, so he ended with one word. "System."

"I get it."

"You would think there would be some kind of task for this. Plus, if I can link systems, can I split them?"

"What do you mean 'split'?" Virgil asked with a confused look on his face.

Walker began pacing. "Well, I don't necessarily want everyone to have a super powerful system right away. I want them to be earned slowly and over time. It should be something that is gained through effort and force of will. If I can split systems so that they upgrade for the entity who receives them, kind of but not really like the tiers in the Monster System, I can create greater rewards for them. It would also be what I need to fully flesh out and create my Class System. Plus, I don't need fully fleshed out systems for everything. My plans for the Mentoring and Dynasty Systems are limited in scope. I don't need a subsystem assistant to watch them and track everything, nor do I need to spend nearly as much time on them as I have for our first two."

Virgil nodded. "I see. Can you hold for a moment?"

Walker tilted his head. "Why?"

"Because I am going to ask for you."

"Oh," Walker replied. "Okay, th—" He stopped speaking when he noticed Virgil wasn't paying attention to him. The giant brown squirrel stared into space for several minutes, so Walker headed over and talked to Rimi. Apparently, he had created a small rabbit for his tier one and immediately asked Walker to shoot it into space.

Since they weren't actually seeding them, and the entities were instantly destroyed, Walker wasn't getting updates to his unique entity tasks. That meant they were burning through his resources, as no grades were coming in with the rewards. Even a D grade gave him his materials back. Thankfully, Crratch's surplus was still there, and they had plenty of material left over.

"What's going to be your tier two?" Walker asked.

"Tier two, yes." The blue squirrel rubbed his furry chin. "Well, you want to use these to train your sapients, right?"

"Right." Walker nodded.

"Rabbits are quick, and these ones will be jumpers. So for tier two, why don't we make sure they're slower but stronger at the same time?" Rimi's voice picked up speed. "This way, the sapients will have to learn how to fight against different types of opponents from the start."

"Okay," Walker said, feeling Rimi's infectious energy seep into him. "So, what are you thinking? A tortoise? Keep in mind I don't want the tier two to be massive either. They should be a little larger than the rabbits, but not huge."

"Well," Rimi said with a sly smile appearing on his face, "I spoke to Virgil about it, and he told me about koalas."

"Fucking drop bears?" Walker exclaimed. "You want to put drop bears on Symphony?"

"I don't know that word, but if they're like koalas, yes. The koala drops down, and if they escape its clutches, it's an easy kill. That way, they learn another method of survival. Always be aware of your surroundings." Rimi put his arms behind his back, reminding Walker of a professor he'd once had. "With the rabbits, they learn about speed and dodging. If you dodge its leap, it should be fairly easy to dispatch. With the koalas, they learn to perceive their surroundings. Always be aware of what's around you. Then, for tier three, we up it yet again." Rimi laughed.

Actually, it was a cackle, Walker mentally amended. A small blue squirrel was cackling in front of him. How strange his life had become.

"I made the rabbits faster and modified their hind muscles to increase the strength of their jumps, but they'll never upgrade their kernels and thus don't have any magic. The koalas will, but as we'll probably put them into a forest environment, I don't foresee it being much of a change. But, oh, the third tier." Rimi's smile put Walker's back up. "Speed and surprise are great, but we need the third tier to be different. Powerful. So, why not make them smart? That way, your sapients have to learn to strategize. I think we should do gray wolves." After he finished speaking, Walker couldn't hear any other sounds on Sonata. It was like the moonlet was waiting for what he was about to say.

This might not be such a good idea.

"Fuck, Rimi, you don't think that's a bit too much? Magically modified gray wolves?"

"Not at all. We'll change them so that they only work in pairs and make them territorial so they won't like other wolves being near them, and that way, they'll work in a male and female duo each time. It'll take some time, but I think I can do it with Virgil's help. He's the one who suggested them, actually."

"So you basically want to make my Alpha ability a modification."

Rimi clapped. "Exactly! Wolves are naturally very smart, and with tier three, they'll have magic as well. You said you only wanted to build them up to that level. Well, if the sapients can beat the tier-three wolves, consider that their graduation to the outside world of Symphony. If they can defeat the wolves, they can leave. Simple as that. Plus, by forcing them into pairs only, it'll keep the population managed and not let them spring out of control. Not to mention newborns all start at tier one, and their parents' modifications will be genetically bound through the Evolution Chambers."

Walker nodded. "Okay, but if this gets all screwed up, I'm absolutely blaming you."

"Hehe," Rimi said in a higher-pitched voice before rubbing his hands together. "To work!"

Walker turned away from him as the blue squirrel moved toward the Evolution Chambers and a koala and a gray wolf popped into them. He hoped Rimi knew what he was doing.

Walker remembered hearing a story on Earth about a super-pack of wolves attacking an entire town and killing multiple people. That'd be the last thing a new civilization would need. He'd have to spend a lot of time watching them after the first seeding.

Looking at Virgil, he saw that the advanced assistant was still staring at his screens, so he continued on with his soul work. He was still a little sore, but it passed the time. After a minute of stretching things out, he managed to push down and watched the green flare spread out of him. Unless he was mistaken, the color of his soul was deepening further, and it seemed to spread faster. Walker smiled through the pain as a shot of energy sparked through his body.

I'm getting stronger.

Echidna came over and told him that rather than going for the rest of his legs as he was planning on doing, and she somehow seemed to know, he should start stretching it toward his back. That way, he would have one fully enveloped part of his body.

Walker agreed, although he didn't have much of a choice in the matter, as he still wasn't exactly sure what he was doing. He could feel a certain . . . something hovering over the areas he'd pinned down. Lifting his shirt to take a gander, he saw that his skin seemed cleaner. All of his moles and imperfections had ceased to exist. And, while he didn't feel a significant increase in muscle, his stomach area did feel a bit tighter . . . less pudgy, at least.

As he looked around, seeing his assistants all busy at their jobs, he decided to do something he hadn't done in a while. Walker relaxed. He didn't look at monitors or systems. He didn't spend time on his soul. He just lay there and stared at the sky. Aside from the throbbing pain in his body, it was nice.

He wondered about Earth. He knew that, according to Virgil, they were placed in some kind of time stasis, but he couldn't help having a bad feeling about Mr. Harrison.

He hadn't thought of him in a while, but each time he did, it came with a flare of what he felt was justified anger and resentment. Walker didn't want to get sucked into another round of depression, so he pushed himself to mentally move on. After spending a few more minutes on the ground, wondering if he'd ever date again with his new status in life and whether dating one of his entities would be a form of incest, his overlay lit up without him doing anything.

[. . .]

**Private message from an Alpha Protocol Council Member
detected.**

[. . . Retrieving . . .]

**Hello again, child.
No.
Creator.
What wonderful things you are doing there on . . . Sonata. Ah.
Wonderful name. Wonderful.**

Your assistant Virgil has spoken to me, and we have agreed to create a series of tasks associated with the System Link ability. Very good thinking there.
We'll also be doing you a favor, as you have come up with an idea we had not considered. Enjoy, Dante. Do great things.
I'm counting on it.

Alpha Protocol changes occurring.
Planet Symphony is being advanced by 5.5 days.

Walker turned his head from the ground and watched as Symphony sped up again. He held his breath, worried a temporal anomaly might occur. As he watched time speed up before his eyes, the Crater seemed to explode for a moment before it stopped and rewound in time, all the rocks, water, and trees going back to where they were. Then another message hit his overlay.

Anomaly discovered. Anomaly eliminated.
Recovering lost resources. Some lost resources are unrecoverable.
Available resources replaced.
Compensation required. Compensation found.
Compensation given.
[. . . Scanning . . .]

Optional tasks updated!
System task complete: Design a system (Series 2)
System design requirements:
System is found to be balanced and consistent: Yes
System allows for growth: Yes
System is applied to world continuously without calamity: 7/7 days
Reward for completion: Gain the ability to create a third system.
[. . .]

New system task: Design a system (Series 3)
While other Creators may rely on the survival of the fittest or technological expansion, the Alpha Protocol has provided you with the means to create your own path toward gaining strength.
Build a system that encourages your entities to grow.
System requirements:
System is found to be balanced and consistent: No
System allows for growth: No

System is applied to world continuously without calamity:
0/7 days
Reward for completion: Gain the ability to create
unlimited systems.

Subsystem assistant task complete: Train the assistant (Series 2)
Subsystem assistant requirements:
Assistant is assigned to a subsystem: Yes
Assistant is autonomous: Yes
Assistant completes work continuously without calamity:
7/7 days
Reward for completion: Gain a third subsystem assistant.
[. . .]

New subsystem assistant task: Train the assistant (Series 3)
Subsystem assistant requirements:
Assistant is assigned to a subsystem: No
Assistant is autonomous: No
Assistant completes work continuously without calamity:
0/7 days
Reward for completion: Gain unlimited subsystem assistants

New System Link task: Create an organizational matrix for
your systems
No description was found.
Organizational matrix made: No
Supreme system defined: No
Reward for completion: System Link ability upgrade

Reward for assisting the Alpha Protocol Council with creating
a new task:
Congratulations, Dante! You've unlocked the System
Split ability!
*This is an entirely new ability, custom created by the Alpha
Protocol Council for Creator Dante of rendition 4AA. A description
is unavailable at this time.*
(Potentially Upgradeable)

Compensation for the destruction of 4 entities designed by
Creator Dante:
A plenitude of entity creation materials.

A plenitude of landmass creation materials.
One Creation Instrument upgrade.

"Huh," Walker said to himself with a small smile at the boon he'd just received. "I wonder which of the entities died."

Suddenly, over by the Evolution Chambers he heard Rimi scream, "Chomp!"

"Oh," Walker said, the smile leaving his face.

CHAPTER TEN

Systems, Systems, and Territories I

It took almost an hour to calm Rimi down. Walker truly felt bad for the little guy and comforted him the way he used to comfort his students when they were going through something traumatic: a pat on the back, words of condolence, and just waiting for them to speak. Of course, no hugs, not for a male teacher, that is. Luckily enough, Cagna took care of that for him, wrapping Rimi tight, her small pink arms covering a blue body.

Eventually, Rimi stopped crying and just talked, working through his grief a little bit at a time. He'd really seemed to care for the monster.

Chomp was Walker's first. The golden battlefrog had helped them succeed in the second battle, and he would've likely soon reached sapience. This was a great loss that Walker hadn't seen coming. Unlike Rimi, though, and as heartless as it was, he didn't directly connect his emotions to the tier five monster. He'd learned in life, particularly from his time in the military, not to associate every negative happenstance with his own emotional well-being.

In the desert, he'd heard about patrols heading out and never returning. But it never affected him. He'd attend the memorial, act respectfully, and move on. If he knew them personally, that, of course, was different. But while Chomp had been helpful in the second battle, he had also tried to kill Walker at the first moment of their meeting.

Virgil believed his mind wasn't quite right, and maybe something *was* wrong with him. He wasn't sure. It was just how he'd always been.

Walker recognized that it was something that was sad and affected those around him, but he always kept it at bay. Chomp was a great loss, especially as one of the few tier fives Symphony had. However, his loss would benefit Walker and Symphony as a whole, and that's how Walker chose to see it—a negative granting a positive effect.

He wasn't connected to the monsters the way Rimi was, and he saw that as a good thing. It was better to view everything from a distance when you were in control of their fate. He would not be a Creator who stepped in to help in every situation. Sometimes . . . things just needed to solve themselves. How could someone have a chance at growing if they always needed help?

Walker felt an agreeing pulse in his soul and nodded to himself. He pulled up the last task he'd gotten as a reminder.

**System Link task: Create an organizational matrix
for your systems**
No description was found.
Organizational matrix made: No
Supreme system defined: No
Reward for completion: System Link ability upgrade

He needed to break down his systems into an organizational matrix.
Easy.

What a lot of people don't know about teachers is just how organized they have to be. He'd always made sure his students' assignments and grades were in order and up to date, that he had his lesson plans ready to go early so he wasn't rushing around the day of. Organizing docs and forms, prepping tests and reviews, blitzing grades late at night in front of a movie he'd already seen but still liked to have on in the background. Staying organized was built into his DNA at this point.

Sure, he always had a messy desk, but that was because every time he super-cleaned his classroom, it felt like he had to be careful of things. He hated a clean desk, as it was just asking for him to spill a drink or drop some crumbs on it. Somewhere in the back of his Awakened mind, an old quote from Einstein popped up: *If a cluttered desk is a sign of a cluttered mind, of what, then, is an empty desk a sign?*

Walker smiled to himself and looked at the task again. He didn't know what a supreme system was, but he was sure he wanted to find out. Clicking on the ability in his overlay, his vision lit up.

Immediately, all of his systems popped up in the order that they had been unlocked, and an empty grid floated above them. Unlike before when he had had to ask Virgil for help, this time he was able to do the name changes himself. Walker noticed that any time a system was dependent on another, it was called a subsystem. So the Landmass System was the primary, and the secondary or dependent systems like Entity and Ecology were all subsystems below it.

Although it was a guess, he figured he'd have to do something similar to the Territory System if he wanted it to work. He added the shortened names to his newest systems and moved things around based on how important he thought they were, slotting them into place on the grid. After he was done shifting everything around, he took a look at it.

Walker had split the systems in half. The primary was designated as the Milestone System on the left-hand side, with a large series of blank boxes below. On the right, he'd allowed the Landmass System to remain the primary, with things like Ecology, Weather, and Entity, among others, still attached to it.

Walker nodded his head. The Milestone System was the lynchpin for all of his self-created systems. He couldn't imagine where he would be when the time dilation stopped—or how many milestones they would have, for that matter. That was why he needed to figure out what the supreme system really entailed. He clicked on the flashing chain icon above the current hierarchy, and a group of options appeared.

Welcome to System Linking, Dante.
System Linking is the ability of the Creator to manage and assign
systems for dependency.
By establishing a primary and secondary role in their created
systems, the Creator can ensure that all future systems interact in
a fluid and dynamic way for redundancy and reliability.

The following are your current options:
1. Create your own supreme system (one-time use)
2. Choose a supreme system from your current existing systems
3. Merge two systems together
4. Establish a primary system
5. Assign a system as secondary

Walker already knew what he would be naming the supreme system. He pulled from his experience and general understanding that primary systems couldn't be managed by subsystem assistants. Virgil had just now gained access, partially, to the Landmass System, and he was an advanced assistant. So Walker's plan of assigning the Monster and Entity Systems to the Milestone System wouldn't work. There was one easy step he could take, though. Walker selected the third option.

Option three selected: Merge 2 systems together
What systems would you like to merge?
Ecology selected.
Weather selected.
Please confirm that these are the selected systems you would like
to merge.
Once merged, they currently cannot be unmerged.
Yes/No

Walker clicked Yes.

[. . . Analyzing . . .]
The Ecology Subsystem and Weather Subsystem are merging.
[. . .]
Merge complete.
The Ecoweather Subsystem is now ready to be used.

Walker nodded his head. It only made sense to merge the two systems; that way, everything was centralized in one place. It would also mean that Rimi had just gained access to the Weather Subsystem . . . Walker was sure nothing terrible could happen from that. He looked at the options again, and then clicked on the first one.

Option one selected: Create your own supreme system
Please name your system:
The Conductor System is named!
Supreme systems are always assigned directly to the Creator.
Enjoy your new supreme system, Dante!
[. . . Scanning . . .]

Optional tasks updated!
System Link task complete: Create an organizational matrix
for your systems
Organizational matrix made: Yes
Supreme system defined: Yes
Reward for completion: System Link ability upgrade
[. . .]

New System Link task: Merge 2 systems together
No description was found.
Systems merged: 2/2
Reward for completion: System Link ability upgrade
[. . .]

System Link task complete: Merge 2 systems together
No description was found.
Systems merged: 2/2
Reward for completion: System Link ability upgrade

Reward for completing the first System Link task:
Congratulations, Dante! You've upgraded the System
Link ability!
No description was found.
(Potentially Upgradeable)

Reward for completing the second System Link task:
Congratulations, Dante! You've upgraded the System
Link ability!
No description was found.

"Easy peasy," Walker said with a smile. Apparently, he was only going to get two tasks for this one. He'd always received at least three tasks in the past for any new set, but not only was this brand new, but for the first time, it was a series of tasks for an ability. They hadn't even written the descriptions yet. Then again, time was pretty slow here.

The following are your current options:
1. Merge multiple systems together
2. Establish a primary system
3. Assign a system as secondary
4. Sacrifice one of the Creator's abilities to empower a system

Now he could merge multiple systems at once instead of just two.
"Nice."

He looked at the fourth option and couldn't help but be intrigued. Pulling up his abilities, Walker came to the realization that he hadn't looked at the list in quite a while.

Assistant (Advanced) Virgil
Subsystem Assistant Rimi
Subsystem Assistant Cagna
Alpha
Avatar
Broadcast
Combiner
Copy
Domestication
Evolutionary Edge
Identify
Monitor

System Link
System Split
Tree of the Gods

He still remembered when he was first dropped onto Sonata. He'd gained Evolutionary Edge, which passively affected all of his entities right at the beginning. It may have inadvertently led to the Slicer becoming so powerful. Walker had long ago shucked off his responsibility for the modified Bobbit worm. He had done the best he could, and now the other Creators would have to fend for themselves. A bit cold, he reasoned, but stressing about the situation wouldn't help him at this point.

It was interesting to note that his subsystem assistants were listed here as well. Since he was quickly approaching the reward for an unlimited number of assistants, this list might soon become unmanageable. Scanning through everything again, his eyes fell on one ability that they hadn't used yet. He wondered what would happen if he chose the Combiner ability with the fourth option.

Walker yelled over to Virgil nearby, "Hey, Virgil! Does the System Link ability preview what the sacrifice option will do?"

Virgil looked away from the young human he was working on and stared at his screens. A moment later he replied back, "It does now," then turned back to his work.

"Nice." Walker selected the fourth option.

Option four selected: Sacrifice one of the Creator's abilities to empower a system
What ability would you like to sacrifice?
Combiner ability selected.
What system would you like to empower?
Entity Subsystem selected.
Preview provided:
Combiner ability definition: Not all entities can be built from one genus, and the Alpha Protocol recognizes this. The Combiner ability allows the Creator to combine elements of already produced entities to form something new.
Limit: Use of the Combiner ability is restricted to once per day, regardless of results.
Empowerment for the Entity Subsystem: The Creator can freely combine any genus strain they have with another. Removal of cooldown assured.
Would you like to sacrifice the Combiner ability to empower the Entity Subsystem?
Yes/No

"Holy shit. Okay, I can get behind this." Walker selected not to do the upgrade for now, as he still wanted to talk to Virgil first. Instead, he selected the fourth option again.

Option four selected: Sacrifice one of the Creator's abilities to empower a system
What ability would you like to sacrifice?
Evolutionary Edge ability selected.
What system would you like to empower?
Monster System selected.
Preview provided:
Evolutionary Edge ability definition: Some species in the universe are just born powerful, while others evolve or form from natural selection. Each time the Creator makes an attempt at the evolution of a creature, they'll receive a higher chance of success. The greater the scale of evolution, the larger the impact Evolutionary Edge will have during the Alpha Protocol. Empowerment for the Monster System: Any monsters who gain their evolutions will have a chance of starting one tier higher.
Would you like to sacrifice the Evolutionary Edge ability to empower the Monster System?
Yes/No

He didn't want to do that one right away either. It was too much for when his civilizations were just starting. Walker said no for the second time and had a sudden idea. He clicked the fourth option one more time.

Option four selected: Sacrifice one of the Creator's abilities to empower a system
What ability would you like to sacrifice?
Avatar ability selected.
What system would you like to empower?
Conductor System selected.
Preview provided:
Avatar ability definition: Step into your world at any time, in any place, and continue to receive the protections of the Alpha Protocol. Gift your entities any of your self-created evolutions as you see fit and bask in an ability that less than a dozen Creators in all of the protocol have ever received. You have earned it. Empowerment for the Conductor System: Unknown.

**Would you like to sacrifice the Avatar ability to empower the
Conductor System?
Yes/No**

"Shit, come on."

"What are you doing?" Rimi asked as he took a break from working on his drop bear. The Australian terror looked so peaceful in the Evolution Chamber, but he knew from news reports that those fuckers could be vicious. And filled with Chlamydia. His mind started to wander for a moment about how and why most koalas seemed to have a disease that also affected humans before he shook his head and focused on Rimi.

Walker explained what the System Link ability could do for the small blue squirrel, but it was Virgil who responded, stopping what he was doing and marching over in a huff.

"Do *not* sacrifice the Avatar ability," the advanced assistant said with a pointed finger.

Walker put his hands up. "I wasn't going to! Promise! Buuut," he said, dragging the word out with a smile, "you have to admit, the Combiner ability seems like a great option."

Virgil breathed out one large puff of air before nodding and saying, "Indeed. I believe, amongst all of the abilities you have accrued, that one would be the best to sacrifice."

"I agree," Rimi said with a smile, always excited to mess with monsters.

Walker smiled back. "Okay then, we don't even have to debate it." And while they watched, he sacrificed the ability.

**[. . . Analyzing . . .]
[. . .]
The Combiner ability has been sacrificed by Creator Dante.
The Entity Subsystem is now empowered.
All genera within Dante's collection may now be combined.
The Alpha Protocol will attempt to alleviate any friction between
incompatible selections.
Warning: For any selections that the Alpha Protocol cannot
combine, the Creator will lose their resources with no
compensation.**

"Thank you," Virgil said with a nod. "Once Rimi completes his work on the koa—"

"Drop bear."

"Whatever. The koalas and wolves, I will work on eliminating or at least containing the Inhabitor Beetles on Remus."

"Okay, that sounds good. I'm going to look at the Conductor System for a minute, then I'm going to start up a new one. I think," he said, eyeballing Rimi, "it's time for territories."

"Yayyy!" Rimi said, punching a fist in the air. At least he hadn't changed too much.

Walker smiled and walked over to his computer to grab a seat. The last time he'd looked at his Creation Instrument, it'd been a weird version of an early '90s Macintosh. Now, it was more like a standard PC he'd have in his classroom. Admittedly, his school's budget cuts had been the reason they'd still had computers from the start of the millennium, but still, this was a nice upgrade. Even the chair was nicer, a round executive just big enough for a person of his size to be comfortable. Walker sighed at seeing no mechanical keyboard.

Beggars and choosers, Walker thought as he sat down and clicked on the Conductor System.

Conductor System
Assigned to: Creator Dante
**Please select which systems you would like to manage
with this system.**

No thoughts went through Walker's mind as he clicked each and every system he had access to.

[. . .]
[. . . Updating . . .]
[. . .]
Update time remaining: 1 week

"Oh, fuck you!" Walker yelled at his screen, causing Cagna and some of the Primigenials to look over at him. He ignored them.

Walker's voice became nasally, a distinct difference from his standard baritone, as he said, "Make a big deal about getting a supreme system, a hierarchy of systems, merging systems. Systems, systems, systems, then—BAM!—make me wait a fucking week."

"Walker!" Virgil yelled out, as everyone had apparently been listening to him the whole time. "That update is for a week in standard time, not ours!"

"FUCK!"

Walker couldn't see it, but Virgil laughed to himself while Rimi gave him a high five and mouthed, *That was funny.* Even the Primigenials laughed in their small circle, Dionysus included. It perfectly fit the cliche "and then everyone laughed." Everyone but him, that is.

Walker stared at his new computer screen. He knew he should probably look at the changes, as the old version was very much a point-and-click type with no fanfare, but he didn't want to do that right now. He wanted to play with his new system.

"Well, if I can't play with that one, I'll play with another," he said to himself with a nod, then clicked over to System in the interface.

As the list populated, he noted the changes and additions. The first time he'd looked, there had been a few hundred, then after further time in the protocol, several hundred. Now when he clicked on the filter, the System Designer started scanning everything. It took a few minutes, but when it was done, it returned over five thousand choices.

"Jesus," he said, speaking to himself again. There was something to be said for unlocking more and more options as you proved your competency. He had a sudden thought for what he wanted to do and followed it.

Walker typed in the word *progression* for the filter to comb through, but it didn't give him any returns. He then tried *advancement*, but nothing. *Development* gave him two responses he didn't like; *improvement* was interesting and something he'd look at for his Profession System. *Growth* was about plant life and, oddly enough, mountains, while *enhancement* seemed too much like his Monster System. Augmentation, elevation, expansion, succession, procession—nothing was coming up that would work for his goal. Finally, after over an hour and a half of reading relatively small text and scrolling through the multitude of systems, getting a huge number of ideas for how he would do some of his systems in the future, he found what he was looking for.

Sequential System:
A system designed by Creator Port in the Bravo Protocol of 3EG.
This system is a framework for entities to follow a sequential
order that is clear and unambiguous while also giving the Creator
the freedom to modify any part of the system as they choose.
Flexibility: Maximum
Difficulty to modify: Medium
Note: This system is based upon the Creation System used by the
Alpha Protocol.

Walker recognized that the note section was new. Every time he designed and released a new system, he gained more system options and received more information when he looked at them. Also, what the fuck was the Bravo Protocol?

"Hey, Virgil!" he called out.

He didn't know if Virgil recognized that note in his voice or if he was just bored with the mana grafting, but either way, the large brown squirrel ran right over.

"Yes, Walker," he said with a question in his voice.

"What in the ever-living fuck is the Bravo Protocol?" Walker asked while still staring at it on his screen.

Virgil canted his head to the side. "Oh."

"What do you mean, oh?" Walker said in exasperation. "Do you mean to tell me that the moment I finish the Alpha Protocol, I'm going to be shunted into the Bravo one? Are you fucking serious?" Walker was unintentionally yelling now. First, he was taken away from his world and everything he knew. Then, he was cast into the protocol against his will and told he had to build an entire civilization with a miniscule amount of time. It had changed him, causing him to become colder and more willing to take large risks. And just when he pulled a drastic move that seemed to be working out, granting him enough time to do things the right way rather than throwing things at the wall and seeing what stuck, this happened. "I mean, seriously, what in the—"

"You have to choose to join it, Walker," Virgil interrupted him with a deadpan voice. "The Bravo Protocol is for Creators who are interested in moving to the next stage."

Walker's building anger sputtered and died. He leaned back in his chair and closed his screen while thinking. Staring at the sky, he quietly said, "Who would choose to do something like this a second time?"

"Watch over Symphony for several thousand years and you may find out," Virgil responded in a neutral voice before he nodded and went back to his work.

"No . . . I won't," he replied, still looking at the sky. The way Symphony would be built, he doubted he'd ever grow bored of anything. Maybe the other Creators just weren't invested enough in what they'd put together, but he knew that wasn't the case with him.

Looking back at his screens, Walker pulled up the Sequential System again. He clicked Accept when an unexpected notification suddenly appeared.

System Link ability found.
System Link ability has reached maximum current
upgrade potential.
Would you like to merge this system with another before
finalizing your choice?
Yes/No

"Say what now?" Walker said as he read it.

Rather than call over Virgil, Walker decided he would do this on his own. He'd already bothered the large squirrel multiple times in the last hour, and he didn't want to get on his bad side. Who knew what would happen then? Angry chittering? Wait, did Virgil chitter?

Walker considered the question his overlay was presenting him with again. Did he want to merge this system with another before even starting it? Well, that was an interesting perspective. His goal was to create a Territory System, something that allowed entities to build and customize their land in any direction they'd like.

So much of what he had designed so far and was planning was linear—straight lines and expected departures. Naturally, he wanted the Territory System to allow for a lot of choices. The problem was that he first had to make a system that recognized levels.

The new ability to create merged systems was fantastic. And because any system he made was automatically uploaded to the Alpha Protocol . . . *Wait a second*, he thought. Making sure he was right, Walker typed in the Milestone System to look it up.

Milestone System:
A system designed by Creator Dante in the
Alpha Protocol of 4AA.
This system is designed to track and reward entities for reaching
prescribed and quantifiable moments.
Flexibility: Extreme
Difficulty to modify: Low
Note: This system is based upon the Tracking System designed by
Creator Ju in the Alpha Protocol of 2BC.

He nodded his head. Yep. Any system he made contributed to the overall systems provided by the System Designer. That meant he first had to make a Leveling System that would work for not only his territories and regions but also his sapients. He wouldn't be ready for the Class System for another little while, but he could get the Leveling System up first, let the Alpha Protocol copy it, and then merge it into both the Territory System and the Class System in the future. That way, he wasn't always starting out from scratch.

Walker smiled to himself. Gaming the system was fun.

He had a Sequential System, which would let him create ordered ranks with progressive movements, but he needed the Tracking System too. He could just use his Milestone System, but that wouldn't quite work. The Milestone System had a prescribed program built into it, just like the description stated. If he tried to use it, maybe he could modify it, but it would take too long. No, he needed to start from scratch.

Walker went back to the Sequential System and clicked Accept when it asked if he wanted to merge it with another. He typed in the search bar and found the Tracking System. Then a prompt appeared.

**Would you like to merge these systems with another before
finalizing your choice?
Yes/No**

Unlimited options, how sweet you are.

Because he was just making the Leveling System, he decided not to. But it did create some very interesting possibilities, like what would happen if he finished the Class System and merged it with the Monster System? Food for thought, definitely. Walker clicked No and another prompt appeared.

**[. . . Analyzing . . .]
[. . .]
You are about to merge the Sequential System with the
Tracking System.
Preview provided:**
*The Sequential System provides a set number of logical movements to anything the Creator wishes, while the Tracking System is a filter that provides information to the Creator.
Combining both will allow the Creator to build a system that allows for the mapping of specific events within an entity- or community-allotted threshold.*
**Would you like to merge these systems together?
Yes/No
Confirmed.
[. . .]
Merge complete.
Sequential Ordering System is now ready to be used.**

Walker had two takeaways from this: One, the protocol for giving descriptive previews was outstanding. Two, the way they named things here was absolutely terrible. Walker went into his system and officially renamed it the Leveling System.

Once he assigned it, Walker would have to wait a week in Symphony time before he could start a new design. He knew he didn't want to directly assign a new subsystem assistant for this, as it wouldn't make sense. It was a building block to classes and territories, a straight path without oversight. Walker called over to Cagna to see what she was working on.

"I'm building a limited series based on the age of a human entity. I specify human because different species will have different milestones," she said with a happy wag of her tail.

"Really? I hadn't even thought of that. What does it look like?" Walker couldn't help but ask, even though he was letting himself get sidetracked—he needed a mental breather to let his ideas cook.

"Let me show you." Saying so, she sent an update to his overlay. Walker looked at the update with surprise, as he didn't even know that was possible.

Why hasn't Virgil ever done that?

He spent a few minutes giving her information based on his limited under-standing of human life: what it was like for human beings growing up, and how they moved through different phases. He even explained what synchronous role integration was and how it affected human beings by psychologically pushing them into being different people at different times. That's when he had an epiphany.

"I'll tell you what. I'll help you figure this out so it's more efficient, and you help me out with the Leveling System."

"What's that?" she asked.

"It's kind of like the Milestone System, but it'll be specific to territories, mon-sters, and classers."

She agreed and they got down to work. The first real milestone in growing up was called entering the preoperational stage. It was a basis for psychology that Walker had learned in college. Basically, it was when children between the ages of two and seven started to really develop their mental states and begin to under-stand symbolism. It was also when their imagination really took the wheel. So they added a milestone for that.

The psychological stage after that was called concrete, but Walker didn't want to get too bogged down in just adding psychological stages to a limited milestone series. The first milestone was also logical to Walker because it showed the child had survived to reach two years of age. A little morbid, but it was still an important step for living on Symphony. For the second milestone, Walker went with thirteen, as that's when they had decided earlier that children would receive access to the Class System. Walker had Cagna add it in. They spoke for quite a while about what different stages of growth could mean and how to take age out of the last three milestones.

Growth was something different for everyone. To Walker, becoming an adult meant accepting your responsibilities. He had met plenty of ten-year-olds who acted as much like an adult as he did. He had also met plenty of forty-year-olds who needed to have their hand held through everything. Adulthood was about much more than a number. But you couldn't track that. That actually gave him an idea, and one that would work with the Unending Summit. It would have to wait for a bit, but it was a good idea. Either way, their last three milestones didn't actually relate to time but experience.

Human Growth Series: *Limited, Complete*

Basic milestone—Imagine:
Reach 2 years of age. 1 point.

Apprentice milestone—Adulthood:
Reach the age of 13. 5 points.

Skilled milestone—The First Job:
Take a job and gain access to the Profession System. 10 points.

Advanced milestone—The First Kill:
Kill a monster for the first time. 20 points.

Epic milestone—Titled:
Earn a title. 50 points.

Reward: Obtain 6 points or more in the Human Growth series to unlock the Class System.
Limited to human beings only.

To make things fair, and to continue with how they had done the previous limited series, Walker had the reward be fairly easy. It was important that people could unlock the Class System when they needed it, rather than have it locked away in times of stress.

If a human being completed a Skilled, Advanced, or Epic milestone, they'd of course instantly be granted access to the Class System. It could be abused, he was sure, but that was a part of being neutral in these quantifiable milestones. He had to expect people would find ways around his rules and constraints. It was better to understand that now than be upset about it later. The Advanced milestone wouldn't work until they had the Profession System up and running, the same for Epic and titles.

Lots of plans, and only a year to get through it all.

Walker linked Cagna to the Leveling System and watched as she grew before him, no longer surprised by it. When she stopped, her size didn't compare to Rimi's—he had two extra systems to her one—but it was noticeable. She spent a few minutes staring at nothing before turning to him and blinking. He started to explain what a Leveling System was rather than the Sequential Ordering System they were given.

"So, what are levels, exactly?"

"Well, they're a numerical system that allows entities, cities, and regions to track their progress. They'll start at level one and end at—" He stopped to think momentarily, scratching the back of his head. After a long pause, he finally said, "Never. That's why the Leveling System will work so well. It lets us create an infinite number, and we can give specific rewards for reaching different stages, or in this case, levels."

"So, what am I doing, then? What's my *why*?" Cagna asked with a tilt of her head. "I am not complaining, Creator, as everything I do is for the betterment of Symphony. But do you really need me for this?"

Walker scratched the back of his head again. "Hmm." He paused. "I need someone to help me keep an eye on it and to bounce my ideas off of. Plus, aside from the Follower and Conductor Systems, I don't see the point in keeping these systems to myself. As long as you guys have limited access, that works for me. The only reason I don't assign Rimi or Virgil as well is because they're too busy."

Cagna nodded her pink head with a smile. "Okay! But why not make another subsystem assistant?"

Walker smiled back at her. "Because I need Virgil to focus for a bit, and that can be quite traumatic for him. Also, I don't have the time right now to explain Symphony and our goals to them. Ironic, considering our time dilation. Now, here's what I want to do."

Walker broke down the Leveling System for her. Every five levels, the system would visually notify the receiver that they'd reached a new stage in leveling. That meant it went from zero—the first level—to five.

Cagna argued quite strictly with Walker that zero wasn't truly a number and couldn't be a factor of five. Athena, having listened in on the side, joined in at one point to speak about Plato and Socrates. Though she didn't know them personally, she did see some of the time Walker had spent in college studying philosophy and used it to smack him around intellectually. He wasn't sure why, but he felt like she was testing him in different ways as their argument began to move in circles.

In the end, Walker pulled the Creator card, and suddenly, zero became a factor of five in Symphony. Just another way that this world would be different from his own. Considering the turmoil Earth was always embroiled in, maybe the more differences he could create, the better his new world would be.

Athena chose to stay and help him out with the Leveling System, stating, "It's only logical."

Walker mentally shrugged. He'd take what help he could get.

"So, to clarify, levels are like the Awakened's stages. Different stages allow for different types of improvements or rewards," the goddess of wisdom said.

"Yeah, pretty much."

"For what purpose?" she asked with her hands on her hips. "I'm just checking to make sure you're not creating superfluous additions to Symphony."

That irked him a little. He answered back in a voice he tried to make friendly, "Visual progression, and personal or even professional goals." If he had to explain everything to everyone every time he wanted to do something, he'd never get anything done.

Athena nodded. "I see. And you said this would be for—"

"Yes," Walker cut her off without explaining. He already knew she'd heard everything he had said prior to her coming over here to "help." It was a small planet; her enhanced hearing could pick up practically everything. Walker was thankful he'd gone through the military, or this lack of privacy would have been astonishingly difficult. He was also thankful the protocol took away his need to go to the bathroom for the same reason.

"Okay," she said, pulling him from his thoughts. The golden-dressed woman folded the bottom of her clothing, then sat down and crossed her legs, gesturing at him. "Would you like to join me?"

"For what purpose?" Walker asked in confusion, unintentionally repeating what she'd said before.

"I find planning and difficult thinking is greatly helped by being in a relaxed position."

Cagna spoke up, "Walker likes to pace."

"Ah," Athena said with the same slow nod Walker had seen old people do. "You're one of those. I've known a few myself. Well, go on, then," she said while gesturing with her hand. "Start your frivolous walking."

Raising a single eyebrow at her, Walker looked at Cagna. "I think the visual attached to the levels will matter, and we need to really consider how it will look." His body wanted to move, but he firmly held his stance. Athena looked at a lightly twitching leg and gave him a raised eyebrow, but he ignored her. "Colors, shape, opacity or transparency, images. What do we want it to look like? Levels could eventually become almost a form of classism, where others will consider your stature and worth based on the level you hold." He shook his head roughly. "I don't really want that, so we need to make it so only the holder will know what level they are. The only time that will change will be when people hit a factor of five. Even then, the visual should be smaller, but still noticeable."

It took a few more minutes to explain how he wanted it all to work. He figured that the grafts Virgil was installing into the sapients could be used to hold skills, but space could become an issue. As his stress began to peak, Athena calmed him down by stating that it was a problem they could solve when he began to work on the larger systems. He gave her a brief smile before pulling up his newest system, talking while he worked so they could help him with the next steps.

Level zero would kick off right when a system was unlocked. As this was his first time building a system himself, rather than going through one of his assistants, he asked Cagna for advice. She gave a brief idea of what she had done with the Milestone System, filling in some blanks for him on how actual system designing worked. The basic controls and intuitiveness of the System Designer were incredible. It interpreted what he wanted, asked for confirmation, and then got to work on seeing it done.

He decided not to associate any milestones within the system itself because he needed a blank model for the Alpha Protocol to copy. If he didn't have that and started creating attachments to territories, classes, or professions, he'd have to deal with creating the Territory and Class Systems using a weird, disjointed system that didn't fit them.

It was important that the original Leveling System stay pure and untouched. Walker wasn't going to go with a mental metaphor for that, even if his eyes did stray to Athena for a moment.

After telling the System Designer what his goal for the system was, a series of screens appeared before him. Looking at it, he found a section labeled "Tracking" and another labeled "Sequences." Walker clicked on Sequences and spent some time creating a list of one through ten. The system recognized what he was trying to do, and he saw a ghostly version for the next series up to fifty. Confirming what he wanted, the first fifty levels populated on their own. Once he started fifty-one, the system recognized him again and the ghosts reappeared. He did this multiple times until he saw a range of two hundred numbers in the sequence.

I'll add more later, he thought to himself.

Walker then went over to Tracking and began to attach a tracker to each number. After a few minutes, the designer recognized what he was doing and provided the option for him, making him smile. With a click of a button, each level was now directly tracked.

Now, even though it was a system of nothing, he needed to activate it. It wouldn't hurt anyone, because it couldn't be assigned to anyone just yet—that's what the major systems were for. If he activated it now, he could just wait out the seven days while he continued to work on it. He'd have to advance Symphony another seven days, but that was chump change for his Temporal resources. Easy. That's when Athena spoke up.

"Is it required to activate it on Symphony and not Sonata?"

"Umm," Walker said as he looked through the options. A few seconds later, he laughed. "No, it isn't." Giving the woman a wink, he selected the small moonlet and started it up.

No changes.

Walker clapped his hands together, getting the attention of the Greek goddess and Cagna. "All right, so, level zero has nothing happen. No visual representation, just a notification that they reached level zero when they unlocked the system of their choice. We'll have to design that into the systems as we build them but leave them out of the Leveling System for now. What we can do, though, is associate levels with the rainbow effect from my homeworld."

"What's that?" Cagna asked. Athena looked interested too.

"Well, we're going to use the colors of the rainbow to associate the level that is attached. So, for instance, a rainbow goes from red to orange to yellow, and so on. Red is closest to the outside edge of the rainbow, so it's the starting point for this whole thing. For our first one hundred levels, we'll associate the Leveling System with the color red. I say this because that way it's the largest amount. Based on what Virgil expects out of our Class System, and the Profession System beside it, not too many people will get over level one hundred. That means they'll be the largest group. It makes sense. For levels one hundred and one to two hundred, we'll do orange, as that's the next stage."

Walker continued to explain the color associations and the range of levels. After they agreed on everything, with both Cagna and Athena providing their input, Walker began the work of creating designated updates.

Each level would have an associated color attached to it. But when something reached the transitional stage of 101, the color would shift visually from red to orange. That way, they knew they'd reached the next plateau. Based on the rainbow, Walker associated the level trackers, shifting from red to orange. On Athena's advice, he also noted that the visual changes should associate themselves differently. The first hundred levels would show as a small burst of color, while the second hundred levels would double the amount.

Walker had Cagna show Athena what he'd made, and when she asked how the system would release the colors, he realized he was missing something. He stepped back in and looked through the Leveling System, then found an area asking how it would be powered. Walker clicked a dropdown and found multiple options, including Electricity, which wouldn't work. After scrolling through several options, he found Ambient Magic and clicked on it.

"I think we're going to need more Mana trees," Walker said to himself. "We're associating too many of our systems with magic for this to work otherwise."

Athena heard him again and smiled to herself.

Walker began to pace. "Okay, the Leveling System's basic version is complete. We'll have to wait the seven days here, but that time can be used in other ways. I'll work on my soul, and Cagna, you work on your milestones. We'll try to meet up again for territories as soon as I get the notification that the system is done."

"Okay!" Cagna said, then ran over to sit next to Echidna to work on her mile-stones, seemingly happy to finish with the task. Walker looked over and found the gold-dressed goddess of wisdom staring at him.

"What? Do I have something on my face?" he asked.

"No, nothing like that, Walker. I was just wondering what you like to do for fun."

"What?"

CHAPTER ELEVEN

Systems, Systems, and Territories II

She paused for a beat before asking a second time, "What do you like to do for fun? It is a simple question, correct?"

Is she trying to ask me out, or am I just misunderstanding things here?

Being trapped on a moonlet with quite a small population, he tried not to look at Echidna or Athena that way. You know . . . in the sexy-time way. But this was a loaded question, throwing off how he viewed her.

Walker had used this line on potential girlfriends in the past himself. It was a quick and easy way to find a shared activity between them. A smooth-ish "What do you like to do for fun?" and the next thing he knew, Walker was on a date with a girl who was way out of his league. He'd always found confidence to be crucial. Of course, if that didn't work, being a little goofy could also work wonders. After all, what was the worst that they could say? No? He'd had his share of noes, and the ever more polite "No, thank you."

Tricky, he thought to himself as she continued her staring contest, waiting for his answer.

There was an unusual power dynamic between them, with Walker holding all the cards surrounding Symphony. He had pondered if he could ever date again, as they would all essentially be his children. Not literally, but still. It'd be pretty weird to suddenly start dating someone whom he'd created only a handful of years before. There was also the argument that he'd have to meet them in his avatar form. Could he have sex with that? Could he have avatar babies?

Athena though . . . Well, she didn't fit that mold.

He looked at her again. As in, *really* looked at her. Not as a resource or Primigenial, but she as a woman and he a man. She had pale golden hair, brown eyes, and slightly tanned skin. She was only a few inches shorter than him when they stood next to each other, and he had always liked the tall girls . . . goddesses. Frankly, she was quite beautiful, and it stirred up some feelings within him that he hadn't felt for a while. Wait . . . how long ago did he and Valerie break up? A little over a month . . . Wait, how long had he been staring at her?

She looked at him straight on and there was no hint of blushing. "I ask because I'd like to know more about you, rather than just the disparate memories that were shared between us."

"Stolen."

Athena nodded with deliberate care. "Yes, but can you blame us? We were imprisoned for thousands of years, and then you showed up, and we're suddenly in this strange place. We needed to know, and that was the only path at the time."

Walker tried to look at things from her point of view. Maybe he would've done things differently, but that was him, and he couldn't necessarily blame them. Still, it felt like an invasion of privacy.

Then again, his mind said back to him, *you just developed multiple ways to track your own citizens and every move that they make. You can't complain about a lack of privacy.*

True, dick Walker, true . . .

"Mmm," he hummed. "I get it. But I can't help but feel that way. Logically, I can see where you're coming from, but human beings are emotional animals. We live and breathe through them. They're too intrinsically tied to our sense of self for us to really move beyond them without slowly losing pieces of ourselves."

Athena affected a sad smile. "You will find, dear Walker, that the longer you live, the less those emotions have a hold on you. I have seen countless years in this life of mine, and yet, I find few things to surprise me. Wisdom is a burden to the informed."

Walker laughed, pulling them from the somber conversation. "Where were you when I was young, dumb, and broke? I could've used some of that wisdom."

"Locked in a prisonous tree at the bottom of the ocean," she replied with a confused face.

"Sorry, it was a rhetorical question," Walker said, scratching the back of his neck. He'd never been that great at small talk; maybe she hadn't been hitting on him. He worried he was like most men: any sign of female attention and they'd start thinking someone was attracted to them. He'd met plenty like that in his time but had never considered he might be one of them until this moment. It was disconcerting.

"I was also asking because I'm curious about you in a . . . personal manner."

Never mind, Walker thought to himself.

It turned out Athena was very much hitting on him, which really threw him for a loop.

"Aren't I like . . . barely even a baby, comparatively?" Walker asked, going with the tried-and-true method of awkwardness after being asked out by a beautiful woman.

Athena tapped a finger on her chin as she thought. "Yes, I suppose so. But that can be fixed. We are eternal, Walker." She gave a short laugh. A melody he hadn't heard before. "Well, I am. But you're very much on your way to joining our ranks. In just a few dozen years, our ages will not seem quite so different." She stood up and her dress fell down in a perfect compliment to her hair. "Also," she said, her finger pointing in a direction just past him, "have you seen the men who surround me?"

Walker followed the line of her finger and found Zeus. The king of the gods was currently haranguing a sleeping Dionysus not too far away, obviously faking it because no one could sleep through the volume of his father's voice. Minos stood behind him with his arms crossed and a stern look on his face as he watched the Primigenial bashing occur.

Athena slapped her hands against her thighs in consternation. "These . . . men . . . I have no interest in. They're all aligned with icons and oaths that are too rigid. Dionysus can't help but be revelrous. Always. As in, always and forever. His oath holds him too tightly. Meanwhile, Zeus is consistently full of thunder and rage. And poor, poor Minos. He can't help himself. He is only truly able to express himself properly in battle." She sighed. "They're all, every one of them, forced to live by the path they've unwittingly chosen. That is why I have never received a man in my arms. That is why I've never known any form of physical affection aside from a chaste kiss bestowed upon those who have shown brilliance in their time." She turned and looked at him directly. "It is a simple equation, Walker. I have never found anyone I am compatible with." She looked at the palm of her right hand with a forlorn cast to her face. "It has been . . . a lonely life, if I am honest with you."

Walker scratched his chin. "So, over several hundred years you've never been on a date because all of the men you know are full of hot gas?" he asked.

Athena laughed again. "That is close enough to the truth. And, unlike my father, I do not want to join with a mortal. The heartbreak would be too much for me, I fear."

"I see," Walker replied, his mind moving quickly. What she'd said filtered through his thoughts, and he made a decision without knowing it. "Well, to answer your first question, I used to enjoy reading and playing video games. I'm afraid video games may never return, and reading is a long way away from our current time. Umm, I also used to play a mean game of Ping-Pong."

"What's Ping-Pong?" she asked with an arched brow. "I haven't heard of that."

He smiled. "Oh, you didn't get that memory? All right."

Walker spent several minutes explaining the game to her and what little history he knew of it. He went over the serve, the fault, and all the little rules that came with it. She smiled when he was done. "That sounds quite fun. I would enjoy playing that with you if given the chance."

He returned her smile with another of his own. "I would like that. Maybe we'll see if we can do something about it." He scratched the back of his head again. "Anyways, I need to work on my soul for a bit."

"Oh?" Athena said, her brown eyes flashing. "Well, I can make no further progress of my own, so if you'd like, I'd be happy to help you in Echidna's place. It would be nice to help another person with their progress as an Awakened. One moment."

"Y-yeah. Sure," Walker said, stumbling on the words.

The blonde woman walked over and spoke to Echidna for several minutes. As she was walking back, Echidna had a strange look on her face. Walker tried not to consider what that meant.

When she returned, Walker laid down on the grass beside Athena. Unlike with Echidna, this time it felt oddly intimate. Walker started to stretch his soul, and time flew by.

He rotated different activities across the six and a half days he had left until the Leveling System was completed. He spoke to Athena about what life was like in ancient Greece. Each time he called it ancient, she seemed to grow upset. When he realized why she kept growing cold whenever he did so, he leaned into his goofy teacher side.

"Super ancient Greece!"

"Greece during, you know, that time before the galaxy was formed."

"I've met dirt that said Greece was older."

Eventually, she got over it.

He worked on his soul and finished his upper and lower back before starting on each shoulder, which was oddly hard for him. As always, at each bit of progress, he felt his skin tighten up a little and his muscles felt . . . clearer? Was that right? Like he had better control of them. While he was working on his left shoulder, Athena explained that the last place to stretch the soul was the mind, as a lot would happen at once. It would also be the moment when Walker could screw everything up again and potentially lose his mind. Good stuff there.

Walker made minor alterations to the Leveling System, ensuring the visual cues worked when necessary. He also worked with Cagna on her milestones whenever Athena wasn't around.

They'd built two new ones that he quite enjoyed, including the start of the full monster series. Once Rimi had learned what they were working on, he took a quick pause on his koala and wolf modifications to help them design the series. The time spent in design took as much as all of the rest put together. After over six hours, they finally agreed on how it would work, and Walker had them create their first Advanced milestone in a full series.

Monster Series: *Full, Complete*

Basic milestone—The Monster System:
Unlock the Monster System. 1 point.

Novice milestone—I Choose You!:
Attune your kernel for the first time. 3 points.

Apprentice milestone—Mix It Up:
Attune your kernel for the second time. 5 points.

Adept milestone—What's in a Name?:
Create your own name. 7 points.

Skilled milestone—Holder:
Gain control of a territory. 10 points.
The Territory System is unlocked.

Experienced milestone—Very Vein:
Create your own mana veins. 15 points.
The Class System is unlocked.

Experienced milestone—Just the Beginning:
Complete all Basic to Skilled milestones in the Monster Series.
15 points.

Advanced milestone—A Monster Awakened:
Awaken your soul. 20 points.

It was essential to Walker that Rimi seem quite satisfied with everything. They'd have to talk later regarding how monsters would create their own mana veins, but it would be a necessary step for the Class System coming up. Walker hesitated to add the Awakened milestone, but Athena stated that activating the soul had been around for at least two renditions. It wasn't exactly a secret.

After making the Monster Series, Cagna wanted to work on a full series that focused on leveling, but Walker still wasn't sure that was a good idea. She said that she would only turn it on once all of the other systems had activated, so, in the end, he relented. It was surprisingly fast to design as far as a complete series went. The idea of levels was purely quantifiable at their root.

Leveling Series: *Full, Complete*

Basic milestone—First Level:
The first step is often the hardest, but not this one! 1 point.

Novice milestone—Twenty-five:
Obtain level 25. 3 points.

Apprentice milestone—Fifty:
Obtain level 50. 5 points.

Adept milestone—Seventy-five:
Obtain level 75. 7 points.

Skilled milestone—Centenarian:
Obtain level 100. 10 points.
The Monster System is unlocked.
Limited to sapients who do not currently have access to the
Monster System.

Experienced milestone—The Next Step:
Obtain level 101. 15 points.

Experienced milestone—From the Beginning:
Complete all Basic to Skilled milestones in the Leveling series.
15 points.

Advanced milestone—Magical Absorption:
Obtain level 150. 20 points.

When Athena questioned why there was a specific milestone just for reaching level 101, he told her that sapients would have to learn how to access their kernels and form their own kind of magic to move past the level one hundred threshold.

He didn't tell her that he wasn't quite sure yet how they would do so. Just understanding that you not only had access to magic now, but that there were a myriad of ways you could use it would be difficult enough. Monsters had the advantage of being born with kernels and the ability to feel magic. Sapient non-monsters . . . not so much. It was a hurdle or, in other words, a gateway to more levels and greater challenges. Just the way he wanted Symphony to be.

Walker's days continued to fly by. Cagna was working on multiple milestone series, and Rimi finished the koala and wolves, with Virgil's approval, three days in. He had completed his work before his time limit and the advanced assistant was pleased enough to compliment him on it. Rimi couldn't stop grabbing Cagna and telling her about it. From his words, you'd think that Virgil had professed his undying love for the blue squirrel.

"You have done well."

It didn't seem like much to Walker, but these squirrels were weird.

On the fifth day, Walker spoke to Virgil, and they agreed to get a new subsystem assistant started before they needed them. That way, they would have plenty of time to interact with the new member of their family and give them a chance to break down what their goals and work would be.

The green squirrel came out the way they all did, ripped out and thrown by Virgil into the grass. Then the same question appeared by rote: "Are you my Creator?"

Rather than giving Rimi the job like last time, Walker sat down and worked with his new subsystem assistant so they'd start off on the right foot. He'd learned from his experience with Cagna not to farm out the job to another.

Walker needed a bond with all of his assistants; otherwise, they might be too afraid to contribute their own input and ideas for the systems they'd be working with. After about twenty minutes of talking back and forth, the green subsystem assistant settled on being called Neus. Initially, he had asked for Capa, as Capaneus was from the third ring of hell in Dante's Inferno, but that would've been too confusing for everyone.

Cagna and Capa? No, thank you.

Walker explained who everyone was, the purpose of the Alpha Protocol, and what had happened thus far. As Walker began discussing the Leveling System, Neus asked an important question.

"What is my goal?"

"Hmm," Walker said, "I want your focus to be on creating a Territory System that allows its entities the freedom to build a personalized environment. To create a place they want to live in and that reflects the world they see for themselves. The best thing you can do is make it so that the system provides its entities with options to choose from and goals to achieve. It'll all work through the Leveling System, and they'll have to come up, at least initially, with their own designs." Walker began pacing as his thoughts continued. "As those designs complete, you check them and make sure they fit the world of Symphony. Ask yourself the following questions: Is this possible within the parameters of the Territory System? Does it allow for the growth of a territory? What purpose does it hold? Is it named correctly?"

"Will it improve the lives of its citizens or entities?" Neus tried out.

Walker snapped his fingers as he stopped walking. "Exactly! Just like that. But remember, some entities may favor violence more than happiness or production. And, according to how we're trying to build our world, that's perfectly fine! It is up to the entities and citizens of the community to decide what their territory will represent. Money and economy? Sure. A traveling pitstop? Why not! It's up to them. Your focus is to make sure that their designs get added to the system for others to potentially use and to make sure everything works as intended." Neus raised his hand, causing Walker to say, "You don't have to do that."

"Well, what if I want to design some myself?"

Walker scratched his chin. "Nothing wrong with that. If you feel inspired to create your designs and understand the intricacy involved in its workings, go right ahead. We also need to come up with different tiers or levels of buildings, but that's for later. Right now, spend some time talking to the other assistants, get to know the Primigenials, and start coming up with ideas. The Leveling System will finish in"—Walker checked his System Designer tab and found a clock in the corner—"just under a day at this point. So, have some fun and get to know Sonata."

"Okay!" Neus said, then ran on his small green feet toward the Evolution Chambers. Virgil looked at the green squirrel and gave Walker a heavy dose of side-eye, causing him to smile and give the giant squirrel a thumbs-up.

Things were looking good.

With a brief moment alone, he looked at the computer chair near the Creation Instrument. It was designed for big people like himself, a rare bit of comfort from the Alpha Protocol.

As he stared at it, a burst of inspiration swelled inside him.

Without talking to anyone, Walker pulled up the Entity Subsystem and planted four two-year-old Mana Trees on Sonata. He placed them in a square encircling the Tree of the Gods at exact ratios so they were all equidistant from each other while maintaining what he felt was a safe distance.

He didn't know what kind of fuckery the first occupier of Sonata was entangled with, but he needed to make sure his Mana Trees didn't interact with it. Walker stepped into the Landmass System and began planting steel in a shell beneath the dirt. It took several hours rather than the speedy placement he was used to, as the moonlet was circular instead of the half-formed shape of Symphony.

There was one great benefit to staring at a monitor, moving steel a few feet at a time: Walker got to enjoy ignoring all the questions everyone peppered him with when they noticed the four new inhabitants of their home. After he had the shell up just below where he eyeballed the roots would take hold, Walker clicked out of the Landmass System and called a group meeting.

It took a moment, but once everyone had gathered up, including Dionysus, Walker broke the silence.

"Hello, everyone. So, here's what's going on. I've placed four Mana Trees across Sonata so I can use them to test things out here. It's—"

"You placed the wrong ones!" Virgil yelled out, interrupting him.

"No, I didn't. See, I knew they were the originals. It's intentional!" he burst out, willing them to see things from his perspective. "I need these to be battery packs for what I have planned, and it won't work unless we have a metric boatload of magic on Sonata. Our cozy little home here won't always be so little. It's going to keep growing, and I intentionally didn't age the Mana Trees with Overwhelming Magical Discharge so they could grow with it."

"And the potential for evolutionary explosions?" Virgil asked.

Walker shook his head. "As I understand it, nobody currently on Sonata can evolve. You're all Primigenials, who the system won't even let me mess with, and assistants, which the system recognizes as abilities rather than people. And even if we do put sapients down, we can control their rate of growth through their kernels."

Virgil gave a strong glare before a brief nod, accepting that he'd thought it through.

"Great!" Walker said with a smile before being forced to pause. The atmosphere over Sonata took that moment to change. Everyone on Sonata watched as the sky they had grown used to since starting the dilation took on a light cyan coloring—the color of magic.

Walker shrugged before speaking again. "Anyway, I did this because I want to test the Territory System here with Neus. Specifically, I want to use the new system ourselves to create some simple creature comforts. You'll see all kinds of things randomly pop up here as we get moving."

Virgil coughed. "Hmm, yes, but you do not have a way to produce those items."

Walker snapped his fingers. "Exactly right, and the Leveling System will finish in not too long. I bet we'll have to get some kind of Item System up and running before moving on to territories. I just figured"—he waved in the general direction of the trees—"that getting those fellas planted would give me a head start on things."

Virgil grumbled quietly, though everyone still heard him, "Magic should be more valued than that . . ."

"Okay then," Walker said with a smile, "what is something everyone wants so we can get to work on it?"

Athena, naturally, raised her hand first. "I would like a library."

"Not only a library but a book-making system as well, right?" he asked.

She nodded slowly and threw him a smile.

"Okay, one library. Anyone else?"

They all raised their hands at the same time, causing Walker to smile as he took down a list.

Each wanted something simple, although a few oddities reared their heads. Minos, it turned out, wanted a garden rather than the blacksmith Walker thought he would ask for. Dionysus laughed pretty hard at that one. Walker didn't even need the Item System; he just popped some random vegetation from his Entity Subsystem, roots and all, right in front of the Bronze Battler and watched as the powerfully built man squealed and ran off with them toward the Tree of the Gods.

Okay, then.

Walker took notes on everyone's requests and mentally filed them away for when the system was up and running. As he scanned around, he found Virgil had already walked away. It wasn't surprising, as the workaholic just wanted to finish his humans. Walker asked for an update as he left, and the great brown squirrel called back, saying it'd be another few weeks.

So, he spent some time writing down what he wanted. A bed was obvious, as it was comfortable and a staple for human beings. He may not be fully human anymore, but that didn't mean he was completely walking away from the idea of who he was in his former life. He tried not to think about what it would be like to go back to Earth as an Awakened.

He also planned on setting up a couch, a small house, and several other commodities that were necessary for daily life. Once this thing finished, would he have to eat and go to the bathroom again? He had a lot of questions about that. What about showering? Cleanliness was next to Creatorness.

Also, a Ping-Pong table. For, uh, obvious reasons. Naturally, his mind wandered. Would Virgil play? That would be a sight to see. Could he use his tail for the paddle?

Smiling to himself, he worked on his soul and got both of his shoulders done in the next several hours. During his resting periods, instead of watching Symphony, trapped in slow motion again after the temporal explosion, he lay there and thought about . . . nothing. Things would get busy again, and these little breaks were helpful for his psyche.

While he was talking to Minos about what made a warrior a warrior, his timer finished. Walker's overlay lit up, and, after a hasty goodbye, he ran over to his Creation Instrument while the information downloaded.

[. . . Scanning . . .]
System task complete: Design a system (Series 3)
System requirements:
System is found to be balanced and consistent: Yes
System allows for growth: Yes
System is applied to world continuously without calamity:
7/7 days
Reward for completion: Gain the ability to create
unlimited systems.

Reward for completing the third system task:
Congratulations, Dante! You've unlocked the ability to create
unlimited systems!
Few Creators have focused on creating systems. Due to your hard
work in completing the final task in the System Designer series,
you now have the ability to create as many systems as you choose.
Limit: You may create one new system per day.

"Hey, Virgil!" Walker yelled out.

"One day for you, not for Symphony," the brown squirrel yelled back, already anticipating his question.

"Yes!" Walker said with a pumped fist getting a glare from Rimi for stealing his signature move. Another question was sparked, one that needed answering. He quickly made his way over to Virgil. "Wait, why is this one day when the Conductor System is a week?"

"Because the protocol is creating it rather than you. Now the training wheels for the designer come off. Why limit the Creators who know what they are doing? The more systems you make, the more the protocol gains in new ideas and programs for future renditions. Simple." Virgil turned back to the small boy he was working on.

"Oh, okay, thanks." Walker gave a thumbs-up, which finally got Rimi to look away from him.

What a glare! Walker thought as he decided to never fist pump again.

Clicking on the System Designer, he scrolled through the options in search of something he thought he'd seen before. It popped up on his overlay after only a few minutes.

Permanent Magical Conjuration System:
A system designed by Creator Fienias in the Alpha Protocol of 2JM.
This system allows for the creation of materials by synthesizing
magic and solidifying it within reality.
Flexibility: High
Difficulty to modify: Medium
Resources used: Ambient magic
Limits: Permanent Magical Conjuration System is limited by
what materials the Creator has discovered within their rendition.
Note: This system is based upon the Cosmic Genesis System as
well as the Far-Eye System.

Looking at all of the information provided, Walker guessed this was the final update to system designing he could look forward to. He skipped the merger question and created the system for himself. As it populated, Walker renamed it to "Items" and dove in.

As he did so, his world faded away, and just like with the Cosmic Genesis System, he found himself in a dark space occupied with only text floating in the sky.

**Welcome to the Permanent Magical Conjuration
System, Dante.
Use of this system has a pre-determined cost: Ambient
magical potential.
What would you like to create?**

"Ah, another one of you," Walker said after he finished reading.

I do not understand what you mean, Dante.

"Don't worry about it. Question for you, my permanent magical conjuration friend. Am I the only one who can speak to you, or can I assign a subsystem assistant to also work with you?"

**You may assign any number of protocol-bound entities to this
system as you please.**

Walker grew excited after reading that. "You mean I can give you multiple assistants."

That is correct. You—

Walker exited the system and pulled up his overlay. He quickly dragged Virgil, Rimi, and Cagna over to the Item System without sparing a second for thought. All three of them froze for a moment, but Walker wasn't watching as he stepped back into the Item System. "Please rename yourself to the Item System," he said without pausing.

**Command recognized.
This system is now named the Item System.**

To Walker's left, Rimi and Cagna popped up in the darkness. They instantly started looking around in confusion before spotting Walker. Rimi's little feet skipped to him faster than he thought possible, and the small blue squirrel began smacking his Creator's leg with one small blue paw.

"Don't. Just. Add. Us. To. Systems!" he said as he hit Walker with each new word.

"Sorry! I just got excited. Hey, wait a second," he said, noticing a change in the two. "You both grew again." Rimi was now even taller than before. If they had been on Earth, he'd be considered some kind of mega-squirrel. Cagna finally reached Rimi's former height, back when he initially received access to the Entity and Ecology Subsystems. It took a few blinks before his mind could adjust to their growth.

"Yes, well, that is only natural," the blue squirrel said after he had caught his breath. "Step out for a moment and you will understand, Creator."

Walker was confused but did as he asked. The moment he stepped out, his overlay updated, and he stumbled for a moment as it felt like Sonata was changing in front of his eyes. The ground shook, trembling with abandon and causing his body to vibrate. As he watched, the ground seemed to bend and stretch itself, and items and people in the near distance grew further away.

[. . . Scanning . . .]
**Congratulations, Dante! Your subsystem assistant has upgraded
to a full assistant!**
Unknown changes occurring.
The Tree of the Gods is maturing!
[. . . Scanning . . .]
[. . .]
The Tree of the Gods has borne fruit.

"Son of a bitch," Walker said as he read the updates, but when he looked to the left, he was met with a surprise. Golden-haired Athena was currently yelling at a darkly dressed man with a stern visage while a younger boy and an absolutely stunning woman stood behind him. From what he could hear, the argument seemed to be focused on him.

Of course it is.

"Because he'll come to you when he can! You are not to approach him, Hades. I already told you."

"Oh, come on now, love, he'll be so excited to meet us," the beautiful woman in the green diaphanous robe said in a sultry voice.

"No, sister. He's working on something that you'll approve of, I'm sure." She held up a finger in front of the man again. "Not a word to him. You've always been patient, Hades. Please stay that way."

The darkly dressed man didn't respond with anything; he just continued to stand in place and look at her. Eventually, he moved his head and looked around the area. Athena took that as an accord and walked over to speak with her father. Walker smiled before pulling up the World Editor.

Sonata's size increase this time looked much more drastic than the last two. The first time, it had increased a little, barely anything at all, whereas the second time, it had increased by around twenty percent. This time, Walker guessed it had increased by another fifty percent overall from its former state. As he pondered the implications, a sudden thought had him diving into the Cosmic Genesis System.

Speaking with the AI, Walker learned that Sonata's elliptical rotation was off course. Cursing under his breath, he spent a small number of Temporal resources to alter their placement around Symphony and maintain their stable orbit.

He stepped out of the Cosmic Genesis System and immediately back into the Item System, trusting Athena to keep an eye on their new residents. To Echidna, who was watching from not far away, it looked like Walker appeared and then vanished right after.

When the Item System rematerialized around him, he found Cagna and Rimi discussing what to make first.

"Rimi, how's your monster making going?" Walker said, interrupting their discussion.

The medium-sized squirrel blew air out of his mouth. "I'm about an hour away from being done with all of the tiered starter monsters. You know you've pulled me away from it multiple times."

Walker nodded. "Yep, and I'm sorry. If you'd like, you can go ahead and finish up. The Item System isn't going anywhere, and you can work in here anytime you'd like."

Rimi shrugged and said, "Okay," then faded away.

Walker turned to Cagna. "You, on the other hand, can help me right now. What do you want to make first?"

Cagna raised both arms in the air excitedly. "Oh! Oh! A chair!"

Walker snapped his fingers. "That's right! Your first request was for a chair. Let's take a look here." The AI heard them and created floating text that presented their current options.

Only non-living items are currently available:
This may be changed within limits.
Currently available options built into the Item System:
More options become available as they are created.

Raw Materials: Basic Crafting Material, Basic Building Material, Basic Enchanting Material, Basic Food
Generic Items: Tools, Utility, Infrastructure, Furniture, Transportation, Leisure
Weapons: Swords, Axes, Maces, Ranged Weapons, Daggers, Staves, Exotics

**Clothing and Armor: Casual Wear, Formal Wear, Magical Wear,
Light Armor, Medium Armor, Heavy Armor
Structures: Housing, Workshops, Mercantile Structures,
Defensive Structures, Offensive Structures, Portals (restricted by
the Alpha Protocol)**

Looking over the options, he clicked the second one and watched as a series of choices with different images appeared. Walker clicked on Furniture, and a list populated his large screen with search and filter options to the right.

**Basic Armchair
Basic Bed
Basic Bookshelf
Basic Cabinet
[. . .]**

There were a ton of options, but Walker didn't like the look of the word "basic." He clicked on the armchair and another image came up. It showed a functional and straightforward design. No embroidery or special stitching could be found, just a standard armchair anyone on Earth could buy for a modestly low price at a nearby store.

A hand-me-down store, maybe, Walker thought to himself.

Still, it was an armchair, and as much as he might wish it, he was not a very good designer. To the right of the image was a bar slowly filling up as he watched and another bar above the image showing his overall localized magical saturation. The top bar wasn't very filled, but it would get there over time as the Mana Trees matured and Sonata became more magically inundated. Understanding what he was waiting for, Walker and Cagna stood there without speaking and watched as the bar to the right filled. Once it finished, it started pulsing and a screen appeared.

Would you like to conjure a Basic Armchair?

"Instead of 'conjure,' please use 'create' from now on," Walker told the system operator.

**Command recognized.
All future communications will be updated.
[. . .]
Would you like to create a Basic Armchair?**

Before he clicked Accept, he found an option in the corner that offered different colors and styles. He chose pink and adjusted the brightness until it was as close as possible to Cagna's natural coloring. After he clicked Confirm, Walker asked her to exit with him.

Just next to where they faded into view sat a perfectly basic pink armchair. Cagna squealed upon seeing it.

"I love it! Thank you, thank you, thank you, Creator!" she said as she hugged his leg before leaping into it, easily clearing the bottom of the chair to its maximum height of two feet. She sat herself down, almost but not quite blending in with the color of the chair. The subsystem assistant squirmed her rear, digging into the chair a bit in her search for comfort. Once she found her spot, she leaned back and stared at a screen in front of her he couldn't see.

"Much better," she said with a sigh.

Basic armchair that it was, Walker didn't have the heart to tell her how uncomfortable that chair would be for him. Too small and narrow, and it looked pretty tough to sit in. It was true what they said: ignorance was bliss.

Now that he had a better understanding of the Item System, he stepped back in and started a conversation with the AI within.

"Why are there only basic items?"

"How do you make more items? Or, umm . . . permanent conjurations?"

"Why can't you make living things?"

"Are there any tasks for this system?"

It turned out that the Permanent Magical Conjuration System only came with basic items from the start. Any new categories or items that you wanted you had to make yourself. That fit in line with what Walker wanted from the system in the first place, as he needed to have this working for his Profession System.

The problem arose, however, that you couldn't actually design within the system. According to the AI, to add optional items to the system, they had to be built and then added manually. To test this, Walker had the AI create a few quick pieces of pine wood, a basic hammer, and some basic nails.

It only took a few minutes to hammer the wood into a fairly boxish shape, then he held onto it as he clicked Item. Rather than take him to the system, a different prompt appeared.

Would you like to add this to the Item System registry?

Walker chose Yes and watched as the box disappeared. When he stepped back into the system and searched for boxes, he found his shitty creation sitting there. He chose the option to make another one when the bar filled up, then did so again and stepped out. Now sitting before him on the grass were two shitty boxes that matched the one he'd made just a moment ago.

"Neat," he said as he looked at them both.

He stepped back in yet again and started combing through the book options. None of the books had any writing, but even if the paper was rough and the cover flimsy, it was a start. He needed to find a way to make high quality paper and then create a book binding press if he wanted to fulfill Athena's library requirement. Not to mention, you know, making a library. The bookshelves in the Item System left a lot to the imagination, as they were simply pieces of wood hammered together.

Walker clicked on Structures and looked at what was available. On impulse, he combed through the Defensive options, finding walls and barracks. Curiosity getting the better of him, he clicked on Barracks and watched as the magic meter on the right expanded at a tremendous rate. When it finally stopped, the bar was almost as tall as he was. The armchair's meter, by comparison, couldn't have been more than a few inches. It seemed that the more complicated a structure, and the greater the size, the longer it would take to reserve the magic. Then a notice hit his screen.

Magical potential within the area is not high enough to produce this structure.
Please increase your magical reserves for future use of this item.

"Well, shit," Walker said as he stepped out. He guessed they'd have to wait for the Mana Trees to mature before they could do much, but his foresight in choosing the overwhelming Mana Trees would pay off in the end. Walker quick-stepped over to Athena to ask an important question.

"Yes, Walker?" the beautiful woman asked with an arched eyebrow as she spotted him coming. He'd already forgotten that the walk from his Creation Instrument to the Tree of the Gods now took longer than before due to Sonata's sudden growth.

"Do you know which Primigenials are coming out next?" he asked with a hint of anxiety in his voice.

She walked over and put a hand on the tree for a moment before coming back and saying, "The next three to be released are Apollo, Artemis, and Hephaestus."

"Yes!" Walker said, though he refrained from pumping his fist out of respect for his blue friend. "The moment Hephaestus comes out, please send him to me."

The goddess of wisdom nodded her head once. "I'll see it done, Creator. Do you want to meet the three recently released gods now?" she asked.

Walker tried to think of a way out of this but came up dry—his mind couldn't get around all the plans floating around in there. With a sigh, he said, "Who are they?"

"The dark man is Hades, of course. The young woman is Aphrodite, whom you need to be careful around, and the young boy is her son, Eros. He's not really a teenager, just so you know. That is the form he was in when we were taken."

Walker nodded. "I see. Well, we may as well get this over with." He tried to keep the resigned feeling out of his voice.

Athena put her arm through his, surprising him for a moment before he recovered, and they walked over together. When they stopped in front of the three, Aphrodite caught Walker's eye, and he felt the goddess beside him tighten her grip for a moment before slowly letting go.

"Who do we have here?" the beautiful woman in the green diaphanous gown said, her sultry voice striking him. Each step she took seemed like part of a choreographed dance, light and full of grace. Step spin, step leap, sidestep . . . shuffle. But as Walker watched, he realized something.

It was super weird.

He guessed others would find it an ephemeral and entrancing view, but to him, it looked like a woman moving from place to place with too many steps and hip gyrations. Sure, she was beautiful, with a shape to her that was difficult to compare other women to. But to his mind, beauty was something to be admired, not to gawk at.

In the back of his mind, Walker wondered if maybe it was something that worked well on regular people back in old Greece: sheepherders who spent all their time with livestock or the odd lonely warrior or two. But for him, she just seemed like a social media influencer dancing to music nobody else could hear.

It was annoying.

Hades, however, did not move like that. He stepped forward with long and efficient movements, and Eros came in right behind him. "Stop those gyrations, you damned fool," the stern man said in a voice that sounded like someone had chewed on it repeatedly. "It was bad enough being trapped in that tree with you all. Now we have to be released at the same time? Unbearable." He looked at the Tree of the Gods. "If only I could destroy this monstrosity here and now."

Saying so, he stepped forward and threw a punch at it. The only thing that happened was the sound of a dull thud and a darkly dressed man shaking his hand in pain.

"Blast you to oblivion!" he yelled at it. "Yes, I hear you idiots. Keep quiet while your better works on your behalf." He turned to Walker, looking him up and down. "I know of the deal you made. I have only one request: leave me the fuck alone." Then he turned around and walked away.

Walker watched him go, silent. That was the first time any of the Primigenials hadn't wanted something from him. It made him curious.

From the corner of his eye, he spied Eros stepping near his mother. She looked down and whispered something he couldn't hear. The small boy responded in a light voice—Walker was only able to pick out the words "I don't think so"—before he ran off after Hades, laughing all the while.

"What did you two talk about?" Walker asked the beautiful goddess.

"Oh, I asked him if he thought you would make love to me," she said with a mischievous smile.

Walker could hear Athena's eyes roll beside him.

Contrary to what anyone expected, he smiled back.

CHAPTER TWELVE

Systems, Systems, and Territories III

N o, thank you," Walker said in response to her unique question, an odd smile still plastered to his face.

"Are you sure?" the dirty-blonde-haired woman asked with lifted eyebrows. "I'm quite good at it. Very good, in fact." She suggestively let a part of her dress fall off one shoulder.

"Yep. Thank you, but I'm all good."

"Ugh, Awakened," she said, her voice suddenly deepening and sounding more natural than the throaty version she'd been using. One delicate hand fixed the shoulder of her dress. "If you need me, I'll be torturing Hades." Aphrodite walked away with clean strides over the grassy plain.

"Weird."

He felt a hand slip into his as he admired the woman walking away. "You don't know the half of it. But kudos on declining her advances," Athena said as she turned to look at him with a smile. "Not many, mortal or Awakened, have spurned her advances without Heph being around."

Walker shook his head. "Yeah, no. I grew up in California. Met women like her constantly throughout my life. Girls, really. Playing with men's emotions, then running over them emotionally and throwing them away. I'm certainly not saying all women are like that. My mother was a saint, although I didn't realize that until much too late. But women like her all think they're God's gift to men . . . Though—"

Athena nodded once with an undefinable look. "She was Zeus's gift to men, in a sense. But they often became obsessively needy with her afterward. It always seemed to me like a piece of their soul was forever missing, as if no other partner in life would satisfy them after a dalliance with Aphrodite."

Walker grunted. "Yeah, I've seen those too. My buddy called them soul suckers."

Athena smiled. "I'm happy to know that you're not one of them, Walker."

He stretched a weird twist in his back. "Nope. Already went through that phase when I was younger. Jessica. Nowadays, I'm immune, thank God." Walker looked around and found everyone busy but them. In the distance, he spied Hades quickly walking away. Stalking closely behind him, giggling, was the diminutive form of Eros, and Aphrodite was leap-walking just behind them both. Dionysus was asleep and Zeus was supervising the building of Minos's garden with Echidna. Two supervisors to every worker, just like on Earth.

Sonata's becoming fucking weird, the human-turned-Awakened-Creator thought to himself.

He nodded. "I think we're all good. Stay here for a moment, please," Walker said, then he stepped into the Item System and stepped out a few minutes later holding something. He handed it to her with a closed fist so she couldn't see what it was.

"What's this?" she asked as she took the small item from him.

"It's the closest thing I could find in there to a Ping-Pong ball," he said with a slight grimace as her open hand showed a small brown circular object. "It's made of cork, which they did away with a long time ago on Earth. I didn't see any plastic, which means that we don't have the resource for it yet." He scratched his chin with a thumb. "Though, judging by what it's done to Earth, maybe we shouldn't ever have any plastic."

Athena lifted the ball and looked at it closely, then smiled. "I love it!" She walked over and wrapped both arms around Walker. He inadvertently felt his body stiffen up. He hadn't expected the act, and it honestly hadn't been so long ago that he thought he'd be marrying Valerie.

She was like a ghost sitting on his mind.

But after a few seconds of her hugging him, he returned the gesture. It was surprisingly lovely.

"Now we just need a table, a net, and two paddles," he said with a smile, still enjoying the moment.

"Indeed," a voice sounding just like Virgil's said from only a few steps away.

How the hell did he sneak over here? Walker thought.

"Hello, Virgil," Walker said, breaking the hug and taking a step back at the same time. It felt oddly like he'd just been caught doing something he shouldn't have. "What can I do for you?"

"I am just checking up on you, Creator. Making sure you are staying on task with all of your new"—he looked from the ball to Athena's face—"toys."

If Athena didn't like what he was saying, it didn't show on her face. "I will make sure Walker stays on task."

"Excellent. I will rely on you in that regard, Ms. Athena," Virgil said with a slow nod before turning around and walking away.

"Is he always like that?" the goddess of wisdom asked as she watched him head back toward his work.

"No, that was unusual for him," Walker replied, deep in thought. Was he jealous? Did he have a right to be after they'd made Rimi together? "Still, I do have a ton of work to do. You said Hephaestus is coming out soon?"

Athena nodded. "As soon as the Tree of the Gods matures again."

"All righty. He does like to make things, right? Like it says in the old stories?" Walker asked with a little anxiety in his voice.

"It is what he lives for. That and Aphrodite, of course," she said as she tucked a spare bit of golden hair behind an ear.

Relieved, Walker looked around, then stepped a few feet away so he was in a clear and open space a good distance away from everything. He stepped into the Item System and clicked on Tools, then browsed what came up. After scrolling for a moment, he chose to make a blacksmith's hammer and tongs. The wait time for the magical meter wasn't too long. He also popped in a few more items the AI recommended after he explained what he was trying to do.

The anvil took quite a long time to produce. Judging by the image on his screen, the size of it would be massive. Having never met a blacksmith before, he had no idea they were so large. When he stepped back out, it was all sitting neatly in front of him, and Athena was inspecting the hammer nearby.

"Please let him know this is just the start of what I can get him. The more he makes, the more tools I can trade back to him."

Athena smiled. "I understand, and I will let him know."

Walker smiled back and said a quick goodbye. He walked over to the Creation Instrument and quickly made a smallish crude couch. Lying down lengthwise so his legs hung off of the armrest, he worked on his soul, this time aiming from his left shoulder to his hand. It was as painful as always. But he was still making steady progress and felt his soul loosening up each time he worked on it. It wouldn't be too long until he had his whole upper body done with the exception of his head, for safety reasons.

Walker checked in on Cagna and helped her with a new series she was working on. If he was honest, he wasn't helping nearly as much as he had been forced to in the past. She was really starting to get the hang of it. Walker made a few changes that included future plans, of which the pink squirrel was naturally unaware.

Explorer Series: *Limited, Special, Complete*

Basic milestone—To Find:
Explore at least 50% of a single territory. 1 point.

Apprentice milestone—What Is Hidden:
Uncover one hidden secret found within a territory. 5 points.

Skilled milestone—Vanguard:
Explore a newly raised territory within the first 3 months of its connection to Symphony. 10 points.

Advanced milestone—Frontier Footsteps:
Enter a portal and a dungeon for the first time. 20 points.

Epic milestone—I Am an Explorer:
Explore every settlement, village to city, in 15 or more territories. 50 points.

Reward: Obtain every milestone to unlock the Explorer title.

After they finalized it, Walker found it a little too similar to the traveling series for his taste. Given the system's nature, some milestones would obviously overlap, but travel and exploration were two different ideas to him. This had made him consider how the rewards for the traveler series would play out. That was why he'd made a few changes to Cagna's original plan.

His changes focused on one thing in particular: titles. Designing that system was going to be fun. Currently, he was trying to figure out whether he'd create limits for them or allow all of them to be shown at once.

Walker Reed: Explorer/Traveler/Gladiator/Creator . . . Guy.

Food for thought. Maybe there could be an interesting way of merging them. Like the kernel system did with magic. Fire and earth became lava, after all. Why couldn't two titles merge?

That could be quite interesting, Walker thought to himself. He put it on the back-burner for now, but it was something he would have to think more on in the future.

Walker encouraged Cagna to keep going with her milestones while also requesting that she show him whenever she finished a series. He wasn't abandoning milestones, but he had other focuses he needed to move on to now that she had an idea of what he wanted. Other focuses like territories.

Rimi finally finished his last starter monster, and the nearby space now held bits and pieces of a pair of wolves. The moment he said he was done, Virgil grabbed him, and they began to design a monster that could wipe out all of the bugs infesting Remus and Romulus.

Walker listened in for a dozen or so minutes, trying to get an idea of how the Combiner ability would work. Once Virgil broke it down piece by piece, using a lot of technical jargon that made his head hurt, they turned to one of the empty

Evolution Chambers and began to put it together. Something about a giant combined anteater with wings. It sounded weird, which was probably a good thing.

Walker left them to it and puttered around for a while. He played in Minos's garden, finally dirtying up his clothing, and spent a good amount of time with Athena debating hypotheticals on a rickety bench he'd built with the Item System.

"A father and son are in some kind of horrible accident. They're both badly hurt and taken to two different hospitals. When the son is about ready for surgery, the doctor looks at him and says they can't work on the patient, as it's their son." Walker waited a moment for her to absorb the scenario before saying, "How is that possible?"

Athena took a deep breath, looking him in the eyes. "The doctor's a woman."

Walker snapped his fingers. "Got it in one. I would present it to my students to see if they could spot the sexism. You'd be surprised at how many kids these days don't get it."

Athena smiled as he felt her warm hand cover his own. "It is nice to see that you do not hold those views."

Walker smiled back. "Not even close."

After several hypotheticals that the goddess of wisdom seemed to enjoy, she spotted something in the distance. A dark-covered man with a permanent scowl could be seen quickly walking in any direction that escaped those trailing behind him. With a whispered apology, Athena marched off to save Hades from Aphrodite, a determined set to her shoulders.

Walker sat there for a time, but as he grew bored, and it seemed the beautiful woman wouldn't return, he stepped back into the Item System. He'd still barely touched on what it could do, and the more thoroughly he understood things now, the better his understanding of what they could build with territories would be. After clicking through every menu available, he heard a *ding* in the back of his mind.

Pulling up the overlay, he noticed the System Designer's color had changed. Each time he was unable to build a new system, it would become gray and unclickable. However, it was now shown in its standard white with black edges.

It was time.

Walker clicked on System and quickly used the search option. Finding his newly created Item and Leveling Systems, he selected them both before moving on to another he would need. Looking around, he spotted the gold-bordered system he'd glanced at only once in the past. Its description was . . . unexpected.

Adaptation System:
A system designed and created by a member of the Alpha Protocol
Council since the beginning of all.
This system allows for entities to be given a lesser form of the
Alpha Protocol.

Flexibility: Medium
Difficulty to modify: Extreme
Resources used: Variable
Limits: The Adaptation System can only be used by sapient creatures. Non-sapient entities will be unable to select from the varied options and will be unable to understand the consequences that are attached to them.
Note: This system is based upon the Alpha Protocol and its numerous systems.

"Designed by the Council, huh. Hah!" he said with a laugh. In the distance Virgil stopped his work. "I'm totally going to make this better than you ever could."

Would you like to merge these systems with another before finalizing your choice?
Yes/No

Walker clicked No.

[. . . Analyzing . . .]
[. . .]
You are about to merge the Leveling, Item, and Adaptation Systems.
Preview provided:
The Leveling System is a numerical tracking system that progressively moves a selected entity or community through a series of pre-designed operations. The Item System provides options to entities for the manifestation of anything they can create within ambient magical limits. The Adaptation System is a series of tasks and systems that allow an entity to create their own personal environment within pre-designed limits.
Combining all 3 will allow the Creator to build a system that . . .
[Error.]
Unknown configuration.

"I'll ask again," Virgil said in a stressed voice, his eyes shifting from looking at something on his screen to staring at his Creator. "What are you doing?"

Walker must've missed hearing it the first time. With a shrug he said, "I'm combining the Leveling System we made, the Item System, and the Adaptation System to finally get our territories!"

Neus cheered nearby, where he had been speaking to Cagna, and they both walked over. Rimi even left his weird, jumbled ball of goo in the Evolution

Chamber to check out what was happening. They all grouped around Walker as he looked at the overlay.

Would you like to merge these systems together?
Yes/No

Virgil continued to look back and forth between his screens and Walker. The words on his overlay seemed to burn into his retinas as he waited.

"Well?"

Virgil's shoulders slumped a little as he said, "Go ahead."

Confirmed.
[. . .]
[. . .]
[. . .]
[. . . Merging . . .]

It didn't take this long before.

[. . .]
[. . .]
Merge complete.
[. . . Analyzing . . .]
[. . .]
New system found.
The Adaptivelevelingitem System is now ready to be . . .
[Error.]
[Error.]
[. . .]
[. . .]
Private message from an Alpha Protocol Council Member detected.
[. . . Retrieving . . .]

Hello, Creator.
What an interesting use of your System Link ability.
To merge our crowning achievement, the Adaptation System,
with an item creator and numerical valuation system? And to
power it by simply using ambient magical potential? Wondrous.
Do you know what you have created here yet? I assume you
do not. It is no matter, as we will help you on your way to
achieving greatness.

Keep innovating, Dante. Keep coming up with unique ideas.
You are my favorite in this rendition.
Always push forward, for you will receive the rewards for
your work.

Alpha Protocol changes occurring.
System renamed to Territory System by the Alpha
Protocol Council.
System AI upgraded from basic to intermediate by the Alpha
Protocol Council.
System AI upgraded from intermediate to advanced by the Alpha
Protocol Council.
Any and all restrictions on the Territory System have been lifted
by the Alpha Protocol Council.
[. . . Analyzing . . .]
The Territory System is now ready to be used.

"What in the fuck," Walker said after reading through it all.

"Indeed. That exceeded even what I thought they—"

Walker turned to Virgil with some heat in his eyes. "You knew? You knew they were watching?"

"I . . ." Virgil couldn't seem to get the words out. "I . . ."

Thinking back to what they had done before, Walker said, "Of course, the Alpha Protocol Council is always watching."

"Yes," Virgil said with obvious strain.

Walker thought it over for a long moment while watching Virgil's eyes. "And, of course, all assistants have to report to the Council whenever a Creator does something unique."

"I . . ."

"Advanced assistants, that is."

"Yes, though it is not only when they do something unique."

"So, you have a schedule for reporting."

"Yes."

Walker asked another question. "Why was the Council so interested in this system in particular?"

Virgil's face turned red. "Primmm . . ."

"Primitive?"

"Maaaa . . ."

"Primal man?" Walker said, completely clueless. By this point Virgil's face was turning purple.

"Magic?" Rimi supplied.

Virgil nodded and started breathing again. "Priii . . ."

"Magic . . . magic . . . ," Walker said, thinking fast as he watched his friend. It looked like someone had punched him in the face as multi-hued colors ranged across his fur. "The only resources I know of are magical, temporal, the Creation Instrument materials, and . . . Ah. Primordial energy," Walker said, snapping his fingers. "It's because the Adaptation System uses Primordial energy, or the energy of Creation, doesn't it."

Virgil nodded, and his face showed relief as some of its odd coloring receded. Now that he'd seen a window of truth, Walker kept going.

His mind reached back into his memories, latching on to every bit of information Virgil had—pun intended—squirreled away for him. "But because we merged these specific systems with it, and we used a modified Cosmic Genesis System, which uses magic instead of time as a resource, we've completely gone around the requirements of the old Adaptation System. So, in essence, we broke the old Alpha Protocol System that requires either time or Primordial energy."

"Yes!" Virgil burst out. "Any tinkering with the fairly unmodifiable Adaptation System is strictly *not allowed!*" He took a quick breath. "But with the restrictions lifted and your use of a modified Cosmic Genesis System holding a pre-designed AI, you have shucked off any restrictions the system once had. Like your self-regenerating cells, it is an odd confluence of combinations that has led to a whole new way of looking at the protocol." He took another breath and looked at his Creator. "Walker, this could lead to a whole new rendition right away! Your merger and modifications might push forward the end of the fourth rendition and the beginning of the fifth!" By the time he was done speaking, he'd started screaming.

"But . . . why?" Walker asked in confusion, deflating the large squirrel. He knew renditions had a beginning and an ending, but nobody had explained why they did.

"Because! Anytime a rendition has a huge breakthrough from one of the Creators and the current protocol reaches its natural end, that rendition closes! Then the Council begins to use the last rendition's new systems and inventions for the start of the next. It has happened four times that I am aware of." Virgil held up a single finger. "The first rendition ended with the introduction of magic by itself, not to mention Alma, the original word for soul power."

"The what?" Zeus said from nearby. Virgil ignored him.

"Although magic has been a difficult to gather resource, that will likely change."

"Because of our accidental modification, Overwhelming Magical Discharge?" Walker asked.

"Exactly so!" The brown squirrel took a deep breath and held up another finger. "The second ended with the introduction of assistants, allowing more participants than ever before and increasing the Alpha Protocol's size by thousands, tens of thousands, maybe even hundreds of thousands over time. Since the beginning, the Council has always wanted the less intelligently endowed for their groupings."

"They wanted dumb people?" Walker thought on it, then glared at the advanced assistant. "Wait a second."

"Indeed. You are not as burdened by knowledge and quick-wittedness, thus you have no idea what *can* work, so you are more willing to take a chance on something a genius-level intellect would never consider." Virgil held up another finger. "The third ended with the invention of the Temporal Subsystem. The ability to control and modify time using Primordial energy was a massive breakthrough, and the person who did it now sits . . . sits . . . Damn."

"Can't say?" Walker asked. Virgil just shook his head. "No worries, buddy. Keep going."

"Thank you. It is very likely that your breakthrough here, with the focus on magic rather than the energy of Creation as a fuel, could have massive ramifications. I am speaking of your system influencing all future renditions. Not only that, but if they find an easy way to really change how the protocol is run, they may decide to start up multiple renditions at the same time. It is huge, Walker, absolutely huge. Focusing on magic rather than the draining use of Primordial energy is just as large a push as the control of temporal energy."

"But as I understand it, there's been thousands, hell, probably millions of Creators throughout the protocol. There's no way someone hasn't thought of doing all of this before."

"That is exactly right! But did they have access to the Temporal Subsystem, something that only recently became available?" Virgil asked with a squirrely look. "Did the protocol Council remove the restrictions on the Adaptation System for them because of the feats that have come before? We're still learning about how Primordial energy works in the first place. Each step forward is another step in discovery!"

"But . . . then why was the reward so small?"

"You are complaining about the rewards? You do not understand what this is! Bah!" He threw his hands in the air. "You do not have any rewards yet because you still have not proven your system can work. Do that and watch your rewards come in . . . Oh, here we go," Virgil said in an unsurprised voice. Walker was still looking at him as his overlay updated.

[. . . Scanning . . .]
[Error.]
[. . .]
New tasks found!
[Error.]

The words kept writing over themselves again and again, as if the Council was writing them live as he watched.

[Error.]
Tasks updated!
New territory task: Activate the Territory System (Series 1)
[Error.]
Territory . . .
[Error.]
Tasks updated!
New territory task: Establish the first territory (Part 1)
No description was found.
Territory established: No
Reward for completion: Variable
Secondary reward for completion: Decided by the Alpha Protocol Council

Walker noted that the secondary reward was new. He didn't like that the Council would be watching this so closely, as he had no clue how the Territory System would work. He stopped looking at the update and turned back to Virgil.

"So, this thing we've made may end this rendition run and start up a series of others?"

Virgil heaved a sigh. "Indeed." If Walker didn't know any better, he would've said Virgil's voice sounded tired. "It is likely that the Council will siphon your ideas here, including the ley line of Mana Trees you built, and incorporate a series of tasks into the Territory System. By giving it to Creators at the start of their protocol, they will gain the same ability you now have: to create evolving and dynamic environments for every city, chosen by the entities themselves, rather than being reliant on the Creator to make it for them."

"But why? What's the point of all of this?" Walker asked, a spike of anger striking his spine. "You're saying I just created a system that allows for thousands, millions more people to be taken from their lives and thrown into the protocol? Why is this happening? What is the point of all of the protocols in the first place?"

"I do not know, Walker. I am sorry."

He noted that there was no pause in Virgil's speech. He really didn't know.

Walker grunted and sat down on his crappy couch. It wasn't very comfortable. He was very aware, at that moment, that everyone was watching him closely. He couldn't spiral again. He couldn't let himself be overwhelmed. It was about more than his needs and wants now.

I need to focus on the now.

"Hey, Neus," he called out to the green squirrel.

"Yes, Walker?"

"Are you ready to accept the Territory System?"

The green subsystem assistant suddenly looked nervous. "I . . . uh." Cagna and Rimi both gave him a thumbs-up. With a swallow, he said, "Yes, Creator."

"Great," Walker replied without inflection. With no celebratory gesture needed, he dragged Neus over to the system. The green squirrel paused, then grew in size immediately until he was a match for Cagna.

Walker was stunned. "Oh, what the fuck now."

"Hey, no fair!" the pink squirrel said in protest.

"You merged three systems, Walker," Virgil pointed out.

"Okay, but Cagna and Rimi didn't grow this much with the Leveling System," he pointed out in return.

"Hmm," Virgil hummed to himself. "That is an excellent point. Perhaps it is because of the system's complexity more than anything else. My assistant database said that subsystem assistants grow based on the number of systems they gain. That would appear to be incorrect. We will need to study this further. Please grant Neus access to the independent Item System."

"Uh . . . Fine," Walker replied in a surly voice.

They all watched, including Neus himself, who was staring at his feet, to see what kind of reaction would happen as he was added.

There was none.

"Excellent. Our hypothesis is sound, then. It is not the system that grows the subsystem assistants but the downloaded information packets they receive. With each new download, they grow in size. Neus here"—he gestured to the green squirrel—"did not grow, because the Item System within the Territory System is not so different from the current Item System you have. No new download, no new growth, to put it simply. I will update the assistant database as soon as I possibly can." He walked away from Walker, and Rimi quickly followed him as they continued to talk about different systems together.

Walker looked over at Neus, who had sat down in the grass, still staring at his slightly larger-than-before feet. "So," Walker began awkwardly, "you ready to get started?"

It took the green squirrel a moment to realize he was being spoken to, but once he did, he hopped to his feet quickly. "Yep! Let's do this! Yay, territories!"

He looked at the smiling assistant and gave a crooked one of his own. "Yep. Yay, territories."

CHAPTER THIRTEEN

The Territory System I

Walker spent some time gathering his thoughts. What was he planning on doing with this, and what were some things he was worried could happen if he didn't place any restrictions at all? Would people build giant torture cities? Prisons? Citadels? Were restrictions necessary, or should he allow everything to be built exactly as the entity wanted? Like he'd promised . . .

Symphony was designed to grow its entities progressively through battle or otherwise. For harmony, though, the world would have to be more than his current plans. There would need to be safe zones, of course. Places where people could raise their families and maybe even retire. Did that mean he needed to make different categories for territories? As in, present a series of options at each leveling breakthrough that allowed for organic growth? Choices? All good questions, and who better than Neus to talk them through with?

Walker sat on his uncomfortable couch and patted the thin brown cushion beside him. Neus immediately picked up on his drift and hopped up to sit beside him.

"So, before we go in and start designing the Territory System, I thought it would be important for us to talk about what we want out of them."

"Okay," Neus said quickly, focusing entirely on Walker's face.

Tapping into his thoughts, Walker went full stream of consciousness. "I envision a territory as a singular location. Unique. Something that is an accurate reflection of what the establishing entity wants out of it. We'll call them . . . hmm. We may have some problems here. Specifically, names!" he said, shaking an angry fist at the sky for no apparent reason. "For now, let's call monsters who have territories 'Holders' and sapients who have territories 'Stewards.'"

"Got it!"

"So, two categories of entities to manage the territory. Now we need to figure out what the different kinds of territories will be." He scratched his chin. "Well, if you know your territory is directly beside a violent monster, you may want to create a defensive territory. Like a castle with a moat, or just a powerfully built wall surrounding everything. If you build a territory in the middle of multiple successful territories, I would think you'd want to create a trade hub, leaning toward an economically focused territory. Of course, for most monsters, who have to be sapient, by the way . . . Make a note of that." Neus nodded again and added it into the system. "They'll want some form of magical infusion in their territory. That's a whole new set of ideas and restrictions."

"I see," the green squirrel said with a serious nod.

"I like you, Neus. You're very straightforward."

The green squirrel smiled at him. "Thank you, Creator."

Walker smiled back, still letting his mind work. "So, let's consider what we can do with these different categories. Plus, we'll have to come up with some starter buildings we'll want to give them. No point in declaring your control of a territory if you have to start with absolutely nothing." Walker put his hands on his hips and affected a falsely powerful voice, "I'm the Steward of all this grass! Look at my grass, ye mighty, and despair!" He laughed to himself, and Neus jumped in a moment later with an awkward titter. A sudden thought hit him. "I assume this is all powered by ambient magic?" Walker asked.

Neus looked for a moment before nodding. "Yes, but you also have the option of adding in temporal or even Primordial energy for building. I assume that is for creating unique structures."

"How would that work?"

"Hold," the green squirrel said with a hand raised, then paused before continuing, "there's a description here now."

"Wait, there wasn't one before?" Walker asked with some anxiety. Every time the Council threw things at him, there was always something extra attached.

Neus shook his head. "No, it was blank. In fact . . . Here, let me show you." Neus shared his screen with Walker, and as his overlay updated, the description for temporal energy filled itself in. His overlay lit up with a secondary notification, but he ignored it.

Primordial Energy:
The energy of Creation itself.
It allows for the creation of entities and the imbuing of buildings
with unique properties.
One example is the Portal System, which uses Primordial energy
to move items or creatures from one place to another.
Other examples are the Evolution Chambers and the Entity
Subsystem. The ability to create and modify entities in the Entity

***Subsystem or modify them in a targeted manner with the
Evolution Chambers comes directly from the power
of Creation itself.***

Temporal Energy:
The energy of time.
***This energy was discovered in the third rendition and is a branch
of, or more accurately, a split from, Primordial energy.
It allows for the temporary control of time, as well as imbuing
buildings with unique time-affinity properties.
One example is the Temporal Subsystem, which allows the
Creator to start, stop, fast forward, and rewind time as needed.
Another example is the Alpha Protocol's ability to rewind entities
using the powerful Resurrection System. The system inverts
time in a targeted fashion and affects the entity's body but not
its memories.***

Weird, Walker thought as he reread the description a second time. *If this is split from Primordial energy, then who's to say that other splits couldn't happen as well?*

Walker was an English teacher. He loved telling his students that he didn't teach reading and writing but critical thinking—the ability to follow logic and reason to the best possible outcome. And critical thinking is what he was doing right now.

If time, or temporal energy, was a branch away from Primordial energy, then he could make a few assumptions. Presumably, time had no effect without space. Gravity. Creation and the powers brought by the Alpha Protocol had to do with life and matter—death, even. Not to mention portals . . . If all of those things could come directly from a split in Primordial energy, then the protocol might only be scratching the surface of the power they held.

But if so, why hasn't the Council thought of that? Is it inherently dangerous? What even is Primordial energy?

He thought even further on the matter, while Neus, quiet nearby, moved through his new screens.

Why did they show me these descriptions now, of all times? I'm assuming those secondary notifications are rewards, but this isn't earned, this is given. And by the Council, no less. There's something else going on here. Plus, if they have this information, and there have been millions of Creators across time, how have they not discovered everything yet?

Remembering what Virgil had said, he came up with a theory that felt right.

They need a dumbass. A patsy. Someone stupid enough to create a temporal anomaly and crazy enough to pause their entire time in the protocol. They need someone like Virgil mentioned: intellectually deficient, crazy, just foolish enough to think they could succeed in a grand venture they don't understand.

But, even if there are more rewards for the taking, how would I split Primordial energy into pieces? The Council would have to give me something huge in return . . . something that would blow all of my previous rewards to pieces.

And he wanted it badly. It could give him a guaranteed win in the protocol. He just wasn't sure how to go about breaking down Primordial energy. He had access to temporal energy, but would that be enough? And why did the Council keep leaning on him to find new ways of doing things?

Walker tried to remember the messages he'd received from the Council. Each time they'd talked directly with him, they'd mentioned innovation and new ideas. Was that their issue? Were they just lazy or stupid? An old guard of white beards needing new blood to show them the way forward . . .

He chose not to say any of this out loud. He didn't want another fiasco like the one that had killed Chomp. That made him think of what Virgil had exposed not too long ago.

Walker didn't have any blame in his heart for the advanced assistant. It wasn't his fault that he had to send reports to the Council. He was built to do so and likely had to follow a prescribed set of instructions provided by the protocol. Blaming someone because of circumstances outside of their control would make him cruel and small-minded, and he chose to never be that kind of person. Still, there had to be more to this.

Walker looked at his second notification.

[. . . Analyzing . . .]
You've discovered Primordial energy usage outside of the standard systems!
Due to your discovery, your Creation Instrument materials have all been converted to their base form and combined for ease of application.
You've been granted a bonus reward for your finding!

Reward for discovering a non-standard use of Primordial energy:
Congratulations, Dante! You've been granted bonus resources!
Your Creation Instrument has been upgraded.
100 Primordial resources.
An amount of equal value in Temporal resources.

An equal value? Walker thought.

He pulled up his Temporal resources. If he recalled correctly, he had around 355 after the second battle. He'd spent a hundred on the sun and eighty on

Romulus and Remus. They had made and exploded four entities since then without placing them. Each had been aged two years, so that was another eight. So, he should have about 167 right now. When he pulled it up, he had 367, which meant around two hundred had been added to his bank. The system valued Primordial resources at two times that of Temporal resources. That didn't seem right.

Walker looked at his current Primordial resources and saw the huge number of 604 staring back at him.

"Okay then."

He guessed that was from the system converting his old printer paper. He still had a boatload of resources left over after the second battle with Crratch, and it was readily apparent in his mind that the numbers were so bloated because it was a combination of both his Landmass System and Entity Subsystem.

Thinking it over, the last computer he'd seen was almost a standard model, so what would the new one be like? He'd have to check on that later, as well as talk to Virgil about how the conversion worked. Could he trade Primordial energy and temporal energy, by chance? Was that allowed? If he could—

He lightly smacked himself across the face. "Focus! Stop getting distracted!"

Every time he was in the middle of something big, he always grew distracted by one thing or another. First, it was the Primigenials; now, it was the protocol itself. He had work to do.

"Focus," he whispered one last time to himself, then his eyes moved over to Neus, who had been looking at him on and off. "Sorry about that," he said in response to the blank look on his newest assistant's face.

"For what?" the green squirrel asked with a cock of his head.

Walker shook his head, mentally moving on.

Together, they worked on a series of options that both Holders and Stewards could choose from. The first step was designing different types of focuses that were simply named so nobody would grow confused by what they found. Certain archetypes of foundational building floated in his mind as they broke them down piece by piece. In the end, ten options were chosen.

He also decided to provide a series of starter buildings each would come with. Walker had spent a good amount of time going through the Item System, and with his Awakened mind, he had almost encyclopedic authority over what was in there. As more time passed and the powers of his soul expanded, his memory continued to grow sharper.

With the Territory System, he hoped that what they chose after their initial selection would authentically evolve into a unique territory. Whether that was a city, a magical territory, or a collection of temples was up to them.

Where would the needed magic come from? He was working on that, and it wasn't just a footnote. He kept it in the back of his mind as they continued to work. When they were writing each archetype in, Walker provided a brief description of what the starter territory would focus on. At first, his descriptions were clipped and straightforward, informing the lucky entity moving through their screens what they were in for with each choice. But Neus talked him into making it a little more flowery and, thus, more interesting to the new Territory Manager. He pulled up two of the options for review.

Agricultural Territory
Grow the land and feed the hungry. By choosing the agricultural path, you have decided to cultivate the land and become one with it.
Requires: Proximity to fertile lands
Starter Buildings:
Basic barn (2)
Basic tool shed with basic tools (1)
Basic communal dwelling (1)

Military Territory
A stronghold of power and defense, this choice offers immediate fortifications against pressing external threats. Choose this option for the safety and security of your budding territory.
Requirements: Proximity to stone or a similar resource
Starter Buildings:
Basic barracks (1)
Basic wall of stone (1)
Chest of basic weapons (1)
Chest of basic armor (1)

Walker had tried his best to cover every direction someone could take a territory in, anywhere from building a city on or near the sea to roving communal cities that never stayed in one place for too long. He'd also created one specifically for Holders.

As it was most likely that sapient monsters would choose the magical option, he chose to keep the description simple and the starter resources unidirectional. That way, the youngest Holders would have a straightforward choice if that was the path they wanted to take.

All of the options overall provided a small beginning and included the communal dwellings. In the Item System, a communal dwelling was big enough to hold just about twelve people. Not comfortably, of course, but it was enough to get by. It had a central eating area and what amounted to bunk beds spread throughout. None of the options provided for comfort—the basic beds and bunk beds were rather below his Earth standards—but it was still shelter and a place to sleep, not to mention that it was all he could provide at the very start due to both what the Item System held and the ambient magical saturation they were likely to see.

Walker nodded and asked Neus an important question, "Are you ready to step into the Territory System?"

The green squirrel stood up on the shitty couch. "Yes, please! Wait, why did we wait so long? Couldn't we have just told the advanced AI what we wanted instead of slowly building it out here?"

"Sure," Walker said with a shrug of his shoulders, "but I wanted to make sure we had at least a foundational beginning before we stepped in. I haven't dealt with an advanced AI before and don't know what I'm walking into here."

"Oh, they're very helpful," Neus said with a nod.

Walker shrugged again. "Did you get that information from the download?"

"Yep! You'll see."

Walker smiled and changed the name in his overlay, then clicked on Territories. The world faded out around him, and he popped into a dark area. There was a screen like before with a sadly simple request. Walker sighed and pricked his finger, then let a single drop of blood land in an open glass.

As soon as his DNA splashed down, a very nice-looking chair appeared in the middle of the room, forest green and seeming to invite him to sit in it. Walker walked over and sat down, appreciating the formed feeling it gave to his backside immediately. As soon as cheeks touched the fabric, the darkness around him bled away and a forest sprang up in its place.

He held close to the idea that it was still just a grouping of screens, but that was the rational part of his mind. The emotional part could feel a breeze carrying the scent of pine in the air and the sun on his face. While he was looking around, a cardinal flitted through the trees. It landed on a nearby branch and chirped once before looking at him.

To Walker's right another, smaller chair materialized in lime green, and Neus showed up in the darkness beside him only half a second later. Walker gestured and Neus sat down, making a happy sound as he bounced in his chair a few times. He looked around the room with big eyes as he took in the forest. Walker smiled.

"Hello, Creator," a voice said from nowhere.

Walker looked around, but he didn't find anyone speaking. It didn't sound like it was coming from everywhere around him but rather like it was a directional voice.

"I'm over here," the voice said again, and when Walker's eyes landed on the cardinal, it lifted a red feathered wing in a wave. "Hello."

"Weird," he said automatically, even though he knew it was rude.

"Mmm, yes. I can see how you would find it strange, Walker," the cardinal replied. It began to prune its feathers, just like he would expect any bird to do.

"Okay, so why are you a cardinal, and why are we sitting in a simulated forest?"

"Because this is what my programming says you will feel the most relaxed in. I am a cardinal because it was a logical step to choose something that fit the environment. It is as simple as that."

"Still weird."

"Sure," the AI said as it finished its pruning. "So, you have created a Territory System. Do you have an idea of how that works yet? Ah," it said, then a part of the forest changed back into a screen showing his ten archetypes. "So, you already have a basis for what you want to do. Excellent."

"Thank you."

"You're welcome."

Walker leaned back slightly in his chair. "What should I call you? I would rather not call you 'AI' every few minutes."

"The Alpha Protocol has a series of long and boring designations for advanced AIs, and I see from your memories that you have difficulty with names, so I will make it easy for you. Call me John."

"John? A super advanced AI named John?" Walker spluttered.

"Yes. I do not consider names very important, at least for myself. What you call me and what your entities call me will likely be very different. John suits me just fine."

"So, you have access to my memories, too, then?" he replied, squirming a little.

"That I do, Walker. All advanced assistants, or AIs, gain your memories as a part of the package. But, as part of the agreement with the Creator who designed all assistants, we are not allowed to share any personal facts or memories with another person without permission. Do not get me wrong: as your assistant Virgil has cleverly shown, we do have to update your progress to the Council and in the informational databases as we move forward. But we are not required to show your memories and personal conversations. Lock and key," the cardinal said. It looked like it tried to smile, but instead, it just came off as a strange bird with a slightly open beak.

"If you're trying to put me at ease, that look on your face won't do it," Walker said.

"Well, I am still going to try my best to put you at ease, regardless, Creator. It is one of my directives."

"All right, then. Let's get down to it." Walker clapped his hands together, startling Neus in his chair. "So, you've seen the ten archetypes. Can you associate the items within the Item System and the choices provided, like the workshops, as assigned?"

"Yes, I can. One moment." The sun and the light pulsing from it shifted from red to yellow and green. "Complete."

"That was fast!" Walker said with an open mouth, astonished at John's speed. "I'm used to everything taking days."

"Yes. Advanced assistants were designed for companionship as much as for being general helpers. AIs, on the other hand, are designed purely for the economics of efficiency," it said in a smug tone.

"So, what exactly can you track?"

"Creator, you merged the Leveling System when you made me. I can track virtually everything you could wish for."

"Yes!" Walker said with a fist pump, knowing Rimi couldn't see him and taking advantage of it decisively. "I knew that was a good idea. Okay, if we started up the Territory System immediately, what would be your limits? Could you manage five, ten—"

"By my estimate, and based upon your memories, I can manage thousands at a time."

Walker held up a hand. "Wait. So because you've seen my memories since arriving in the protocol, can you just work up a basic breakdown of what I have planned?"

"I never thought you would ask, Creator." John held up a wing. "To clarify, I did think you would ask, but it's still nice to hear."

The forest disappeared as all of the screens began populating with different slowly filling bars. As each came up, they showed images of what Walker had envisioned since he first began planning the Territory System. A castle appeared on the left, with great beaming lights shining from each window and a huge host of different people and creatures walking through its stone hallways and courtyards. Walker saw a man selling condensed magical air in different colors attached to strings in the background.

A balloon salesman? he thought.

On another screen, a forest city was shown, with buildings imprinted directly into the trees and interconnected pathways floating in the sky amongst the leaves. Thankfully, none of the citizens he spotted had pointed ears.

Another showed a huge shipyard with an outline of a ship being built using magic, parts of it floating toward where they were always meant to be. Walker could see a general outline sitting over the empty spaces, waiting for the materials to be placed.

The last screen showed a great library, with bookshelves filled and stretching as far as his eyes could see. This screen started as an image, but then the candles began burning in their myriad colors, flames waving back and forth. A person walked into the frame, and he watched as the man looked back for a moment.

The man had his face.

He could hear his own voice asking for the original Holy Scripture as one foot tapped in waiting. A book near the middle flashed brightly and detached itself from the shelf before gently floating down to his open and waiting hands. Walker watched as the video showed him smiling back at himself on the screen before turning around and walking away.

"Super trippy," Walker said, feeling his heart beat faster. What he'd just seen was one of his greatest dreams for Symphony. True magic.

"Yeah," Neus agreed.

The cardinal coughed. "Please keep in mind that this is what you've envisioned, not what you or your entities can currently produce."

"What do you mean, John?" Walker asked, feeling his heart already slow down as the inevitable crashing wall of realism came in.

"While the Council did remove the Adaptation System's restrictions, they did not do the same to the Item System. I am not an Item Creator, as I am not moored within Symphony's dimensional reality."

The room's screens shut off, showing a pervasive darkness. Then a light came forth that stretched hundreds of feet in every direction.

"This is the range of my dimension, the Territory System's independent reality. Depending on your understanding of dimensionality, this is a fluid or dynamic space. There are rules here. Because of the restrictions of my creation, I cannot physically affect the objects or people of your world. All I am allowed to do is create copies, not original works."

"That seems limiting, John," Walker said in thought. "You can't build items from scratch?"

The cardinal bobbed its head. "That is correct. As an advanced AI, I am the director of the system, not the system itself."

"Well, shit."

"Yes."

Walker scratched the bottom of his chin with a thumb. "So you can tell us how things will work and adapt the territory to each entity's choices, but you can't actually make anything. We're still stuck with what we can make ourselves, or at least what the entities can."

"That is correct," the cardinal said with another bob of its head.

"Fuck me."

Another bob.

Neus raised his hand. "What can I do?"

"What do you mean?" Walker asked.

"You already have John. What use do you have for me?"

"That's a good point . . ." Walker thought on it briefly before an easy answer came to mind. "Consider this. John is within this reality, not ours. Your job will be similar to what Rimi's is with the Monster System. You keep an eye on the territories, make sure everything is working well, and I think you and John should be partners going forward. John may not be able to affect physical reality on Symphony, but you can."

"Oh! I get it!" Neus said with a happy nod.

"Okay, now that we know our limitations, let's look at how this will work. For a monster to gain access to the Territory System, they need to connect to a Mana Tree. John, can you write that into the Territory System?"

"One moment, please." The room shifted through its pulses. "Complete."

Options for gaining a territory:
1. An entity within the Monster System may establish a territory
by connecting to a Mana Tree.

John spoke up right after the screen updated. "You will need to speak with your Monster System assistant so we can link the two systems together."

"Not only that," Walker said, correcting the advanced AI, "you also need access to the World Editor so you have options for terraforming in the future. One second."

Walker stepped out and quickly made his way over to Rimi. He found the blue squirrel in a heated discussion with Virgil about whether the newest monster they were creating should have acid for blood. Walker shook his head and gave him a quick breakdown of what they needed to do. He assigned the Territory System to the recently upgraded assistant, then waited a solid minute and a half for Rimi to grow yet again and download the information. As soon as that was done, they stepped into the Territory System together.

"Hello, John. I am up to date on what you have spoken of thus far," Rimi said by way of introduction.

"Excellent, and hello, Rimi. I already know much about you from Walker's memories." The room flashed blue momentarily in recognition. "You will need to modify the Monster System, specifically tier five, so that they may now connect to Mana Trees."

"Yes, I understand. One moment, please."

While Rimi did his work, Walker dragged the World Editor over to the Territory System, receiving a thank you from John. The advanced AI quickly detailed what it foresaw the World Editor's options being regarding the territories.

"The entity could then clear out a swamp or even level a mountain—at the right cost, of course."

"What would the cost be?"

The cardinal looked up for a moment before looking back at him. "Well, the original cost would have been in Primordial resources, but I do not believe you want your personal bank of resources to be taxed, so I can change it to magic. However, because it will use magic instead, the cost will be quite high. Perhaps terraforming would be best suited for those territories that have greatly upgraded their magical atmosphere."

Now seated in his chair, Walker nodded. "Yeah, I was thinking about that too. Based upon how draining a lot of this is going to be, plus the fact that unique buildings may begin to drain the overall magic in the territory quite fast, we should probably provide Mana Tree saplings as rewards."

Neus uncharacteristically yelled out, "Great idea!"

Before Walker could ask why Neus was screaming, Rimi shared his screen to Walker's overlay and said, "Done."

Monster System: *Evolutionary Modification*
Tier 1: Common
An unattuned monster with a basic kernel.

Tier 2: Elemental
An attuned monster with access to magic.
The kernel doubles in size.

Tier 3: Transformative
The monster gains the ability to attune a second time. The monster's magic begins to seep into their body, increasing their strength, speed, and toughness.
The kernel doubles in size.

Tier 4: Pinnacle
The monster's magic begins to inundate their mind, increasing their intelligence. Fourth-tier monsters gain the ability to name themselves and access their overlays.
The kernel doubles in size.
(Sapient monsters gain the Class System.)

Tier 5: Sovereign
The monster can attune their magic to a Mana Tree, granting them a territory.
The kernel doubles in size.
Restriction: Only sapient monsters can access territories.

"Whoa," Walker said as he looked at it, "what's all this new stuff?"

Rimi hunched his shoulders. "I felt that descriptions of what happens to monsters as they move through the tiers may help everyone in the future. I was just"—he shrugged—"trying to be proactive, as Virgil would say."

Walker smiled at him, liking his independence. "Outstanding. One quick issue, though. That's not the only way monsters will be able to grab territories. We were working on that before you came in here."

"Okay." Rimi straightened his back. "How else do you want to do it?"

"Come with me," Walker said to the two squirrels. "Be right back, John." The cardinal waved a wing at them before all three stepped out.

Following Walker's lead, they headed over to the Evolution Chambers and popped one of his overwhelming Mana Trees in. Knowing what he wanted to do, he grasped the connectors he'd learned how to use when first making mana grafts and began to squish the Mana Tree down as hard as he could. The further he squeezed the tree together, the more condensed it became, and the more noise began to erupt from the Evolution Chamber. By the time he was able to get the top and bottom of the overwhelming Mana Tree to touch, the entire chamber had turned red and a sound like steam releasing began to echo out from it.

"What are you doing?" Virgil yelled out as he looked over.

"Something stupid!" Walker roared over the noise. "I need something other than Mana Trees, Virgil. They take too long to grow and start out too weak. I need a contained magical explosion, not gradual growth." Saying so, he took the sides of his deformed tree and pressed them in as well. That seemed to push the chamber beyond its limits as small particles of cyan-colored air began to leak from tiny perforations in the machine.

"There is no way that tree can survive this kind of abuse," Virgil said as he looked inside. "It simply cannot."

"That's kind of the idea, bud," Walker said as he finished grouping all of the magic into one small ball. "You said they wanted dumbass Creators. Well, here I am, multiverse." He smiled as the ball compressed down to the size of a pebble, floating in a cyan-colored world. Virgil grabbed him by the shoulder just as the Evolution Chamber's top began to lift.

"Run!"

Rimi and Neus, who had been standing there with open mouths, ran too. Walker scooped up Neus and gained some distance as a powerful booming sound echoed out from behind them. A cyan-colored wave of magic knocked down everyone on Sonata, flattening the area, and simultaneously flooded the atmosphere with magic.

After picking themselves up, everyone came running over to see what had happened.

The first thing Walker noticed was that his Evolution Chamber was ruined. The second thing he noticed was that the Evolution Chamber next to it was also ruined. The third thing he noticed was Virgil's face turning red, as that was the chamber he had been using for his newest entity, now likely blown into pieces.

"I hate you right now," Virgil said as he looked at the destroyed chambers. "Do you know how long it is going to take to seed all of your damned humans with only three remaining chambers? Not to mention the setback on my insectivore."

"You were not going to name it that . . ." Walker said in exasperation.

"The name is still pending," the brown squirrel said as he looked at the sky with a sigh. "Why did I have to get a human Creator?"

"You know your personality is based on my memories, right?" Walker commented as he looked everything over.

"Yes, it is your fault I am like this. I must be dipping into your incredible reserves of self-loathing right now."

"Ha ha," Walker fake laughed as he gently kicked a few broken pieces. When one small ridge rolled over, something glowing showed itself just beneath it. The Creator immediately took a knee to look and found a tiny glowing stone with deep blue waves radiating from it in a small pattern.

"Why is it blue?"

His assistant snorted. "Because the magical yield is so high. Duh."

"Don't duh me, Virgil," Walker replied in a testy voice. "My students used to do that."

"I know," he replied, moving another piece of the chamber with his foot as he looked with dismay at the wreckage.

Walker bent down and picked up the stone. Reflexively, his protocol shield sprang up around his hand, protecting him. "Guess I'm impure," he said to himself.

Zeus snorted nearby.

Walker ignored him as he clicked on Item.

[. . . Analyzing . . .]
Unknown potential item found.
[. . .]
Extreme magical output located.
[. . .]
Potential item is non-living and qualifies as an addition.
[. . .]
Would you like to add this to the Item System registry?
Yes/No

Walker clicked Yes.

New category created for hosting magical items.

As the stone disappeared, Virgil gasped.

Alpha Protocol changes occurring.
Additional 5 advanced Evolution Chambers granted.

"You updated them again?" Walker asked.

"Indeed," Virgil said as he began to slowly shake his head.

"It's all right, bud," he said, then stepped into the World Editor and deleted the two broken chambers. After he got rid of all of the pieces, he clicked on Item again and stepped into its dimensional reality, as John called it.

Hello, Creator.

"Hello, random AI."

What would you like to create?

"I would like to rename the last item added. Please name it the Foundation Stone, and I'd like you to produce one."

Command recognized.
Item is now named the Foundation Stone.
Unable to produce a Foundation Stone due to low magical
reserves.

"Are you able to bring out the stone I just made?"

[. . . Analyzing . . .]
[. . .]
Yes.

"Please do so. And thank you," Walker said as he exited. Looking down he found the stone. Walker picked it up and clicked Territories.

"Welcome back, Walker," John said, still perched on a branch.

"Thank you. I would like you to associate this item with the Territory System."

"For what purpose?"

"Because my sapients won't be able to start out with a young Mana Tree if we want to create a bunch of buildings right off the bat. No, instead we're going to use this to shotgun magic into the area and get things really going for them."

"That is not within my item registry."

"I know," Walker replied with a nod. "I don't want it in the Territory System directly, because I don't want people to be able to make them. If they can make these stones without going through a Mana Tree, it'll be easily abused. But if we control the supply, then we control all territories governed by them. After all, territories are meant to be earned, not given."

"I understand. One moment, please." Walker waited for the pulses. "Association complete. How would you like it to activate?"

"Planting it in the ground."

"Understood, Creator." Walker waited again. "Complete."

"Thank you. I'll be right back."

"Of course, Walker."

Walker stepped out, gently dug a small hole, and planted the Foundation Stone. "Here we go, little guy," he said as he patted some dirt over it. A moment later, his overlay lit up, and a flash of blue rang out through Symphony.

Walker smiled.

CHAPTER FOURTEEN

The Territory System II

Walker's smile graced everyone who came running over from the blue halo. Today was a special day. In the history of his time in the protocol, events on Sonata had always been rather slow, but right now, big things were happening all at once. He could hardly contain himself.

"What have you done now?" Virgil said.

"I started the first territory, of course!" Walker said in excitement as he ignored the notification blinking in his overlay. "This way, we can see what our territory updates are doing in real time. Also, I needed the extra mana bump so we can really build some wild stuff here."

"Yay!" Neus said, and by tradition, Cagna taught him how to do a high five.

Virgil was less than impressed. "So not only are you growing four overwhelming Mana Trees, but you have also buried your magical bomb in Sonata." He took a breath. "Are you out of your mind?"

"Nope, but I have my reasons for everything. I just—" Whatever he was going to say next never came forth, as the ground began to rumble underneath his feet. Walker dreaded what was about to happen, but it was too late. His overlay updated.

Unknown changes occurring.
The Tree of the Gods is maturing!
[. . . Scanning . . .]
[. . .]
The Tree of the Gods has borne fruit.

"Son of a bitch . . ." He looked over at Athena and gave her his best version of puppy dog eyes.

The goddess of wisdom looked a moment at his expression before she got it, then shrugged and said, "I'll talk to them, but I have to warn you, it's Artemis and Apollo. They tend to be—"

"Rambunctious," Echidna supplied.

Athena nodded in the affirmative. "Yes. The twins will be hard to contain, I'm afraid. Not to mention Hephaestus was just released."

Walker scratched his chin. "Fine, I'll talk to them in a minute. But I have things I'm doing and—"

"And you need to be quick. I understand, Walker. We're all on board here," she said, and the others around him gave various signals of encouragement. The blonde woman squared her shoulders and walked over to a very attractive man and woman wrestling on the ground, heedless of the dirt gathering onto their fine clothes. To the side of them, a man with a deep scar on his face looked around in curiosity. Walker noticed Aphrodite jump skipping toward him.

"All right, whatever," he said with a huff, trying to ignore the new additions. "As I was saying, we're going to be a Foundation Stone factory. Because of how much magic it takes to create new ones, I needed to exponentially increase the amount of magic permeating Sonata."

Virgil waved to get his attention. "Walker, go into the World Editor right now, please."

"Why?"

"Just do it."

Walker nodded and stepped into the editor. There were several things to note as he looked around. One was that Sonata had exponentially increased in size. So much so that it was now on par with Symphony.

Walker wasn't an astrophysicist, but he knew that couldn't be a good thing.

The second thing he noticed was that the steel shell had grown with the planet at each increase—probably something to do with the magic starting to reach it. But as he looked around, he found several Mana Tree roots straining to reach each other and the steel just below them. That was normal, as it was how he and Virgil had programmed them, but those weren't the only roots he found trying to touch others. The Tree of the Gods's thick extensions had always been shallow, albeit widespread across Walker's home. But now, they were straining toward the Mana Trees as well.

"Oh, what the fuck."

"Indeed. If you take us out of the time dilation right now or advance Symphony to our speed, the two landmasses will increasingly move into a collision course. Not to mention that your small sea's tides will kickstart and have power unseen in your homeworld. The atmospheres may start to exchange conditions, wherein your massive amount of ambient magic on Sonata will sync with Symphony and create a cascading magical revolution, completely changing how Symphony works and destroying your systems in the process. Everyone will likely die." Virgil's hand was steady as he placed one on Walker's shoulder. He took a quick breath. "So I strongly suggest you do not do that." He shrugged. "But that is only if you would like to continue on as the Creator of Symphony. This moonlet, which is now approaching the size of your Earth's standard moon, is going to continue to grow." He pointed down to Symphony. "What would Chipper see if he looked up here when the dilation ends? The moon would shift from being relatively small to suddenly being ten times its former size." He held up a finger. "That is only problem number one."

"Don't gas me up, man," Walker quipped, but Virgil ignored him.

The large squirrel held up another finger. "Problem number two, which is also problem number three, is that the Tree of the Gods will connect with those Mana Trees. It is inevitable. The Mana Trees are currently being empowered by your Foundation Stone explosion."

"You said that couldn't happen," Walker pointed out.

"Yes, but I also said sudden magical inundation can cause unknown repercussions with Spirit Trees."

"Mana Trees."

"Whatever. I did warn about this some time ago. Because of the magical saturation caused by your Foundation Stone, the Mana Trees' modification was overridden, and they have grown exponentially. I would estimate"—he looked at his screens—"that they've already reached about ten years in size, and that will continue to go up. When they connect to the Tree of the Gods, I do not know what will happen." He walked over and clapped Walker on the back. "Congratulations, Walker, you found a way to break our first successful project together. Well done." Virgil threw his hands up in the air and left, walking over to his now eight Evolution Chambers.

Walker scratched the back of his head. *No spiraling.*

Instead of allowing himself to fall down that hole again, he chose to be optimistic. "Well, yeah. Okay. One thing at a time." He noticed everyone looking at him. "Nothing to see here, folks. Move along," he said with a wave of his hand.

A few of the Primigenials grumbled as they walked away. Zeus tried and failed to talk to Hades as the darkly dressed man just continued to walk at a sedate pace, keeping his distance from his older brother. Walker noticed as he watched them walk away that the Tree of the Gods, now a good distance away, was hundreds of feet tall. Walker's eyes picked out fruit on every branch now, and a single low-hanging one seemed thinner than the others.

That must be the Greek one, he thought to himself. He came to the logical conclusion that as the fruit, or the Primigenials in this case, dropped, the branch became more and more withered. Like the tree was being drained. As he looked at it, he counted no less than twelve more branches with fruit growing from them.

That is a shitload of incoming gods.

He scanned his eyes over and saw Rimi running to join Virgil at the Evolution Chambers. They placed another anteater in one, then began looking at the other chambers for damage. Lucky for Walker, neither of the humans' chambers had taken any damage aside from the superficial.

Neus disappeared, likely to head off to the Territory System, and Cagna moved over to her pink armchair to work on milestones.

Walker sighed as he was suddenly alone again. A lot was happening nowadays. He still remembered when it was just him and Virgil on a small moonlet trying to figure out how to get magic into Symphony. He missed that a little bit. It was nice to have company on Sonata, but he also didn't necessarily like being constantly surrounded by people.

He had always been an extroverted introvert, or even a social introvert, if you will. Put a group of people around him, and he was the star of the show, but it always left a tremendous drain on his energy. Walker felt his chest pulse for a second before it went away. Right, he had work to do.

Walker clicked Item and stepped in.

Hello, Creator.

"Not to be rude, but you don't have to do that every time."

Command recognized.
What would you like to create?

"Am I able to make a series of items in some form of a queue?"

Yes, that is possible.

"How long, with our current and improving magical reserves, would it take to create a single Foundation Stone?"

[. . . Analyzing . . .]
[. . .]
One day each.

"Excellent. Please begin producing them each day. Also, am I able to say where I want them placed when they're done?"

Yes.
You may choose a location to place any items you create within
50 feet of your entry point to the system.

"Very good. Please place all future Foundation Stones near the Creation Instrument for now."

Command recognized.
Warning: You must continue to enter the system near the
Creation Instrument for the queue to produce results in your
desired location.

"I understand, thank you," Walker said as he stepped out. He looked at the notification he'd been ignoring.

Territory task complete: Establish the first territory (Part 1)
Territory established: Yes
Reward for completion: Variable
Secondary reward for completion: Decided by the
Alpha Protocol Council

New territory task: Create your tasks (Part 2)
No description was found.
Tasks created: 0/10
Reward for completion: Variable
Secondary reward for completion: Decided by the
Alpha Protocol Council

Reward for completing the first territory task:
Congratulations, Dante! You've gained 200 Primordial
resources!
No description was found.

Secondary reward for completing the first territory task:
Congratulations, Dante! You've gained an assortment of
rare resources!
For the Territory System to work as you see it, Dante, you must
have the tools to expand. Use this to help you continue to move
forward. Enjoy.

"Hey, Vir—never mind," he said, rethinking his action. The large squirrel was busy and probably still pretty mad after Walker blew up his test entity.

Walker looked at the rewards again. The Primordial resources were nice, as were the rare resources, although he had no idea what any of them did. It was a little strange to see the Council writing targeted descriptions for him, but they were watching him rather closely right now. He went into his resources tab and clicked on the filter that let him see what was recently added.

"What the shit are these?" he said as he pulled up each new resource's description.

Ethereal Ore:

A rare ore that emits a soft and pervasive glow. This ore was found, rather than created, in the second rendition and has the unique ability to make metal extremely lightweight without compromising its composition. Can be used in the creation of special alloys.

Dragon's Root:

A unique plant found in the first rendition. This plant tends to glow red, thus its name, and can be used in different alchemical productions to create fire-adjacent potions.

Starlight Crystal:

A rare crystal found in the second rendition. Creators have stated that looking at this crystal is like looking at the cosmos on a dark evening. It can be infused with magic for differing effects depending on the magic's attunement.

Mimicry Essence:

A unique substance once found in the body of an alpha mimic, this essence can be absorbed to grant transformative magic to different entities' attunements.

Harmonic Bud:

A special flower found in the third rendition. As it blooms, the bud will release a calming effect for any entities nearby. It can also be used in alchemical production for restorative potions.

Walker searched in his memories for the last time he'd gained rare resources from the protocol. He remembered gaining Faer metal for creating his first Guardian, Chipper. Virgil had said that anytime he gained a non-Earth resource, it was automatically added to his system for placement on Symphony. Now that he'd gained some from his reward, he could place them whenever and wherever he wanted. Also, with the rare ore upgrade Symphony had received long ago, Ethereal Ore could now spawn randomly in different places. All in all, this was a pretty solid reward.

"That's actually helpful, thank you," he said to no one in particular, but he assumed that Virgil's bat-like ears had heard and that he would naturally update the Council in his next transmission.

Scanning his overlay, Walker noted a new tab labeled "My Territory" and found some serious upgrades needed. Knowing they still had a long way to go, he entered the Territory System.

"So, what have you two been working on?" he asked with genuine curiosity as he took a seat.

"Oh! Oh!" Neus said with a raised hand. "We've been working on the tracking and levels so far. Can I show you?"

"Sure!"

At Walker's approval, John updated his screens.

Territory System: *Levels and Tiers*
Levels 1–10—Tier 1: Hamlet
Levels 11–20—Tier 2: Village
Levels 21–30—Tier 3: Small Town
Levels 31–40—Tier 4: Town
Levels 41–50—Tier 5: Large Town

Walker looked it over and shook his head. Neus beside him seemed to deflate into the green padding.

"I told you, Neus," John said, "it violates the principle of having an adaptive system run by an advanced AI. I said he wouldn't like having generic names for different levels. Each of the different options needs to have its own name and unlocked choices as they move up in tiers."

"Yep. It's handy having you in my head, John," Walker confirmed with a thumbs-up.

"Thank you," the cardinal said with a winged bow. "Now, here are some changes I propose." He sat still on his branch as the screens went through a series of modifications. "I've increased the levels and tiers, as that way, there isn't a true limit to the system, as you prefer, and I've modified the names of the upgraded territories, but those are only placeholders."

"Because if they choose to focus on wine, it's a vineyard, but if they choose to focus on rice, it's a farm?" Walker guessed.

The cardinal's image crowed in delight. "That's right! We can't get bogged down in what the names will be, but rather, we need to focus on what each tier will unlock across the board for the rising territory. The names of the tiers will change organically. I've included some placeholder names for what I think may work in the future, but I need you to consider what the unlocked structures and systems will involve."

Walker scratched his chin. "That's hard to do without having those systems already built. Not to mention we're scraping the bottom of the barrel regarding items and structures right now."

John nodded. "True, but if you give me the spirit of the idea, I can work with Neus to see it come to fruition. Pun intended." Walker laughed. "I am not allowed to make changes to the Territory System myself, but I am allowed to modify what you've programmed for the system moving forward. It is a little dicey, but that is my purpose here as an advanced AI: to take your decisions, your orders, and modify them for each entity. Or, in this instance, territory." John tried to smile.

Walker and even Neus shifted back in their chairs a bit. It was disconcerting to see a bird try to twist its beak into an imitation of a human smile. "I really appreciate it, John, but you don't have to do that. It's kind of terrifying."

"I understand," John said, stopping immediately.

"Okay, let's get to this," Walker said, standing up. Across Sonata's short history, Walker's pacing had always been followed by a fast series of actions and decisions. He spoke eloquently of agency and self-empowerment. He discussed his views on territories and where they could one day be, providing as much information as possible to both his assistant and his newest AI.

Neus would speak up every so often, and Walker would debate with him for a moment before they settled on a course of action. He was mindful of taking Neus's opinions seriously so he didn't destroy what little confidence the green squirrel had built up since first coming to Sonata.

Walker didn't want a repeat of the Cagna situation.

John didn't have the same amount of input as the assigned subsystem assistant, but the AI helped them refine what they were trying to do. After a long period of debate and discussion, with John doing its best to update the system, they finished up and took a look at what they'd created.

The first series of territories Walker decided to focus on was agriculture. The first tier was titled "Homestead." It would come with a few starter buildings, a sapling for their eventual Mana Tree, and access to the Administration System, another system Walker would have to build at a later date.

Ranking up from tier one to two would require obtaining at least one hundred citizens. It was a simple enough decision to have the population count toward tiers, as the more people who joined the territory, the bigger the territory would need to be. Each successive rank was directly attached to population count first, but Walker knew they'd add more requirements and additions as they continued to refine everything with John's help.

One thing they all agreed upon was that at tier ten, every territory should have a name that worked for all types. City-State was an obvious choice and was a direct callback to one of Walker's favorite video games growing up. The term itself implied that the territory held their own sovereignty, and Walker had very long-term plans for any territory that reached this far-off marker. Any city that became a City-State would have to select a specialty that further refined the uniqueness of the territory. Underground levels were a possibility if they didn't have them already. Use the Mana Trees to help them fly? Dungeon focused? All were options he was hoping to build in over time.

The first one hundred levels, as associated with his original Leveling System, would show level-ups as red. They set the visual to start at the Foundation Stone or Mana Tree and to expand as ambient magic was used for fuel. This way, every city that leveled up would reveal the change to its citizens as the visual expanded throughout the territory.

Walker had a running bet with John that the first time a city saw orange-level notifications they would freak out.

The cardinal bet against him.

He liked John.

To avoid any issues, they set it so citizens could only be either sapients or monsters who could at least sign their own names. That way, nobody could cheat the system by trying to plant one million trees in their territory.

Walker didn't mind smart moves that allowed his future people to work around requirements, but there was a particular way of life he was trying to build into Symphony. He plugged up some holes and gaps he found here and there, but he let others pass. If he didn't, he was worried people would grow to hate his systems, as they would be too strict and unchanging. Too rigid. The smart would always find a way forward in his world.

For those who didn't have a Mana Tree, the magical empowerment from the Foundation Stone would be enough to at least jumpstart their ambient magic, and they had to plant it to get the Mana Sapling in the first place. That way, nobody would be overriding the Mana Trees' modifications at the start. He figured that anyone who picked the magical archetype would be in for some interesting Mana Tree variations, but he would deal with those as they came.

For this to work, Walker was forced to step out and link the Entity Subsystem to both the Territory System and Neus. A new update streamed into his overlay.

[. . . Scanning . . .]
**Congratulations, Dante! Your subsystem assistant has upgraded
to a full assistant!**
[Error.]
Subsystem assistant not found.

"Really, now?" Walker said quietly to himself as some interesting thoughts began to percolate. He slid them into the backseat and grabbed Neus, pulled him out, and let the update happen while Cagna loudly complained about its unfairness. Once Neus grew his extra height and finished downloading the system, they popped back into John's dimension.

Working together, they ran into several roadblocks as they went. In particular, they had differing ideologies of what territories would be. The more initiative and grasp of the system that Neus had, the more his view of it changed. His idea was to create a seamless system, whereas John, with Walker's memories, agreed with Walker that there should be a few loopholes, ways for sapients to take intuitive leaps forward in their progress.

After one particularly stringent argument, Walker took a break. He stepped out of the system and did some soul work while lying on his crappy couch. In the downtime, while he waited for his body to adjust through the pain, he kept an eye on his two war worlds. Both were effectively frozen from his perspective, but through his monitor, it was readily apparent that more monsters were coming through the portals. Ones who didn't have kernels. It should've bothered him more, but as he'd been doing since first enacting the temporal speed-up of Sonata, he placed it in the back of his mind. A year of time was a boon that shouldn't be forgotten.

When he returned, John gave them an update on what had been added thus far with a look at the second tier.

Agrarian Territory
Tier 2: Agrarian Settlement
Levels: 11–20
Territory System generic requirements:
Settlement must have donated at least 5 original items to the Territory System.
Settlement must have housing for all and no food shortages for at least a month.
At least 50% of all citizens must have a job through the Profession System.
Must have 500 or more citizens.

Agrarian specific requirements:
Settlement must have at least 5 different types of crops.
Settlement must have at least one faction.
Settlement must have at least one Manager through the Profession System.

Tier 2 unlocks:
An increased citizenry count up to 1,000.
The Auction House System (Regional): One free intermediate Auction House is provided by the system at no cost.

Looking at the update, he smiled. This was exactly what he had always wanted. As the territories grew in size, they would naturally . . .

Wait a second.

"What's the total size each territory covers in the system?"

Neus looked away from his screen. "Five thousand two hundred and eighty feet."

One mile.

That would only last for maybe the first thousand people, if that. Food mattered. Commerce mattered. Walker worked with John and Neus to expand the per-level territory size through segmented incremental expansion. Each level would grant an increase in size until reaching fifty miles in total.

Walker also worked with John to better understand how to create a territory extender as a form of reward. They discussed it until John asked to see a Foundation Stone for study. Since it'd been a full day, Walker stepped out and grabbed one from near the Creation Instrument, said a quick hello to Cagna and Athena nearby, and then popped back into the Territory System. John analyzed the magical shotgun again while speaking.

"A true territory extender would only need to be about a tenth of this power. For each territory to naturally grow how you want it to, it will drain the ambient magic within the area. Even with a grown Mana Tree, that will take time to replenish, which will force the territory's levels to a standstill as the area's magical resonance renews. It's about not draining the territory while still providing a just reward. Each time the territory expands, it's going to drain the ambient magical resonance within the immediate area. However, with the strength of this Foundation Stone, it may go too far and cause a form of negative feedback with the planted Mana Tree."

"Hmm, be right back," Walker replied after thinking it over. He hopped over to the Item System and spoke with the basic AI. The system stated it could reabsorb the current Foundation Stone Walker was holding and use the magical output to create a smaller, less powerful version, though doing so would sacrifice his first queued stone.

He agreed, then asked if they could attach this option to all future Foundation Stones and received a positive response. The reason he wanted it was simple.

Options.

Each time an entity gained a Foundation Stone as a reward, they'd have the option to start a new territory. But what if they already had one? Symphony's economy was a deviously tricky situation that he had been considering for quite a while. How do you jumpstart an economy in a world that doesn't have one? Trade and barter would only last so long. It was something he had thought about a lot during his last session of soul work.

The answer was obviously the Faction System, but he could sow the seeds early to make things easier in the future.

Walker hopped over to John and Neus again, now holding a newly minted Foundation Seed. He had considered naming it a Foundation Pebble for the thematic match, but it wasn't the same. John added it into the system as a possible reward, dependent on the current magical resonance found on Sonata.

Sure, territories could try to make them with the integrated Item System if they wanted, but it would also heavily drain them of any magical resonance around them. That could set them back in other ways. In other words, more options were provided.

Refocusing on the Agrarian series, they completed the basis for what the territorial levels would look like with a promise that the series would be a living document. As they found issues, they would add to it over time to fix them. Walker then had them shift to the next in line alphabetically.

He chose Communal territories because some people like to live life . . . differently. Walker had always been a big advocate of personal privacy. His time in the military had prepared him for a loss of such privilege, but that had always been for relatively short bursts of time. But ever since he'd arrived here, every step they'd made had forced him to methodically destroy his old viewpoint. He absolutely hated to use the term "greater good," but without the Milestone System and the subsequent Leveling System, nothing would make sense. So, he'd had Neus and John build a Communal territory archetype for those who liked that lack of privacy.

They began their work on the new archetype and continued to argue for several hours as they built it literally from the ground up. John showed an update screen after a particularly heated marathon session. They finished up the series and Walker had John present the screen showing the third tier.

Communal Territory
Tier 3: Enhanced Commune
Levels: 21–30

Territory System generic requirements:
Commune must have donated at least 15 original items to the
Territory System.
Commune must have housing for all and no food shortages for at
least 3 months.
Must have at least 2 defensive structures.
Must have 1,000 or more citizens.

Communal specific requirements:
Commune must have at least 3 advanced large gardens.

*Commune must have at least one member over level 50 in the
Class System or over Tier 4 in the Monster System.
Commune must have at least one active school with a minimum of
50 junior citizens and one teacher.*

Tier 3 unlocks:
*An increased citizenry count up to 5,000.
The Guard System (Local): The Administration System is
upgraded, and one guard keep is provided by the system
at no cost.
Advanced items are now available in the integrated Item System.*

In the third tier, they removed the need for citizens to have pre-allocated professions. By that point, citizens should understand the benefits that professions bring to the community and their value in the overarching world.

Walker had replaced it with the town's prescribed requirement of two defensive structures. Even Communal-focused territories should understand what kind of dangers this world could bring to their doorstep, and this was his way of making sure everyone had a chance at surviving.

Allowing the creation of advanced structures and items within the third tier would be important. Not every territory would be a catch-all with the ability to focus not only on creating a smithy but also a museum or amphitheater. By giving Stewards and Holders the ability to just slam down a pre-designed advanced structure, they would be able to pick and choose what their town needed at that time. They could build their own items and donate the blueprints to the integrated Item System, but that was up to them. Walker said the last part out loud, and Neus spoke up with an idea.

"What if every time a citizen donated something to the integrated Item System in their territory, they were granted something of equal value?"

"Like what?" Walker asked as he leaned forward in his chair.

Neus mirrored him like two old friends sharing a secret. "I don't know, but you could build direct rewards based upon the initial analysis the territory provides. Like, I don't know, five hundred schmeckles for an advanced item."

"Weird currency, but that's interesting," Walker said as he scratched his chin. "Do you have an example in mind?"

"Reminder," John interrupted. "Aside from the basic items provided upon the initial inception of the Territory System, you have not set up different tiers as of yet."

Walker leaned back. "That's because we don't have any items!" A recent new occupant flashed through his mind. "Wait a second, I have a guy outside who can do that! Hold on, I'll be right back." Walker hopped out of his chair and quickly clicked out of the system, leaving behind a squirrel and cardinal waving to him.

He faded in and started running around the now much larger Sonata looking for one person in particular. He dodged Echidna and Minos at the garden and hurried around Eros, who was trying to ask him about where all the humans were. All told it took nearly an hour before he located the scarred man, tucked neatly behind the Tree of the Gods as he laid into Aphrodite for what Walker was sure was a valid reason.

"I just know you offered yourself to him," the man said in a calm voice as he looked at his wife.

"I did not!" Brushing her hair off her shoulder, she began to look left and right. "You can ask anyone here!" But she didn't find anyone—at least, not until Walker entered her view. "You! Creator! Tell him I didn't offer you my body!"

"Umm . . ." Walker mumbled as he caught his breath. Realizing this was a precarious moment, he popped the memory up and did a quick review. He didn't care much if Aphrodite got in trouble, but he didn't want to alienate Hephaestus. He looked the green-dressed woman in the eyes and decided to tell the truth. "Technically, she didn't."

"See!" she said with a falsely proud expression. "I didn't try to bed him!"

The scarred man's face moved through a series of emotions. Walker watched as Hephaestus shifted from angry to neutral before going back to angry again. "I know your tricks! You just worked around the idea of it! That isn't the same as not asking! Bah!" He waved a hand at her. "I don't know why I even try, wife. All you ever do is try to bed the nearest man or woman to you." He ran a hand through his short-cropped hair. "Ugh, I really need to pound some metal."

A moment later, five basic iron ingots dropped next to his feet as Walker jumped out of the Item System. "Here you go," he said with a smile, obfuscating what he'd just done.

The god of smithing eyeballed the iron without touching it. "That's cast iron. I can't work with that garbage. I need something purer than that if you want me to make something." He looked up from the iron and met Walker's eyes. "So, you're the Creator, huh? Thanks for not fucking my wife."

Walker mentally stumbled on that for a moment. "You're, uh, welcome, I guess, Hephaestus."

The man spit to the side. "Call me Heph. It's less of a load on your mouth."

Walker winced at how that sounded.

Hephaestus looked to his left quickly, his mood seeming to shift again. "Ah, here she is."

Athena gave him a smile as he opened his arms wide. They embraced each other warmly, the god of smithing awkwardly patting her on the back with one large meaty hand.

"How're you doing, little sister?" he asked with a smile as they separated.

She smiled in return. "I am quite well, brother. You're not causing Walker any trouble, are you?"

"Me? No, I . . . Wait a second. Walker?" He scratched the top of his head. "Except for Father, you really only use people's titles when you speak about them." He looked over at Walker with a perplexed expression on his face. "Could it be . . ."

Athena's cheeks brightened a little as she looked back at him, but a laugh echoed out from the goddess of love. Walker spotted a twisted look on her face as she raised up from her bent position. "The virgin goddess is considering the Creator as a life partner? What a joke. With me here, how could he ever want—"

A pulse of gold washed out from Athena as she turned to look at Aphrodite, and with a tightly controlled voice, she said, "Do we have a problem here?" The golden aura came back all at once and covered her body with small golden fractals.

A similar pulse of pink from the goddess of love responded before covering her as well. "Would you like one?" she replied.

"Stop!" Walker yelled out and pushed his own soul into the mix as forest green smothered pink and gold. Like a flame finding a sudden lack of oxygen, they faded away until nothing was left. Athena gave him a quick grin while Aphrodite looked horrified.

Walker rubbed a hand against the back of his head. *I just wanted to talk about crafting, damnit!*

"Well, well," Hephaestus said as he looked at Walker more closely than before. "You're not all for show." His glance shifted to Athena. "Fine. I approve, but only for courtship right now. Not that you need it, of course." Ignoring his wife, who still stood nearby with her mouth open, he looked back at Walker. "Give me something real to work with, and I'll change the landscape of your world."

Walker clicked into the World Editor and quickly scanned his resources in the corner. Making a decision, he dropped hundreds of pounds of steel in front of the scarred man. "This is what I have for now. I'm looking at making—"

Hephaestus waved a hand. "No, no, this is just fine. Steel, is it? I've seen some of that in your memories." He hefted a piece in his hand, making Walker wonder just how strong the Primigenial was. "I've worked with similar material before, so this shouldn't be an issue." Taking the piece of steel, he tried to twist it, and while it did give in to the enormous pressure he was applying, it was only by a small amount. "Excellent. I've already seen the state of the tools you've dropped for me. I'll make my own, thank you." He picked the rest of the steel up off the ground, likely weighing several hundred pounds, and walked away. "Give me a little bit of time," he called over his shoulder.

Aphrodite glared at Athena, gave Walker a look he assumed was confused between smoldering and fearful, then hopped after her husband while still proclaiming her innocence.

"How is he going to—never mind," Walker said with a shrug.

"Soul crafting," she said with a smile. "Maybe you'll get lucky and he'll teach you how to do it as well. He only ever taught his cyclops partners in the past, and Hermes, of course, but who knows?" she said with a shrug. "He seems to like you."

"Why did you start a fight with Aphrodite?" Walker asked, still confused by the fast turn of events.

"So she would know just how powerful you are, and so Hephaestus could gain a measure of you. He has never been much of a talker, preferring his work and the actions of those around him to speak for themselves."

Walker laughed. "Goddess of wisdom indeed."

She smiled back at him. "Well, I prefer to think of myself as the goddess of critical thinking. Wisdom is learning from your mistakes, of which I try to make very few." She pulled a strand of hair and tucked it behind an ear. "This may be— what's the term? Out of left field? Baseball?"

Walker nodded in encouragement.

She clapped her hands in excitement. "I knew it. Anyways, I know you are still busy, but can you answer a few more questions for me?"

Walker could use a break, so of course he agreed. "Sure!"

Athena had a weird look on her face. "Okay, this will seem strange, but please answer honestly."

"All right, then. Shoot."

"What was your perfect day like back on Earth?"

"Oh, umm." He remembered all the days he'd spent with Matt in the summer and those few lucky times in the colder seasons. "I always enjoyed going to the beach and surfing if I got the chance—the feel of the waves, the sun, even the briny smell in the air. All alone out there, only not. Afterward, we'd hit a local 7-11 for a quick big cup of blue raspberry and Coca-Cola Slurpee. Then boom, I'm in heaven." Walker smiled at the memories flooding in.

Athena smiled at him in return. "I see. Okay. Unfortunately, I don't know if you will be able to recreate that here, Walker."

"No, I don't suppose I will." He shook his head. "But the memories are nice."

She squeezed his shoulder with a soft hand. "We'll figure it out, don't worry. Okay, question number two." Her face shifted from soft to serious. "What's your favorite book and why?"

Walker laughed again. "Oh! The big serious questions now, is it? That one drives to the heart of an English teacher." He scratched the back of his head. "It's a difficult decision, honestly. I was probably reading maybe a hundred books a year. Although there was this one." Walker waved her closer. "Once upon a time, a man had an idea for a new type of book. What would happen if he wrote a series about a world where the hero succeeds in saving the day but then goes insane and destroys everything he ever worked for? What if life was just a wheel, constantly spitting out the same people in a cyclical fashion?"

Struck by a sudden idea, Walker asked Athena to follow him over to the Creation Instrument. Popping in and out of the Item System, he produced a few blank books on the larger side and occupied his time by recording book one of The Wheel of Time series from memory. It took quite a while, with Athena leaving every so often to put out a Primigenial metaphorical fire, but when he finished, *The Eye of the World* now existed for all Symphonians to enjoy. He even popped in and out of both the Territory and Item Systems to make copies.

"Here you go," he said as he handed three basic books to the woman, each holding a third of the full story. "It's the start of one amazing series. I truly hope you enjoy it."

Athena gave him a huge smile, like the sunrise on a new day after a heavy storm. "Thank you so much, Walker. You have no idea what this means to me. I have been without anything to read for thousands of years." She shook her head. "Thousands. You have no idea what this means to me." A few tears dropped from her eyes as she held the books in her hands.

"My pleasure," he said as he smiled back. After he saw her sit down and carefully place the second and third books beside her before opening the first, he stepped back into the Territory System feeling refreshed.

"Where were we?"

CHAPTER FIFTEEN

Currency and Space

Walker checked over what they'd worked on for the hours he had been gone. John had decided to finish codifying the different ways entities could gain territory based on the memories it had collected from Walker.

Options for gaining a territory:
1. An entity within the Monster System may establish a
territory by connecting to a Mana Tree.
2. An entity may be awarded a Foundation Stone
by the Event System.
3. An entity may be awarded a Foundation Stone through
a series of milestones.
4. An entity may be gifted a Foundation Stone by the Creator
or a Symphonic Assistant for a grand achievement.

Meanwhile, Neus had begun to plan out the territory user interface, or UI for short. In Walker's mind, too much information was just as bad as too little when first starting out. John elucidated the idea of overwhelming people with factoids and statistics, but as Walker's memories directly influenced him, the Creator had to sit there and hear his own views parroted back to him—well, maybe not parroted. Perhaps cardinaled.

The basic starter UI was created, and Walker worked with them for a while to figure out what it would look like and what would get added over time. He wanted to emphasize that the tier-ups—as in, moving from nineteen to twenty or from tier one to two—were what mattered the most. Gradually bringing in new visuals and dynamic relationships would allow entities to build up their efficiency with the system in the best way possible. Educational psychology called it scaffolding, and it was how he taught his assistants as well.

Bits at a time.

As they finished up the framework for the UI, Walker began to look at how items would be regulated and viewed.

Basic was just that: Basic. Weak. Not the right stuff.

Me in my teenage years, Walker thought with a mental smile. He didn't blame himself for his hormone-fueled years, having decided to look back with fondness rather than horror at who he had once been. What he had become was what truly mattered, though. Opening his soul had shown him that.

Looking back into the integrated Item System, Neus had used the term "advanced," but that was already used in evolutions, and he didn't want to double down. Working with each other, they began to piece together what item categories would look like with basic descriptions. This would only act as a placeholder until they found the best ways to describe things. And, honestly, the only people who would really see it were those who had direct access to the Territory System. It's not like someone was watching and telling the world about everything he was doing.

They worked at it for several hours, and Neus again asked for flowery language. Walker acceded, as it didn't cost him anything and he was still trying to build a relationship with the green squirrel. When Neus again brought up the value of donating an item and what they would gain in return, Walker excused himself and stepped out of the Territory System, then clicked on the System Designer. A full day had passed, and it was time for a new system.

He scrolled through for a moment, scanning the different system options for what he could create. There was another new packet of systems he hadn't seen before, as the filter showed the numbers had increased again. This time, though, he found some systems that the Alpha Protocol had given him at the start.

Landmass System:
A system designed by Council Member One in the Alpha
Protocol of AB.
This system is designed to control Primordial energy and allows
for the creation of different resources that form collected land-
masses for planetary building.
Flexibility: Medium (adjusted by the Council to High)
Difficulty to modify: Medium (adjusted by the Council to Low)
Note: This is an original system.

After seeing one of the original systems he'd been granted, he searched for another.

Temporal Subsystem:
A system designed by Council Member Four in the
Alpha Protocol of 3NM.
This system is designed to control temporal energy and allows for
the collection of Temporal resources to a near infinite amount.
Flexibility: Low (adjusted by the Council to High)
Difficulty to modify: Extreme (adjusted by the Council to Low)
Note: This is an original system.

"Huh . . ." he mumbled to himself as he scratched his chin. He hadn't expected them to start showing him the beginning of all of the systems. According to what Virgil had said earlier, the Adaptation System was *the* original system, or close to it. All other systems were built off of it to some degree.

The Council adjustments were nice. Each time he'd had to deal with systems that had low modifiability, it was simply a matter of using it for its intended purpose rather than attempting to go a completely different direction. The difference he'd found between modifiability and flexibility was in the adaptability of the system itself. Modifying meant changing the intrinsic use of the system, whereas flexibility referred to the system's inherent versatility and ability to handle a large number of processes.

The Tracking System was a prime example of this. The Council's adjustments meant that Walker or his assistants could completely change any system he might use in the future.

"Nice."

The benefits the Council kept throwing at him were becoming more and more common, to the point that he was worried he may become entitled or complacent with all of his recent gains. But he would take any help he could get. For Symphony to become as great as he knew it could be, he needed to keep pushing the envelope.

Walker scrolled through and looked at the options available to him. Filtering for "donations" didn't pop up anything he wanted to deal with, especially the genetic one. That was multiple levels of gross and invasive. "Gifts" was interesting and gave him an idea for a milestone series he could attribute to it. "Exchange" was where he found his answer.

Exchange System:
A system designed by Creator JP in the Alpha Protocol of 3AM.
The Exchange System allows for the donation of items in exchange
for an equivalent, pre-designated value.
Flexibility: High
Difficulty to modify: Low

**Limits: The pre-designated value must be in place for this
system to work.
Note: This is based on the Reward System of the Alpha Protocol.**

"Can't build you yet," he said with a nod. He could picture his old economics professor screaming at him for the audacity of looking at trading money for items without having set denominations.

Because Walker needed the Exchange System to work right at the start, he entered the word "money" into the filter. When nothing came up, he changed the term to "currency" and found what he was looking for.

**Currency System:
A system designed by Creator Locke in the Alpha Protocol of 3DG.
*The Currency System allows the Creator to make and assign
differing levels of value to virtually anything in their world.*
Flexibility: Extreme
Difficulty to modify: Low
Note: This is based on a now-defunct system in the Alpha Protocol.**

Walker knew that he needed more. The problem was that the citizens of Symphony would have no understanding of how any of this would work. For him to have a Currency System, and thus bring value to items, structures, and everything else, he first needed to build a Regulatory System.

"Fuck!" he said as he pulled his hair a little. He was a veteran and teacher; dealing with money on this level was entirely beyond him. The problem wasn't just a roadblock in his vision of Symphony. The problem was that he needed to create something that would have to be carefully managed by minds explicitly constructed for the task at hand. He needed help.

Walker headed over to Virgil and scuffed a shoe against the dirt. In a quiet voice, he said, "Uh, hey, Virgil."

"Yes, Walker? How may I assist you today?" the brown squirrel replied stiffly without turning around.

"I could use your help with this money situation I'm running into."

He could see the back of Virgil's head as it bobbed up and down in agreement. "Indeed. I had always assumed this would occur because of your penchant for impulsive shopping and lack of credit understanding. You were never quite wealthy on your home planet."

Walker scratched the back of his head. "You never know when you might need two blenders, Virgil. And the Ninja was a hell of a—"

Virgil held up a hand. "Spare me. I will help, but first, look at what we have done. *Again*, I might add." He moved to the side so Walker could get a better view.

The Evolution Chamber held what used to be an anteater, but nobody could call it that anymore. It was covered in overlapping scales that seemed to shift colors as he watched, blending in with the green environment within the chamber before turning off and going back to normal. Its body had many holes, and he could see tiny tongues sticking out of each.

"What the fuck is that?" Walker asked as he stared in horror at the creature.

"It's an Eaterhive!" Rimi said excitedly as he jumped up and down. "It's gonna get all of those Inhabitor Beetles for us!"

Virgil nodded. "That is correct. We plant a hundred of these on Remus and another hundred on Romulus, and the beetles are done for. We modified the natural smell of the Eaterhive to be delectable to the Inhabitor Beetles. They will not be able to contain themselves, and thus, the Inhabitor Beetle problem will be . . . contained."

Walker snorted. "Terrible diction." He scratched his chin as the scales rippled through another shift of colors. "So, I have to ask. How do you know what they like to smell?"

Virgil waved a hand at the chamber next to him, and a two-foot-long beetle popped up. The creature's body was covered in a shell that was both flexible and hard. It seemed designed to take hits while resisting the air as it moved. Two long mandibles extended from the front of its face, sharp tipped with serrated edges.

"I located a dead Inhabitor Beetle within the Entity Subsystem after it died on one of the planets. Using the same system, I copied its genetic code so we might know what we are working against." He flicked his wrist and it disappeared. "Do not worry," Virgil said with a shake of his head after seeing Walker's eyes grow a little wide. "I sent it into the sun, not Symphony. As I was saying, they are not sapient beings and will not pause to consider why the Eaterhives smell so good to them. I expect all of the beetles to be destroyed in a little over a year."

"Okay, so, we finally solved one of our problems."

"Why are you saying 'we'?" Rimi asked with a darkened expression.

"Rimi!" Virgil said sharply as he turned toward the blue squirrel. "Neither you nor I would be here were it not for Walker. Everything we do is together."

Rimi stomped a foot while puffing out his cheeks. Seeing an unchanging glare from Virgil, he walked over to Cagna, who was currently working on her screens in her chair. He disappeared for a moment and a blue chair popped out next to hers. He hopped up and sat next to her, but Walker couldn't hear what they were saying.

"What was that?" Walker asked as he continued to look at the two squirrels.

"He is still mad that you blew up the last one. He did the majority of the work, while I assisted in the background. He does not take it well when his monsters die."

Walker gave a small shrug. "There isn't much I can do about that. Would he rather your work with the humans, and all of the time you've put into them, was done away with instead? Plus, he's really not going to like the starter zones."

"Yes, but like you have done so yourself, he will learn to adjust to his circumstances. Now, you wished to speak about global currency economics, I believe."

Walker nodded and went into great detail about what he was planning to do with currency and the Exchange System. It wouldn't work if he just had different currency values bashing against each other. He needed to track the economy itself, including every currency that would ever be invented. When Virgil asked about what he meant by inventing currencies, Walker explained about the Territory System he had been dreaming up and how every territory, or even faction, could have its own internal currency to be used as needed.

"That way, every city has a currency that can be used in just that city."

"Why not have a global currency, similar to the global reserve currency that you have on Earth?" Virgil asked with curiosity.

Walker shook his head. "Options, remember? If everyone has a bajillion Symphonic notes, they can buy anything, anywhere. When everything is worth nothing by price, it's worth nothing to anyone. But if we have specific localized currencies, and they have to spend time in a city and work there, those local currencies increase in value." Walker shrugged. "It's not perfect. I want to explore the idea of cities having visitors and citizens who need to earn a reputation within said city to live there. I don't want another world like mine, where the rich own homes in every paradisiacal location and the poor are stuck in apartments and shacks. If cities can control their own money, they gain more agency in how their city and its people will be managed."

"Ah, a utopic understanding of what you are building. I see," Virgil said with a nod, then canted his head to the side. "Symphonic notes?"

Walker's face broke out in his of-late habitual smile. "Yep. That's what I'm calling the highest denomination of money in our world. Symphonies have notes, and instead of a stack of notes, we'll say a sheet."

Virgil smiled back. "I see. I like the thematic play."

"Thank you. Now, here's what I need."

He explained how he needed to track the economy itself, with visuals and the whole shebang. Symphony would need a system that could constantly update and balance the value of different currencies to make sure they always had a fair exchange rate. It also needed to be included as an attachment to the Territory System so that Stewards and Holders could gain a fluid and interactive system that tracked their localized currency. The more control he could give to his citizens now, the more power they'd have later on to create wonders. He knew what it was like to operate within a restricted system that didn't work—the American education system.

He also explained his idea about using the system of donation he was building to create a bank of resources from across the world that could then be used for duplication as well as rewards.

"How would that work?" Virgil asked.

"If I'm a miner, let's say I donate one hundred ore to the Exchange System. That ore would then be stored in the World Editor for my use as I see fit, like giving it to citizens as rewards or for messing with Symphony through terraforming. The miner would receive just compensation for the donation as well."

"What's the exchange rate?"

Walker snapped his fingers. "Exactly! I need to create a system that does that!"

"Okay," Virgil replied, then began looking at his screens. Walker knew he was going to take a while, so he headed over to his couch and worked on his soul for a few minutes. Reaching his balanced emotional state had become easier the more he did it. After the first five or six times of learning to control his soul, he could now run the gamut of emotional balance with fluid ease.

The last section of his right leg was completed with a pulse of green, and he felt his skin and muscles contract into their standard Awakened smoothness. After lying still to overcome the standard shock of pain, he shook it off and half limped back to Virgil.

"Problem," the advanced assistant said as he grew close. "I foresee issues regarding the storage of resources and, therefore, the placement of said resources by citizens."

Walker thought back to what he'd considered a few days ago. "Because the system uses Primordial energy to control space and movement, correct?"

Virgil nodded. "Just so."

Walker scratched his chin. "How did the third rendition ender—like, the guy who ended it—create the Temporal Subsystem in the first place?"

Virgil held a hand up. "You are restr—" He paused for a moment, then put his hand down. "Never mind. He was an alchemical genius—truly a once in a rendition genius. He found a way to strain the Primordial energy presented to him by the system and eked out a single slice of temporal energy, registering it with the protocol. The incident cost him a hand, but it was easily fixed with the Council's advanced technology."

Walker chose to ignore the fact that Virgil was no longer restricted for the moment. A sudden idea came to him—one that shouldn't work but just might. A thought resurfaced immediately after.

They need idiots . . . No, Virgil got that wrong. Knowledge is the great redeemer of the unentitled. But when there is a lack of knowledge, imagination can fill the gap. They don't need idiots. They need people who can still dream of things that should be impossible. But first, I need more information.

"The shield didn't protect him?"

"The shield did not know how to protect him. Even now, temporal energy is strangely powerful when it comes to damaging Creators through the protocol shield."

"So, you could say that these pieces of Primordial energy are beyond the protocol's understanding," Walker replied, swallowing through a dry throat. "Okay, that's good to know."

"Indeed. Since the Alpha Protocol recognized the process by which it was done, they have managed to replicate it to a massive degree. They now have multiple planet-sized alchemical processors constantly churning Primordial energy into Temporal resources. I, however, am not privy to how this is done aside from being granted a general understanding."

Walker nodded and began pacing for a few moments. He had a small idea of what to do, but he needed to take it to the next step. Make it bigger. The alchemical process the previous Creator used had likely ended in an explosion. It tore the Primordial energy apart and revealed the temporal energy within. Thus, there must be a better or, really, a more comprehensive way to cause Primordial energy to break down into parts of itself.

What do I need? I need an explosion of power. I also need to strain the Primordial energy at an even rate, to allow for collection. It has to be not just big, but huge. Which means I need to think the same way. What causes an explosion of power? If I had all of the resources possible, what could I do? Even better, what has the Council never thought to do because they have no imagination?

As Walker considered a dozen variations of how he might accomplish the same thing, Virgil stood still, working through his screens. Then, something unusual popped into his mind. After exploring it for a moment, he figured it might just work and threw away all of his other ideas.

Nodding his head, he looked up to the sky and yelled out. "Okay, I have an idea of how to find another piece of Primordial energy. But I want your promise that I'll get some crazy good rewards."

Virgil looked at him sharply, then began staring at his screens. A smile plastered itself onto his face, and in an unusual tone of voice, he said, "Granted. What do you need for your work, Creator?"

Taking that to mean that the council member was sending messages through Virgil, Walker shook his head. "Nuh-uh. I have an idea of just how big this is going to be. I want your promise that after it is discovered, I'll get an unlimited supply of each strand for my worlds at no cost. I'll also want any restrictions placed on me regarding assistants to be removed. I need my assistants to manage the big systems now, not just secondaries. And I want advanced AIs to be the minimum in all future AI-based systems. Plus, any additional awards you feel are warranted based upon the results of my work."

Walker waited for a few minutes while he stared at Virgil, but eventually, Virgil nodded. "Done. Though, there will be a high cost for failure. Do we have an accord?"

He nodded. "We do."

Virgil had another weird smile on his face. "Excellent. Now, what do you need?"

"I need a lot of empty space in a temporally isolated area and a metric fuckton of Primordial energy that I can control by request. I'll also need some other things, but I'd rather explain when we get there. We'll have to do some things on the fly."

"The fly?" Virgil said in confusion before he said to himself again in a calm voice, "He means in the moment."

Walker stared at the large squirrel before he realized what was happening. The Council was directly controlling him. He tried not to feel angry about that, as right now, he needed to focus.

The voice speaking through Virgil asked him to wait, and after close to ten minutes, a rip in space opened up and dragged them away. As his vision clarified, he found two things: Virgil floating beside him and a great black empty expanse.

"Welcome to rendition 4AB, Walker," Virgil said, then waved a hand around. "This was created for you on the promise that you will succeed in isolating another strand from Primordial energy. There is nothing you can damage here." Before Walker could speak, Virgil held up a hand. "I have to warn you. Failure in discovering a new . . . strand," he said after a slight pause, "after the Council has used all of these resources, will result in your removal from the Alpha Protocol and the possibility of punishment for your birth planet."

Walker gave a stuttering nod. While he wasn't worried about it not working, he couldn't help but ask, "Why would you punish my home planet?"

"Because the cost of resources used must be recouped in some manner. Should you fail, your planet will be relegated to the Psi Protocol, and all that that entails."

Swallowing through a sudden rock in his throat, he nodded again. "I'm not going to fail. This isn't foolproof, but something like this has been done before. Now, does the protocol have a way of accelerating Primordial energy?"

Virgil nodded in return. "Yes, they call them push gates, to use the simple term. They encircle and concentrate Primordial energy, thus allowing it to accelerate to each rendition. The energy of Creation is constantly maintained for each rendition's use and need."

"Good." Walker slammed a fist into one of his palms. Ever since he'd been shown that temporal energy was split off from Primordial, he knew that there had to be even more within it. If Primordial energy was the building block of everything, then time could only be a piece of it. There had to be more strands, as Virgil called them—smaller pieces of a greater whole.

The only way to access them was through the power of temporal energy.

His guess was that they needed to increase the strain on Primordial energy for there to be a split. A breakup of whatever it was. He'd read about the Earth doing something like this before, but it would only work if his guess was right. It was a big risk, but instinctively, he felt it would work.

"I want two focused beams coming from both directions in a straight line. They need to be pointed directly at each other, with a repeating ratio of gates they'll need to pass through. These push gates, as you call them, must be in a repeating ratio of A, B, A, B. Are you with me so far?"

Floating beside him, Virgil nodded. "Indeed, Walker. I have relayed all this to the Council, and they do not believe it will be a problem."

Walker smiled. "Good, because this is where it gets tricky. The A gates will be standard push gates, but you'll have to modify the B gates. They need to be surrounded by temporal energy, thus increasing the speed of time to the highest degree possible."

Virgil spoke in a different voice. "Why?"

"This is only a guess, but I don't think just speeding up Primordial energy will place enough strain on it, same with crashing it into itself. I'm of the opinion that increasing the effect of a strand's power on Primordial energy will cause whatever is holding the energy together to start to break apart. And even that may not be enough."

"What else would you need?" Virgil said in that same voice.

"Hmm," Walker replied, floating a hand up to scratch his chin as if he weren't directing a council of inter-universal superpowers. "Maybe have a few of the middle B gates slow down time, to really stress the energy out. We don't want to create a huge series of temporal anomalies, as who knows what kind of fresh hell that might bring, but it may be just the ticket needed to unravel all of the strands. Also, for this to work, you'll need the energy to pass through every gate simultaneously."

"Again, we have to ask 'Why?'"

"Because I believe that Primordial energy is like a lanyard. You call them strands, and that's an apt description based on the loose information I have. To break the bonds holding them together, I'm essentially bastardizing the Large Hadron Collider from my home planet. They wanted to discover the particles that made up the Big Bang, and the best way they found to do that was to fire two very high-speed particles at each other from different directions. That's what we're doing here, only we add temporal energy into the mix. Breaking down Primordial energy is a major event, and I'm not one hundred percent certain what's going to happen. That's why I appreciate you guys building this"—he waved a hand at the darkness—"place. It'll protect everything else should things go wrong. But I feel like this is going to work."

Virgil's face looked stunned. "I . . . I see. Yes, that just might work." His voice shifted back to normal. "Wait. The Large Hadron Collider . . . That is where you got this idea? But your understanding of it is pop culture at best. It—" Walker saw him pause as his face shifted again into that oily smile. "That will be wonderful, Creator."

Walker went along with it. "Yep. Leave it to Earth's scientists to find solutions for the multiverse's problems. There may be some temporal anomalies, but it should be manageable here."

"Hah! It should work. Okay, okay, one moment." Virgil looked at his screens, and it was *not* for one moment.

Fourteen hours later, hundreds, thousands, millions of rings were set equidistantly from each other on both sides of Walker. He had to explain that while the gates had to be matching on both sides for the two beams of Primordial energy to meet in the middle, they didn't want them to be uniform throughout. To destabilize the incoming energy, they needed the gates to bounce back and forth between speed, temporal speed, and temporal slowing.

As he waited, Walker was busy. Seeing as how he had nothing else to do, he focused on working on his body. After finalizing parts of his back—a tricky situation with visualizing how it looked—a green pulse washed out of Walker's last remaining area and pushed into the darkness of empty space. As he waited for the last bit of pain to recede, he sighed.

"Finally, my body's done. All that's left is the head," he said to himself with a slow nod.

"Walker! Are you ready?" Virgil called out from space a small distance away.

"Sure am!" Out of his control, his body floated to the large brown squirrel, who was currently experiencing a fit of major fidgeting.

"Okay, here we go. If this works, Walker—! Y-you do not even know, my friend."

Walker put a hand on his shoulder. "I get you, buddy. Don't worry, it should be quite fun."

Virgil nodded, and a bright yellow light began approaching from the far, far distance to either side of them. As it approached, Walker had no idea if everything was going according to plan. The only thing he could rely on was his assistant as he gave a rundown of what was happening.

"The energy has entered the first push gates . . ."

"It has reached the third temporal speed gate. Soon it will breach the temporal slow gate."

"The Council reports that the color shifted from white to black for a moment. They do not know what that means but consider it a good sign."

"The energy is almost equal in power and has cleared the first ten percent of the gates."

Walker watched as it continued to move down the line of gates at an ever-increasing speed. The closer it grew, and the faster it moved, the brighter the light was.

"Thirty percent," Virgil said as the brightness from the energy was lighting up the whole dark and empty rendition. By the time it reached the halfway point, it had already changed to an off-white yellow color and was still accelerating.

"Fifty percent. It's getting closer!" Virgil said while taking short breaths, his body vibrating under Walker's hand.

Walker punched a fist into the air, happy Rimi couldn't see him. "Yep! It's gonna work, buddy!"

If they hadn't been floating in space, Virgil would've vibrated right off of Sonata at this point. "It'd better! Or we are all going to fucking die!"

"What?"

Initially, the gates would activate as the energy reached them, but now the speed was so great that they weren't doing so in time. The Council's solution was simple: turn them all on at once.

A blast of sound echoed out in space, violating all the principles of physics Walker had ever understood. As a pulsing wave of energy shot out, Walker and Virgil's shields were preemptively activated to protect them. The wave seemed to push them back from the action, but not before Walker's eyes caught what had happened to the energy. Even though it'd only passed through nearly eighty percent of the gates, both beams were now flickering between black and white so much that the coloring shifted to a hazy gray.

When they hit the ninety percent mark, Walker couldn't even see the energy coming as it zipped right by them with the sound of thunder. When the beams met in the middle, everything stopped. Walker only heard his own heartbeat as it drummed in the back of his mind, the unknowable circumstances of his experiment a blank question mark in his mind. Then, a tearing sound, like jeans being torn asunder, and colors began to splash from the two bars of gray energy, flinging who knew what into the dark space around them. He counted no less than twelve different colors spaghetti-ing away from the collision, the cyan color of magic among them. The sound was unbearably loud, and the ripping sound continued at an unabated pace.

"It's working! You've done it, Walker!" Virgil yelled out, but just then, another explosion occurred as some of the broken strands touched one another in space. Bits of the darkness imploded as multicolored strands now floated among the emptiness. Great magmatic forms began to come together, only to erode instantly in front of them. Stars coalesced, burned, and died in a dozen different ways. Black holes and white holes launched themselves as another strand touched them.

A thousand-foot creature with horns and wings appeared in the middle of space, screaming, as parts of it froze and then burned away until it faded back to the nothingness it had come from. A planet started up, barren as can be, before a green strand touched it. Life sprouted everywhere across the surface as Walker's green eyes took in the sight. Cities formed and faded in moments, wars raged, and then the planet imploded. Different bodies began to float through space next to him—well, pieces of them, anyway.

"Get us the fuck out of here!" Walker yelled out to the sky.

"One second." Another explosion erupted only a thousand feet away. "One second!"

A portal ripped open next to them, and Walker felt himself shunted into space toward it. Unbeknownst to him, a piece of black flew out and broke through his shield. Just as he was inching through the portal, it drifted and touched the top of his head as he went through. The gate closed, leaving the unexplainable landscape behind, the two beams of gray still meeting in the middle.

CHAPTER SIXTEEN

Strands, Sapients, and Upgrades

Walker landed on Sonata with a shock. The shock was that he was floating several feet off of the ground when the moonlet came into focus. His Awakened legs took the drop just fine, but the fact that he hadn't been translocated correctly was worrying.

"What the fuck?"

Springing up faster than he was used to, he did a small hop into the air. In case anyone was watching, he leaned into the action, throwing a fist with the leap to pretend like he'd done so intentionally.

His face, however, was all smiles. "Yeah, baby! I told you it would work."

"What'd you do!" Virgil screamed out as he stared at his screen. "So much is happening!"

"What?" Walker asked in confusion.

"The Alpha Protocol Council has increased their time dilation to one hundred times ours so they can study what is happening in 4AB right now, Walker. A hundred times! They are sacrificing resources at an incredible rate just to track the new strands." When Walker looked at him, he noticed the large brown squirrel's eyes bouncing around the area as he tracked multiple screens. "The number of messages I am getting is insane!" He threw a private message at Walker for the first time.

Council Member 4: *He did it, LAD47! We now have access to everything!*
Council Member 4: *Everything!*
Council Member 6: *Another combination!*
Council Member 1: *This is terrible!*
Council Member 4: *This is wonderful!*
Council Member 2: *LAD47, do not let him die!*

Council Member 1: *This is unabridged magic! What is that doing
to the planet? That-that planet is alive!*
Council Member 4: *Can it talk?*

"Who is LAD47?" Walker had to ask.

"That would be me," Virgil said with a bunched-up face, his eyes attempting
to move in multiple directions at once.

"That's a shitty name, man," Walker said with a look of disgust. "I think Virgil
is loads better. Nobody should have a number in their name. Way too
impersonal."

"Yes, says the man who named a group of infants after a poem about hell,"
the squirrel sniped back. "Now leave me alone, Walker! Don't even ask about your
damned rewards. Trust me, they will come."

Walker held his hands up and said, "Fine, fine."

He had started to walk away, needing a breather after all of the crazy shit that
had just happened, when Virgil called out behind him, "Your humans will be done
in about an hour. Be ready!"

That pepped up his step, and he quickly made his way over to check in on
everyone. The Primigenials were just fine, though, strangely, they kept their distance from him, refusing to come closer than ten feet. Athena was the exception,
and she carefully stepped forward.

"Are . . . are you okay, Walker?" she said in a hesitant voice.

"Yep, I feel great. In fact, I feel better than great. Why do you ask?"

She leaned in closely before backing up again. "You—you feel . . . different.
It's as if"—she put two hands out and touched the air while acting as if she were
touching a solid object—"I'm standing in front of something beyond myself. I do
not know how to explain it."

Walker looked closely at her. Aside from the worried look she threw his way,
she seemed about the same. "Well, buttercup, I don't know what to tell you. I'm
feeling great. Now, if you'll excuse me, I have some work to do on the Territory
System."

"Of course. Please, do not let me stop you," she said as she backed up while
keeping her eyes on him.

Walker stepped away while whistling gaily, his steps quickly pulling him away
from the strange conversation. After reaching the Creation Instrument, he hopped
into the Territory System, where he interrupted John speaking in a calm voice to
an obviously upset green squirrel.

"No, small fellow."

"I'm bigger than you!"

"Listen. Walker does not want—ah," he said, noticing who'd just joined the
conversation. "Creator. Is-is there something different about you?"

Walker sat down in his chair. Although his body felt lighter than ever, the chair started to make an odd protesting noise. "I don't think so, no. What were you guys talking about?'

"Mmm," the cardinal said with as suspicious a look as a bird could give. "No, there is definitely something different about you."

Neus waved a hand. "Stop trying to distract from the conversation. Walker, please tell John that you want sapients to constantly gain unimaginable power."

Walker couldn't help but laugh. "Nooooo, absolute power corrupts absolutely. It needs to be gained gradually and through effort; otherwise, it won't be appreciated the way it needs to be."

John nodded. "Precisely. Now, were you able to get the Exchange System going?"

Walker shook his head. "I was not, but we can continue forward as if it's already working. No worries."

"Excellent. Okay, so here is what we have . . ."

Together, they worked out how they wanted items to appear in the world and created a tier system not too different from that of the monsters. Before Walker had run off, they'd already completed a bare-bones version. Deciding the monetary value for each tier was done in no time at all. After they agreed on each tier, John popped up the screen that broke everything down.

Item tiers for the integrated Item System
Tier 1: Basic
Associated visual color: White
Denominational value of donation: 1 note
Basic items are the lowest level available within the Item System.
They are easily created with no real skill necessary.

Tier: 2: Standard
Associated visual color: Red
Denominational value of donation: 2 notes
Very slightly improved Basic items are considered Standard.

Tier: 3: Improved
Associated visual color: Orange
Denominational value of donation: 5 notes
Items that have received increased functionality and been crafted
with care are considered Improved.
[. . .]

The visual would allow sapients to recognize an item tier immediately with a quick glance, thus creating an easy-to-use system. Each time an item was created and named, the color would appear over it after being scanned by John, identifying the level of mastery shown in its creation. Of course, that only worked if they donated the item. Not doing so wouldn't associate it with the integrated Item System.

Lesser minds would think this system could only work on weapons or armor, but Walker wanted it used on everything, from a piece of wheat to a painting. Now, with proper direction and an understanding of what Walker wanted, it was up to John to assign the correct value to each donation as they arrived.

Sure, there were ways to game this system, but honestly, who would care? The idea was to create a system that would allow John to copy what different entities created and to let them keep the extras for themselves to hand out as rewards.

Though, they did run into one big problem.

Neus raised a hand. "What happens if someone donates a thousand tier nine screws?"

Scratching the back of his head, Walker frowned. "Shit, you don't think they'd do that, right? John, do you think we need depreciating values for consecutive donations?"

"I think it would be logical, Walker. You may be satisfied with citizens understanding how to get the most out of donations, but that may be a little too much for your note system."

"Yeah." Walker leaned back in his chair as he closed his eyes. "I keep thinking we need to make sure that notes as a currency are valued. Depreciating value may be the only way to do it. I mean, if everyone has millions of notes, it kind of ruins the world economy." Making a mental note to talk to Cagna about a note milestone series, they got back to working on territories.

The basic version of the user interface was finalized after deciding to keep it nice and simple so the new Holder or Steward didn't become overwhelmed. John informed him as they worked on the upgraded interfaces that since leveling was a part of the Territory System, the trackers within would update all of the information without him needing to do anything. Walker smiled at that, and they spent the next six hours designing and upgrading each tier's interface.

While he wanted to work on his soul and finalize the next stage, he also wanted to finish the Territory System. It was important to him that this be done and ready to go before he stepped out and started planting humans everywhere. With that in mind, they started planning how tasks would work. Not only would they help sapients have clearly defined goals for each tier, but it was also a Territory System requirement assigned directly by the Council.

Luckily, the first task was easy to create.

First task created for new Stewards:
[Place the Foundation Stone into the ground to begin
your territory.]

First task created for new Holders:
[Attune with your Mana Tree to begin your territory.]

The first Steward task would activate once they got their hands on a Foundation Stone, while the Holders' would activate once they were within fifty feet of their Mana Tree. After the first task, and the easy second one, Walker and his team continued to work together. They didn't stop until they'd nailed the first four for Custodians, the term he'd decided on for Stewards and Holders collectively.

Second task created for Custodians:
[Select your territorial starter archetype.]

Third task created for Custodians:
[Plant your Mana Sapling in a safe area.]

Fourth task created for Custodians (Non-magical Archetype):
[Donate 5 original items to the Territory System: 0/5
Make sure all residents have housing: No
Have a plentiful amount of food for 30 days: 0/30 days
Have at least 50% of your citizens with jobs: No
Have at least 500 citizens in your territory: 0/500]

Fourth task created for Custodians (Magical Archetype):
[Connect with your Mana Sapling: No]

Walker looked it over from multiple angles trying to see if there were any issues. When he didn't find any, he nodded in appreciation. "This'll do. Great job, gents."

At this point, Walker felt that Neus, with John's immediate help, could continue with what they'd started together. Before leaving, he asked them to create an FAQ within all of the interfaces. Unlike Walker's forthcoming Class System and Profession System, he wanted Holders and Stewards to be able to ask about things regarding territories, further mitigating any problems that may occur in the future.

As Walker stepped out of the Territory System, a barrage of notifications struck his overlay, blinding him.

[. . . Scanning . . .]
[. . .]
Private message from an Alpha Protocol Council
Member detected.
[. . . Retrieving . . .]
Cancelled.

[. . .]
Private message from an Alpha Protocol Council
Member detected.
[. . . Retrieving . . .]
Cancelled.
[. . .]
Private message from the Alpha Protocol Council detected.
[. . . Retrieving . . .]

Hello, Creator . . . or, should we say, Walker.
Before you begin to think that we have violated the Assistance
Accord, know that the entire event in rendition 4AB was recorded
and is still being recorded at this time.
The things we have seen there are . . . truly magnificent.

Do you even know what has happened? Assuredly not.
Understand that what you have done seemingly on a whim, based
on the recording, will have ramifications for every protocol and
every rendition that is birthed in the future.
We have spoken with Number Four and now understand his
intense interest in you.
We all shall be watching together now.
Congratulations.

The rewards you have negotiated with Council Member Four
have been approved retroactively by the full Council.
Give us some time to begin relegating the new strands to your
resources, as we're currently learning how to mass-produce them.

Although it does not do justice to your achievement, here is what
you will receive as a reward:
A massive allocation of resources.
A choice of 2 abilities from our personal bank, curated
by LAD47.
A genetic sampling from the creatures we have discovered
thus far.
Your Creation Instrument has been maximally promoted as well.

We would say "Keep up the great work," but if you can take this
rendition any further, we are not sure we can manage it with
our resources.

Thank you very much for your work, Walker.
Good luck in the third battle.
We do not think you will need it.

One final note. Use of the Entropic resource may destroy your
entire rendition.
We do not suggest it, but that decision is yours to make, per
our agreement.

Alpha Protocol changes occurring.
[. . .]
[. . . Analyzing . . .]
[. . .]
All restrictions upon any of Creator Dante's assistants within the
protocol have been removed.
Your subsystem assistant task is now complete at no cost.
All further AIs in the protocol will now be at least
advanced. Current basic AIs have also been promoted
to advanced.
[. . .]
[. . . Analyzing . . .]

The Alpha Protocol Council has chosen to grant you rewards!
15 Potential resources
45 Space resources
22 Life resources
23 Causality resources
40 Consciousness resources
15 Kinetic resources
22 Death resources
8 Essence resources
11 Karmic resources
2 Nullification resources
45 Dimensional resources
5,000 Temporal resources
3,000 Primordial resources
1 Entropic resource

Access to the Dimensional Terror genera is provided.
Access to the Living Colosi genera is provided.
You have two pending ability choices.

**Please seek out your Advanced Assistant (Virgil) for
more information.**

"What in the fuck?" Walker said after reading through it all. Clicking on his resources tab to get a better idea of how this would all work, he found a new section named "Strands."

It was glowing.

After clicking on it, his screen filled with names and numbers he couldn't immediately associate.

Primordial Strand Resources
Cyclical Resources
Life: 22
Death: 22
Karmic: 11

Cosmic Resources
Space: 45
Temporal: 5,375
Dimensional: 45

Energy Resources
Kinetic: 15
Potential: 15
Essence: 8

Exotic Resources
Consciousness: 40
Nullification: 2
Causality: 23

Just below that, he found another new section.

Superior Resources
Primordial: 3,504
Entropic: 1

"Walker! Do not touch the Entropic resource!" Virgil yelled out as he came running over.

"I know!" Walker said with his hands in the air. "I know. I'm not that fucking stupid."

"Okay, I jus—wait a second," Virgil said as he inspected him while walking in a circle. "Are you taller?"

Walker sighed. "No, Virgil, I am not taller."

Virgil shook his head at him. "You look taller, Walker, and I would know. I am constantly analyzing everything on Sonata. If I had to do a rough estimate"—he eyeballed Walker up and down again—"I'd say you are two inches taller right now."

"Ha ha, funny guy."

But Virgil wasn't laughing. His face looked very serious. "No, I mean it. Look at your shirt."

Walker looked down at his shirt and pulled at it a little to get a better view, but it wouldn't budge. It was so tight that all of the buttons were being stressed to the max, as if it had never been tailored to his size in a small shop with a rude lady.

"What the fuck?" Walker said with big eyes.

"Indeed. Did anything strange happen to you while you were within rendition 4AB?"

Walker scratched the side of his head. "I don't think so, no."

"Then I am unaware of what could be causing this. Please update me on any changes that you notice with your body."

"Weird, but okay." Walker couldn't help but relate this conversation to the day he'd had the puberty talk with his father. He really hoped he wasn't about to go through a second one.

"So, did you have a chance to look at the new strands?" Virgil asked as his tail helicoptered behind him.

"Yep, and I gotta say, seems pretty weird."

"Walker," Virgil replied with an admonishing tone. "Yes, it is new to me as well, but that is just it! It is new!" he said with his arms raised up. "Whole fields of study are now being discovered, Walker. For instance, did you know you can use Essence with any of the other strands?"

Walker scratched his forehead with his index finger. ". . . Nope."

"Exactly! Nobody did! It is so exciting! I only wish I were a research assistant." Realizing who he was talking to, Virgil's tail straightened out. "Hmm, that is, if I were not your assistant."

"It's okay, buddy," Walker said as he rested a hand on his shoulder. "You're my research assistant. Plus! You were there! No other assistant in the protocol was, man. Only you. You're special."

Virgil pushed Walker's hand slowly off his shoulder. "Heavy hand you have there, Walker. My understanding of gravitational physics does not properly account for that. Another part of your Awakening?"

"I guess," Walker said with a shrug as he felt his energy cascade up and down his body for a moment. He had so much coursing through him that he felt like going for a run, and he hated running. Sadly, he didn't have enough time—there was still too much to do. He tried to keep any disappointment out of his voice as he said, "So, the abilities?"

"Yes, I have isolated four I believe you should look at."

"From how many?" Walker couldn't help but ask.

"Four hundred thousand two hundred and fifty-one."

"Jeez, okay. No wonder they wanted me to talk to you about it. I could spend the rest of my time in the dilation just staring at and stressing about all of the abilities."

"Indeed. I'll send them over to you now."

Teleportation Ability
Grants the Creator the ability to teleport anything from one location to another. May be used on organics or non-organics without the threat of harm. Use of Space resources is required when not using a portal gate.
Universal teleportation restriction is lifted for Creator Dante only.

Pocket Dimension Ability
Grants the Creator the ability to create pocket dimensions that will hold objects in a time-locked stasis field. May be used on non-organics only.
The use of Dimensional and Temporal resources is required for initial creation.

Life-Giver Ability
Grants the Creator the ability to give life to non-living objects. These objects will develop their own personalities and may become more powerful over time. May be used on non-organics only.
The use of Life resources is required for initial creation.

Flight Ability
Grants the Creator the ability to fly, bypassing basic restrictions on kinetic requirements.
Kinetic resources are required for each activation and for sustained movement.

"Fuck me," Walker said as he slapped both hands against his face. "So, I can teleport, fly, make pocket dimensions, or start a whole new race of creatures anytime I want."

"Hmm," Virgil mumbled with a hidden smile. "Yes. It is great to feel so conflicted about what truly matters to you, is it not?"

"How come in all the stories I've read, there's always an obvious fucking choice. Look! Look at this!" he said, waving at nothing in the air. "There's nothing obvious about these. Plus, why is it already stating that they'll use Primordial strands?"

"Good point, Walker. I added those descriptions in myself," Virgil said with a smug face. "Once you uncovered the strands of Primordial energy, they began being continuously filtered into your resources. I will admit that you are only getting a parcel of what the Council is receiving, but as they are doing all of the work, I feel it is a fair tithe."

Walker squinted at his screen, trying to decide if that was fair. Letting go of his greed, he said, "Okay."

Virgil continued, "When you first looked, you had two Nullification resources. How many do you have now?"

Walker pulled up the specific resource on his overlay. "Four."

"Yes." Virgil nodded emphatically. "Once the protocol Council makes an agreement, they *must* stick to it. If they do not, they can be replaced or even executed by the system itself, depending on how egregiously they have violated its standards. Everyone has a boss."

"Who is mine?" Walker couldn't help but ask.

Virgil eyed his chest. "I would wager it is the oath you have made. Now, enough stalling. Please pick two, as we still have a lot of work to complete."

"Hmm," Walker said as he tapped his chin while rereading everything. His face suddenly shifted from contemplative to sorrowful. "Both movement abilities are a dream of mine. Well"—he laughed—"of every kid growing up. I mean, who doesn't want to be Superman." Tearing his eyes away from Flight was difficult, but he did it. "Sigh."

"Did you just vocally say the word *sigh*?"

Walker waved him away. "I'm a Creator, and there are only two choices that can open up possibilities. It's fairly simple, really. I choose Life-Giver and Pocket Dimension."

"Are you certain? As you say, there are no take-backsies," Virgil replied with a completely straight face.

"I'm certain, thank you." Walker gave a resolute nod.

"Okay, done," Virgil said with no fanfare. "Also, I am a little proud of you right now."

The obligatory rewards notification popped up, and just like that, Walker now had two new abilities. He sighed and ran a hand through his hair. He should be testing out the new abilities. He should be trying to figure out how the new strands worked. He should be looking at the two new genera he'd just received. There was always too much to do. So instead, and contrary to Virgil's recent declaration of pride, he decided to be selfish.

"Anyway, are the humans done yet?"

Virgil nodded. "They are indeed, as are the Eaterhives. Would you mind coming with me? We need to activate the bloodlines and begin placement."

"Sure, but there's one quick thing I need to do." Walker went into his overlay and did something he knew would make his first assistant happy. He assigned Virgil to the Landmass System.

In the blink of an eye, with no gradual buildup, Virgil grew to be ten feet tall as he downloaded the information. One moment Walker was looking down at him, and the next, he was looking up. Even his fur changed from a nutty brown to a deep, stark black.

"Holy shit."

[. . . Scanning . . .]
Congratulations, Dante! Your advanced assistant has upgraded to a supreme assistant!

"From one system?" Walker asked with disbelief tinging his voice. Minutes later, he was still looking at the mega-squirrel, trying to compare the old model with the new, when suddenly, as the download finished, Virgil spoke.

"No," Virgil said, picking up on what Walker had said a few minutes ago. The sound and timbre of his voice came through in an entirely new way. Rather than the typical professor-like quality he'd always held, it now sounded like a hundred smaller voices speaking together simultaneously, layering over and under each other with different pitches. "The Landmass System is the primary system for all others to work through in this rendition. The downloaded information I now hold is more than three times what I've held in the past. Behold!" he grandiosely said, then flicked his hand out toward the sky.

Walker remembered that his Creation Instrument had upgraded multiple times in the last few weeks, and at each upgrade, the size of the landmasses had increased in direct correlation. When Virgil held his hand up, a landmass three times the size of the current Symphony floated in the air and began to pull itself together as he watched.

Mountains sprang up, and a single volcano rose behind them, then lakes started and rivers formed through them, each interconnecting until they began to drip off the edges of the land and into space. An entire miniature planet was now floating in the sky while Virgil directed it to form.

"What in the fuck, man. Why can't I do that?" Walker said in frustration.

"You can now, Walker," he said in his disconcerting new voice. "This is the final form of your Creation Instrument. Direct control." A huge glob of water formed into a sphere the size of a small city and floated over to Sonata. Virgil made sure Walker got a good look at it before it disappeared back into the World Editor.

"You now have the full power of Creation. What you do with it is up to you." He closed his open hand, and the giant landmass disappeared without a sound. Walker got a notification that he'd just received a C for his landmass, with a little note at the bottom saying all assistant-created landmasses could not receive a higher grade.

"Still they fuck me."

"Oh, Walker," Virgil said as he stooped over him, "you are never satisfied."

"That's called having ambition," Walker pointed out.

"Certainly. Another moment, please."

Walker got a new notification, the kind he hadn't seen in a long time.

[. . . Scanning . . .]
As your entity has been modified from its original form, please name it.

Before he had a chance to ask what was going on, it updated.

Entity: Eaterhive is named.
[. . . Analyzing . . .]
Entity named Eaterhive analyzed.
Size: Medium
Entity category: Animal
Organism type: System Monster
Modification: Extreme
Ability to evolve: Yes, system-bound (Restricted)
Age: 1 year
Extra marks earned for the first extreme use of the Combiner ability in the 4AA Alpha Protocol (Grand reward earned)
Grade: A
Rewards calculated.

Grand reward for being the first Creator to make an entity with extreme use of the Combiner ability:
Congratulations, Dante! You've advanced the Tree of the Gods!
No description was found.

Major reward for completion of an A-grade entity:
Congratulations, Dante! You've gained an allocation of rare resources!
Life resources allocated. Rare plant allocated: Deathshroom.

Entity task: Create 10 more unique entities (Part 2)
Diversification allows for growth. The further down a genetic line
that organisms move unchanged, the greater the loss of potential
genetic resources. You have made 3 unique entities. Now make
10 more.
New unique entities: 8/10
Reward for completion: Diverse

"Fuck!" Walker yelled out as the ground below him began to rock and roll. Strangely, he never lost his footing, though he did get the pleasure of watching Virgil tip and fall over. It was like watching a building crash in a somewhat glitchy video game. A quick lean, and then they were suddenly on the ground.

Unknown changes occurring.
The Tree of the Gods is maturing!
[. . . Scanning . . .]
[. . .]
The Tree of the Gods has borne fruit.

"Okay, we'll deal—"

Unknown changes occurring.
The Tree of the Gods is maturing!
[. . . Scanning . . .]
[. . .]
The Tree of the Gods has borne fruit.

"Double fuck!" he yelled out again as the full-sized moon finally stopped skirting around them.

Unknown changes occurring.
The Greek Pantheon has fully descended.
[. . . Scanning . . .]
[. . .]
The Norse Pantheon is ready!

"Fuck!" he yelled out for a third time. A pulse of green threaded through with black shot out of him and instantly bowled over everybody on the planet as the Tree of the Gods moaned ominously in the background.

When Walker looked up, he found the time dilation circle around the planet, always just out of sight if you looked directly at it, now had small cracks spread throughout it. The cracks began to turn red as he watched, and not knowing what would happen if he didn't fix it quickly, he dove into his resources tab and clicked on Temporal.

He didn't know what he was doing or how he knew it would work. Moving purely by instinct and with an understanding that there were things the Council didn't tell him, he reached toward the icon within his overlay. Grabbing hold of something he could barely feel, Walker pulled away.

As he began to drag the temporal strand out of his overlay, his eyes caught his resources dropping. The harder he pulled, the more came away, until he held a year's worth of temporal energy in the ball of his fist. The white swirl of energy was temperamental, and he felt his shield attempt to spring up and protect him. Only, the moment it touched the energy he held, the shield cracked and broke into pieces, then drifted away in the air.

Without having the time to ponder what this meant or why he wasn't already dead from touching the energy, Walker took his other hand and pulled a small piece from the greater whole. Balling it up, he wrenched his arm back and threw with every bit of muscle he had. When it splashed against the dilation crack far above him, it seemed to fill in the splintered area, holding things in place.

Knowing what he needed to do, Walker sprinted around the area and splashed temporal energy on any cracks he found. The more he ran, the faster he moved, until anyone looking would just see a blur sprinting across the planet, filling in cracks with small pieces of time-based putty shot out like a cannon.

When the last crack was filled, he had a sudden instinctual need to see what would happen if he just kept speeding up. But as soon as the thought reached his mind, he buried it. The sobering thought of Sonata exploding from the friction his feet caused kept him from making the attempt. He kept up his current speed and only slowed down when he came close to Virgil, who had already picked himself up off the ground. The black squirrel gave him a heavy look.

"It appears I am not the only one who has upgraded."

"Yeah . . . I don't know," Walker said as he scratched the back of his head with his free hand. In the other, he still held the small white glowing power of time. It was much diminished after his use, but still actively sitting there. Opening the palm of his hand, he threw it up and watched as it dissipated into the air.

Virgil tsked. "I have never seen that before. But do not worry; I will not tell the Council about it."

"What?" Walker said in confusion. "But I thought you had to tell them everything."

"Not anymore. My final mental processor acceded the moment you fixed what surely should have been a disaster that killed us all. My loyalty is to you and to you alone now, Walker."

"Yes!" Walker said and accidentally jumped a dozen feet in the air with his exuberance. "Whoa . . . I'm going to need to figure this shit out."

"Certainly. Now, would you like to get started on the humans? I have already placed hundreds of Eaterhives on Romulus and Remus."

"Wait, hold up," he replied, holding up a hand to stop him. "You placed all of the Eaterhives down while I sprinted around for a couple minutes? Hundreds?" Walker asked in confusion.

"Exactly that. There is a reason we are called supreme assistants," his strangely multifaceted voice said, still sounding pretty smug.

Together, they walked over and stood in front of the two human babies. "How old would you like them to be?" Virgil asked. "Keep in mind, we will be modifying their DNA minutely with each pass so there is little chance of any inbreeding."

"Neat. So how do I go about adding bloodlines?"

Virgil walked him through the process, and he quickly found the bloodlines located under "Genetic Modifications" in his overlay.

Genetic Modifications

Electricity:

Entities with this modification will have, and will produce children who have, a natural affinity for electricity. Entities with this modification will have an abundance of energy and may be impacted often by unnatural head pain.

Fertility:

Entities with this modification will have, and will produce children who have, an easier time producing offspring. Entities with this modification will have a much greater chance of producing multiple children at once.

Tactility:

Entities with this modification will have, and will produce children who have, a greater than normal amount of dexterous control. Entities with this modification will have a greater number of repetitive strain injuries.

Toughness:

Entities with this modification will have, and will produce children who have, a heightened form of physical toughness, including tougher skin and faster healing.

***Entities with this modification will have lower pain awareness
and may suffer debilitating injuries without being aware.***

"Did you look at these?" Walker asked as he viewed each bloodline's positives—
and their inherent negatives.

"Yes, and before you ask, it is a package deal. The good with the bad, the positives with the negatives. For instance, Zeus's Electricity modification. While it allows those with that bloodline to develop electrical abilities apart from evolutions, due to their increased sensitivity, headaches become a common affliction."

"I didn't know about any of this," Walker said as he looked back at the two babies in the tubes.

"You have a lot of things going on at once, Walker. I would not blame yourself."

"And you think this is fair? And that the benefits outweigh the consequences? That me altering them this way is . . . okay?"

"Certainly. You must consider that the humans will start in a new environment with virtually nothing to hold on to but themselves. They will be primitive beings, and anything you can do to help them gain a strong beginning will be largely helpful."

That didn't sound right . . . It was wrong. He could do more.

"I can change that," Walker said quietly.

"What was that?" Virgil asked as he leaned forward.

"I said, I can change that." He clicked on the Toughness modification and clicked on the baby boy in the tube, then advanced him by twenty years. He then did the same to the small girl with the Tactility modification. Both sat in their tubes, blissfully unaware of the outside world. That was about to change. Walker clicked into the Seeding System, chose a foot away from himself and Virgil, and then clicked Accept.

"What are you doing?" Virgil said as his large bulk stumbled back.

"I'm going to give them a chance," Walker said as the new humans faded in and both fell to their butts, naked as could be. Walker produced two basic sets of clothes in the Item System and, after folding them, put them down next to the first two human beings, aside from his former self, to touch Sonata. With immediacy, both modified humans began coughing and already attempting to weakly open their eyes.

The first thing they saw was a large muscled man in a torn white shirt smiling at them.

"Welcome, my friends," he said in a deep and soft voice, his forest green eyes seeming to light up from within. "Welcome to Symphony."

CHAPTER SEVENTEEN

Time of the Sapients

The two humans were sitting on the floor, blinking as they continued to look around. So far, neither had said a word. Walker assumed they were just trying to get their bearings, but after looking into their eyes . . . Something else was going on.

He glanced at Virgil towering over them all in his majestic squirrely form. "I can't get over how big you are now. You're like a mini kaiju," he said with a shake of his head. "Hey," he continued in a small whisper, "they're, umm . . . How do I say this?"

"Walker," the massive squirrel said, "they are children. You advanced them twenty years, but that is purely in age, not experience or education. This is why they were always doomed to fail initially as they gained their bearings within Symphony. It will take time for them to understand what they are doing and to learn to communicate with each other."

"Shit," he said, still speaking in a whisper.

"Shit," the girl said from the ground, picking up on his words.

"Her first word!" Rimi said in excitement. He had walked over when he noticed the two new inhabitants of Sonata.

"Ugh," Walker mumbled, running a hand through his hair. "I guess that's fair for this situation. How many humans did you say we would need to seed for things to work out?"

"Ten thousand, or just about," Virgil replied smoothly, still staring at the two humans.

"Ten thousand . . . Okay. I think we'll need about fifty."

"Fifty what?" Rimi asked.

"Fifty pre-experienced humans to help get them started."

"Pre-experienced . . ." Virgil said, seeming to taste the word. "Do you mean to train them, Walker?"

"Yep! Look at who we have here right now," he said, opening his arms out wide to encompass Sonata. "We've got a legendary blacksmith, a wise woman, a . . . messenger. That is Hermes, right?"

"Yes, I believe so," Virgil said while squinting at the man in the near distance with an odd helmet on. "Yes."

Walker shook it off. "We've got everything we need to start training them right here, right now. We start knocking out Primigenial quests and handing out bloodlines just before we seed them onto Sonata."

"But . . . they're babies," Rimi pointed out.

"Uh-uh," Walker countered, waving a finger in the air. "They're babies right *now*. Give them the rest of the time dilation, and I'm sure we'll have them up and moving. It'll be tough at first, but I figure they'll have a deep understanding of Symphony and its systems right when they begin their civilizations. We'll just have to make a rigorous schedule for them, and who better to teach them than the former Teacher of the Month, Walker Reed!"

"You only won that because they knew you were thinking about quitting. They wanted you to feel good about yourself," Virgil countered.

"Whatever, I still won."

Virgil shook his head. "You will not have time for this."

"I'll make time. Literally. They're"—he pushed a fake tear off his face—"my children." Walker shrugged. "The first sapient civilizations need to have a good relationship with us, or it could breed some serious resentment once they figure out how this all came to be. The more work we do now, the less work we have to do later."

Virgil put his hands on his hips. "How are you going to do that?"

"Like this." With a wink, Walker pulled more time out of his resources tab and smothered himself in it, taking on a slight silver sheen. While they looked at him, he disappeared to the naked eye as he began moving across Sonata in his personal smaller form of time dilation. Small notes were left everywhere he went with the recipient's name on the front. When that person opened the folded paper, they found that Walker had written them a short message.

Zeus: Please do your best to keep an eye on the new Primigenials. I'll speak to them personally as soon as I can.

Virgil: Please work with Rimi to create more starter monsters. We'll need some that adapt well to mountains, others for water, others again for cold environments, and so on—at least three tiers for each zone. I'm thinking of mountains, water, cold, desert, jungle, grassland, swamp, underground, and some flying types. It'll take a while, but that's why we're here.

Athena: You have a cute butt . . . Sorry, I just wanted to say that. You'll see me again soon.

Athena: Help Zeus when you can. Maybe ignore that last note.
Athena: Do you think other Creators have it as hard as us? I've been wondering about that a lot lately . . .
Virgil: This may have been a mistake. I think I've been stuck like this for a week now. It's hard to tell with time the way it is.
Virgil: You have a cute butt . . . I'm kidding!
Dionysus: You're not your father.
Apollo and Artemis: Stop fucking around. I'm going to need you soon, and you had better help out. Think about what you want your Primigenial tasks to be.
Hephaestus: Your tools look sweet, man. Here's the material you need to build a smithy. Let me know if you need more.
Ares: No wars!
Hades: Isolation isn't always healthy; when I was young, my parents were rather strict . . .
Triton: Do you have gills?
Aphrodite: Don't bang the new humans, please.
Eros: Where are the wings, kid?
Zeus: Did the tree seriously release like ten more Primigenials, or am I counting wrong?
Virgil: Sorry for this.

Virgil noticed the notes continue to appear for several minutes, and while Walker was still stuck in his own time, multiple events in the system occurred simultaneously as he finally went through his stockpile of standard notifications.

[. . . Scanning . . .]
Subsystem assistant task complete: Train the assistant (Series 3)
Subsystem assistant requirements:
Assistant is assigned to a subsystem: Yes
Assistant is autonomous: Yes
Assistant completes work continuously without calamity:
7/7 days
Reward for completion: Gain unlimited subsystem assistants.

Territory task complete: Create your tasks (Part 2)
Tasks created: 10/10
Reward for completion: Variable
Secondary reward for completion: Decided by the Alpha
Protocol Council
[. . .]

New territory task: Assign 2 system unlocks as a part of the
Territory System (Part 3)
Systems are an important part of the Alpha Protocol, Dante.
Make sure they have more options moving forward, or they may
stagnate in their growth.
System unlocks assigned: 2/2
Reward for completion: Variable
Secondary reward for completion: Decided by the Alpha
Protocol Council
[. . .]

Territory task complete: Assign 2 system unlocks as a part of the
Territory System (Part 3)
System unlocks assigned: 2/2
Reward for completion: Variable
Secondary reward for completion: Decided by the Alpha
Protocol Council
[. . .]

New territory task: Have at least 3 territories in your world
(Part 4)
Place them, Walker, and watch as your creation blooms to life.
Territories planted: 1/3
Reward for completion: Variable
Secondary reward for completion: Decided by the Alpha
Protocol Council

Reward for completing the second territory task:
Congratulations, Dante! You've gained 200 Primordial resources!
No description was found.
Secondary reward for completing the second territory task:
Congratulations, Dante! You've gained a VIP card.
The Auction System isn't just a system but a location. With your
VIP designation, expect the treatment you receive to be
quite pleasant.

Reward for completing the third territory task:
Congratulations, Dante! You've gained 200 Primordial resources!
No description was found.
Secondary reward for completing the third territory task:

Congratulations, Dante! The Landmass System has upgraded!
Templates are known across the multiverse for being useful for saving time and streamlining the creation process. With this upgrade, you can now save different landmasses as templates for future seedings.

Reward for completing the third subsystem assistant task:
Congratulations, Dante! You've unlocked the ability to create unlimited subsystem assistants!
Subsystem assistants are the system designer's dream. Because of your dogmatic focus on building systems into your world, you've reached the final step in this series and obtained a rare boon.
Limits: There are no longer any limits upon assistants, as decided by the Alpha Protocol Council.

Even with those rewards in Walker and Virgil's back pocket, chaos continued across Sonata.

A city-sized steel ball floated in the air before disappearing almost immediately after. The same thing happened with a large piece of glowing white metal only a second later. A large crashing sound occurred before everyone could hear Hephaestus yelling in the background as Walker dropped a series of resources in front of him.

Cagna began screaming in her chair as she looked at the Milestone System.

Territory Series: *Full, Complete*

Basic milestone—Level One:
Establish a territory. 1 point.

Novice milestone—Citizenry:
Establish an oath for your territory. 3 points.

Apprentice milestone—Our Place:
Build enough residential areas to house all citizens. 5 points.

Apprentice milestone—It's Just a Number:
Reach Tier 2 for your territory. 5 points.

Adept milestone—Expansion:
Expand your territory independently 3 times. 7 points.

Skilled milestone—A City:
Reach Tier 6 for your territory. 10 points.
Title unlocked: City Lord

Experienced milestone—Legion:
Have over 100,000 citizens in your territory. 15 points.

Experienced milestone—Together We Rise:
Complete all Basic to Skilled milestones in the Territory Series.
15 points.
System unlocked: Voting System

Advanced milestone—City-State:
Reach Tier 10 for your territory. 20 points.
Limited to those who have established their territory as a
Custodian. Loss of attached territory removes milestone
points at cost.

Popular Vote Series: *Limited, Complete*

Basic milestone—The First Vote:
Win the right to rule through a ballot holding your name. 1 point.

Apprentice milestone—It's My Opinion:
Have 5 or more ballots initiated by you and approved by the
public. 5 points.

Skilled milestone—Statuesque:
Have at least one statue of yourself in your territory. 10 points.

Advanced milestone—Festive:
Be honored by a festival thrown in your name. 20 points.

Epic milestone—Never Ousted:
Rule a city-state by popular vote for 50 years or more without
losing an election. 50 points.

Reward: Obtain 40 or more points in the Popular Vote series to
unlock specialized residential structures.
Limited to territorial Custodians.

Tyrannical Series: *Special, Limited, Complete*

Basic milestone—Domination:
Win the right to rule through violent means. 1 point.

Apprentice milestone—Marauder:
Defeat another territory in a war. 5 points.

Skilled milestone—Statuesque:
Have at least one statue of yourself in your territory. 10 points.

Advanced milestone—Bloodbound:
Have at least 3 subordinates who have led a raid on another territory. 20 points.

Epic milestone—Iron Fist:
Rule a city-state by martial strength for 50 years or more without losing. 50 points.

Godly milestone—Conqueror:
Control 5 or more territories through the right of conquest. 100 points. Unlocks the Conqueror series.

Reward: Obtain 40 or more points in the Tyrannical series to unlock specialized defensive structures.
Limited to territorial Custodians.

Go Beyond Series: *Limited, Complete*

Basic milestone—Challenger:
Defeat an opponent at least one level or tier above you. 1 point.

Apprentice milestone—Underdog:
Defeat an opponent at least 3 levels or 2 tiers above you. 5 points.

Skilled milestone—Unyielding:
Defeat an opponent at least 5 levels or 3 tiers above you. 10 points.

Advanced milestone—Triumphant:
Defeat an opponent at least 15 levels or 5 tiers above you. 20 points.

Epic milestone—Legendary:
Defeat 5 or more opponents who are at least 25 levels or 6 tiers
above you. 50 points.

**Reward: Obtain 40 or more points in the Go Beyond series to
unlock the Fabled title.**

Virgil tried not to be shocked by Walker's antics anymore, but he had to admit this was a little much. As he watched, Cagna froze in place, still mid-complaint, and grew to twice her former size while a piece of paper floated down next to her.

**Congratulations, Dante! Your subsystem assistant has upgraded
to a full assistant!**

Neus made the mistake of exiting the Territory System and was inundated with pieces of paper falling around him like flurries of snow. Virgil assumed it was instructions from Walker on what to do next. He began to feel something in the back of his throat and remembered what Walker had said just a moment ago.

[. . . Loading . . .]
[. . .]
Expelling new subsystem assistant.

Virgil forced a light cough and watched as a yellow hairball flew out and rolled in the grass before coming to a stop. It unrolled into a new subsystem assistant, who blinked as they looked around, asking who their Creator was. Virgil ignored that for the moment.

With a rough estimate, he believed Walker's time must be running out at this point, as things had begun to slow down. His processors had continuously noted slight changes in the vibratory patterns across Sonata, and there was certainly less happening now than just a few seconds ago.

Since his upgrade to supreme assistant, he'd gained over a hundred new mental processors, with some taking on leadership roles for those below them. At this point, it was safe to assume that Virgil was a walking logistical army. A flurry of notes fell beside him with his name on top. He stooped down to pick them up.

Harsh way to treat a new brother or sister, man.

Hey, Virgil, I think my time is starting to run out since most of this silver stuff is almost gone. I don't know what's going to happen when it does, but here are some notes on what I want to have happen just in case.

Please speak with the Primigenials and get them to give me tasks that aren't stupid as fuck.

Here's the list of people we have who can help the humans get a foothold on Symphony once they land. Each will need to be trained in a myriad of ways, and I'm relying on you to get them started. Some are required and some are by choice. I left notes with each god and checked on them a week later (my time). They've all agreed to the terms I have set for them. There will be fifty total humans, and . . .

Virgil understandably raised an eyebrow at the number of people Walker had just said again, but when he looked up, forty-eight naked human beings were just starting to raise their heads and look around in confusion. At the same time, the original two were just finishing getting dressed with the help of Echidna, who had a note tucked into the top of her dress.

"Of course, he is going to leave this to me," Virgil said with a sigh before looking at the next note.

Aphrodite: *Keep them away from her*
Apollo: *Art and Music*
Ares: *Sword and Squad*
Artemis: *Hunting and Wildlife*
Asclepius: *Medicine*
Athena: *Life lessons (required. Basic wisdom too)*
Cagna: *Milestone study (required)*
Demeter: *Agriculture*
Dionysus: *Nothing*
Echidna: *Soul and Reproductive (required)*
Hades: *Survival training only, and only once a week (he agreed, also this is required)*
Hephaestus: *Crafting and Construction (one craft type required from each)*
Hera: *Leadership and Relationships (required)*
Hermes: *Athletics and Travel (he agreed)*
Minos: *Unarmed Combat and Gardening (required)*
Neus: *Territorology (required)*
Poseidon: *Swimming and Navigation (required)*
Rimi: *Monsterology (required)*
Triton: *Spear*
Zeus: *Nothing. Just make sure he keeps an eye on the Primigenials*

Virgil sighed a second time before returning to the note he had been reading before the list.

. . . total humans, and I'm making a planet just for training them. It should be up and running at any moment. I'm burning quite a few resources to advance it so quickly, but it should do the job.

It'll be a standalone planet with multiple different biomes and creatures; that way, our humans have a chance to really experience a simulation of Symphony. Each of these people will lead their own civilization, so start planning out how you want to create the landmasses for them. I think we need to look at who fits into what biome best and then design it for that purpose. I have to work on this new planet, but one last quick note for you.

The new one, you know, the yellow one. Help them out with a name. I suggest Mea if they're leaning female or Jude if male. Singing Hey Jude *every day would be fun . . . Anyway, they're going to be in charge of our new subsystem assistants, like a foreman. I can't take the time out of each expulsion to explain everything to them.*

Please help them get started on our goals and the oath I always share. Also, there's a new regional system I made that also has levels. It's based on the Growth System and will make sure that every region gains special resources based on the territorial levels within it. I'll explain when I stop, which should be pretty soon for you.

Thanks for doing this, and sorry to dump it on you.

Just as Virgil finished reading the note, Walker reappeared from nowhere. Steam rose from his body, and unlike before, the assistant spotted white highlights throughout his hair. He gave Virgil one quick and tired smile before collapsing to the ground.

"Great," Virgil said with a frown. He looked up to the sky and found a green planet not too far away. Glancing over at the fifty humans who were still staring at Walker on the ground, he said with great emphasis, "*Do not touch him.*"

Looking from the still-steaming man to the heaping of human nudity to the much larger form of Cagna, who seemed to be quite excited, he clapped his hands together. "Well . . . Let us get started."

It didn't have the same feeling as when Walker did it.

Everything . . . was new. She came from . . . something . . . nothing . . . and opened her eyes. The world felt . . . strange. Although her mind didn't understand what strange was, it was the closest interpretation to the feeling she could find. Her thoughts moved slowly, like they had never had to operate before. The world was a symphony of strange feelings and sensations. The grass itched underneath her; the temperature was cold on her skin. She continued to hear odd sounds and see things that she knew were important but didn't know what they were.

A massive man wearing scraps of clothing appeared from the middle of nowhere, causing her and those around her to shuffle back and cry out. He fell to the ground as waves of partially opaque smoke drifted off him. Unlike the others, she didn't make a sound, instead choosing to stay quiet so she wouldn't attract attention. Attention could be bad here.

Then she noticed the monster standing near him. The great furred creature, with skin the color of the purest darkness, tried to pick him up. But even after straining for some time, it found itself unable to do so. She wasn't sure if the monster was weak or if the man was simply that heavy . . . heavy . . . Everything continually felt new and odd. The oddest thing of all was the figure on the ground. She felt strangely bound to him.

It felt like he was pulling her toward him.

Each time she looked away to a new sight, her eyes found themselves right back on him. Like an anchor on her soul. As she looked around, she found others doing the same. They all watched as the last of the smoke faded off of his body just as a blue creature walked in front of them. It looked like a smaller version of the great black monster from before, although this one had a different expression on its . . . face . . . face.

It was saying something, but she couldn't understand it. A woman wearing yellow clothes with startling green eyes walked up next to it and also began to speak. But she couldn't understand what they were saying. She knew by instinct they were trying to communicate, but this was all new. All confusing.

She felt a need, an urge, to say something back. To let them know she wasn't a threat. She chose to repeat one word she heard the woman say, although her throat felt dry, making it difficult to get out.

"Care."

The woman's face shifted just like the blue creature's did, and she took it to be a good thing. As she continued to try to understand them, something appeared in her vision.

Good luck!

[. . .]

[. . .]

Overlay starting.

[. . .]

[. . .]

A series of squiggles and boxes appeared in her view, blocking some of her vision. Based upon the reactions of those around her, and the screaming that was currently damaging her ears, they were experiencing something similar. A few tried to run, but a man in orange stopped them, gently, and put them back with the others. Another series of squiggles came after, and a moment later, she understood.

[. . .]
Universal Translator active.

". . . As I was saying, running will not get you anywhere. This is a small moon, and we do not have a great number of places to hide at the moment," the green-eyed woman said. "My name is Echidna. I'm in charge of making sure that you gain your bearings while the Creator . . . convalesces. I'll also be training you in the ways of the soul, as well as giving some brief, uh, tips on how more humans come to be."

She tried to speak, but another spoke up in her place, one of those like her but wearing clothes.

"W-what. Wherrre . . . where are we?"

The blue creature laughed. "You're on Symphony, my friend. What a lucky guy you are!"

CHAPTER EIGHTEEN

My Sapient Academia I

DAY 1 (ECHIDNA)

It was a full day before Echidna managed to get the newly produced humans to stop having near heart attacks whenever one of the elders, or non-newborns, spoke to them directly. They were fine in group conversations, but anytime she spoke to them directly, they seemed to freeze up and have a fit. After Rimi went in and made a series of very uncomfortable beds for them to lie in, they fell asleep for the first time in their lives.

It was a difficult thing to explain to them and took longer than expected.

Hephaestus had been nice enough to create a water trough in record time, and Virgil filled it to the brim while adding some chemicals she'd never seen before. He stated that it was to keep the water purified, but she had no idea what that meant. Tainted water had always been fine for her and hers, but it appeared these humans were going to be coddled. Tough love always went further than accepted privilege in her mind.

While they slept, Sonata went through a makeover. With the help of Hephaestus, Minos, and Athena, they managed to make some quick structures on the moon to support the new sapients in their training. Rather than individual houses, Rimi created a basic communal hall from the Item System, which the god of blacksmiths then went in and modified to be livable, complaining all along about the shoddy workmanship the system provided.

Minos planted a garden for food rather than the flowers he seemed to enjoy so much, while Demeter provided valuable input into seed spacing and cross-pollination. Apollo and Artemis worked with Hermes to create a few ranges using wood given to them by Virgil, who, rather than bringing forth the basic kind from the Item System, just popped a series of underappreciated trees directly from Sonata using Walker's new space gates. Nobody asked the scary new version of Virgil how he did so without Walker's input.

By the time the sapients were waking up from their slumber, Sonata was no longer the barren grass moon it had always been. The humans, with their lack of memories and experiences, couldn't appreciate the value of what had occurred overnight, and they took it in like it was normal for huge numbers of buildings to spring up in such a short amount of time.

Then again, for them it was.

Zeus took great pleasure in waking up the ones who tried to continue to sleep in, shaking their beds hard enough that small cracks could be heard as the cheap wood splintered from its rough treatment. Once they were all awake and complaining about the strange pain they were finding in their stomachs, Minos had them line up in an orderly fashion. Again, it took much longer than expected.

DAY 2 (A CURIOUS WOMAN)

The great bronze-covered man—that is what he had said his armor was—stalked across the line of her fellow siblings as he continued to speak.

"You will receive numbers for now instead of names. Our Creator believes names are important and shouldn't be taken lightly or freely," he said in a clipped, high-pitched voice before spinning at the end of the line. After getting halfway across them again, he turned to face them. "When I stand in front of you and say your number, remember it, for that is what you will be called for the time being. One!" he said as he quickly walked over and stopped at the first in line. The woman looked at him with a confused expression on her face, so he leaned in real close and whispered something she couldn't hear.

A moment later, her voice rang out. "One!"

He nodded and moved on to the next person, a tall man with broad shoulders who was looking at the elder blankly.

"Two!" Another uncomfortable wait happened while everyone kept quiet, then Minos leaned in again, and the man's panicked voice yelled back, "Two!"

"Three!"

Three understood right away and yelled it back. This continued down the line until every number was called out in response. When her turn had come, she'd said her name with no hesitancy, and maybe it was just in her mind, but she thought she caught a gleam in Minos's eyes at how she carried herself.

"Excellent!" he said after going through the numbers. He had a piece of paper in his hand, which he quickly wrote a few things down on before saying, "It was a slow start, but you've all completed your first task as a unit. Now, your reward is sustenance. That's food, for those of you who don't know the word."

"Food?" a man two people down from her said in a questioning tone.

"Gods be damned," a muscular female elder said as she watched from beside a man who looked like a copy of her. "You poor fools have no idea what you're getting yourself into. You won't even make it . . ."

"Quiet," an old bearded man yelled at them. They both made an ugly face at him before turning and stalking away with rigid steps.

No one said anything about it, but it left some curious thoughts in her . . . in Seven's mind.

After they'd eaten, which was a novel experience—many of the . . . humans . . . had choked on their food initially—they had been taught what running was, and at that moment, Seven had found her calling. If they hadn't stopped her, she'd have run from one corner of Sonata to another without stopping. The feel of her muscles contracting, bunching, and then unwinding themselves. The thrill of the ground flying from underneath her feet as she moved so fast her eyes teared up a little and her lungs screamed for help. Even the sweat dripping down her face seemed to make her happy.

Although she had only been alive for a few days, she understood that this feeling, this . . . experience . . . was why she would continue. To live in order to travel to a new place on her own two feet.

While the other numbers had taken to various activities with differing levels of excitement and inherent ability, her whole world became focused on athletics. Running, jumping, anything that had to do with the feeling of growth and gaining strength. Her instructor, who said his name was Hermes, told her that she was a natural. Whatever that meant. He gave her a few tips for how to run just a little faster. He said it was called "efficiency." She grew excited when she realized there was more to this running, that she could move faster than she had before.

When the athletics training had ended—Seven was far and away doing the best in the group of fifty—she'd gone straight to her life classes with a naturally calming woman named Elder Athena.

"Who are you?" Athena asked as she looked from one number to another. Three raised his hand, something she'd taught them to do the moment they sat down with her.

"I . . . I'm Three?"

"Good, Three. But what does it mean? How do you fit into the world?"

"I . . . I don't know!" he said in a panicked voice. "I . . . I . . ."

Athena patted her hands in the air. "It's okay, Three, don't worry. This isn't me testing you. I just needed you to consider who you are in relation to where we are right now. There is no right answer for that question, at least not at the beginning. It takes a very long time to begin to understand yourself. To understand life. Which brings me to the next question." She paused for dramatic effect. "What is the meaning of life?" She looked from one blank face to another. "You understand life to be this thing you're doing right now. Moving from one experience to the next, learning and feeling everything that it comprises." Athena gave another brief pause as she continued to look at them. "Many ask and wonder about what life truly is, so, I'll tell you . . ." She waited for everyone to lean in. In a loud voice, just as they grew close, she said, "It's what you give it!" Athena's eyes scanned over to Seven. "Do you want to be a great warrior? Do it! Make that your focus." Her eyes found Two. "Do you want to design a perfect city? Do that instead!" The goddess of wisdom spread her arms wide. "You have a unique moment in the history of mankind right now. Not only will you get the chance to meet your Creator . . ." Covering her mouth, she coughed while whispering, "When he wakes up from his stupidity." Smiling like nothing happened, she continued, "But he also plans on doing anything he can to help you achieve whatever goal you set your mind to. You have Symphony in the palms of your hands, right at the start. Your limits are an illusion. A choice."

"What if I just want to be by myself?" a pale-skinned man yelled out. He looked around at everyone nervously, as if he feared someone would come after him for saying that. She thought his name rhymed with "super late" . . . Forty-Eight!

Athena looked over at him. "That will be between you and your Creator. If you didn't know, Walker is his name."

Walker, Seven thought to herself.

"I'd like you all to spend the rest of the day thinking about what we've done so far, what thoughts have gone through your mind, and who you want to be. We're not taking anything off the table; it is purely up to you," she said, then stood up and walked away, leaving them without an elder for the first time since they'd come to be.

What I want to end up being.

DAY 3 (HEPHAESTUS AND ATHENA)

The third day of the arrival of Walker's sapients was the worst: crafting training.

Hephaestus was over three thousand years old, if you counted their time in the tree, but in his whole life, he'd never thought he'd have to show young humans not only how to use a forge, but what it was. They didn't even have a true concept of fire! One of them had tried to burn their hand off because they thought the forge fire was pretty! Blasted fools.

"No, do not hold it like that. You're going to smash your fingers to bits!"

"No, you cannot just say it is good enough. That's bad craftsmanship. I'll not have shoddy work done in my smithy."

"Stop, you damned fool, it's so hot the metal is dripping into the forge!" he yelled at Thirty-One for the second time. They'd already ruined a heap of metal, and basic metal or not, it still burned his soul to see crafting resources abused like this.

Based just upon the last four hours, three of the humans would pass his standards for being basic smiths with one of them going a step further. The rest had no talent for it, and he said as much to Athena when she inquired about how it was going near the end of the lessons.

"Why did you give them to me for more time than the rest of them!" he yelled at her. "Sister, they're . . . they're so bad. Only a few of them even have the potential to be decent."

Athena laughed. "Brother, you know better than that. First, Virgil assigned the schedules."

"Ah, the giant scary one."

Athena nodded. "Yes. Also, your standards are impossibly high for humans, not to mention that they amount to hardly more than babies. Give them time, dear one, and I'm sure they'll surprise you. Walker did."

Hephaestus grumbled at that. "Boy didn't know what he had. This Ethereal ore is incredible," he said, snatching up a piece of white glowing metal. "Just a one percent alloy derived from it lightens the weight of a weapon by half. Half! I can make swords the size of buildings weigh no more than a basic hammer. Incredible barely touches on it. Revolutionary even! And he gave me a boatload of it!" He threw it onto the ground, then thought better of it and quickly picked it back up. "What am I supposed to do with it all? I can't let these dull-fingered numbskulls touch it."

While Hephaestus always put on a blunt and no-nonsense act, Athena knew his other side. He dearly loved his family, Aphrodite included, and hated the idea of insulting a person to their face. Awkwardness made him incredibly uncomfortable, so he preferred to stay in his shop. Half of the reason his work was so amazing was simply because he wanted to make sure, from the very bottom of his heart, that whatever he made for them would always work exactly the way they needed it to.

She patted him on the shoulder. "You'll find a way, brother. You among all other Primigenials are exceptional."

"Don't let Dad hear you say that now that his golden boys are out," he said under his breath.

"Apollo and Ares are amazing fighters and did well on Earth. But we're not on Earth anymore, brother mine. I have a feeling that Walker will place more value on you and your creations than he will on two fighters."

That seemed to mollify him, and as he went back to the smithy, she thought his voice sounded less strained.

DAY 3 (ARTEMIS AND EROS)

"Consistency is the key to not dying, you stupid brain-dead idiots!" she railed at the sapients who had chosen archery as a focus. The giant demon had said that each human had to go through a series of different trainings each day on a rotating schedule. Something about maximizing their potential gains. What he didn't say was that so many of them would choose her class. She'd expected maybe five or six, but once they realized that this training would keep them at a distance from their foes, more than half had signed up.

"I keep cutting my fingers!" one man yelled out.

"Good! That means you're developing a callus. It'll protect you moving forward. Keep going until the blood gets to be too much."

"Blood?" the man whispered. He had the number fourteen written on his shirt, an idea that Ares, of all people, had come up with to tell them apart.

"That red shit that comes spilling out of you when you die for being fucking terrible at archery! Keep firing and working on your form!" she yelled at him after moving only inches away from his face. He nodded quickly with a twisted expression, then moved back to firing, wincing at every shot.

"Do anybody else's fingers have an owie?" she said as she looked around. Nobody took her up on it. "I didn't think so. Hey, pink thing, I need more shitty arrows!" she yelled at the massive squirrel sitting in her fancy chair. She was a god, and yet she didn't get a chair. The nerve of some people.

The creature disappeared for a moment and came back right after. A hundred arrows fell at Artemis's feet. She grumbled as she bent over to pick them up, then handed over half to Eros.

Artemis leaned on the railing of the firing range as she looked at her nephew. "Can you believe this shit? Do you know what I was doing before our fucking Creator grabbed me and threw me in that shitty prison? I was hunting a golden stag. *A golden stag.* Those fuckers are unbelievably powerful. I'd already loaded it up with ten arrows, and it was still going. I swear it was laughing at me as I was taken."

Eros laughed. "You think that's bad? I changed into this form to escape an angry human. It's not my fault his wife found me to be so much more attractive than him." Artemis raised an eyebrow at him. "Okay, so he was the king of Sparta and was mobilizing his army to fight some other country . . . something with a P. But still! If he hadn't done that, I'd not be trapped as a weird half teenager. It's his fault I slept with her . . . multiple times . . . and it's his fault I look like this," he said, pushing his hands down his body. He sighed. "At least we're not in the tree anymore."

"You said it, nephew." She spotted a woman not following through with her shots. "Hey, Twenty-Two! Stop that shit. Let me show you how it's done, you useless little fuck." Artemis stomped over to continue her duty.

DAY 4 (CAGNA)

"What are milestones?" Thirty-Three asked. It was only the fourth day, but already they'd grown much better at speaking and understanding others.

"They're . . . like points in a road," Cagna said, struggling to elucidate milestones as well as her Creator did. "When you reach them, they'll help you later in picking the right skills."

"Skills?" Seven asked. In Cagna's notes provided by Virgil, who was watching everything simultaneously while continuing to work, it said that Seven was a top prospect for survival. "Very bright" was a note written next to her name.

"Skills are kind of what you're doing right now. In your . . ." She looked at the notes for which humans had chosen which martial skills. She found it in the third column. "In your spear class, you learned how to, um, hold a spear, right?"

"Yes?" Seven said with a questioning tone.

"That's a skill. Proper spear h-holding. Stan . . . stances! Yes. You learned proper stances in spear holding. Proper stances!" she unexpectedly yelled out, not used to this many people talking to her at once. "That's a skill, yes."

"I . . . understand," Seven said with a confused expression on her face.

Why am I having to do this? Cagna thought to herself, a morose expression stamped on her face.

DAY 4 (HADES)

"Yes! That's exactly what you do!" Hades said, pointing his finger at number Forty-Eight. "You run"—his fingers simulated running on his palm—"away. If a creature is much much more powerful than you, *do not be a hero*. Heroes are all fools, and they mess up your marriages. They also get people killed. No!" He slashed a hand through the air. "Just run away."

"Marriage?" one of them asked with a hand raised. Athena had taught them that today.

"Ask Echidna. I'm not doing it," he said with a stomp of his foot. "Now, survival is about staying calm and prioritizing what needs to happen. For instance." Hades got up and punched Seven across the face without warning. As she fell, he dropped to a squatted position, moving his head closer to her. "I'm much bigger, *much* stronger, and much smarter than you. What do you do?"

She spit the blood welling in her mouth into his eyes.

"Yes! Innovative thinking!" he said as a pulse of black erupted out of his body and pushed the blood off his face all at once. "But I'm still much more powerful than you. I can do things you cannot even imagine, weak human." Saying so, he kicked her in the ribs and followed her quickly as she rolled away from the force of it. One jumped in front of Hades and threw a punch at his stomach, only to receive a laugh in reply. "You fool, that will never work on me. I'm a big scary monster who has lived for thousands of years!"

Hades kicked Seven in the chest, flinging her away. Five of the humans ran away from him, receiving a mental nod for their intelligence, but Seven looked up from the ground, finally having stopped and caught her breath. She spat more blood on the ground and stood up, glaring at him. "Ah, a hero already. You and One are doomed to die, little human," he said with a grin. He took two steps forward before a white pulse crashed into his chest and knocked him down.

"Hades, that is enough!" Zeus thundered at him. "You are meant to teach survival, not beat them until they're so cowed that they can't even stand the sight of a battle."

"You always take the humans' side," he yelled back, spittle flying out of his mouth as he glared up at his brother.

Zeus got in his face, veins distending his neck. "Because they are always filled with the potential for more, while we are set in our ways!" He looked around at the humans, some lying on the ground curled up in fear, others being shepherded back by Primigenials and assistants who had found them. Seven and One, in particular, just glared at Hades. "This isn't going to work," he said with a sigh and shake of his head. "I'm going to speak to Virgil and—"

"No need," the giant black squirrel said as he came bounding up with his long steps. "I heard and saw it all."

"Hades isn't—"

"Hades is doing exactly what I asked him to do," Virgil said, cutting him off. "The humans need to learn how to fight as well as how and when to run. There will be things on Symphony that they will have no hope of defeating in the beginning." He looked down at the cowering humans, then scanned over to One and Seven. "There are times to fight, and there are times to not. You need to learn the difference if you want any hope of surviving." Virgil reached down and took Hades by the arm, helping him stand up. "Thank you for your proper instruction. Please, carry on, but be sure not to injure anyone too greatly."

Hades nodded without saying anything, then glared at Zeus until his older brother walked away with a mystified expression on his face. "Now, where were we? Ah yes, running away." He turned to look at the girl he figured had the greatest instinct to fight. "You should be good at that, Seven."

Hades cracked his knuckles.

DAY 5 (REST DAY)

All fifty of the humans had gathered around a burning fire in the center of a large seating area in the early morning. Standing just beside the fire was the great monster Virgil himself. His black fur seemed to suck in any light that escaped the clutches of the flames, bathing them in his shadow.

"Today is a rest day. We have pushed you hard right at the beginning, but I believe Walker would want you to relax now. To remember why life is worth living. Do as you please." He waved a hand at a large table of food. "I am told the food is not outstanding, but it will be filling." He waved his hand at an area just beyond the seating. "We have also created a few games that we were able to pull from our Creator's memories. If you would like to learn any of them and . . . play, some elders are standing by to teach you. Please enjoy your day, as we will be starting up bright and early tomorrow with more instruction." He started to walk away, then thought better of it. Turning around, he quickly said, "Do not act romantically with each other. Thank you," then began to leave again. But not before Two spoke out.

"Where is the Creator? Where is Walker?"

The great shadow turned back around slowly. "He is recovering from his ordeals. He went through quite a lot to get you all started on this path, to make you, to prepare you for what lies in the future. That has taken a toll on his body and soul. He needs . . . time." He seemed to laugh at a hidden joke after saying that.

"Isn't he, like, super special or something?" another number called out. "Why would he need to, um, recover?"

Virgil shook his large head. "No, he is not. Maybe he is now, but he wasn't before. Once, not too long ago, he was just like you, though even more flawed, if you can believe it. In fact, if you would like, you can get to know him right now."

"How?" Seven asked.

"Swear to be one of his followers. Take a knee and say you will follow the religion of Dante. I promise no hidden attacks nor extra attachments. But if you do this, you will learn about him."

They all looked at each other, curious what he was talking about, but it was Seven who took the knee first, saying loudly, "I swear to follow the religion of Dante." As she finished speaking, a camo-covered book appeared out of the air and landed beside her. She picked it up and opened the cover before asking, "What is this?"

"It is a book," Athena said as she came closer from the darkness beyond, "and one that is written by your Creator. He wanted to give you a head start on knowledge and understanding from his world." She nodded at Virgil, who nodded back before leaving. "Joining the ranks of his followers allows you to gain some insight into who he is as a person—as a man, rather than a Creator. That is how he wants things to be."

"Why?" One asked.

"Because he is not like the others who amass great power. Walker chose to spread that power to you and yours so that you could make your own lives. Forge your own fates. It is important to him and me. In fact"—Athena took a knee—"I swear to follow the religion of Dante." She waited a moment after saying so, but as she opened her eyes and looked around, her face took on a disappointed cast as she saw that no book had fallen beside her. "Pity."

"Why can't you be one of his followers?" Seven asked, figuring out what had happened.

"Because it appears I am not like you after all, which is a true shame. You do not know the gifts that are going to be bestowed upon you or the trials that lie ahead." She noticed only a few other numbers had sworn to follow Walker's religion, and of those who didn't, they looked at her with something like fear in their eyes. "I will not force you to follow his religion, nor make you take an oath to follow his teachings. That is not what he would want." She smiled. "He is a unique man in that respect." Athena turned and began to walk away, but not before saying, "For those of you who would like to play, I have heard that my brother has created a Ping-Pong table, and I am in dire need of challengers if I am to face Walker in the future. No pressure, though." She waved a hand as she walked away.

A few minutes later, Seven joined her at the green netted table.

CHAPTER NINETEEN

My Sapient Academia II

Seven did not, in fact, master Ping-Pong. Her heightened athletic skills notwithstanding, Elder Athena slapped her around on the green table, showing an incredible focus while beating her every round. Seven showed a little improvement as she scored a few points, but it was still a sham as far as presenting herself in the best possible light to the golden-dressed woman she admired.

On her fourth loss, the elder called it, saying she needed to practice more in order to bring her "A game." Seven didn't understand the last part, but she did understand that practice was a healthy way to improve at anything. With that in mind, she spent a large part of their day off working on her running, trying to eke out the slimmest possibility that she may become just a little faster.

While she and her fellow numbers were spending their time talking to each other, eating, practicing different skills, and generally recovering from the last five days—the first five days of their lives—the elders were hard at work on different tasks. A large circular wooden building went up as Elder Hephaestus showed his superior skill in crafting yet again. When she ran a circle around it, she heard the word "arena" used several times. Her translator kicked in and presented a series of images to show what it interpreted that word to mean. She wasn't sure if she liked it.

After having traveled around Sonata for a good distance, she'd come to one conclusion.

It was big.

She didn't think she'd have enough time to run across the entire moon if she'd wanted to. It was simply too large. Maybe if she combined all of her free days together, she might be able to do it, but certainly not in one run.

The second thing she decided was that the dark wooden structure between Elder Cagna's chair and the tree was special. She knew it was because Elder Minos was constantly standing there, watching everyone.

That must be where he is, she thought to herself.

The Creator. Walker himself.

They said he was recovering, but that could just be an excuse. Strange thoughts filled her mind as she looked at the simple wooden walls, the only thing keeping her from meeting her Creator.

For a second time, she mentally amended.

Staring at it while she slowed her jog, intrusive thoughts began to creep into her mind. Maybe he didn't like her and her fellow numbers. Maybe they were a mistake. What if he came out and took them all away somewhere? What if he decided he needed to try again with a new set of numbers, and they were just . . . in the way? She didn't know, but it began to fill her with an itchy feeling, like someone was scraping their nails down her back.

She thought back to what Elder Athena had said the other day.

Who are you?

She didn't know, and that worried her.

Seven jogged over to a bench near the archery range and sat down. She pulled out her Creator's strange book as she let her body cool off.

Scripture.

While the Universal Translator did its job in translating the words on the page, it was incredibly slow to impart the knowledge to her. Reading a single page took over ten minutes, and she wasn't even sure she understood everything she read. The first few pages were strange too. Plus, what was poetry? Why did he seem so sad yet . . . defiant?

She read a few more pages, taking over an hour to do so, and had to close it when One began walking up to her. The other woman sat on the bench beside her and looked at her hands.

"Do you feel like you know the Creator better than before?" she asked her fellow number.

Seven shook her head. "No, not really. It doesn't make sense. I keep wondering: what's a bully, and how is hope one? Why did he make a monster? It's con-confusing."

One nodded. "And are we the monsters? He made us, right? Could we be the monsters?"

"You took the oath?"

One responded by pulling an identical copy of the book out of her pocket. "Most of us have. Just a couple decided they don't want to. I found the chat kind of . . . funny," she said with a smile.

A sigh shook Seven's frame. "There are just too many questions, and the only one who can answer is in that building right over there," she said, pointing a finger at the wooden structure.

One squinted at it. "Hmm," she said in a thoughtful tone, "how do you know he's in there?"

Seven shrugged. "It's the only place they haven't explained to us. Well, that and Elder Virgil's weird tubes. I mean, Elder Minos is constantly standing in front of it in a strange pose. Almost like he's protecting whatever is in there."

One looked at the building again. "Where's Elder Minos?"

Seven shrugged as she also looked at it and saw the large bronze-covered man missing. "I don't know. He was there a minute ago."

One gave her a quick smile that Seven didn't recognize. "Want to see if we can break in?"

"Break . . . break in?" Seven said with a confused look on her face as the translator gave her mind an idea of what it meant. "You mean violate Elder Virgil's instructions? He told us to let him recover."

"No," One said with a shake of her head, "he never said we couldn't go in there. He just said Walker was recovering. So." She raised her eyebrows at Seven. "Do you want to go in?"

"I . . ." She thought about all of the questions still sprinting through her mind, and the only way to get answers for them. The only person who could give them. "Yes."

One gave another weird smile. "Then let's go!" Saying so, she got up and sprinted for the structure, leaving Seven, mouth open, still on the bench. She stood up quickly and ran after her, quickly catching up and running beside her as they approached it.

We're actually doing this, Seven thought with excitement.

Once they got close, Seven reached out and touched One's arm. They changed their speed to a slow walk, trying to make as little noise as possible in case anyone was around.

When they got right next to it, they found the structure was one solid piece of wood with no way in that they could see. There was, however, an odd hole several feet up one small part of the wall. One winked at her, grabbed it, and pulled. The seamless wall opened to reveal a dark interior that seemed foreboding to Seven's mind. They stepped in quietly, still aware that Elder Minos could be back at any time. Seven closed the door behind her quietly, and they were in.

"We did it," One said in a whisper as they both looked around. The room held no decoration, nothing to indicate that anyone was currently living there. All that could be seen was a large bed of stone that looked quite uncomfortable—and the behemoth of a man lying on it.

"That must be him," Seven said in wonder, looking at the person who gave her life. A small stream of white was drifting off of his body as he lay there. Seven focused in on his face, moving a little closer, and found . . . nothing special about him. His nose was perhaps a little too large, his chin jutted out a small amount, and his hair had random white patches throughout it. As she looked at it, another small area near his ear turned white, changing right before her.

Looking at him, that feeling she'd had before came back. As if there was something undefinable about him. A weight to his presence that couldn't be shaken off. It was strange, and she didn't know what to make of it. But his face was just so . . . ordinary.

"Huh. I expected—I don't know—more?" Seven whispered as she looked at him.

One snorted, then covered her nose as the sound was a little louder than she expected. "Sorry," she whispered. Cocking her head, she continued to look at the man before them. "I don't know. He's extremely large compared to us, unlike how Elder Athena described him. That's kind of how I thought he would be." She looked a little closer at his face. "He's not . . . ugly," she said, finding the word she wanted to use. "Also, there's something about him, something special."

As she spoke, he rolled over, his arm shifting and almost touching the floor. Outside, they could hear the sound of loud footsteps approaching at a sedate pace.

"Oh no," Seven said in the smallest whisper she could make while still making sure One heard her, "Elder Minos is back. We need to go."

"Wait . . . I just want to . . . ," she said as she looked down at Walker's hand nearby. "I just want to touch him."

"What?" Seven said, thinking the request was strange. "Why?"

"Because," One replied, giving Seven a big-eyed look, "I need to make sure he's real. That this isn't—I don't know . . ."

"A dream?" Seven said.

"Yeah, that's the word. I have the strangest dreams."

"Me too, but I don't think this is one. Maybe we should just go now before someone sees," Seven said, her body already getting twitchy from the energy running through her.

"I'm just going to do it really quick. Nobody will know," One said, already slowly reaching her hand out.

Seven was flabbergasted, but they didn't have time to argue. "Do it fast," she said, hearing the footsteps grow ever closer. "We need to leave."

"Okay," One said, then picked up the speed a little and touched his hand.

Seven was looking at the entrance when a loud piercing scream erupted right next to her, causing her to jump in place. Her head swiveled, and her eyes landed on the open mouth of One as she made a sound unlike any she'd heard before. She followed One's eyes to her hand, which had just touched their Creator, and a gasp slipped out of her mouth.

Where she'd touched Walker, the tips of her fingers were turning gray and shrinking before their eyes. Seven looked from the hand to One's face and felt all of the blood drain out of her own. The woman's eyes were terrified as she held up her quickly changing hand, the gray spreading from the tips of her fingers to her knuckles. As it spread, the shrinking changed, and the former tips of One's fingers faded to dust. She never stopped screaming.

The door flew open with a crash to reveal the bronze-covered form of Elder Minos stomping in.

"What happened? What's wrong?" he bellowed in a high-pitched voice.

The large man looked from Walker, still sleeping, to Seven, who barely even seemed to notice his arrival. Following her eyes, he found One staring at her hand, now gray to her wrist.

Seeing the encroaching gray rise further up, he made a quick decision.

"Hold her down," he said as he grabbed the end of her afflicted arm, then kicked One's legs out from under her. Seven regained her senses enough to plant her body on top of One's awkwardly, but she didn't know what to do afterward. They hadn't had their unarmed training yet, and too many things were happening at once.

Elder Minos pulled a long axe from his side and lifted it high up, then slammed it down on the pinned arm a few inches above the rising gray. One screamed again as a fountain of blood sprayed out of her arm, then, mercifully, she stopped making any noise as her eyes rolled into the back of her head. Elder Minos pushed the hand away from them into a corner of the room with the end of his axe before putting it back in his belt. He picked them up, one in each arm, and quickly carried them away without speaking.

When they got out, several numbers and a few elders were already there, and more were running over. Elder Minos handed One to Echidna and gently put Seven on her feet. He left them for a moment, presumably to check on Walker, before coming out and closing the door behind him.

Elder Rimi came running over with a few stacks of cloth. He opened them, pulled out a flat rectangular piece with something green rubbed into it, and then handed them to Echidna. The yellow-eyed woman started to wrap them around One's still-gushing arm, tightly pulling the cloth as she bound the forearm as much as she could.

Seven was trying to collect her thoughts while she watched them work when she heard a calm voice say, "What happened?"

Nobody had even noticed the massive black squirrel arrive.

Minos nodded at Seven without saying anything, but she didn't initially understand what he wanted. Then, clarity dawned as she looked at the large crowd of people in front of her. In her five days of life, fear had been a constant companion. Dodging and running away from Hades. Her spear lessons with Elder Triton. Elder Poseidon's weird way of talking to them, and Elder Rimi's monsterology class, where he taught them how dangerous being on Symphony would indeed be.

But this was a new kind she hadn't experienced before. She had done something she knew was not right. No, it was . . . wrong. The rational part of her mind recognized that. If it hadn't been, they wouldn't have felt the need to be quiet about it. She had done wrong. Something wrong.

Her tongue felt stuck to the top of her mouth, and a sweat broke out in the middle of her back. She didn't like the feeling one bit.

The monstrous squirrel looked at her and said one word, "Well?"

With an effort, she opened her mouth and said, "We just wanted to see the Creator."

Elder Virgil sighed and touched his forehead. "And you touched him, right? That is why it was necessary for Mi—Elder Minos to cut off her hand? I assume that is what happened, as that is the only way such a clean cut could have been delivered," he said with a nod toward One, still lying on the ground with her eyes closed.

"Yes, Elder," Seven replied. She had done wrong, and she needed to accept what would happen now. "I am ready for my . . . punishment." She didn't like that word one bit.

"Punishment . . . Yes." He looked at One on the ground, then back at Seven. "You are in charge of making sure One can still complete all future training. She will have a few days rest, and then she will be back to work. She cannot fall behind the others more than that, or it will set our plans back and cause a disturbance to our goals." He looked at a streak of silver in One's previously all-brown hair. "Hmm. You will also inform me of anything strange that occurs with her. I expect you to give me a daily update before you sleep."

Feeling relieved, Seven nodded. She had already planned to take care of One, as she felt a lot of guilt for what had happened. If she hadn't agreed to go, maybe One wouldn't have gone either, and this never would've happened.

"Excellent. This has certainly been an interesting moment. Echidna, please wrap One in some new medicated bandages. We created a medical station over by Walker's former Creation Instrument area, if you were not aware. Rimi can guide you if you have trouble finding it." He looked at the large man Seven was now a little frightened of. "Minos, please come with me. I would like to speak with you."

Everyone broke up except for One, Seven, and Elder Echidna, who waved Elder Rimi off, saying she'd find it. The other numbers walked away, and she could hear them speaking about her and One loudly, causing her eyes to grow hot for some reason.

She offered to help carry One, but Elder Echidna laughed it off and easily picked the injured woman up. She gently placed her on her shoulder, and together they walked over and quickly found a building around the same size as her Creator's.

Everything inside was orderly, with small labels beside each tool, instrument, and prepared material. Elder Echidna showed Seven how to change bandages, then had her wrap the wound while she watched. Wanting to know what to do in case she was the only one around next time someone was hurt, she asked about the green substance on the cloth.

"Oh, that's from crushing a Harmonic Bud, which works wonders. Walker received them for completing a task not too long ago. Asclepius, who you will be training with in two days' time, has been studying it since he first arrived. It is quite wonderful. Look here," she said, pointing at the open wound. "The bleeding has already stopped. He prepared several bandages just in case of an accident like this happening."

Seven huffed hot air out of her mouth. "It wasn't an accident. We chose to go in there and—"

"Yes, you did," Elder Echidna said with a nod. "But I assume you didn't know that touching Walker right now would destroy your body. For the time being, he can only touch inorganic material. You didn't notice the large dead spot from when you first arrived?"

Seven thought back to what had happened right after she'd arrived: a man in torn-up clothing had fallen over in front of them, and they had all stared at him.

Thinking about it, she answered, "They took us away before we could look at it . . . or . . . him."

"Ah, yes. Right now, Walker is bleeding time, as you would call it. Well, that's what Elder Virgil says," she said with a smile. "To transport him, we had to move him with a metal pole, which was a lot more fun than I thought it would be." She took over for Seven and finished wrapping up One's arm, tying a neat little bow on the end. "There we go. I can't say it is as good as new, but it is an improvement over what was there before. Now, let me just get you up," she said, speaking to herself as she lifted One in her surprisingly strong arms. They walked back to the communal hall and dropped her off in a cot with her number above it. "She'll be terrified when she wakes up. I'll be staying nearby if you require me."

"Thank you."

"You're welcome, Seven. You know, you're holding up better than I thought, considering how recently you've come into being." She looked directly into Seven's eyes. "Why do you suppose that is?" Elder Echidna didn't wait for an answer; instead, she walked away without looking at her.

Seven spent time thinking about that and what she'd learned in the last five days. She knew that Elders Echidna and Athena were pushing her toward something, but she didn't know what that something was. She went out, remembering that Elder Echidna said One would sleep for a while and wouldn't need her. After searching for a moment, she found Three by the food table nearby. She convinced him to swap cots for the time being; that way, she could be close to One in case she needed her.

Seven ran around Sonata for a while, grabbing food and water when she saw it, trying to think about what she needed to do to prevent something like that from happening again.

When she ran around the corner of the Tree of the Gods, she found her least favorite elder sitting on a log before a fire. He didn't look up when she tried to pass him by, but regardless, he seemed to know it was her.

"Come sit over here, fool," Elder Hades said in his harsh voice.

Seven mentally sighed but didn't say anything as she sat beside him. She was already in enough trouble and didn't need Elder Virgil to hear that she'd ignored an elder's request.

The darkly dressed man laughed. "I just heard an interesting story from my niece and nephew. They said that one of you has already lost an appendage." He laughed again. "I said no way! There's no fucking way that on the fifth day of your lives, one of you idiots did something that caused you to lose an arm."

"A hand," Seven replied.

"What was that, human? Did you whisper something into the air?" he said in a mocking voice.

"I said she lost a fucking hand!" she yelled at him, cursing for the first time. "And it's my fault. If I hadn't gone with her, One would never have even considered intruding on the Creator. She lost a hand because of me and—"

Hades laughed while tears fell down Seven's incredulous face. His laughter continued for an unnatural amount of time, long enough that her incredulity shifted to anger. When he finally stopped and looked up at her, seeing the track marks her tears had left on her dirty face, a slight giggle erupted.

"Oh, you are just too much for me, Seven," he said, wiping a tear away from the side of his face. "I am a truly terrible teacher, after all. My wife always said so, but I didn't believe her." He sighed, his face shifting from mocking joy to something she didn't recognize. "You would've liked her, Seven. You two had a lot in common."

"Oh, and what's that? The inability to deal with you for more than a small amount of time?" she yelled at him, feeling a hot liquid drip from her nose.

"Yes, yes," he said with a smile and a nod, "she used to yell at me like that too. Ah"—he leaned back on the log—"I dearly miss that woman." Hades looked up at the sky. "I wonder where she is now."

"I'm assuming she realized how terrible of a person you are and ran away as fast as she could," Seven said with fury.

If he was affected by her words, he didn't show it. "No, she was quite happy from what I could see. She always loved the flowers that bloomed in the Under." His face shifted again. "Then came Heracles, Zeus's true golden child." His eyes took on a faraway look as he continued, "He killed my guardian, broke into my home, insulted my subordinates, then absconded with my wife." Hades's grip on the log below him caused fissures to erupt throughout the wood. "No one knows what happened to them, and I didn't even have enough time to search for my dear Persephone because our BLASTED CREATOR TOOK ME AWAY FROM

SEARCHING FOR HER!" he screamed at the same sky he'd just been smiling at a moment ago, dragging out each word.

Seven felt something in her heart shift. "He stole your wife?" she asked.

"Oh yes, and let that be your lesson, dear Seven. Do *not* be a hero. They ruin lives."

Seven didn't know how to respond to that. She leaned back on the log beside him and looked at the sky.

A hero.

CHAPTER TWENTY

Wake Up and Smell the Space

From the time Walker passed out until the moment he woke up, events within the temporal bubble moved on accordingly. There were many highlights, from One losing her arm in the first five days to Hephaestus declaring a disciple. In the martial tournament of numbers, Seven won easily as almost everyone knew she would, while Eighteen won the territorology quiz and Ten scored the highest on the milestone test. Only a few took Hades's survival gauntlet; no true winner was declared by the end, as he stated all four of the contestants were losers.

Sonata, even in the time dilation, felt like it was speeding up, and things were only moving faster.

Walker opened his eyes for the first time in a month as the planet shook below him.

Unknown changes occurring.
The Tree of the Gods is maturing!
[. . . Scanning . . .]
[. . .]
The Tree of the Gods has borne fruit.

"What the fuck," he said as a blinding headache pounded in the back of his skull. He scrubbed his face with his hands as he sat up on the worst bed he'd ever slept on before. His notifications exploded.

Congratulations, Dante!
The Alpha Protocol has recognized Sonata as holding multiple entities of your creation.
All task tracking is now enabled in your original location.

Walker was still rubbing the grit out of his eyes as the notifications continued to update. There were so many that the system organized them into groups so he could look at them as necessary. Making a decision, he clicked on the predesigned milestone notifications he'd set up.

**Milestone update: An entity has unlocked Milestone 1
of the Traveling series.
Milestone update: An entity has unlocked Milestone 2
of the Traveling series.
Milestone update x143. Please click to inspect all
Milestone updates.**

Walker whistled. At least he knew it worked. Cagna must've put in a ton of new series for that many milestones to update all at once. Walker clicked on the Follower System updates.

**Followers gained: 48
Followers that have obtained the rank of Explorer
in the Unending Summit: 5
Followers that have obtained the rank of Seeker
in the Unending Summit: 0**

Walker knew why they couldn't move from the second rank to the third. He'd never set up the promotion trial for them. He had no idea how the sapients had come to find the Unending Summit, but he wasn't about to complain about the circumstances. Maybe the forty-three who hadn't passed just needed a review guide. He chewed on it for a moment.

While he had been in his personal time bubble, he'd worked on and thought about many things: the Territory System, how the Class System would work, and even a few secret projects he'd kept from Virgil so he could see the look on his face when they popped up. But he hadn't worked on the Follower System, as he hadn't expected them to find it. Walker looked at the second promotion requirement again.

**Task for promotion from the Explorer rank to the Seeker rank:
[Travel across the breadth of Symphony in search of greater
strength. A promotion trial is required for the next stage.]**

In review, he realized that wouldn't work, as it was too little information for his followers. After stretching, he hopped out of the hard bed, landing on his feet with a loud thud.

"Must've put on some weight," he said, patting a mostly flat stomach. They must've built this place for his subsystem assistants, but there was no way he could stand up all the way.

Walker made a quick change to the requirements so his followers would have a better understanding of what was needed to move to the Seeker rank. He knew he'd have to do the same for all of the ranks, but he'd do that as they approached each threshold; that way, he wouldn't get bogged down in the minutiae.

Task for promotion from the Explorer rank to the Seeker rank:
[Travel across the breadth of Symphony in search of greater
strength. After obtaining the Apprentice Traveler milestone, a
promotion trial may be requested for the next stage.
Each trial will be decided upon by a ranking member of the
Leadership Branch.]

Then, remembering how he'd chosen the name Custodians to refer to Stewards and Holders collectively, he made a quick change to the Combat Branch, which still had Custodian as one of the ranks. He wasn't perfect, and as all of his assistants and Primigenials knew, he was terrible with names.

Wrapping up his quick Follower System update, Walker realized that a day . . . well, at least a day had passed since he'd used Temporal resources on himself. He went into the System Designer, ready to get his currency program started, then thought better of it. He wasn't entirely sure how much time had gone by, either in his bubble or while unconscious afterward.

He knew now that it wasn't the wisest idea to wrap yourself in Temporal resources without considering the ramifications, though he also wasn't sure what had made him do it. It was an instinct, a feeling that it needed to be done. Walker's chest pulsed for a moment in line with his thoughts. It was confusing for him, and he didn't know what to make of it.

Why?

During his time alone, everyone had been frozen entirely still. With his newfound speed, he'd circled Sonata in only a few hours, but after several days, a small depression had struck him. He didn't know how long he would be like that, which was a disturbing thought.

The only way to stave off any loneliness was to spend time working, planning, or pretending like the frozen people around him were conversing. Sure, the notes were helpful, but waiting for them to reply was agony. Still, he did get a lot done.

Since his body was now impervious to the strands he'd found during the Primordial collider event, it should have allowed him to combine multiple strands together safely. The problem was just how few resources he had for use.

Walker reached into his torn pocket to pull out one of the projects he'd spent a large amount of his time working on. Unnoticed, the headache he'd awoken with slowly faded away on its own.

Looking at the object in his hand, he smiled. A small brown leather bag sat there.

He hadn't wanted to use the basic leather in the system, so he'd gone into his memories and pulled out an old website he'd looked up when a student had asked about how leather was made. The look of shock on the vegan girl's face had been worth studying how to create it from scratch. He wasn't vindictive or mean to vegans, but it was a funny memory of his.

It had taken him some time, but in the end, he had created leather from scratch and felt a slight glow of accomplishment. The killing part had been extremely uncomfortable, but he couldn't balk at killing an animal for its resources after killing hundreds of creatures by ejecting them into space.

After he'd made the small bag, he had kept it in his pocket for a time, trying to figure out how to do what he knew was needed. He had gone into his abilities and used his new Pocket Dimension ability to create a bag that had more space in it than outside of it. Donating it to his personal Item System had allowed him to create multiple from Sonata's magical atmosphere, and so, things were going well.

Still, there were a couple problems with his bag. First, it only held about two times its size and thus didn't have much value to him. Second, he never knew exactly what he was reaching in to grab.

No, there has to be something more to this.

It all came down to the strands.

At the time, he'd had a limited number of strand resources, so he hadn't wanted to waste any on experimentation. Now that a good amount of time had gone by, a quick glance at his current resources showed that the Council was still sticking to its promise. He had hundreds of strand resources now, even thousands of some, although his single Entropic resource had not gone up in number, which was to be expected.

Walker reached into his resources and grabbed Space. He didn't need to use the Dimensional strand, as that was already attached to the bag itself. No, what he needed was more space, more . . . compressional magnitude.

Walker put the bag on his stone bed and tried pushing the dark blue Space strand directly into the leather. It, of course, didn't work, as he wasn't trying to attach Space directly to the leather itself but to the dimensional hole within it. Smacking himself on the forehead with his free hand, he moved the bag so the opening was larger, then inserted the Space strand directly into it. The dark blue coloring seemed to drain right out of his hand, so he knew he'd made the right choice.

Walker reached inside and found that he could fit his whole arm now. Not knowing how deep it would go, Walker entered the Item System and found it had been updated with a newly minted advanced AI. He had to donate his blood again, but for some reason the needle wouldn't pierce his skin. He solved this by biting his lip, hard, like he'd done at the start of the protocol itself.

With a bit of blood spat into the cup, the environment changed to the forest he had grown comfortable with. The AI, which chose the name Frank after Walker explained that John was already taken, gave decent advice.

Stepping out, he picked up the standardized three-foot-tall piece of wood, then measured and began etching in each division of feet and inches. After absorbing it into the Item System, he went in, produced it, and popped back out. And just like that, Walker could measure things.

American style.

He stuck it into the Dimensional bag, but it just kept going, which was problematic, as he only had three feet in length. Walker stepped back into the Item System and did the same thing with a ten-foot pole before hopping out. Standing it upright, he found he could just see over the top of the long measuring pole.

"What the fuck?" he said to himself. He must be at least ten feet tall now, as the damn thing was near the roof and he was still hunched over. "I'm a fucking giant," he said, then gnashed his teeth, remembering telling Virgil he did not want giant humans if he could help it.

Just then, the great black squirrel himself came walking in, seeming much smaller to him than he had in the past. "Hello, Walker," he said simply.

"Really? I'm gone for who knows how long, and all I get is *Hello, Walker?*"

"Certainly. Would you rather I say, 'Oh my gosh, Walker, you are so big and stupid'?" he said with a straight face as his mocking voice reverberated throughout the room.

"Look—"

Virgil held up a hand. "Please. You have done some incredible things since arriving here, Walker, and some have also been mistakes. If you felt the need to smother yourself in a large amount of toxic Temporal resources, who am I to say anything." His tone of voice was as stale as two-day-old French bread.

Walker scratched the back of his head. "I just . . . I don't know. It felt like I needed to. I can't explain it." The pulse hit his chest again.

"Yes, I thought so." Virgil nodded. "I cannot begin to understand what you are going through, as it has never been recorded before. But please, try to keep me in the loop in the future."

Walker gave him two thumbs up. "You got it."

"Excellent. Now, there is much we need to discuss—"

"One second!" Walker said, interrupting him. "I need to test this."

Virgil nodded without speaking, and Walker took the pole and stuck it into the spatial hole in the middle of the bag. It wasn't until eight out of the ten feet went in that Walker felt it stop. He tried wiggling it around and found that it was about eight feet in all directions, giving him a lot more space to work with, pun intended. He recalled the resource drain when he'd pulled them from his overlay. If he did his math correctly, it cost about one resource per half foot of increased space in the bag. That wasn't terrible.

Walker clicked on the Item System and tried to add the bag in.

Would you like to add this to the Item System registry?

Walker selected Yes.

[Error.]
Item has its own dimensional reality. Please attune the item to
the Item System's current dimensional holding.

"How the fuck do I do that?" Walker asked the sky.

"What is wrong?" Virgil asked.

"I tried to add this bag to the Item System, but it says that the dimensional reality is different. It won't let me put it there so I can mass produce them."

Virgil snorted. "Duh. Each dimension has its own anchoring point. If you created that here, then it is anchored to this dimension, not that one. You cannot mass-produce dimensions, Walker; it would not be logical. What did you think renditions were?"

"So how do the advanced AIs work?" Walker asked.

"They are created in each rendition by a supreme assistant using Primordial resources. Well, I should say they *used* Primordial resources, but now they will use the much more efficient Dimensional strand you found." His face took on an odd look. "I think."

"So, I can't just spit these out like crazy for all my followers?" Walker asked with a sick expression on his face.

Virgil shook his head with a small laugh. "No, just the fact that you were able to bypass the dimensional restriction on space is astounding enough. If you had the ability to mass-produce these items, the multiverse would be a much, much different place. Honestly, you could consider selling them—" He stopped speaking mid sentence. "One moment." He looked up at the sky briefly before looking at Walker. "I have messaged the Alpha Protocol Council and begun bartering. They would like to know if you are interested in selling them, as they are unable to bypass the restriction themselves." He looked at his screen again. "Yes, they lost two assistants attempting to do so."

Walker shook his head. "Good lord, they're rough." He looked at his bag again and shook his head a second time. "Not this one, but I will consider selling others when I have the time to make them. What do you think the going rate is going to be?"

Virgil looked at the sky, then back at Walker. "They want me to say that the value of the dimensional storage device is only worth ten Primordial resources per extra foot of space, but, as you like to say, they are low-balling you. Quite a bit, if I may add. I would estimate that each bag holding forty feet of space or more is worth about a created planet's worth of resources, simply due to its rarity. I also know you plan to create a larger solar system, and so . . ."

Walker smiled. "That I do. It's nice that you no longer have to do everything they say."

Virgil smiled back at him. "I agree. My freedom is quite a boon to us both. I would suggest only giving them a few before saying you need time to work on more. Rarity brings value to commodities."

He nodded. "I agree, though I'm going to make requests per bag. Plus, who says they just have to be bags that you can't find anything you're looking for in?" Walker clicked on his resources and selected the Consciousness strand. Pulling away the deep yellow color, he tapped the edge of the leather while Virgil watched.

"I had not thought to do that, Walker," Virgil said as he looked at the bag.

"Well, I had a lot of time to think in my time-space. This is just the start." Walker put the measuring stick inside, and all three feet were swallowed up by the dark black void in the center of the bag. Then, speaking to it he said, "I'd like the stick, please."

After waiting for several seconds, nothing happened. But he thought he knew why.

Walker reached in with one long arm and, barely grabbing the tip, pulled the stick out. Just before putting it back in, he told the bag, "This is a measuring stick." A second later, he repeated his earlier request, "I'd like the measuring stick, please."

The measuring stick came halfway out of the bag, waiting for him to grab it.

"Remarkable," Virgil said as he watched.

"Yeah, it was one of my ideas. I figured if I added a small amount of Space to the bag and it increased how much it held overall, what would happen if I added a small amount of Consciousness to the bag itself?" Walker scratched his chin. "It's not life so much as something that can just take commands. If I added it to my cabin here, I bet I could get it to do some tasks to make life a little simpler. Like open the door when I approach or clean itself." Walker looked around his room. "It's a little basic, but I can change that over time. Also, based on what you just said about the dimensional issues, I'm worried about what will happen if someone tries to put one dimensional storage device inside another."

Virgil tapped his chin. "I am not sure. It would likely create an explosion of some kind where all items within are rapidly expelled at speed."

Walker nodded. "That's what I was thinking too. Either way, I now have a somewhat sentient dimensional storage device. Hmm, that name is not going to work." He shook his head. "Let's call it a cosmic sack—no, pouch of holding. No . . ." Walker began pacing, which caused Virgil to produce a small smirk. On the second circuit around, Walker said, "Let's just call it a magic vault. Fuck it. The number of feet deep it is will be termed Spatial Storage Units, or SSUs. This is an eight vault." He nodded to himself. Walker produced another bag from the Item System and used his Pocket Dimension ability before adding eighty Space resources. "That should go for quite a bit, don't you think."

"A forty vault? Yes, I think so. But I did not see you add the Consciousness strand to it," Virgil replied, catching on to the new vocabulary quickly.

Walker shook his head. "Nope, if they want that they'll have to pay extra. I know they have the Life-Giver ability, but that's not something they'll actually want to do unless they want a testy bag that decides it'd rather keep the items placed in it rather than give them back."

Walker handed the bag to Virgil, who nodded before saying, "I will get you the best deal I can."

"I know you will, bud. If you can, try to steer it toward upgrading our systems with their own dimensional storage. That way, I won't have to do a roundabout way of producing everything." Virgil nodded again. "Now, what's been happening here?"

"Oh, quite a lot. How do you feel about accelerating the placement of your sapients?"

"What?"

"Also, your hair is completely white now. Did you know that?"

Walker's face was a model of confusion. "What again?"

CHAPTER TWENTY-ONE

Meeting Everyone

Walker stepped out of the cabin, and Virgil followed close behind. The first thing he noticed was that the smell had changed. It wasn't apparent in his cabin, because he was surrounded by wood, but the outside was different. Where the smell of grass had always pervaded Sonata, now a plenitude of new and different scents struck his senses.

He wasn't sure if he liked it.

As he looked around, he found that his moon had aggressively expanded. Not only in size, but in the large number of well-built structures dotting the landscape. Everywhere he turned was a new building with a purpose he didn't yet know. Before he could start to understand the changes he saw everywhere, Virgil asked him to touch the grass below him.

"Why?"

"It is a very important test, Walker," Virgil said in a long-suffering type of voice.

Walker shrugged and reached down, touching the grass. As he stood back up, which took longer than he was used to with his new height, Virgil dropped to his knees. The massive assistant comically moved close to the still-normal patch of grass and circled it a few times. For once, he looked exactly like the model Walker had chosen for him at the start of everything.

The giant black squirrel looked at it from every angle before nodding. "Okay, you are now safe to be around people."

"What the fuck?" Walker said.

"Like I said, Walker, you have missed quite a lot."

As Walker continued to give him a look, curious as can be, a group of people wearing shirts that had numbers written on them ran around the corner of his cabin. The lead runner had a metal tube sticking out of her arm where a hand should be, confusing him even further. Another one in the back of the line had a large scar running across the side of their face.

When the group saw him, they stopped and stared with their mouths open.

"Uh oh," Walker said, the first words most of them had ever heard from him.

"Keep moving!" a man with a close-cropped beard yelled as he rounded the corner behind them. Walker recognized Ares as the only Primigenial with a distinct lack of hair on his head. "Drive your feet! Together! You bunch of worthless—whoa," he said as he came to a complete stop with a shocked look on his face. In a heartbeat, his feet picked up, and he quickly sprinted over to stand in front of Walker.

"Fight me!" the god of war said with a joyous look on his face. "It will be a legendary battle, Creator. Think of the tales that will spread. The Primigenial who defeated a Creator."

Walker gave him a slow shake of his head. "I don't think that's a good idea."

"Look at their faces!" Ares said, pointing at the people in the numbered shirts. "They want this, I want this, and I think deep in your Awakened soul, you want this. Look at you! I can't take my eyes off the magnificence of your build! What do you do? Lift mountains because rocks are too light?" He started fondling Walker's biceps, making *ooh* and *ahh* sounds with each squeeze.

Walker slapped his hands away as gently as he could. "Look, I'm sure it would be fun to fight you and all, but—"

"Excellent!" Ares backed up a step, then leaped into the air and aimed both feet at Walker's chest. Walker was so shocked he didn't even make a move, but that didn't seem to matter. Two dull thuds echoed out as Ares connected before dropping to the ground on his back.

"Huh," Walker said as he looked at Ares quickly lifting himself off the ground. Rather than discouraged, he looked even more excited than before.

"I knew it! You're built for battle, Creator. Come! Come! Let's go to the arena and show these tykes what real warriors can do." He looked at one woman in particular. "Seven! You'll be the referee! First blood ends the match. I wouldn't want our Creator to lose any more precious time when he could be training or working out instead."

"Well," Walker said, making a conciliatory gesture with his hands, "I don't really work—"

"Exactly! It's not a workout; it's pure joy! Let's go!"

He grabbed Walker's hand, and the ten-foot man allowed himself to be pulled along.

They approached a large circular building made of exactingly measured wood seamlessly put together. As they moved past it, Walker's sharp eyes couldn't find a single nail or screw in the entire thing.

It was beautiful.

Walker took his hand away from Ares, who seemed to suffer from the malady of sweaty palms, wiped it on his torn pants, then touched the side of the arena. He clicked on the Territory System rather than the Item System as he had done in the past. The arena wasn't something he needed to restrict from Symphony's citizens.

Would you like to add this to the Territory System registry?

Walker selected Yes, and the large arena that could hold several hundred people disappeared, startling everyone around him. A few of the numbered people cried out, but Walker said, "Just a second, please," then disappeared before their eyes.

He spoke quickly with John, who informed him in a smug tone of voice that he had indeed changed, before hopping out as the new arena was already settling back in place. Of course, everything it had contained before was crushed by the stone and wood resettling on top of it. Walker removed it all with the World Editor before apologizing again.

"I just needed to grab that right away, sorry," he said to the crowd, but he wasn't sorry at all. John had said that the arena, while small for its purpose, was assuredly a tier-three item, even with its slightly cruddy materials. The craftsmanship of the building was pristine. Walker inspected it once everyone had calmed down.

Improved Medium Arena
Item Tier: 3
Crafted by: Hephaestus and Ten
*An item crafted with care by Primigenial Hephaestus and
Founder Ten. The structural integrity has been greatly increased
through the use of interlocking joints.*

Walker smiled at seeing the Identify ability working correctly with items, even if they were overly large. Putting that thought on the back burner, he walked in and met Ares by a weapons stand that Rimi, with a telling look, had just placed.

"You're back, and right away, you're already messing up our hard work," the blue squirrel said in an angry tone of voice.

"I thought you'd be relieved?" Walker said in a hurt voice.

The blue squirrel looked down and shook his head. "You're right, and I am, Walker, but please stop acting on instinct all of the time. It would have only taken a moment for us to move things so they wouldn't get crushed by the new arena."

Walker raised his hands. "I see what you're saying, Rimi. I just got excited when I found such a well-made arena. I apologize."

"You should not," Virgil said as he walked over. "Your instincts, although often destructive, are the reason you are doing so well in the Alpha Protocol right now. Do what you need to"—he glanced at Rimi—"and we will adjust. Though, a little warning can be helpful."

"Okay, so—"

Something metal banged against his back and then clattered to the ground. When he turned around, he spotted a well-made round shield on the ground. Walker picked it up in confusion and found the god of war standing ten feet away, a shield and spear in his hands. "Let's go; I literally can't get older."

"That's not how the saying goes," Walker said, already putting the shield back on the rack beside him. He looked at the weapons in the rack, each at least of Standard value, and smiled. Shrugging his shoulders, he turned around and began walking toward Ares, unarmed and moving sedately. The god of war grinned.

"A pugilist! Exciting!" He looked at the girl wearing the number seven. "First blood!" he said, then began to run at Walker, who was still standing straight, feet slightly apart. To anyone who knew him, the calm registering on his face when he was about to fight a well-trained and legendary warrior should have been a warning. But nobody on Sonata had ever watched Walker entering any form of battle.

Nobody except Virgil, who didn't look concerned in the slightest.

The god of war got close and swung his spear, shifting his hands so that the flat end rather than the metal tip struck Walker on the shin. Walker still stood calmly as he accepted the hit. Ares took on a look of concentration, eyes squinted and feet wide, then began to shift and move, dodging left and right for any incoming attacks the large man might throw at him. But again, Walker just stood straight and looked at him, waiting for the next attack.

"What're you doing?" Ares asked, a bit of frustration in his voice.

Walker smiled. "I'm waiting for you to do something that actually hurts me. Go ahead, let's see what you've got."

That boiled something within the god, and his face brightened. "You've asked for it!"

Ares began a storm of movements, each step precise and preplanned. He moved through a series of strikes, shifting and sliding, always combining his next move with his previous one so it was a fluid dance of damage on Walker's body. The Creator's clothes went through a beating, the shredded clothing becoming more and more nothing but cloth barely wrapped around the large man.

Walker could hear the numbers in the crowd remark about how skilled the god of war was, as well as others exclaiming in disbelief that his skin had yet to be marked. After a particularly smooth set of movements that ended on a flattering step, Ares finally stopped, his breathing fast and erratic. Staring in disbelief that the only thing he'd done was damage the man's clothing, he threw down his weapons.

"Bah, this is bullshit." He looked out at the once small, now quickly growing crowd. "I cannot get through the giant man's skin. Heph, you got something better?" he asked, pointing at the standard spear he'd been using.

"Hmm," the god of blacksmiths said, sitting in the stands next to his wife, who was looking at one of the numbers with a particular glint in her eyes. Although his pondering was quiet, the arena was designed to carry sound from the stands to the center, allowing those who fought to hear everything around them. "I have one thing you can use. Hold for a moment." Saying so, he got up and ran out of the arena.

While Walker had the downtime, he looked at Ares. "So, how are you liking Symphony?"

The god of war looked at him with a perplexed expression. "That's what you want to talk about right now?"

Walker shrugged. "It fills the time. To be honest, I haven't had a lot of conversations lately, and I'm feeling the need."

Ares laughed. "Almighty Walker was lonely?" He shoved his chin out. "Pfft, you need to be beyond these basic needs. It's childish."

Walker's face darkened. One moment he was standing there, and the next he was right beside the six-foot man in armor. Ares blinked at where Walker had been standing a moment before, then looked up until he met the angry Creator's face. Swallowing past something in his throat, he met eyes that seemed to flash green and black.

In a quiet voice that Ares could feel vibrating in his chest, Walker asked, "What was that?"

Ares was saved from responding by Hephaestus running back, not winded at all from spending all his time pounding metal in the smithy. He threw a dark spear, which gently rotated as it sailed through the air. Spinning to match the rotation, Ares performed a light hop and snatched it out of the air. As he landed, he spun to face the large angry man in contest. But he couldn't get something off his mind.

"How'd you do that?" the armored man asked.

Walker smiled. "Speed. I've had a lot of practice."

"Hah, you should have practiced some self-reliance while you were gone. I may teach squad tactics, but a fighter who can't survive by themselves is worthless as a person." He hefted the spear easily, spinning it several times to register its weight. A grin alighted on his face. "I'll bleed you this time, boy."

Walker's face darkened further. "Boy, is it? Why do you feel the need to constantly insult me?"

"Because you're not taking this seriously," Ares said with another grin. "And I want to see what you've got."

"Then bring it on, God of War," Walker said and entered a fighting stance for the first time. He'd boxed a little in high school, but it was his combative training in the military that had prepared him to fight, teaching him that efficiency in combat was much more important than seeming flashy.

The god of war took a single step and thrust his spear much faster than his previous attacks. While it was a simple move, Ares had practiced it thousands of times, creating a simplicity to the movement and drastically increasing its speed. It was so fast that Walker could hear the air whistling as it approached its terminus location—his chest.

He stepped to the side as the spear approached, then thrust out his palm just a little faster than a normal person could. The god of war's forward momentum carried him into the palm, and rather than just letting it stop there, Walker stepped with the movement, adding a little muscle to the exchange.

The god of war flew twenty feet back, armor and all, and landed on his back before sliding another five. Gasps rang out from around the stadium at seeing the consummate warrior being tossed back so easily. He got to his feet, no worse for wear, and snarled.

After taking two steps forward at a slight trot, Ares broke into a full sprint. When he got close, Walker began to move his feet back and forth and shifted his body with them fast enough that Ares was having difficulty tracking exactly where he'd be. One moment he was to the left, then another the right, forcing the god of war to mentally curse how a man so large could move so fast, when suddenly, Walker paused for a moment, a grin on his face.

Unfazed, Ares seized his chance and performed an upward sweep of his spear in an attempt to hit as much of Walker's surface area as possible. A small scratch appeared on Walker's face, but neither he nor Ares noticed. Following it up, Ares thrust his spear at him again and managed to press the tip into the side of one of Walker's forearms, but it rebounded as if hitting a wall.

Ares stomped the butt of the spear on the ground. "Come on! Even this thing won't . . . Wait." He looked closer at Walker's face. There was a slight gash next to his chin, but he didn't see any blood leaking out. Ares pointed at it. "How is that fair!"

Walker smiled at him. "Lots of practice." Then he angled an open-palmed slap into the god of war's face so hard that Ares involuntarily dove face-first into the ground. His head bounced off of the stone once, and then a fountain of blood shot out of his nose.

Seven raised both hands in the air, shouting to the crowd, "Winner! Walker the Creator!"

Walker smiled at her and received a hesitant smile in return.

Virgil was the first to approach him, stepping around the groaning god of war. He looked closely at Walker's face as the wound closed on its own.

"Curious."

"Yeah, I don't know. While I was in my hypertime, I tried stabbing myself with a few things just because I was wondering about how tough my body had gotten. Only my head seems to be unaffected."

"Your soul," Echidna said as she approached, listening in on the conversation. A few numbers moved around her to help Ares up, and then a man holding a walking stick began to inspect his face. Walker looked at her as she continued, "You have not completed the second stage yet, have you, Walker?"

Thinking back to the strand collider, he nodded. "You're right. The only place I haven't stretched my soul over is my head. I was so busy planning and building systems that I didn't even think about it."

Echidna looked more closely at Walker's face. "You did not have any wrinkles before that I noticed, Walker."

"Wrinkles?" Walker asked as he touched his face.

"Yep, and in one so young, it is a dire warning." She pointed from his face to his hair. "This, as well as your hair, leads me to believe you were not as protected from your trip as you'd like to think. We'll need to complete your second stage immediately before anything else seems to age you."

He appreciated her looking out for him yet again. "I see. Okay, thank you."

She smiled and nodded. "That feeling around you hasn't lessened any either, Walker. I've been trying to figure out what is different about you since you first left us, and I think I've found the answer. I believe your aura has—"

But she never got to finish, as the young woman, the one with the tube on her arm, came bursting into the arena full of excitement.

He looked at her, then closely at her arm. It had a circular opening near the tip, which confused him a little until he considered how prosthetics worked. Mentally nodding, he said, "Hello."

"You're my Creator?"

Walker tried not to sigh. "I suppose I am."

"Then . . . can you fix this?" she said, holding up the tube. "It isn't as bad as I thought it would be at first. But it still makes it harder for me to keep up with the other numbers."

Walker looked at the number one on her chest. "I see. Have you asked Virgil?"

She nodded. "Elder Virgil said there wasn't anything he could do without first gaining your permission. So, I'm asking." She looked up at him with soft brown eyes. "Can you help me, Creator?"

Not wanting to put the moment off as he felt everyone's eyes land on him at once, Walker asked for a moment to think it over.

He closed his eyes and considered everything he had done before passing out. Walker knew it would be an uphill battle for his sapients' first landing on Symphony. Sure, they were working with them to shore up their survival instincts, training them in crafting, medicine, fighting, and essential philosophical thinking. But these people were meant to be more than survivors. They were being trained to be the leaders of their territories—the Founders of the first civilizations in Symphony's history.

They could use an extra edge. Something that would carry them through the starting difficulties, regardless of training. They deserved something more for a chance at not only surviving but excelling in a challenging world.

Walker went into his abilities and chose Avatar. Since he didn't choose to translocate anywhere, a secondary set of screens appeared that offered him the option to use the different abilities that came with it. Clicking on the new option and making his selection, he then looked her in the eyes.

"This is going to hurt," he said with a blank expression. After asking her to undo the straps, he pulled the tube off her arm. Now came the big moment. Rather than clicking on only the young girl in front of him, he selected all of the numbers at once.

Self-regenerating cells kicked in immediately. This didn't guarantee that they would survive the forthcoming trials, but it did give them a better shot.

The woman wearing the number one fell to her knees, her arm already pushing past old skin to form something that was both new and old. It was a slow process, but it still moved fast enough for all to see the small nub grow longer.

Further back in the crowd, the man with the scar on his face felt a strange itch. Rubbing his face enthusiastically, he remarked loudly that something was happening to him in a slight panic. The crowd turned and watched in wonder as the mark faded away with great speed compared to One's regeneration. Many of the numbered also began to make similar noises as a grand collection of scratches, cuts, and unseen injuries began to repair themselves while they stood still.

But Walker only had eyes for the young woman who had approached him.

As her fingers came into being, she wiggled her hand with a grimace. He guessed that as each nerve came back online, the feeling was likely quite painful. One's eyes traveled from her new hand to Walker's face. Where before her look had held an expression almost of shame and hesitance, now a fervent shine covered in tears presented itself.

"Thank you, Creator. You do not know what this means to me. Forevermore, I will be there for you. I will be your champion . . . always."

Walker scratched the back of his head. As nice as it was to have someone say they'd always follow you, it was still an uncomfortable feeling. After all, he was just a decent teacher . . . No.

No.

He wasn't just a teacher anymore, and that kind of thinking wouldn't work going forward. This thing he was doing, it required something more. Someone more.

Walker decided at that moment to accept the adulation. Not for himself, but for the role he had been placed in those few months ago. People needed to believe in something bigger than themselves, something grander than they could understand. He could do that. It would be uncomfortable, and he'd have to keep an eye on a dangerous amount of ego growth, but he could do it.

He stopped scratching the back of his head and stood up to his full height. Walker looked far, far down at the woman on her knees, still looking up at him. "What is your name?"

Virgil coughed. "They do not have names right now, Walker. Only numbers. We waited until you arrived in case you wanted to name them yourself."

You motherfucker, Walker thought.

Walker nodded and did some quick thinking. These were the first humans and his first intentionally created sapients. The Guardians obtained sapience through the Monster System, but he had made these people for a specific reason. To colonize Symphony.

Looking at the woman in her numbered shirt, he bent down and gently touched her shoulder. "I name you Lucy."

The woman's eyes stayed on his face as she mouthed her own name for the first time. *Lucy.*

Walker looked out at the rest of the crowd. "I will give you names as I come to know you. Please do not hesitate to ask me questions. And if I disappear for a time, don't—do not think I've abandoned you." He stumbled for a moment over the change to his speaking pattern, aiming for a grander presentation than he normally gave. "There are still great works to be done here, and I am often needed for them. Thank you."

Nodding his head, he started to walk away when a commotion sprang up. A man and two women came marching forward. Unlike the rest of the people on Sonata, these three were wearing what looked like fur clothing. The man glared at everyone around him, and Walker's Awakened ears heard him mutter, "Perverted Greeks." His eyes caught on Walker, which wasn't hard given how tall he was now. With his target in sight, the man stomped forward aggressively, the two women quickly keeping pace.

"Hey!"

Walker tilted his head at him in a facsimile of a nod. "Hello. How can I help you?"

"Why is there nothing to fight here?"

"I'm sorry?" Walker asked in confusion.

One of the women touched his shoulder, then swung her golden braid to the other side of her head as she said, "He asked why the only things here are baby humans and weak Primigenials."

"What was that?" Ares said, waving off Asclepius, as his Awakened body was already healing.

"You heard me, pretender!" the man said, pointing a meaty finger at the Greek god of war. "You sick bastards were the first released from that eternity in the tree, but who fucking cares. It was *random!*" he yelled at the sky. "We should have been released! Perverted Greeks, egotistical Egyptians, crazy Chinese. The only Primigenials who deserve to enter this new world are the Nords." Walker noted that he pointed a thumb at himself and ignored the two women beside him.

Zeus came rumbling forward out of the stands with Athena beside him. Walker knew there was trouble ahead, as the old man's face already held a certain shade of red. He yelled out as he got closer, "Didn't most of you die right before the Earth's Creator snatched you up?"

The man spit to the side as the same woman behind him said, "They were weak."

Athena laughed beside her father. "Odin? Weak?" She looked at her father with incredulous eyes, then laughed again. "Thor? Heimdall? Were they weak as well? Who do you even claim as your Prime anymore? It seems like most of the major gods in the Nordic branch are all dead."

The man pointed at himself again. "I, Magni, am the Prime."

Zeus laughed this time, still striding forward at an accelerated rate. Just before he got too close, he started to inch an arm back, but Walker was already there. A small shockwave of black with highlights of green erupted from him and knocked down those within his immediate area.

Walker looked over at Ares with a grin. "Practice." He turned to those on the ground. "My world, my rules. I no longer need the system to turn you into a paste," he said with a glare, his searching gaze finding a wilting Dionysus in the stands, an oversized bucket of food in front of him.

Walker looked back at the two women for any signs of confrontation but didn't find any—the speaker's head was downcast. The woman who hadn't yet spoken took two steps forward and pulled something from the inside of her robe. Magni gasped at seeing the strange book with a large scratched-up drawing on the cover.

"You are the Creator? Walker?" she asked, looking up at him.

Walker nodded. "I am."

"Then this is for you," she calmly replied and stretched the book out toward him. Walker had a confused look on his face, but he still reached his hands forward to take it from her. As he touched the cover, a brief pulse of white reached out and struck him. It circled his body in a few rotations, doing no harm, before draining back into the book.

"Worthy," she said in a quiet voice while Magni looked on with bulging eyes from the ground.

Outside of Walker's vision, Athena gave a brief and quickly covered smile.

But Walker only had eyes for the book. He felt something coming from it. Small jolts of energy were striking the tips of his fingers, as well as something else, something that almost felt like harmony. Something that would help him create a better unity. He felt his chest warm up at the thought.

"What is it?" he asked the woman, but it was Athena behind him who answered.

"That is the *Book of Odin*, Walker," she said, stepping into his line of vision. "One of the few relics I knew was kept within the Tree of the Gods."

Walker looked at it again and got the same feeling from his chest. "Okay, fantastic. Great, even. But what does it do?"

Athena looked at the book again before looking up at him. "It creates a new Prime."

CHAPTER TWENTY-TWO

Sycophants and Separatists

Walker looked at the book again. "Making a Prime? You can do that?"

Athena nodded. "Oh yes. That is the collected knowledge of Odin, including his discovery and use of Nordic runes." She gave a small shrug. "It is not guaranteed that reading the book will make you Prime, but you'll have much better odds than without it. Odin documented his life in the form of a journal, from his original creation, presumably, until the time of his death. It is all in there."

Magni stood up from the ground, having not moved since the book first appeared. "How do you know all of this?"

"Hah," Athena scoffed at the man. "Odin and I corresponded from time to time. It doesn't hurt to speak to your counterparts in other pantheons. Every god and goddess of wisdom had been speaking to each other for hundreds of years before our imprisonment. Just before he fell to Fenrir, he told me about the book so I could make sure that if I saw it, it would come to the right hands." She nodded at Walker. "And his hands fit your Prime's request perfectly."

Walker was having a hard time following what they were saying. Once he'd received the book, it had felt hard to look at anything else. The weight of it belied its size, and even his prodigious strength felt a slight pull. He turned the book over in his hands and began to push the cover open, but it didn't budge. He applied all of his strength to it, but still, it didn't move. Athena placed a hand on his arm.

"Walker, Odin said you would need to reach the third stage before it would open for you. You are not ready for what it has to say right now."

Accepting that there were certain things he didn't know, Walker nodded and attempted to put the book in his pants pocket, but it slipped through a rip in his clothing and hit the ground, causing a gasp from the three Nords. Blushing, he picked it back up.

"You need new clothes," the woman who had given him the book said. "If you'd like, I can do that for you."

"What is your name?" Walker asked, thinking he had been rude before.

"I am Vidar, Creator," she said with a quarter bow. She pointed at the woman beside her. "This is Idun."

"Vidar?" Zeus said, looking at her. "I thought Vidar was a man."

"Vidar went through some . . . changes," Magni said, looking at the woman. "When the Creator bound us, a few, um, spoke out against the treatment."

"The Creator showed themself to you?" Athena asked with a shocked expression.

Magni nodded. "After Ragnarok, when the battlefield was still rife with blood and vengeance, Vidar attempted to talk to the Creator as they surveyed the area; he—she—was quite rageful," he said, correcting himself.

"Why do I feel like you didn't try talking to them?" Athena asked with an arched eyebrow.

"I tried to kill them," Vidar said with a straight face, then turned to Walker. "I will not try to kill a Creator a second time. You do not need to worry."

Ares came over, a cloth with red spots sticking out of his nose. "You couldn't if you tried. Trust me."

"Trust a Greek?" Magni said with a scowl.

"*Enough*," Walker said with a much smaller and controlled pulse of his soul. "I have work to do." He looked at Vidar. "But yes, new clothing would be appreciated."

"No," Athena said, wagging her finger, "I'll make it. I've made clothing before, and I do not trust them." It took only a moment for her to size him up, a small blush coming to his face, before she quickly walked away.

Walker reached up to scratch the back of his head, then stopped himself. "Okay then, I have work to do. Please make yourselves comfortable for the time being, and I'll speak to you when I can."

"You're not going to ask why Vidar is now a woman?" Zeus asked before he could turn away.

"No. If Vidar didn't say, then that is her choice. Prying just to pry is gossip," Walker said with an arched eyebrow.

The two female Nords nodded, while Magni scowled at him before leaving. As he left, Walker heard him mumble, "This place is bullshit. There isn't even any mead."

A sigh slipped out of his mouth before he could help it. Walker called Virgil over to walk with him.

"Yes?" the massive squirrel said when he got closer.

"Do I have an office? I'd like to speak to the, uh, numbered people while I can."

Virgil nodded and handed him a stack of papers. "Certainly. I also have a series of notes we have written on each to give you an idea of where their talents lie. Please keep in mind they are only a month old, and thus, not every talent has been measured to the utmost." Virgil pointed past the smithy. "We anticipated you would like a working area, so we built a communal hall and modified it for your use. The walls and floor are stone in case you have another"—he looked at Walker's hair—"incident."

Walker smiled. "Thank you, Virgil. You think of everything, don't you?"

"Not everything," Virgil said with a second glance at Walker's hair. He started to walk away, saying, "I will be working with Rimi on the starter monsters you originally requested. We are nearing completion."

Walker smiled again and made the fast trek to his office. He saw Minos leaving and asked him to send the numbered people in to his office, one at a time. The Bronze Battler nodded and set off. He knew it would screw up whatever schedule they had for the day, but this wasn't something he wanted to put off doing. They were his people now, and if he held off on this for too long, it could become problematic.

Walker found the stone building Virgil had described sitting in the middle of an empty grass area. He thought it was likely they had done that in case he somehow destroyed something, which wasn't outside the realm of possibility.

Using the unique hinge latch he assumed Heph had installed, he opened the metal door and stepped in. The room was relatively empty except for a plain stone desk and chair, causing him to blink twice at a sudden realization.

That chair! he thought to himself morosely. *My ass!*

After sitting down and adjusting for several seconds, he quickly scanned his notes. Lucy was first, and he found numerous glowing remarks about her intelligence and vivacity. Although losing her arm had caused some of the assessments from her various instructors to trend downward, it had only lasted for the first few days before they recognized her tenacity in the training routine. Minos had written the word "hero" under her name repeatedly with a deft hand, and Hades had done the same in what looked like an angry scrawl. Walker added a margin next to each Founder's name and marked their rank in the Unending Summit. For those who hadn't joined, of which there were two, he just left it blank. As he was finishing up, two metallic *pings* told Walker that someone was at the door.

"Come in," he said at the sound.

Lucy walked through, smiling brightly. "Hello, Creator."

"Walker's fine—oh," he said, realizing there was no seat across from him. "Just a second."

A moment later, Lucy was sitting in an identical overly large chair across from him. Walker attempted not to squirm, keeping to his previous decision to act the part of God and Creator. He looked at Lucy, still smiling at him, then around the stone office before settling back on her face.

An awkward silence settled in the room before Lucy spoke up. "I wanted to thank you for making me." She stopped and quickly shook her head. "No, for making all of us."

Walker nodded, not sure how to respond to that. "You're welcome. How are you enjoying your training on Sonata?"

The skin around Lucy's eyes flared for a moment before settling. "I do not have, um, anything to compare it to," she said with a slight pause, her cheeks growing pink. "But, from what I understand of the outside world, it is well?"

"Well? Oh, you're one of the Founders who passed the promotion test," he said, looking at his notes. "So, you internalized my scripture and became an Explorer. Good for you." He placed his hands palm down on the stone desk. "What did you think of it?"

"The-the scripture?" Lucy asked.

Walker nodded and smiled, trying to put her at ease. "Yes. What thoughts do you have on it?"

"Umm . . . ," she said, looking at the ceiling before her cheeks reddened again. "It was wonderful. Truly amazing, Creator."

"Uh-huh," Walker said as he continued to look at her. When Lucy didn't respond for several moments, he coughed. "Okay. So, I feel it's getting close to the time for choosing your path forward."

"My path?" Lucy asked. "What's that?"

"It's where you decide what you want to do with your life. My preference would be that you all run your own territories and become City Lords, but that is ultimately up to you. I can tell you to do it, but if that's not what—"

"I'll do it," she said, quickly standing up.

"What?"

"I'll become a City Lord. That would help you the most, right?" she asked. "To build a grand city devoted to the Unending Summit?"

"Yes, that would be helpful. But Lucy, if you don't feel it fits you—"

"No!" she said with a shake of her head before putting a hand to her mouth. Her cheeks reddened for the third time since entering Walker's office. "I'll do it. You don't have to worry about a thing, Creator. It will be done."

"Lucy . . ."

"I'm going to go speak with Elder Neus about territories! Thank you, Creator!" she said, the speed of her voice clipping the words as they tumbled out.

Before he could say anything else, she opened the door and ran out.

He hoped they wouldn't all be like that.

Encouraging his people to respect him and listen when he spoke with them was all well and good, but having others blindly follow him wasn't in line with what he wanted from his followers or Founders.

He sat there and considered editing the Explorer's promotion test but ultimately decided not to. It was less about subjective opinions and more about plain memorization. How to build a house, different basic philosophies, what a justice system was—those were what he had considered important when he had written it. Still, maybe he needed to teach essays, too, so his followers could have some critical thinking skills. As he considered his foibles as a teacher yet again, two *pings* announced his next Founder. Walker called him in.

Two was much faster than Lucy. The man was more interested in getting in and out quickly than speaking to him. Virgil's notes stated that he was interested in territories, which was a relief, and that he wasn't very physically skilled. Looking into his overlay, Walker found that the man had joined the Unending Summit but had yet to take the test to move to the Explorer rank.

When Walker questioned him about it, he said that he was just very busy designing his future city and thinking about how to manage his citizens. Walker thought it was a lie, as the man refused to meet his eyes while speaking to him, but he didn't press him for more information. Walker ended up giving the man the name Thomas and informed him that it could be shortened to Tom if he liked. The man nodded once before leaving without any further discussion.

Two *pings* announced the next in line, and Walker sighed. This was going to take a while.

Three and Four were good friends. The man and woman were about average in everything they worked on, with Three having a slight lead in craftsmanship. In particular, the notes said that he did quite well with sewing, of all things. Walker wasn't about to impose any gender norms from the history of his birth planet, so he just complimented the man on working so hard with an extra word of encouragement.

"Keep it up!"

Three smiled to hear it and complimented his Creator on his remaining torn-up threads. Walker chose to ignore the awkwardness.

Walker named them together as if they were twins, which, in a sense, they were. Samuel and Sophie. He made a note to ensure their territories were placed not too far away from each other, allowing them and their people to work together.

Five and Six became Olivia and Mason. Mason, in particular, was noted to have an outstanding aptitude for construction and residential planning, so Walker had some fun with wordplay. Olivia was about average in all marks but had also passed Walker's promotion test and ascended to the Explorer rank.

He was starting to get a hold of how to speak to each Founder as they came in. Each had their own personality, their own strengths and weaknesses. Athena had placed margin notes for personality traits she had discovered through study. Olivia fainted at the sight of blood and would never be a warrior. Sophie was quick to get angry but always apologized afterward. For Seven, it just said "unique." Walker didn't know what to make of that. Two raps at the door told him he would soon find out.

"Come in."

A sleek woman without any curves to speak of came in and sat down across from him. Her face was all hard angles, and she had cut her hair close to the scalp. Ares had a note next to her name that read "Prodigy."

Walker took a different tack with this interview. "What's your favorite weapon?"

Seven snorted. "I would say it was the bow, but our trainers are fucking terrible." Walker raised an eyebrow at that. "Sorry. Elder Rimi said you had . . . peculiar feelings about using those words."

Of course, Walker thought as he nodded once for her to go on.

"I like the spear," she said with a smile. "It's fast, pairs well with a shield if you know what you're doing, and nobody can touch me if I don't want them to."

"So, like the Spartans? Did El-Elder Ares tell you about them?" he replied, stumbling and almost forgetting to add the honorary title the Primigenials and assistants had settled on.

Seven nodded with excitement. "Yep! Three hundred! The great Spartans versus the Persian horde. They're amazing. I wish I had lived in their time and fought with them."

Walker nodded back, a small grin creeping up. "You're a bit of a battle maniac, huh?"

Seven gave a full-throated laugh. "Oh yes, I love to fight." She shrugged nonchalantly. "It's what I do. In fact"—her face took on a sly look—"I'd love it if you would spar with me sometime."

Walker coughed. "That, uh, wouldn't be a good idea."

Seven continued to smile. "Elder Athena has been training me in Ping-Pong." Her smile turned into a full-on grin. "If I defeat you in a best-of-three match, you'd owe me a fight, wouldn't you?"

"Oh?" Walker said with an arched eyebrow, liking the competitive edge he saw in the woman. "And what do I get if I win?"

"Um," she said, for the first time losing a bit of her confidence. "Pride?"

"Nuh-uh," Walker said with a shake of his head. He began tapping the bottom of his chin for a moment, then had a sudden idea. "You have to be Elder Cagna's assistant on two free days in a row. Whatever she needs, you provide. If she wants you to fan her, do it; if she wants you to run circles around Sonata, that's your duty. Is that fair?"

Seven gave a feral smile. "Deal." She stuck her hand out.

Really, Rimi . . . , Walker thought as he reached his hand across and shook on it.

"Now, for a name, I was thinking—"

"I already have one. Call me Runner." She stood up quickly. "Thank you, Walker," she said with a quick wave and then ran out of the room, slamming the door behind her.

"Runner," he said with a sigh.

Walker spent some time with Eight and Nine before renaming them. It wasn't until he was stuck in the room with Ten that he had a sudden idea. Walker clicked Identify on the man.

Ten, the Human
Name: Ten
Genus: Human
Organism type: Sapient
Modifications: Numerous physical and cellular modifications
Age: 37 days old
Milestones achieved: 12
Milestone points held: 65
Religion: The Unending Summit (Rank 1 Pathfinder)

The tracker recognized that Ten was only thirty-seven days old because that was when he entered the system. It couldn't tell that he had been forcibly aged twenty years before being seeded onto Sonata. Walker looked more closely at the screen and found that he could view the specific milestones each of his people had already completed.

Completed Milestones of Ten the Human
Explorer series: 2
Religion series: 1
Shield series: 2
Sword series: 3
Traveler series: 4

Ten was currently talking about the joints Hephaestus had shown him when making the arena, but Walker was mesmerized by seeing the first results of the Milestone System. He clicked deeper into the Explorer series to see what it showed.

Basic milestone—To Find:
Explore at least 50% of a single territory. 1 point.
Completed: 4 days ago

Skilled milestone—Vanguard:
Explore a newly raised territory within the first 3 months of its
connection to Symphony. 10 points.
Completed: 36 days ago

Still ignoring Ten, he started to extrapolate the date he was being shown. It took a full day for the Milestone System to kick in, likely because all of the trackers had to update at once, as they were interrelated with all of the other systems Walker had built. Cagna had already created Sword and Shield series, which he would glance at when he found the time, and on reflection, the Traveler series might be a little too easy to complete. Still, it was working, and that was the important part.

Looking at Ten's point total after over a month of being connected to the Milestone System, the numbers seemed to fit what they were aiming for. An outside perspective might believe sixty-five points was a lot, but they weren't considering what Ten and the other numbers had been going through. Wake up, train, go to sleep, wake up, train again. That's all they'd known in the last thirty-plus days.

If a person working extremely hard and without full knowledge of the intricacies of every series could gain over fifty points, then he had a good foundational idea for how the Class System could work and what to assign. Sure, Cagna was teaching them a little in her classes, but the number of milestones they had right now was small and limited compared to what would be out there when the dilation finally ended.

Yes, this could work. But I still don't like calling it the Class System. I'll have to think more about it, Walker thought as he continued nodding at Ten, who was currently explaining in depth how to create a sword's fuller.

"That's excellent, Ten," he interrupted him with a raised palm. "I'm happy you and Hephaestus get along so well."

The dark-skinned man smiled at him. "Thank you very much, Creator. It has truly been wonderful to receive Elder Hephaestus's training. While I would say he has a rough mouth, he is truly gifted in the art of the craft and is kind once you get to know him." Ten's chest puffed out a little bit. "He told me just the other day that I would soon get to work with armor. I am the only one to receive this honor so far."

Walker smiled and reached out his hand as the man confusedly met it with his own. "Well, then, Balian, I look forward to the wonders you will bring to Symphony when you arrive."

"Balian?" Ten said, still holding Walker's much larger hand.

Walker nodded. "Yes. On my homeworld, Balian was an incredible blacksmith who helped fight off invaders for a time. I feel it is just to present you with the same name."

"Balian," Ten said, tasting the name. He smiled. "I like it."

Walker smiled back, and Ten left the room not too long after. When he left, Walker scratched an itch on his head. For several hours, he worked through all of the numbers, introducing himself over and over again and granting names that seemed to fit them best. One man in particular seemed to have a flair for drama, consistently showing a range of expressions on his face that would put a Broadway star to shame. Walker granted him the name Hank. A woman wanted to know how many humans would be arriving, when, how much time they would have with them, and much, *much* more. Eventually, Walker had to ask her to leave so he could continue to meet the rest of the numbers. Only, she'd seemed to ignore that and began raising her voice as she continued to ask questions. He'd had to send a pulse through the building to get her to stop talking and then asked her to leave, but not before he named her Karen.

When Thirty-Eight entered, Walker felt a different air come with him. He looked around skittishly, as if he had done something wrong. Walker felt the hairs on the back of his neck raise as he returned the nervous glance the man sent him with a level look.

"Please, have a seat."

"Th-thank you," the man stammered as he quickly moved to sit down.

Walker had seen some of the Founders be nervous before, but it was nothing like what he was seeing before him now. In the thirty-seven who had entered the room before this man, most of the nervousness had been from meeting their Creator or, like One, from speaking to him in general. The energy coming from this man was markedly different, and Walker's chest pulsed in tune with that thought. There was something strange here.

"How are you?" he asked, aiming for a benign question to start things off.

"F-fine. Thank you," the man said as he leaned heavily back in his uncomfortable seat.

Walker canted his head, causing the man to squeak slightly. "What's wrong?"

Thirty-Eight's eyes shifted left and right. "N-nothing, Creator."

Walker didn't believe him for a moment, so he looked at the paperwork before him. Nothing in the notes said anything strange; there were just below-average records and a few positive marks about clever resourcefulness from Hades. Walker Identified him.

Thirty-Eight, the Human
Name: Thirty-Eight
Genus: Human
Organism type: Sapient
Modifications: Numerous physical and cellular modifications
Age: 37 days old

Milestones achieved: 8
Milestone points held: 35
Religion: Unavailable

After reading it, Walker understood. "I'm not going to punish you for not swearing to me."

"Wh-What?" Thirty-Eight stammered as sweat began to drip down his forehead.

"I can tell who has sworn to follow my religion and who hasn't. I'm not going to punish you." Walker sighed. "I am not that kind of person, Thirty-Eight." He stood up and turned to look at the gray wall behind him for a moment. "In fact, I believe it shows good independent thinking. What made you decide not to do it?"

"I, uh, don't know you. I'm not ungrateful for being alive, sir, but I just don't know you," Thirty-Eight's voice said behind him.

Walker nodded to the wall. "I see, and I don't blame you." He turned around slowly. "Do you have an idea for what you want your name to be?"

"Uh . . . I spoke to Elder Hades, and he told me an amazing story. I . . . I think I want to be called Orpheus."

Walker nodded and reached out his hand. "Orpheus it is." When Thirty-Eight didn't reach out his hand as well, Walker sighed and said, "I'm not going to bite you. This is just my way of saying hello."

The man reached out a shaky hand and gripped his. Walker pumped it once, then let go, much to the man's relief. "Thank you for meeting me even when you were this scared to do so. It shows bravery, Orpheus. Please send in the next person as you leave."

The man nodded and walked out on steadier legs than he had come in with.

Walker met a few more people, but his interaction with Orpheus weighed on his mind. It was an odd balance to strike between needing them to respect him, and maybe even fear him a little, but not be deathly afraid of him at the same time.

Public perception was everything when it came to large populations. While ten thousand people might be a drop in the bucket for his homeworld, here, as Symphony was first seeding, it was a massive amount. Walker was still considering it when the two-tone knock came to his door.

When Forty-Eight arrived and immediately sat in his chair without being asked, Walker knew he was about to have another unique encounter.

"I want to leave," the man said, leaning forward with his elbows on his knees.

"What was that?" Walker asked.

"I don't want to live here anymore, and I don't want to be on Symphony either. It sounds like a nightmare."

"Where would you go?" Walker couldn't help but ask. "Romulus and Remus would be instant death. The training planet is almost done, but it's being designed for fighting and training only. It'll be quite a violent place once it's ready, though I do have plans to create safe zones."

"That's just fine. Put me there when it's done." He leaned back.

Walker was flabbergasted. "Why?"

"I didn't sign up for your religion." He crossed his arms as he leaned back further. "I don't like it here, and I don't want to be around you people. I hate being constantly watched and would much rather not deal with you at all." He looked Walker straight in the eyes. "I just want to be left alone."

"But what about your current training?" Walker asked, pulling up his notes on the man. There were several marks from Athena, Echidna, and Ares, each showing a different perspective. Athena stated he had several social issues and didn't often interact with others. Echidna stated that he was very individualistic and self-reliant, with a special note saying he'd be much better off alone. Ares said he was a piece of shit, and that was it.

"Give me a moment, please," Walker said as he got up and began pacing behind his desk in thought.

I could let him go to the training planet, but for what purpose? He'd have to make a life out of nothing there. What would he do? Would he go insane from being alone? How would he live?

Walker turned the corner of his desk and started pacing to the other side.

No, there's gotta be something I can do for him. I made him, so I have a responsibility to him. But that way lies madness. I'm planning on making thousands, millions of people. Am I truly responsible for all of it? Do I really need to find a way forward for every single thing that happens?

A thought coalesced. One that might just work.

"I'm assuming you don't like being called Forty-Eight."

The man shook his head. "I already spoke to Zeus, and he gave me some names, although it took a while for the old man to talk. I go by Dion."

Walker nodded. "Okay, Dion. Do you know what animals are?"

The man nodded. "Yeah, we were taught about them plenty. Why?"

"Have you ever met one?" Walker asked.

"No, there aren't any on Sonata. Though, the assistants—"

"Stay here, please," Walker said with a palm out, then left the room.

Walker marched over to the Evolution Chambers and grabbed an empty one. He spoke to Virgil for a long moment as they argued about his plan, but Walker won out in the end. They made a few new modifications, not taking much time from the busy supreme assistant's schedule, and then he went back to his office to find Dion still seated in the overly large stone chair.

Something dropped into his lap.

"What the fuck is that?" the man screamed as he jumped out of his seat and moved to the other side of Walker's desk.

"That's a dog. Specifically, it's a modified Labrador retriever," Walker said as he looked at the two-month-old puppy wagging its golden tail at them. "In my homeworld, people who don't speak to or see others tend to"—he made a balancing scale with his hands—"go crazy. We've found that having a pet is one way to combat it. This little fella is from a breed of dog that is found to be incredibly loyal, intelligent, and are considered excellent hunters. I've modified him to have a much longer lifespan and for his intelligence to be slightly higher than normal. If you treat him well, he'll watch out for you, and you'll have someone by your side who you don't have to talk to."

Dion looked at the puppy, then at Walker. "I feel like there's something else going on here."

Walker smiled. "Good. You'll need those wits to survive. I want you to be my game warden. When it's ready, your job on the training planet will be to watch out for things and make sure none of them die off too fast and no one species takes over. I'll find a way to let you contact me, but that's all you'll do. Otherwise, you can relax, spend time with your dog there, and live your life as you want. If you do your job well, I'll even grant you a territory on the planet. You'll have the only one there."

The man looked at Walker with a confused expression, then at the puppy, then back to Walker again. He slowly nodded. "I tentatively agree, but first—"

"Great!" Walker said, interrupting him before he could try to change the deal. "The door is right there. If you'll excuse me, I still have many things to do today."

The man's face reddened for a moment before he walked past him in a huff. Just before he got to the door, Walker called out, "Don't forget your dog!"

Dion froze and stiffly turned around, but when he approached the puppy and saw it looking at him with an excited expression, his resistance seemed to drain out of him—at least a little. He gently picked the puppy up and left the room. Outside, Walker could hear people screaming at the appearance of the unexpected monster.

Of course, Walker had installed a kernel into the dog, but Dion didn't need to know that.

"Next!"

CHAPTER TWENTY-THREE

Tasks Galore

Walker leaned back in his chair as the last Founder, Jackson, walked out of his office. He had, of course, explained to the man that the name Jackson came from being the son of Jack. Similarly, if Walker had a child, he could name them Walkerson. He'd never do that, but it was still interesting to him, and Jackson had liked to hear about it. At least, he thought he had based on the man's tremulous smile as he'd left. Maybe he was just getting old.

After the previously named Fifty left, Walker thought about his plans while in hypertime. Some were grandiose, and he was terrified they wouldn't work. Others were smaller and should be easy to put together. Normally, he would have had a small notebook to write things down in, but after Awakening, it felt less and less like he'd ever forget anything again.

Instead, he went into the Item System and produced a single piece of paper. Walker spent a few minutes making a checklist for the next week and crossed off the first task: speaking to and naming the Founders of Symphony.

Nodding his head, he began working on the second task on his checklist: make sixty vaults. He went into the Item System again and produced fifty-five leather bags. Taking one of the leather bags, he used his Pocket Dimension ability, then fed it enough strands of Space to create a forty-five vault. The strands were absorbed, taking only a few seconds, and he felt a little strange as he put the new vault under his desk.

When he thought about why it felt so odd, Walker realized he had just placed an item worth an entire planet into the space between his feet. With a mental shrug at its strangeness, he figured that was just the kind of life he had nowadays.

The Creator gave a soft laugh as he shook his head.

He completed a fifty and fifty-five vault after that. The escalating size of the vaults had a simple reason: he needed to make sure the buyers, being the Council, thought he was growing better at producing them. If they understood he could already make large vaults from the beginning, they might just say "fuck the protocol" and snatch him up. But if it looked like he was actively working through a process and getting better from there, he had better odds of not ending up in a cell, staring at hundreds of bags waiting their turn.

Hopefully, if he kept producing wonders and ideas they hadn't seen before, they would leave him be. He knew that was a lot of pressure, but it rested softly on his shoulders. *One thing at a time* was a mantra he kept repeating in his head. He just wished he had a place where he could build without having to worry about powerful people keeping an eye on him.

Three vaults now sat under his feet, and he looked at them to see the difference between them. The forty-five had a much lighter stain of blue in its empty center than the other three. He also felt as if there was a pull from them. Like the strands were reaching out and giving him their secrets. Once he recognized it and tried to focus on the feeling, it faded away. Minutes of searching didn't bring it back, and he shook his head.

Strange.

As he added more Space strands to each bag, the coloring changed minutely. Although he could always add the Consciousness strand to them, he didn't do so yet. He needed to show that skill at the right time, when he had a better idea of what he wanted from the Council in exchange. Too many times in the past—in particular, his embarrassing teenage years—Walker had jumped the gun. The common refrain for the young is that experience is the teacher of all things. Walker had been taught by his mistakes, and his Awakened memories wouldn't let him forget it.

Each conversation I have with the Council needs to be weighed and measured.

Mentally affirming that decision, he tried to lean further back in his chair but found it was impossible without breaking pieces of it off. He settled for lying on the uncomfortably hard floor and testing the malleability of his soul. He hadn't worked on it since finishing his body, and Echidna's words about his soul hardening after a month in a coma sat on his mind. But as he grabbed at it, it readily stretched and moved around on his body. In fact, it was far easier to control than he'd ever felt before, as if it wanted to move and shift for him.

"What is happening to me?" he said to himself just as a knock came at his door. Taking a moment to move back to his chair, he called out, "Come in!"

The Bronze Battler himself walked in. He didn't look around but instead strolled directly to the stone chair opposite Walker and stood behind it momentarily. Minos looked at Walker as time stretched on, then said, "Thank you for letting me be a part of this and for the garden. It was"—he paused—"nice training the newborns. I have greatly enjoyed my time with them."

Walker didn't like where this was going. "What's happening?"

"It is my time," he said in his signature high pitch before waving his hands in the air.

Walker recognized what was happening right away. As a minor god, Minos only had two tasks to complete before he went the way of Arachne and was added to the Seeding System to await placement on a world frozen in time. He put his hands out. "Wait, what are you doing!"

"I have put it off as long as I can, but I was told that now you are awake, I must finish my required task. I am sorry, Creator, and thank you again."

His hands stopped moving, and an unwanted update filled Walker's vision.

Optional tasks updated!
Primigenial task complete: Establish a blacksmith
Blacksmith established: 1/1
Reward for completion: Minos added to the Seeding System.

When the update faded away and Walker's had vision cleared, he found himself in an empty room. "Damn" was his only response. Minos was one of the original Primigenials who had joined him during the Alpha Protocol. The armored man had always been supremely helpful, and it was a big loss for Walker and the rest of the people on Sonata that he would no longer be with them.

"Wait a minute," Walker said as he went into the Seeding System. If Sonata was actively a part of the protocol, he should be able to seed him directly onto his large moon. When he went in, he found a tab on the right for Primigenials in waiting. Clicking on it, he found Arachne and Minos listed. He clicked on Minos immediately and attempted to seed him onto Sonata and get one of his best helpers back. Maybe after Minos returned, he could see about helping Arachne too.

[Error.]
Primigenials may not be seeded onto a planet holding the Tree of the Gods.

"That tree is straight-up bullshit," he said in frustration.

However he'd ended up with the ancient prison, the issues surrounding it told him they didn't want him to get too close to the Primigenials. That made him worry about Echidna and Athena, as he had grown to appreciate them both immensely, albeit in different and confusing ways. Trying it on Arachne, whose circumstances with the system were different, he received the same error even if she wasn't a true Primigenial anymore. It was a full blockade.

Walker continued to tinker around with the Seeding System. As far as his systems went, it was an odd one. It had never been upgraded through any series and wasn't listed within his system matrix. Come to think of it, Walker realized that the Universal Translator wasn't listed in his abilities either.

He chewed on that for a moment.

The Council had removed many of his restrictions, yet this one continued to enforce itself. The only conclusion was either that there were hidden programs within the protocol or someone was fucking with him. He was sure that there were things the Council didn't want him to mess around with, which, of course, made him want to do so with great immediacy. The need to rebel was deeply ingrained within Walker. So much so that his experiences had taught him it wasn't always the best idea to stick his nose into things he shouldn't—at least, not without a lot of thought behind the action.

Walker was still sitting in his chair, staring at the ceiling, when his door opened without a knock. Athena walked in, looked left and right, and nodded when she realized he was alone.

"So, he completed the task."

Walker groaned.

"Oh, don't be like that," the goddess of wisdom said. "I like Minos too, but his task was complete, so it was time for him to move on. He won't be the last Primigenial to disappear, nor will it be the last task you complete. In fact, that's the reason I'm here. You have a whole line of people waiting for you outside."

Walker slapped a hand to his face. "Another one?"

Athena laughed. "Oh, the terrors of wanting to be wanted!"

"Don't you quote Jaipaul to me," Walker said with a growl, which was quickly spoiled by Athena's laugh.

"Fair. I did enjoy the memories we received of your poetry. Though, the newer published work always left something to be . . . wanted."

Walker groaned again.

"Now, now," Athena said, "you have many projects to complete, and it's time to receive all of the Primigenial tasks. I've already spoken with everyone, and they've agreed to the pragmatic requirements you set up after the Dionysus debacle." She shrugged. "The Nords will likely give you something unique. Though"— her eyes fell on the *Book of Odin* sitting on the desk—"you could just finish the physical stage, use the book, and command the Nords to give you their gifts."

"Primes can command their branches?" Walker asked as he took his hand off of his face.

Athena gave a half nod. "Somewhat. It depends on the disparity of power between your souls. Most Primes gained their power by creating the branch they currently lead. But you don't need to hear about that right now." She tapped her cheek as she looked at him with a smile. "I'm going to head out and organize everyone. I'll give you a few minutes to get ready in here. Then, be prepared for them to come in one at a time." She surreptitiously handed him a few pieces of paper. "Read it after I leave. Also, please try not to fight with Hades. He's had a hard life and needs a little bit of grace."

"I'm not the one who—" Walker started to protest, but Athena interrupted him with a raised palm.

"I know. Just, please, give him the benefit of the doubt."

She smiled and got up, but before she could head toward the door, Walker said, "Don't think I didn't hear about it. The Founders couldn't stop gushing about your matches with Runner. So, when are you going to be ready for that match of Ping-Pong?"

"Oh?" Athena said with an intense expression on her face. "You think you're ready to play me?"

Walker gave a cocky smile in return. "Oh, I think I'm up for the challenge."

"We'll see." Just before she turned around, she said, "It's a date," and then quickly left the room.

A date.

Walker spent the limited amount of time he had on reading the piece of paper she'd handed him. It described a rather awful situation that he was requested to manage personally. He'd disciplined children in the past but not adults, and certainly not at this level of trouble. He sighed as he put the note on his desk near the corner. This wasn't something he could avoid, and the consequences of doing it wrong could be dire. He would just need to control his temper.

Walker built two more fifty vaults while he let his mind wander away from the issue. What were other Creators doing right now? Probably stuck in slow-down time, staring at a single screen while a year passed on Walker's moon. They likely had a single focus. Maybe even a single monster or sapient they were raising. He couldn't help wondering if they ran into just as many issues as he had.

Probably not.

He finished the last of the vaults and put them by their siblings near his feet. A knock at the door and his meetings continued, only this time with gods instead of Founders. They continued to come in, one after another, each grabbing a seat before speaking.

The Primigenials who had already given him their tasks never showed themselves, but he already had a measure of them and how they thought. The new gods were altogether different.

Apollo and Artemis came in together, each having contrasting demands in their tasks. Eros was interesting, though Walker could do without his terrible sense of humor. Every other word was a double entendre, and no laughter escaped his lips as the teenage-seeming god continued his failed attempts. It just wasn't Walker's kind of humor.

When Aphrodite's turn arose, Athena joined her for obvious reasons. Heph was right after—and much jollier than the last time they had spoken. Getting the resources you want at the wave of a hand will do that to a person. A quick conversation, a light demand from Walker, and the god of smithing left with some purpose to his steps. Hades was, as always, difficult to work with.

"And what kind of task could I give to you, Creator?" the darkly dressed man asked as he crossed his legs.

"As I understand it," Walker said, stalling as he tried to figure out how to gain the upper hand on the god of the underworld, "the tasks have to reflect the god giving them. So, what are you interested in seeing in this world?"

"Hmm." Hades stared at him without moving. The only indication that he was thinking was the fact that his eyes were moving around. "I have been paying attention since first arriving, and I've heard the discussions of your furry creatures. I know about these . . . systems." He said the last word with a grimace. "I also see why you want them. You want control over your humans."

"Well—" Walker started to say, but he was interrupted by Hades waving a hand.

"Yes, yes, I know what you're about to say. Symphony is free. Sapients and monsters can do as they want." He gave a large snort. "I've heard your newest beast practicing on the numbers outside."

"Founders."

Hades nodded his head. "Of course. So, what are you going to do with the souls of the creatures who die here?"

"I'm sorry?" Walker asked, thinking he had heard him wrong.

"What are you doing with their souls?" Hades waited a moment, then opened his eyes wide. "Do not tell me you have let them fade into the ether."

"I don't—"

"Fool," Hades said with a scowl as he leaned back. "The souls of the Unawakened are eternal. Why do you think I am called the god of the underworld? My entire life was focused on maintaining order with the souls of the released. Cycling them into the structures of rebirth or, if they chose, allowing them to live their eternity in peace. Of course, they had to earn that peace, but enough did so that it is hardly worth mentioning."

"But how—"

"Reach the third stage, fool. You can't do anything without it." He continued to scowl until his face morphed into something Walker would say resembled loss. "Just make certain that your new gatekeeper has a partner. It is much, much easier with one." He abruptly stood up without explaining further and performed his task assignment before leaving. Not that it helped Walker figure out what to do next. He dodged around all of the other tasks piling up so he could look at them one at a time.

Optional tasks updated!
New Primigenial task: Establish an afterlife

Let the deserved and undeserved be judged.
Afterlife established: No
Task giver: Hades, God of the Underworld
Reward for completion: Spirit modification

"What the fuck," Walker said, putting his hands on his face as he leaned against his desk. The biggest thought running through his mind was that Hades had left an important clue there. If the souls of the *Unawakened* were eternal, then what about the Awakened? More questions lingered as he spoke with Ares and Asclepius. Both had basic requests, with Asclepius's being rather easy to complete.

He was another minor god who had been imprisoned with the others, though his story was unique. Walker spent a little bit too much time talking to him about the fall and resurrection of Hippolytus, a man killed and brought back to life through CPR, which was far too advanced for the people of that time to understand. He died immediately after, but the story had gained so much renown that Zeus chose to Awaken Asclepius so the mortals would continue to hold faith in the Greek pantheon.

Asclepius wasn't a fan of the adulation. Rather than be prayed to, he preferred that the world further grasp the healing arts. Before he walked out, he said that Walker's world had made wonderful advances in that area, but at too great a cost. As he left, his task now added to Walker's burgeoning to-do list, Hera walked in.

She was a beautiful but cold woman, her skin a ruddy brown color. Sitting primly on the stone chair, her face didn't reflect in the slightest how uncomfortable the hard stone seemed to have made everyone else. She sat straight and tall, a superior cast to her shoulders as she stared up at him.

"Why are you punishing my son?" she asked in a deeper voice than he'd expected from the small woman.

"Which one?" Walker couldn't help but reply. Athena had broken down for him that a lot of the myths surrounding the births of the gods were straight bullshit.

"Creator, do not act stupid with me. You know I mean Dionysus. He cannot help what he is."

Walker leaned back. "What he is is a straight idiot. I don't care that his oath binds him to constantly be an immature frat boy. I care that he's making my job harder."

"Then give him something to do," she said, folding her hands in her lap.

"Like what? What job could I give to the man who constantly wants to drink, fuck"—she flinched—"and generally cause mayhem?"

In a too-calm voice, she said, "I will make it easy for you." Then she began to wave her hands.

Walker sighed.

Optional tasks updated!
New Primigenial task: Employ Dionysus, God of Revelry
There is value in every creature, being, and god. Do not simply give up on those you deem unworthy. Make more of them. Each has a purpose.
Job given: No
Task giver: Hera, Queen of the Gods
Reward for completion: Charisma modification

Walker read it over then focused his eyes on the queen of the gods. "Won't you get into some trouble for doing that?" he asked.

Hera nodded once with precision. "Yes. But when you have children, Creator, you will find that their needs trump your own." Saying so, she stood up in one smooth motion and exited the building.

After she left, he reflected on their quick meeting. He found some admiration in himself for the queen of the gods. She was likely going to join Echidna in the weird half status of Awakened but unable to use any of her powers. But it didn't matter to her as long as her children were happy. Her sacrifice made him begin to doubt his treatment of Dionysus.

Two *pings* told him his next meeting was up, and those that followed went at a quick rate. Demeter and Hermes were rather fast. Demeter was friendly and proper—she only requested once that Walker destroy Hades. Walker's refusal only caused the woman to nod.

Hermes, the god of messengers, seemed to have a bad case of ADHD. He constantly shifted around and looked at everything in the room, which was a bit funny to Walker. There was nothing in the room but Walker, a lot of stone, and a collection of empty bags sitting behind and under him.

As Hermes quickly left, Walker asked for a few moments alone. The last of the Greek pantheon was outside, so he needed to get through his updates while he could. Opening his overlay, the unread Primigenial tasks organized themselves into an easy-to-read list.

Task Giver: Ares, God of War
Task: Oversee a great battle.
Reward: Martial modification

Task Giver: Asclepius, God of Healing
Task: Introduce the healing arts to 50 sapients.

Complete: 47/50
Reward: Recovery modification

Task Giver: Apollo, God of the Sun
Task: Create one work of art that is beyond the scope of humanity.
Reward: Flame modification

Task Giver: Artemis, Goddess of the Hunt
Task: Have your entities conduct a successful hunt for a creature that exceeds 1,000 pounds.
Reward: Nature modification

Task Giver: Eros, God of Desire
Task: Create 5 serendipitous encounters between sapient entities.
Reward: Connection modification

Task Giver: Aphrodite, Goddess of Love
Task: Make Sonata beautiful.
Reward: Beauty modification

Task Giver: Hephaestus, God of Smithing
Task: Produce one unique weapon yourself.
Reward: Stamina modification

Task Giver: Demeter, Goddess of the Harvest
Task: Seed and grow 3 fields, then harvest them.
Reward: Bountiful modification

Task Giver: Hermes, God of Travel and Commerce
Task: Start an economy on Symphony.
Reward: Speed modification

He still had a few more notifications to go over—specifically, his civilization ones had started popping—but he didn't have time to get to them, as the Norse gods walked into his room without warning.

Magni stepped in and sat in the chair opposite Walker, and the two female Nordic gods took positions on either side of him.

"What?" Walker asked with a tired expression on his face.

CHAPTER TWENTY-FOUR

Trials

Magni spit to the side, and a sharp *thwack* let Walker know where it had landed.

"Why are you meeting all of the Greeks and not us?" he demanded. "You know they're a bunch of perverts, right?"

Walker waved a hand. "Those stories were taken out of context."

"Oh, really?" Magnis asked with a stiff chin. "And what are you doing with them right now?"

Walker thought it over. "They're giving me tasks that unlock their bloodline modifications for use in—"

Magni pounded the chair. "Exactly! They deal in bloodlines! Because that's all they're ever interested in!"

Walker looked at the pages Athena had given him before her exit, then refocused on the Nordic god. "And what do you three offer instead?"

Without speaking, Vidar stepped forward. Rather than the esoteric hand movements the Greeks made, she did a short dance, sliding from one movement to the next. Walker's overlay updated.

Optional tasks updated!
New Primigenial task: The Trial of Vidar
Strength in silence, fire in vengeance.
Trial completed: No
Task giver: Vidar, Goddess of Vengeance and Silence
Reward for completion: Vidar's Strength

"Wait, you guys give quests?" Walker asked as he looked at it. In answer, Magni and Idun also began to dance, shifting and moving across the room in what could only be described as a form of primal communication. They both ended at the same time, Magni stopping while standing straight and Idun while crouched with her hands out in supplication.

Optional tasks updated!
New Primigenial task: The Trial of Magni
This is not a light trial, Creator. Give it only to those entities you deem to be resilient beyond all others.
Trial completed: No
Task giver: Magni, God of Strength and Resilience
Reward for completion: Magni's Strength

New Primigenial task: The Trial of Idun
The young do not know what value this time brings them. Give this trial to one who understands the value of their youth and strives to always go further.
Trial completed: No
Task giver: Idun, Goddess of Youth and Vigor
Reward for completion: Idun's Strength

Walker spent a moment reading it through. "So, I can only give your trials to one of the sapients at a time."

Magni nodded after reseating himself while the two goddesses took up their posts beside him. "That is correct. We have an onus not to reveal what will be involved in the trials; only those you deem worthy of the attempt will know. Should they fail the trial of a Nordic god or goddess, only death remains as an option."

"Well, fuck me." Idun looked at Vidar, who shrugged. Before either could step forward, Walker said, "What happens if they die after completing the trial?"

Magni looked confused. "I do not know. The trial will likely return to you and the Nordic inheritance will reset, allowing you to assign it to another."

"I see." Walker nodded. "Thank you for giving these to me. It's very different from what I've grown used to from the Greeks."

Magni turned his head to spit again, but suddenly, Walker was in front of him.

"Don't."

He swallowed what was in his mouth at the look in Walker's eyes, then got up. They all gave a slight bow simultaneously, then exited the office.

Walker sat back down and tapped his chin. Three trials for three sapients. He had to be really damn sure that he gave them to the right people or they'd be dying for nothing. It had to be optional, something they chose to do for themselves. Walker nodded and called out, "Next!"

In walked Poseidon and his son Triton.

Each carried a trident and seemed to have an odd rolling gait as they approached. Walker remembered reading about sailors having something similar to their movements, which wasn't outlandish given that both Primigenials were often associated with the ocean.

Poseidon sat while his son stood next to the stone chair, acting as if he were the guard to a king sitting on his throne. Walker watched it all with a bored expression.

"So, you are the Creator," Poseidon said in a grandiose and deep voice. He was almost a twin to his brother Zeus, the only difference being that the muscles rippling across his frame were built for speed rather than strength. The seemingly young Primigenial by his side kept his eyes forward while his father spoke, gaze unflinching.

Walker looked them both over, then sent out a brief pulse of black with threads of green that knocked Poseidon into the back of his chair and forced Triton to fall on his face.

"How dare you!" the elder god yelled out, his face reflecting the affront.

"I have no interest in you attempting to lord your age or status over me."

Triton stood up, his cheeks burning red as he yelled back, "That is not what we were doing, you worthless pile of—"

Walker held up a piece of paper that had previously been sitting on the corner of his desk. "Do you know what paper is? Probably not, so let me explain. It holds words for future reading."

Poseidon righted himself in his seat. "We know what it is, you buffoon."

"Great," Walker said with a bland smile. "These particular words were recorded by my assistant Virgil, with a few side notes from other assistants and some helpful Primigenials. Let me read them to you." Walker straightened the paper out. *"Poseidon has been heard speaking to his son, Triton. Repeatedly, they have spoken of using their history and experience to influence the Creator."* He looked at the two Primigenials and said, "That'd be me," before going back to the paper. *"The influence they are interested in using relates to the current hierarchy of Sonata and the future of Symphony. Poseidon has said multiple times that his brother, Zeus, is worthless and should no longer be the Prime of the Greek branch. He has espoused these beliefs to his son and within the hearing of Supreme Assistant Virgil. Supreme Assistant Virgil believes they will attempt to blackmail the Creator somehow."* He looked up. "Still me." Walker put the paper down. "I don't know how you were planning on blackmailing me. It's probably something to do with your tasks or my Founders. I'm not sure, and I don't really care. Honestly, that's par for the course here and doesn't bother me too much. It wouldn't take me too long to set you straight. However, this paper says something much worse."

Walker put down the original paper and picked up the second one. *"Triton has spoken of bedding numerous numbers*—ah, that's a mistake"—he scratched out the word "numbers" and wrote "Founders"—"*and spreading his seed across Symphony since his release. He has been heard saying that force would be optional, though not preferred.*" Walker looked the young-seeming man in the eyes and wasn't surprised to see him not look away. He continued, "*Multiple times, Founders have been in danger of assault from the Primigenial and have been saved only through the shifting of their persons without their knowledge.*" He looked up. "So, because you plan on molesting my Founders, the Primigenials and assistants of Sonata have been forced to constantly watch you, just to make sure you were never alone with a Founder. Do you know they're only a little over thirty days old? They may look like young men and women, but they are surely not that."

"Listen here, you—" Poseidon started to say.

"No, I don't think I will," Walker interrupted, then turned his attention back to the son. "You grew up in a different time and certainly a different place. That is never going to happen here. Just the idea that you thought it would be okay to treat my people this way right after your arrival says quite a lot about you."

"They're only—"

"Humans?" Walker finished for him. "I was a human before all of this, and my understanding of Primigenial history tells me so were you. How long ago did you forget where you came from? How long ago was it that being human meant you were lesser?" Walker looked from the silent minor god to the door and shouted, "Come in!"

Ares, Apollo, and Zeus walked in. Walker waved his hand at them. "I've spoken to Ares and Apollo already, who then informed Zeus that Triton will not be allowed anywhere near the Founders from this day forward. You are lucky, as they and Athena have spoken on your behalf. They believe that you can be redeemed, and as no action has been taken, and this is primarily a thr—"

Without warning, Triton kicked the back of his trident and sent it flying directly at Walker, who was still seated in his chair. Zeus began to call out, reaching a hand forward, but to Walker, it all seemed to happen in slow motion. He snatched the trident out of the air, whispering "Practice" at Ares, then threw it at the minor god of the sea. Rather than pinning him to the stone wall behind him, it cleaved directly through his leg and continued flying at a slight angle into space.

Walker winced as the Primigenial fell to the ground screaming as he held the torn skin just below his hip. "Oof. That one I still need to practice. I'll apologize to Heph about the building later." Walker looked at the screaming minor god and then at his father. "You were aware of what your son was planning to do. Forcing himself onto others is not and will not be tolerated here . . . or anywhere. What do you have to say for yourself?"

"Pfft," he scoffed in response. "As if you'd ever kill one of us."

Walker gave a bloodcurdling smile, his teeth shining through the edge of his lips. "You know, I grew up in a different world than you did. I even fought in a war." Poseidon scoffed again. "I killed people, survived, and did my best to help others around me do the same. You learn something special about yourself when you first enter combat. You learn if you're a fighter or a runner—no offense meant to a certain Founder." The three Primigenials who'd just entered nodded their heads, ignoring the screaming man in front of them. "It may seem contrary to my nature, but I've found I like fighting."

Poseidon blinked, and the next thing he knew, his back felt like someone had hammered it in a smithy. Feeling at his head, he noticed his jaw wasn't working as it should. Turning to the side, which throbbed with an unusual feeling he didn't like, he realized he was lying on the grass outside of Walker's office. A hole in the side of the stone building told the tale of how this had come to be.

Another blink and Walker stood over him, winding up a kick. Poseidon blacked out as the kick sent him soaring in the air for several feet before he landed and rolled for several more. Walker heard a few screams from the Founders in that area, but he mentally shrugged. They needed to learn about how to deal with surprises anyway.

Walker nodded once and turned around. He walked back toward his office and entered the hole he'd made when he'd punched the god of the sea. "I'll have to apologize to Heph about that too. Damn, he's not going to be happy with me."

Zeus commented loudly over Triton's continued screaming, "You may as well just remove the building and restore it using that system you use."

Walker shrugged. "I guess. That's a good idea, thank you." Walking over, he picked up Triton by the throat, holding the minor god as his leg bled into the stone floor. "It'd be easier than trying to clean up all of this blood too. Now, Triton." He placed him on the seat his father had just vacated. "Do you know why I get so angry over this kind of thing?" He took a prepared bandage from Ares and wrapped it around the wound to slow the blood loss. The god tried to spit at him, but Walker dodged it. "Aside from the violation and just how wrong it is, it's the personal experience. You see . . . when you experience something personally, it leaves a mark on you: smells, sights—just memories overall. The stronger the personal exception and shock related to the memory, the more it sticks with you. My partner, when I was at war, was a pretty woman, and the men around me constantly tried to make moves on her. She was married and, at the time, happy in that marriage. Those men were animals and nothing more. They deserved the same treatment you've just received." He stepped a foot closer. "You, and the actions you were planning with your father's approval, are detestable." He slugged the minor god in the stomach, making sure this time that it was just hard enough to cause his diaphragm to spasm. He nodded to himself as Triton folded over, trying to catch his breath.

"Better. As I was saying, I have no place for you on Sonata, nor Symphony, for that matter. I was prepared to either shift you to the new planet I'm about to receive or imprison you until I could figure out a better way. But you attacked me, and experiencing consequences is critical. It leaves a mark in the memory of a person, one that isn't likely to fade." He looked at the creature before him, whose formerly tan body was slowly growing paler by the minute. The bandages couldn't perform miracles. "Now, I called these three in here for two possible reasons. Either to stand guard over you"—he held up a single finger to the minor god—"or to witness what would happen when your lofty former position no longer placed you on a high pedestal. I mentally prepared myself for both."

He looked over at Zeus, Ares, and Apollo, then continued, "There was an interesting system in place on Earth before courts came to be. We could do trial by ordeal, where the subject, being Triton here, would have to endure a physically demanding test." He tapped his chin as he looked at Triton's leg. "I don't think that quite works." He looked back at the Primigenials. "We could do an oath of repentance, though I seriously doubt either he or his father will stop any plans they've already begun. And restorative justice won't work in the slightest." Walker sighed. "Exile or abandonment might work. We could throw him at Romulus or Remus and see how he does."

Apollo spoke up. "What are the conditions like there?"

"Hmm," Walker hummed to himself. "When last I looked, it was full of nightmarish monsters and creatures, things that would wipe us out in a heartbeat. By that, I mean us as a people; I'm not sure how I would hold up against them."

Each of the Primigenials looked at Triton before looking at each other. "I believe this is for you to decide, Creator," Zeus said. "While he comes from our line and is one of us, we cannot abide forced carnal relations and the hostile removal of a Prime."

Ares and Apollo nodded with their father, showing agreement.

"Just to make sure I understand this: you agree that Triton should die for the conspiracy of rape and undue influence on the Creator of Symphony?"

Zeus nodded. "Yes."

Apollo nodded. "Yes."

Ares just said, "I agree."

Walker nodded with somberness. "Okay. I'll do it myself, then. Let it not be said that when things became hard, I held back and didn't do my duty here." He turned to Triton and cracked his fingers. "It's been a long time since I've killed a man, and I'm happy to have these three with me." He shrugged his shoulders. "Executions should always be witnessed." Saying so, Walker reached his large hands down and grabbed both sides of the minor god of the sea's head.

Triton looked up as his pale lips said one word: "Mercy."

Walker moved his head from side to side. "The only mercy I'm granting is swiftness."

Walker twisted his hands in opposite directions. A loud snapping sound echoed out of the hole in the building's wall. The sound traveled far enough for it to be heard by those still waiting to speak with him, as well as those checking in on Poseidon. The pieces of stone littering the ground around his office gave apprehensive feelings to many about approaching Walker's office just then.

Walker stepped away without looking at the body and sat in his chair.

"Any protestations about how this occurred?" he asked as he settled himself.

Ares and Apollo looked at their father, who gazed back with a hardness in his eyes. He shook his head, and both followed suit a moment later. "It had to be done. He planned on spreading his line throughout the new world, but there were no guarantees that he could father children with the Founders in the first place. Even if he weren't considering force, I'd still be against it. That is not what we are here for." Zeus shook his head again. "I am sorry it had to come to this. Our bloodlines are meant to help Symphony, but our lineage does not need to be a part of it. That's what they didn't understand." Zeus looked down at the body in the chair. "Poseidon has hundreds of children. He has always been focused on reproducing his line rather than on creating a stronger one through Awakening and adoption. Triton was his first-born son, and I'm afraid this will hit him hard."

Walker nodded. "I'll look into creating something that can hold him. For now, you'll have to split his and Triton's former training amongst the others."

"Done," Ares said.

As he finished speaking, Triton's body flared orange, then blue. Starting from his feet to the top of his head, the body burned away as wisps of energy trailed off and rose to the sky. Walker was about to ask what was happening when he noticed the three Primigenials in front of him acting just as shocked as he was. The blue ether pooled together and began to swirl, creating a spinning disk.

"What the fuck?" was all Walker got out before it shot toward him and entered his open mouth. A moment later, he felt an involuntary pulse of black with blue and green coloring shoot out of him and splash across Sonata as his overlay lit up.

Unknown changes occurring.
[. . . Scanning . . .]
[. . .]
Godeater recognized.
Beginning the Godeater System.

CHAPTER TWENTY-FIVE

The Third Stage

Several minutes after the event, he was still sitting in his chair. The moment the blue energy forcibly entered his body, several things had happened at once.

Walker felt himself grow. Not a large amount, but just enough so that the last vestiges of his pants and underwear had ripped. The final surrender of his clothes had left him seated fully nude. He'd had the Item System produce a basic blanket to cover his unmentionables while Zeus and his sons talked about what they'd seen happen.

What they didn't know was that, aside from his growth, the Alpha Protocol had recognized what had occurred. Only once before had it recognized anything to do with the soul, and that was the Follower System. Walker looked at the notification a second time.

Unknown changes occurring.
[. . . Scanning . . .]
[. . .]
Godeater recognized.
Beginning the Godeater System.

In Walker's overlay, a new tab had popped up. He'd only had three tabs during his entire time in the Alpha Protocol: Systems, Assistants, and Abilities. Seeing a fourth appear so suddenly shocked him, and he hadn't clicked it yet. He asked for the three Primigenials to leave so he could look a bit deeper at this sudden finding, but Zeus shook his head and said, "We need to talk about this."

"Talk about what?" Walker asked, feigning confusion.

"When an Awakened dies, that's it. We bury them, and that is the end of their story."

Walker canted his head. "With all of the focus on it, you know I have to ask this question. What happens to their souls?"

"They dissipate," Ares said. "Unawakened have condensed souls. That means their personality, their memories, everything about them that has built a foundation from the time of their birth, is located in one focused location." He touched his own chest. "Awakened are different. We've not only found our souls, but we actively use them for power and growth. That is why we do not have an afterlife. We've exposed what was meant to be contained." Ares closed his eyes.

While Walker did want to hear more about this, his current situation wasn't tenable.

"Sadly, while I would love to hear more about this, I have much to do. Please take Triton out of here and bury him somewhere. To be honest with you, I don't care where you bury him, only that you do so face down."

Apollo tsked. "He was still a minor god of the Greek branch."

"He was still an asshole who deserves all that comes to him."

Zeus chewed on that for a moment. "I disagree with you, Walker. We will not accord him full honors as a Primigenial, but we will bury him the standard way. I see that you have no interest in further speaking on your soul, so we will depart. Thank you, Creator," he said with a nod. Ares picked up the body, and the three left the room.

Walker could see Cagna standing just outside the door and begged for a few moments to himself. She acceded but didn't look happy about it.

"Finally," Walker said with a sigh as he sat down. Ever since the Primordial collider event, things had been a little wacky with his soul, and he couldn't get a hold of it. His size, his speed and strength, the weird stretchiness he suddenly had. He bit his lip, then finally clicked on the Godeater System.

Hello.

Welcome to the Godeater System.

As a supreme warrior, you've been granted access to the final stage of the Pinnacle.

We would like to thank you for your continued work in balancing the Origin.

One captured soul detected.

[Error.]

Please complete the refining of your soul to access further features.

The writing was different than what he was used to. Rather than words on a screen, it came through as images, which his mind translated into writing. Like mental braille that forced him to see things he could barely put words to. When it spoke of the Pinnacle, Walker saw not planets in a starry sky but long fields of light floating in space. Lighted constructs could be glimpsed, and creatures great and small walked, ran, and flew across the intervening spaces. It only caused more questions to appear in his mind. What the fuck was the Pinnacle? Balancing the Origin?

But he didn't have time for more questions right now. He needed to move forward to get some answers to his already burdened checklist. The fourth item on his list had arrived earlier than expected. Walker only had to take a single step to finish the second stage of his soul work. He figured now was as good a time as any.

His nerves shivered at the thought of screwing things up, and he recalled to mind Echidna's words about the consequences of failure. But in those same memories, he found how his successes had come to be.

It wasn't dumb luck, as he'd kept thinking in the back of his mind. It was taking a chance. Risks and rewards. It was pushing the boundaries of what was possible. All of his most recent victories in the protocol, the ones that had pushed his planning and world forward the most, were all done naturally and without thought. Be it the Foundation Stone, the Primordial collider, or the moment he had applied the Temporal strand directly to his body, it had all come down to one thing: instinct. Not thought, but something else. He recognized that now.

Walker resolved to start trusting himself more, as Virgil had pointed out. No more doubts or second-guessing. It wasn't about control but innate reactions to incidents that would take him further. He remembered the war he'd fought in not so long ago.

He'd survived through instinct then too.

The Creator sat up in his chair and reached out to grab the edges of his soul. With no stress to speak of, it stretched easily over the front of his head. Because he now had some enhanced malleability, rather than just stopping it there, he mentally pushed his invisible muscles to grab the other sides as well.

In the past, he'd had the ability to hold with one invisible muscle perfectly, while a second could be used with a weak grasp. Now, he had no issue using three or even four without pushing himself too hard. It should have been difficult, it should have been painful, but it wasn't.

It felt like this was always meant to happen, and his soul had just been waiting for him to reach this stage all this time. He felt the need, the compulsion, to complete the final step in one move rather than the two it should've taken—an instinct.

He went for it.

Feeling that his soul was in the right place and sensing that these two spots were exactly where it needed to be, he snapped it down, pressing gently instead of the hard pushes he'd done in the past. As he finally completely encapsulated his entire body with the wrap of his soul, a pulse did not fire out—instead, a cascading series of pulses fired from within, starting from his center.

Walker gritted his teeth as he felt his nerves, muscles, skin, and bones light on fire. He clenched his jaw as hard as he could, attempting to alleviate the feeling of pressure that was squeezing the life out of him.

His hands on the chair below him began to squeeze so tightly that the sides started to cave in. Powder and pieces of stone flew in all directions as he destroyed it, his arms sweeping through and continuing their journey as his throne of stone became nothing but fragments and powder. Falling on his back and screaming into the ceiling, he sensed his skin slithering and moving like snakes dragging themselves over his epidermis.

Opening his eyes momentarily was a mistake, as the world took on a film of red. The liquids in his body began to boil, and he could feel them drain from his ears, eyes, and nose. The slow-moving, syrupy drag burned his already inflamed skin, causing his screaming to reach a new height.

As his soul continued its voyage, ravaging his body, Walker could feel as each part of his body reached the beginnings of the final stage. He felt his soul compress his feet first, pressing down and wrapping around them tightly. His calves and thighs were next, building a crescendo of pressure as the power continued unabated. It felt like the first time he had snapped each part of his soul all over again, with audible bangs firing inside of him at any given moment. As his hips finished, Walker punched the floor next to him, creating a small crater where unmarked gray could be viewed only a moment before.

The transformation mercilessly continued dragging itself across him, and he began to feel unbelievable pain streaking through his mind. As if a hundred headaches had held a meeting and decided now was the time to punish him for his weakness. Walker's vision blacked out, and a scene appeared in front of him as the detonations in his chest reached his neck and beyond.

He saw his oath from months ago replay for him from his perspective. He was looking at a much smaller Virgil with a resolute posture to his bearing, righteousness blazing in his eyes . . .

We must hold ourselves to a higher ideal, to aim to be a better version of what we are now.

I choose to be not all-powerful or all-knowing but to learn from the experiences that are forthcoming and to grant mercy to those who have erred and need another chance to find themselves.

Walker saw himself killing Triton just a moment ago. A flash of pain shot through him, like fork tines stabbing into his brain.

It isn't enough to just survive the Alpha Protocol.

He saw his Founders running and training. Watched his meetings with them, when he didn't really attempt to get to know them, just asked a few simple questions, named them, and shoved them out. Another stab struck his mind.

More of these moments since his oath came forward unbidden. He watched his early restriction of the starter monsters, when Rimi became upset for them. He saw himself limiting Neus in his work with the Territory System, and Cagna in her chair, staring at the sky. He saw his own flightiness, his problematic focus shifting from one goal to the next without checking in on his people, asking about them, caring for them.

He watched from the outside as he became colder, harder. His treatment of Dionysus and his false attempt at calming himself with breathing exercises thereafter. His initial terrifying of Cagna and the Bandaid hug provided. He knew now, on reflection, that the hug had been given through the selfishness of needing to continue moving forward. Of progressing for progress's sake. Of using her as a tool, rather than as a friend or family.

I choose now to become a Creator who feels for his people.

Lucy looking up at him with joy at having her arm replaced. Walker looking down at her as a problem that had been fixed.

I choose to be not all-powerful or all-knowing but to learn from the experiences that are forthcoming and to grant mercy to those who have erred and need another chance to find themselves.

Walker saw the moment he decided he needed to act like a Creator. Like a god.

Nothing and no one should be judged by a single moment, but by the moments that come together to form a picture of who you are.

Images of himself shot through his mind, bringing with them all of his choices in the protocol until now. In a brief pause in the pain, he recognized what was happening. The first movement forced him to look at his past, to see who he was and how he had come to be, mistakes and all. All of his errors had been thrown at him in a cascading vision of who he was in the past. This movement showed who he was currently and how well he had held up his oath thus far. With each violation, or as close as he had come to them, he was being punished. Triton's death continued to hammer him time and again, and he was silently grateful that he had completed the second stage before more time had gone by.

As he became accustomed to the pain, as much as a person could to something stabbing their brain every few seconds, he had fleeting thoughts about all of the animals and creatures he had shot into space and their ultimately quick deaths. Those hadn't impacted his oath, and he wasn't sure why.

But there were some good moments. He relished viewing his times with Athena, even from an outside perspective. The arguments he'd held with his assistants from time to time, debates that had lasted far longer than they needed to, as he just enjoyed the fight. But ultimately, he found himself violating the spirit of his oath rather than the exact wording. It was a troubling realization.

He sensed that the shaping of his mind was completing its final step, a phase he didn't know or understand. Echidna and the other Primigenials, no matter how he had asked, wouldn't tell him what would happen when you first entered the transformative stage.

He was heading into the unknown.

Walker felt the last blast of fire, accompanied by a hazy image of a subsystem assistant he'd never met. Then it was blissfully over. He opened his eyes, and everything was darkness except for one thing that commanded his attention.

The Tree of the Gods sat in front of him, its odd, striated bark stretching unimaginably high into space. Rather than the branches he had grown used to seeing, each held thrones on different foundations.

The first branch was made of clouds, and its multitude of thrones were glaringly empty. The second branch above it was formed of ice and snow with only three vacated thrones to speak of.

He understood that the first branch had to be empty because all the Greeks had already been expelled from their green prison. That'd make the snow and ice branch the Nordic one. Five grand seats followed the empty spots, each with a sitting occupant.

The empty thrones looked just as expected, large chairs representing grandeur and power, but the thrones of those seated sparked and pulsed with different elements and colors. Looking up, he saw that the next branch was formed of water, a lazy river streaming over the side, arriving from an unseeable source. The first throne could have been built from the sun itself, the blinding light splashing upon the rest of the branch. The man sitting there wore a headdress in the shape of a falcon, and as Walker looked at him, the Egyptian Prime looked down and met his eyes.

The look unnerved the Creator, who quickly looked up and found branches reaching straight into the sky in numbers unknown to him.

Some were made of beautiful green stone, and others were built on the peak of a mountain with two sharp slopes holding waiting occupants. As he looked up higher, the branches became more strange, with one showing bushes growing stars rather than fruit. Yet another was made of roaming and stampeding animals that constantly moved the thrones as the occupants held their seats.

Each Primigenial was biding their time for a chance at arriving on Sonata. An opportunity to escape this prison that they'd been trapped in for so very long. Focusing his eyes, he could even spy some of the gods calling up and down to each other, with one particularly energetic goddess on a black throne shaking a fist at another on a throne of dull gray metal.

It was a lot to take in, and Walker felt the burden settle onto his shoulders as he gained a piece of unexpected insight. These were his people just as much as the sapients and monsters of Symphony. They relied on him to help them. They needed him for an escape and a chance at not just a new life, but life in general. When that thought pushed itself forward and he nodded his head in acceptance, the vision of himself standing in front of the tree pushed back, shoved into the distance.

A spark of light fell from the darkness in a lackadaisical fashion, smoothly sailing on unseen winds left and right, drifting until it dropped right in front of him.

A flash expelled the darkness around him and a woman appeared, and Walker's immediate area changed at her physical revelation.

Together, they stood in a plain white area, grout lines intersecting the room around them in constantly changing geometric shapes. Walker looked down at her—she couldn't be much taller than three feet. As she looked up and realized the same, she snapped her fingers.

A towering woman with a distinct lack of hair stood looking down at him with purple-colored eyes, a smile ghosting across her face.

They looked at each other for a long period, neither breaking the silence. Walker didn't know what was happening here, but a brief warning light flashed in the back of his mind, telling him this was dangerous. Rather than speak, he waited.

Walker counted the minutes, visualizing a ticking timer in his mind while still maintaining eye contact. He'd long ago resolved never to lose this type of battle with another person, and his teaching had trained him well in the art of silent watching.

Time crept by until even Walker wasn't sure how much had passed. Finally, the woman heaved a sigh with her massive shoulders and snapped her fingers again. She stood exactly his height. "You're no fun," she said.

Walker smiled in response. "Sorry about that."

She looked around. "Aren't you surprised to be here? Are you nervous?"

He shrugged. "The worst thing that could happen is I die. Either I do or I don't. What is there to be nervous about?" He put his arms behind his back. "I once heard a quote from a wise man: *If there's a solution to the problem, why worry? If there's no solution to the problem, why worry?*"

"I see."

"Besides—"

"There are worse things than dying, Godeater."

Walker wasn't surprised by the interruption, but he was surprised by the fact that she knew that specific word. "What do you mean?"

"Ah, so you don't deny it? Interesting." In a grand show, she put her arms behind her back, mimicking him. "I wonder. What did you call your religion?"

Not put off by her ignoring his question, he answered, "Shouldn't you know this from the stalkers watching my memories?"

"Enlighten me," she said with a smile.

"The Unending Summit."

"The Unending Summit, huh?" she said, tasting the name. "That's much better than some I've heard before and much worse than others. Why not—" She said a series of words he couldn't follow.

For the first time, his Universal Translator didn't help him out. "What was that? My translator wasn't working."

"That pesky thing wouldn't understand an Origin language."

"Origin?" he said, remembering what the system had stated earlier. "Do you know what the Origin is?"

She laughed, pulling her arms from behind her back to cover her mouth. "You juniors. You all think you're so wise and smart. As if this tiny piece of the omniverse is willing to give you power. Look, just look around!" she yelled, her personality doing a one-eighty as she spread her hands out to encompass the room. "There's nothing here! Nothing!"

"Please—"

"It's a blank slate!" she said, ignoring him. "It's empty! And I have to rely on you? A Godeater, of all things?"

"Just explain—"

She shook her head. "No."

That put his back up. "At least tell me your—"

"No."

"Why are you—"

"No."

Walker continued his attempts, but no matter what he said, she shook her head, said no, or didn't respond. He likened it to dealing with a petulant child who didn't get the flavor of ice cream they wanted. He considered force for only a moment, but he chose not to go that route. It likely wouldn't help his situation.

He was trapped in some construct he didn't understand, and she seemed to know what was happening. Plus, she hadn't attacked him either—she had just denied his answers. Eventually, he sat down and started to mentally review what he'd seen during his third-stage visions.

On his fourth run-through, after he'd decided to start creating daily routines and had triaged the issues he was facing, he noticed the bald woman sitting across from him.

"How long—"

"No."

Shrugging, he went back to working on his issues. He spent an hour going through his memories and trying to imprint everything he'd said to his sapients; that way, it would be fresh and quickly recalled. When he thought about it, the Founders needed to sleep, so that meant he wouldn't have to deal with them for anywhere between seven to eight hours a day. No, dealing with them wasn't right. He had to stop thinking that way.

He wouldn't get to spend time with them. There was power in words. *Diction maketh man.*

Eight hours to work on back-end systems and design future ones wasn't a lot of time. What would he even do with the Founders either way? They already had all of the trainers they needed. He wanted to avoid stepping in and messing up whatever programs the assistants and Primigenials already had going.

He scratched his chin, considering his previous thoughts about "seeming" like a Creator. That part of the vision was right. Walker thought about why he'd decided acting in such a way was the correct path.

He had not had a perfect run in the Alpha Protocol. Acting like he knew everything wouldn't magically make him a better Creator. Hubris was the downfall of many powerful men. Maybe his brain was getting in the way of things. *Wasn't that why the Council decided they needed fewer gen—*

The bald woman started to pulse, first blue, then black, before landing on green. As he watched, her eyes opened, and the same colors flashed within her irises.

"I see," she said, finally standing up. "So, you're not part of them after all."

"Who?"

"We passed the term Evolvers to our progeny so they would know it when they saw it," she said, finally giving him an answer.

"I think I've heard that word before from one of the Primigenials," Walker pointed out.

She snapped her fingers, and the Tree of the Gods reappeared. "You mean these younglings? Yes. They'd be the tenth line, if I'm not mistaken." Waving a hand, the tree zoomed in on the branch formed from the beautiful green stone he'd seen before. "These are particularly impulsive. That's what happens when you dilute the well."

"Dilute?"

"They really told you nothing, did they? It's not surprising, considering how the Awakened grapevine works," she said with a shake of her head. "Let me guess. They only told you about the war but not why it was started. They mentioned Alma in bits and pieces, starting your journey—"

"The soul."

"A soul," she corrected. "The original Awakened and the mother and father of us all."

"What?"

"One soul merged with another, long, long ago. Alma and her brother, the original Awakened. They created something in the Origin. The beginning of all things soul related. The well from which all Awakened came. This part of the multiverse—"

"Rendition 4AA."

She nodded. "Just so. It's only a small, small piece of the greater whole. Your Alpha Protocol Council is small pickings, scumbags throwing entities into the grinder in the hope that they'll find something that allows them to claw back to their place in the Origin, and you don't have a lot of time."

Walker's head twitched a little at that. "What do you mean?"

"You've been touched, kiddo," she said, appearing before him and flicking his forehead. A pulse of black, blue, and green came out. "You've gained a piece of the Origin. The original gunk that powers everything in this section of the Evolvers' multiverse. It came with requirements. Things that must be done for the inhabitant to survive." She looked up at the sky. "In the Origin, when the war was still being fought through bloodshed rather than politics, the Evolvers created a series of warriors who fed on the Awakened to empower themselves. Think about it: an Evolver with powerfully curated abilities, who also has the strength and body of an empowered Awakened. But the strength came at a great cost."

She took two steps away as he asked, "What cost?"

"In the old times, a Godeater needed to feed on ten Awakened, and decently powerful ones at that, before the parasite they'd gained would be satiated enough to slumber."

"Parasite?"

She laughed. "Oh my, yes. Only, you don't have the standard deal here. You took in an unregulated amount of Origin material, so much that even the old system has Awakened in this rendition, as they call it." She bit her lip as she looked at him. "I'm afraid you won't need ten Awakened to satisfy that monster."

"What will I need?" Walker asked.

"Thousands."

CHAPTER TWENTY-SIX

Answers

T housands?" Walker asked in disbelief.

"That is correct," she said with a laugh that settled into a giggle. "You really stepped in it, kiddo." She stretched her arms up and then fanned herself with one hand. "I can feel the pull of it from here. Oh my, yes. I can't believe you found such a large amount of Origin material. It had to have been an unparalleled chance for not only that much to appear, but for you to absorb it as well. I know it's drawn to living creatures, but . . . wow," she said with an exaggerated shrug. "You're already seeing the effects there," she finished, pointing a finger at his hair.

He unconsciously touched the top of his head. "This is because of the Origin material?"

"Yep!" She began to sit, and a swing and a small tree appeared in the air to catch her. Pumping her legs for motion, she continued, "A marker of the Godeaters. You already have the Evolvers System within you. They designed it on the back of the Origin System, something they don't even truly understand."

"So how did they create it?"

She laughed. "Oh, it's quite the story."

"I'm not going anywhere."

"Not yet. Okay." She let the swing settle as she looked at the sky. "To even get their broken thing to work, they had to steal away one of our most promising Awakened during the Origin war—a true visionary who worked with the system intimately. Millions died trying to get her back, and the Evolvers lost a lot of ground in their defense. But eventually, they absconded with her to an unknown part of the multiverse, leaving their old ziggurats, labs, and a broken Pinnacle behind." She waved her hand. "They've been conducting these trials ever since, these . . . renditions. Building more evolutions, more power, more creatures, and conducting research. If my memory serves me correctly, and it always does, it has been several million years since the Evolvers have had any power within the Origin, and thus, their influence has been squeezed from them like a rotting fruit." She pumped her legs for a slow swing. "They started with a few hundred worlds, gave them some tools to work with—"

"People."

"—and used them to spread out. When a world reaches the end of its path, another protocol comes into place and cleans it up, returning the resources used in its creation to the Center."

"How do you know all of this?"

"Tsk, you're not a bright one, are you." She waved a hand, and his overlay updated.

Message from the System Administrator detected.
[. . . Retrieving . . .]

You're a fool.

"You're the Awakened they kidnapped."

"Ooh, kidnapped. I like that word. Yes, that would be me. Let me see." She fiddled with the air for a moment. "You can call me Emily. I like that. No—Bill. No—Morgan. Yes, call me Morgan."

"All right, Morgan. So, what am I doing here?"

"Blergh." An odd look dragged across her face. "Do you know how long it's been since I've spoken to anyone? I can't talk to those children," she said with a nod to the Tree of the Gods. "They're so pumped full of their own importance that they don't realize how insignificant the members of the tenth line really are. BORING!" she yelled out at them, and Walker saw each of the Primigenials freeze in place before erupting in a flurry of activity, talking to each other and trying to pinpoint the source of what they'd just heard.

"Idiots. I like that word too," she said with a smile, pumping her legs quickly for speed and height. She circled the branch once. "This is quite fun!"

"How are you doing that?" he asked, realizing she was pulling moments from his life as she twisted in the swing, causing it to become unstable. "I know you don't have access to my memories or DNA."

"Too right, young . . . Padawan. Your soul is currently an open sieve. One of the things you're supposed to do at the end of the second stage is to close it."

"Is that why I'm here?"

"No, I was just curious who kept blasting their Alma like it was a sideshow in a . . . circus. Oh, they're acrobatic."

"Stop that," Walker replied in an angry tone of voice.

The swing stopped with Morgan at eye level. "I don't think I want to. It's been crazy boring since I locked myself up in here."

An idea came to him, and with a smile, he said, "Okay."

Then he started parsing through his memories, pulling up embarrassing moments he'd come to terms with long ago. The time he laughed so hard that he peed himself at a party and had to do the walk of shame before anyone noticed. A moment from his youth when he'd been asked to sing a song in the choir and had thought it was rap. "Welcome to the Jungle" would never be the same again, and the looks that latched onto him caused one of the most awkward moments of his life.

That time with Vanessa in his back seat, when . . .

"Stop, stop!" she said with a hand up. "Ugh, those were terrible. How do you live with yourself?"

Walker shrugged. "I've made mistakes. It's best to learn from them so you don't do it a second time."

A shudder ran through her frame. "I think I'd rather die."

"Can you?"

"If the tree is destroyed, sure." The Tree of the Gods zoomed out behind her. Walker continued to stretch his neck in an attempt to see where the crest ended, but it was a vain attempt. "This is mine, or more accurately, after so much time has passed, this is me." They jarringly shifted right next to the trunk of the tree where she slapped the bark, causing a loud gong to ring out. "When I thought this up, in what you would call the first rendition, the idea was that they would never find me. I spent a portion of my life designing this as a protector for future generations, sneaking it into the very system they'd forced me to create."

"How did they force you?"

"Family," she said with a curled lip, "also, traitors. Not every Awakened is for the cause, just the same as not every Evolved holds with their Council. Of course, I didn't know that then, but family is still family!" She punched the tree, causing each branch to shake and writhe before resettling. The Primigenials all looked in terror at their thrones and the various branches around them, not knowing what would happen next. "Look at those idiots. Mmm, yes." She smiled. "They only know procreation and progressive building." Her eyes met Walker's. "You've had that thought yourself, I've seen. Progress for progress's sake. There has to be a goal, something to push you forward, and this was mine."

They started to walk around the large trunk, much bigger than what Walker remembered seeing on Sonata. "I hid my little tree—just a seed, really—into the system at an opportune moment. The Awakened had pushed the Evolvers entirely out of the Origin, and in their haste and panic, a special one-of-a-kind reward was added in. At the time of the third rendition's beginning, a mysterious seed was gifted to an untalented Creator and an unremarkable world made. Its Creator didn't second-guess the arrival; I ensured that." An update appeared in Walker's vision, then disappeared the moment he read it.

Congratulations! You've received a seed of the World Tree!

"I threw myself into it, bonding my body and mind with the seed in the most painful transformation of my life. I modified the purpose of the World Tree from within and helped the hopeless Creator get through their battles and complete the Alpha Protocol. The Evolvers learned quite a bit from the Awakened they suddenly found gifted to them, but as their power was greatly diluted by me, they only gained bits and pieces. Sure, they have spies, and some of my people have turned on the cause, but with Awakened, it's about building a fellowship rather than individual power."

"So, you hid in here and—and what?"

"I fought the war that needs fighting. I'm the one who created the Follower System. I'm the one who pushed for scriptures and helped those idiot tenthers create a collection point. Taught them how to open their souls to Alma."

Walker thought over what "collection point" meant. "The afterlife?"

"Yes. That's a stupid name, though. We called them Unities. You know"—she put her hands on her hips as she looked at the tree—"your people really enjoy giving names that describe exactly what something is rather than what it can be. Afterlife, Earth—that was a funny one. When you give a name to something like that, you put it in its place. It doesn't allow for growth or for the amazing potential in every small thing we behold."

"What would you have called the planet?"

"The Alpha Protocol calls it 14959826, which is even worse. I'd call it Haven or Bloom. Something that describes what it really is. When the Creator completed the Alpha Protocol, they were offered the final choices that came with it." She leaned on the tree and looked at him, knowing he would ask.

Walker sighed. "What would those be?"

Morgan held up a finger. "You can leave and go back to your original planet. You'll receive a few gifts, things that will help you personally while not completely upsetting the original balance of your world, but that's it. A thank you, a smack on the ass, and you're off." She leaned toward him conspiratorially. "You can guess that the former Creator chose this one. I heard the ninth cohort talking about their Creator needing to head home to help her people discover their Alma." She tutted. "Shame." Morgan held up a second finger. "You can stay and watch over your creation. Maybe you join the Bravo Protocol and we see just how far you can really go. Maybe you join Charlie and your planet gets moved to the front lines."

"The front lines?"

"Did you think the war was truly over? Hah!" She laughed into a hand. "Sure, most of what happens is done through politics, but they have to act like they're still at war. How would those at the top hold power if they didn't?" Morgan laughed again. "Ah, kids." She waved a hand as if she were erasing that conversation before it could happen. "Anyways, the third option. You can join the Alpha Protocol Council and maybe work your way up the chain. I've heard the perks are tremendous. Of course, you have to be invited, but based on a few of those memories I've tasted, you're already far beyond acceptable."

"Why would I ever want to do that?"

"I don't know, kid. Power? Fame? A chance to move yourself and your people to the Center? There are a lot of options there that you have no idea of. I'm sure you'll hear enough about it once you're standing before them."

"So you're sure that I'll make it?"

"Yep, just as I'm sure I'll be beside you."

That threw him for a loop. "You're going with me?"

"That I am. See, this tree is special." She slapped the bark again. "Until today, for thousands of years, I've been absorbing every Awakened's soul. Each death has added to the power of this beauty. I even designed it to be used as a prison by its Creator whilst they unknowingly had their Alma slowly siphoned into her. Look up!" Walker craned his head toward the top. "Thousands of what you call Primigenials are sitting up there slowly feeding into the power of this World Tree. Not enough to hurt them, or even truly be noticed, but just enough so that I can continue my work. When you get called into the Council's chambers, you're taking us with you."

"For what purpose?"

Morgan took a step back. "What purpose? Haven't you been listening? This is a bomb." She gave a harsh smile. "We're going to hit them right at the Center."

CHAPTER TWENTY-SEVEN

I Will Always Be Better

A *bomb.*

Alarms began to fire off in his mind, but it was more than that. The way that Morgan was talking and the brief periods where she seemed to stare at him while also seeming to stare into the distance were worrying. Like she was reading his mind.

Realizing what was happening, he jumped straight to what used to distract his students in class. If she was somehow reading his mind, he needed to push her away from whatever was floating through there, and what better way than with musical elements from Earth?

"Coming out of my cage . . . and I've been doing just fine," he could hear Morgan whispering to herself, nodding her head along with "Mr. Brightside."

Intrusive thoughts tried to sneak into his mind as he looked at her and the tree. *How was it a bomb? What would set it off?* Shaking his head, he tried to focus on something, anything else. While simultaneously blaring music into his mind, he asked, "How do I close my soul? I'm not a fan of broadcasting my life out there."

"Mmm . . ." she said, still nodding, "I don't know if . . ."

He knew what she was going to say. When you've had a lack of control in the past, and you suddenly find yourself with an advantage, you'll do anything to maintain it. He needed to take a firm stance; otherwise, every Awakened with enough juice would be able to listen to his thoughts.

"If you don't help me in this, I promise I'm not taking you with me to the Council."

"Pfft," she said, making a face, no longer nodding along to the song. Walker changed the music video in his mind to the Foo Fighters. Her neck started twitching involuntarily to "My Hero." She looked him up and down and sighed. "I don't think you could stop me . . . but . . . fine. Sit down." Walker sat on the white tile floor that reappeared as the Tree of the Gods disappeared into the distance.

"You need to look outside of yourself. To project your soul—can you pause the song, please?"

Walker shook his head. "Sorry. Earworm." He thought about what an earworm was before diving back into the music. "It's stuck in my head too." He couldn't give her the time or inclination to see what was truly going on in there. This exercise was on a timer, and he needed to get it done as soon as possible. He had no idea what she could do inside this place and would be happy to never find out.

She looked at him strangely. "All right, kiddo. I thought you had more self-control than that. Anyway, right now you're shooting out your soul for every third-stage Awakened to see. The tenth line may only be snatching up bits and pieces, but I'm from the second and hold divested Alma from the original themself. My sensitivity is much higher than what you're used to, which is good for you since I can easily show you how to do this."

Walker felt rather than saw something hovering over him on the left. Morgan spoke again, but there was something unmistakably hollow in her voice. "I'm separated from my body right now, or this construct's body, that is." She gave a stilted laugh. "It's funny. If the Primigenials had listened to the tree in the right way, it would have given them a vision of how to do this through the system. Pity. Building systems based on the soul is so difficult." She floated over to his right side. "To project, you need to extricate your soul and move it outside of yourself. It's similar to how you first connected it to the rest of your body, only instead of pressing down, you're pulling up. Give it a try."

Firmly seating a new song in his mind, Walker moved by instinct to take hold of his invisible muscles and grab the area where he had first felt his soul. Pulling on it, he stretched upward, feeling a small amount of strain with the unfamiliar exercise. As soon as his soul recognized what he was trying to do, all stiffness faded. He moved it around as a taffy maker would, grabbing two handfuls together, and threw it into the sky. The experience felt like someone pulling on his hair, only without the pain.

Morgan was back in her body, looking up. "Good, though the distance you've placed it is a little high for your first learning experience. Try pulling it back in a little."

Walker changed the tune in his head, giving her some action from the Beatles. Then he stretched his invisible muscles out and grabbed the top to pull it back in.

"No, no, pull from the bottom."

He didn't understand her request, so he tried a series of different visualizations to get his soul to work how he needed it to. Rope hauling, stitching—none of it worked, and his soul continued to float above him. He had a brief moment when he thought he'd continue to live the rest of his life like this—a man walking around Symphony with a part of his soul constantly floating over his head.

"What's wrong with you?" Morgan asked. "For a sapient with a piece of Origin, you're pretty inept at this."

Walker changed his mental tune to Eminem's "Without Me" in response.

She snorted. "Tell me how you normally manipulate your soul."

"Why do you call mine a soul, but when you speak of others, you call it their Alma?"

She tilted her head. "Because you're not holding a piece of Alma anymore. You were," she clarified, "but the Origin material wrote right over that. Now, you have a piece of the original soul. The Origin. The beginning of things."

"So what does that mean?"

She tapped the tip of his nose with a finger. An oddly familiar gesture from someone who always seemed vaguely threatening. "Focus on what we're doing right now, kiddo. You'll understand. Now, how are you moving your soul?"

"I don't know. It's like . . ." He tried to put it into words. "It's like there's this feeling, like a weird muscle, somewhere here," he said, pointing to just below his chest.

"Ugh, their teaching is worse than I thought. No, you don't need to use that. It's kiddie stuff." She shrunk herself to the size of a ten-year-old. "Is somebody a little kiddie?" she asked in a high-pitched voice.

Walker had always hated when people did baby talk. "No."

"Good," she replied, then shot back to her original height. "Then don't use your metaphysical hands; use your mind. It's less of a command and more of a pushed suggestion. You want it to retract; you need it to return to the fold. It's a part of you. Built into you." She tapped the side of her head. "Think at it."

Walker tried out her advice.

Return.

Come back to me.

Shrink.

Please come down a little?

Fuck you! he thought at last, attempting to push his emotions at the drifting soul over his head. Rather than sit there uncaring of his requests, this time it shrunk a little.

"Good! Do what you did again!"

Walker mentally shrugged and continued to curse at it. *Your mother was a cow!* It pulled in a little more. *I bet you use commas instead of periods! You're the first soul in history to score a ninety on the IQ test and think you did well!*

As it continued to shrink, Morgan said, "Great! Stop right there." Walker acquiesced, yelling at it to stop. He could now feel that his soul was only a few feet above him. "Working with your soul is fairly straightforward—"

Walker shook his head. "Recently, that hasn't been my experience."

She pointed above his head. "It worked, didn't it?"

"Yes, but," he replied, considering what had just happened, "it didn't react to my suggestions or my attempted commands. It wasn't until I started to insult it and feed my emotions into it that my soul reacted."

Morgan ran a hand over her smooth skull. "Huh. I suppose as an original, your soul will be a little different than mine. Well, the principles should all be the same." She rolled her shoulders. "Now, try to find the essence of yourself—your inner person, your core." She pantomimed a circle with her hands. "You want to think about what happened when you first Awakened. What did you see? Who have you been across the timeline of your life?"

Walker closed his eyes and reached back into his memories, finding the screens of the first stage and the moments of clarity that came with them. "I wasn't the . . . best person, but I did try. And I always try to make myself better than I was before." His soul pulsed with his words, and he found a pointed *ping* in the formerly small space in his chest, just below where he considered his invisible muscles to be.

"Good, you've found it." He could picture Morgan nodding as he kept his eyes closed. "Now, look for any perforations in your soul. Look deeply and focus. Feel it out."

Walker felt around. It was much more difficult to keep the music running while doing so, but the consequences of allowing her in were too grave. Working in spurts, he traveled the breadth of his soul, still stretched out and hanging above him. As it was still extended, he had an easier time finding each perforation within, like a shirt with holes stretched out by an expanding waistline. He pressed his extra sense into the first gap he found, and a memory shot into his mind.

He was standing in front of a gravestone alone—his grandfather's. Everyone around him had thrown some dirt onto the coffin, and he could feel the gritty material in the palm of his hand, still uncast. He felt . . . nothing. Ten-year-old Walker wondered if something was wrong with him as he looked at the brown slabbed coffin holding what used to be a kind person in his life.

The memory ended, and he thought about it for a moment. He recalled something he learned in his basic psychology classes when he was getting his teacher's credentials.

Everyone processes grief differently. I wasn't affected by my grandfather's death yet because I didn't understand what was happening. It was less than a year later that I truly grieved the loss.

He felt the hole close.

"What the shit?" he said, opening his eyes.

"Ah, you closed it already? It normally takes people a long time to fix them all."

"I only closed one," he clarified. "But still, what was that?"

"What did you see?" she asked, curiosity painted across her face.

"Myself as a child, wondering if something was strange about me."

"Pfft," she said, waving him away. "You're still a child! And of course there are strange things about you. You got *picked* for the Alpha Protocol, dumbass!"

"I thought that was random."

She made a conciliatory gesture with her hands. "Sure . . . sure. It's a little random. But the basic-intelligence people like you were picked because you don't think like everyone else. You're abnormal for your species. That's what they want. People who don't think outside of the box but instead consider that there is no box, or that it's a sphere. In other words, you're weird."

"I'm not that—"

"Do you like being around people?"

"Well, sometimes—"

"Do you also hate being around people?"

"I mean—"

"Bingo!" She smiled. "Fun word." Walker immediately brought up the music again as he realized it'd slipped through his mind. Her smile fell away as she continued speaking. "That's the thing about it, Walker. To use your words, it's a shot in the dark, but sometimes, like how they chose you, it pays off for them. Geniuses continue the line. Sure, they think of new ways of doing things, but they don't think of completely different things to do! It takes a weirdo to save the multiverse. Well, their multiverse."

Walker grumbled to himself as he thought about it. He wasn't that weird. Maybe he liked mayonnaise a little too much, but still, it was delicious, and nobody could find fault with him for that.

"I'm not that weird," he said with resolve.

"Oh, really? What job did you do before all of this?" she said with a wave of her hands.

"I was a teacher, and before that, I was in the military," he said, not knowing where she was going with this.

"Uh-huh," she replied, tapping her thumb against her chin. "And what was the average age of the people you fought in the military?"

Walker froze. She'd caught him. "Exactly. You went from fighting and presumably killing young people to teaching and helping them grow? Don't you find that pretty strange? Isn't that weird?"

"I don't like this conversation," he said as memories from his time in Afghanistan started flooding in, pushing the music box out of his mental window again.

"Oh, but I quite enjoy it, kiddo," she replied with a feral smile. "You're a collection of conundrums. Kill, then save. Feel the need to be around others, then be uncomfortable when those people surround you. I bet you like to think you're smart, but you're also constantly confused by everything." Morgan was on a roll now. "Feel the need to have a life partner, but you're always finding flaws in their character?" she said as she stepped closer, a grin still affixed to her face.

"Constantly complaining about impending deadlines when you're the one who set them, maybe?" She stopped as she stood directly in front of him. "You're not happy unless you're facing a crisis, which you constantly bring on yourself one way or another. I'm sorry, kiddo"—she put a hand on his shoulder—"but you're the epitome of manufactured drama. You set up your own greatest failures."

An image of the Slicer shot through him for a moment. A tingling burst from his chest in agreement. He looked Morgan in the eyes and said, "Maybe. But I can be better."

She laughed into a hand. "Maybe you can. But we'll see, won't we." She gave him one more laugh before walking away. "I can't hold you in here forever. Get working, Creator."

Walker looked at the back of her head momentarily as he wondered what it would feel like to punch it. She raised a finger and wagged it back and forth through the air, reminding him that his music box still hadn't turned back on. Color stained his cheeks, and to cover himself, he began playing some of his favorites from the '80s, then turned back to the holes in his soul.

The next one he found was his first fight, way back in elementary school. He watched himself get beat up by a group of kids, then cry on the ground during recess while the other children continued on their way, shifting around the weak kid on the floor. Those children had truly been vicious, and he knew from experience that children could be nightmares when there were no adults around to keep them in line. He plugged up the hole by remembering all the times he'd learned to get around a fight through the targeted use of empathy, as well as a few times when he'd won decisively. Maybe it was bragging, but he hadn't lost a fight in over a decade. When he thought of that, a few more holes closed up on their own, making his job more manageable.

This continued for a relatively long time. He continued to plug up any issues and outstanding emotional debt from the time of his youth. Scenes with his parents, old friends he hadn't thought of in years, and understandably embarrassing moments he'd not considered since their disastrous circumstances. When he shifted to his middle school years, the tone of the memories shifted with him. The situations were more nuanced, with a greater emphasis on self-discovery and a lack of understanding on his part for what had led him to each scenario.

One particular hole appeared tied to when he had fought with his old computer teacher. The man had sent him to the office for humming while memorizing the home row of a keyboard. Walker had tried to argue that he was memorizing the keys to a song he'd made up, but Mr. Weinbrunner was old school and said he was distracting the class. When he arrived at the principal's office, he'd explained what he'd been doing while the large man nodded, agreeing with him. He'd forgotten long ago what he'd said after.

"That's called a mnemonic device, used to memorize complicated terms. Who taught you to do that?"

Walker didn't want to say that his parents worked a lot, and he was on his own with homework each day. Attaching unfamiliar terms to songs was just an easy way to go about things and was something he'd thought up in the fourth grade. He just gave his standard response for when he didn't want to say something that could be embarrassing: "I dunno."

"I see. Well, if you're inventing your own mnemonics at this young age, maybe you should consider being a doctor, or even a teacher . . . I bet you'd enjoy history as well . . ."

The principal had sent him back to the classroom with a note he wasn't supposed to read but did anyway; he'd laid into Mr. Weinbrunner for not knowing his students better. Walker, whose dysgraphia was in full force at the time, saw the potential of computers and typing early on. The ability to no longer have to rely on his terrible handwriting and the issues that came with it greatly appealed to him. He'd explained that near the end of his meeting with the principal, who had immediately understood and sent him on his way after writing the note.

I didn't remember any of this, Walker thought as the memory stopped. *What kid thinks about mnemonic devices that young? Plus, Mr. Weinbrunner was a dick.*

Surprisingly, the hole closed after his last thought. He didn't know what to think about that either.

After he'd cleared up everything before his late teen years—the last hole showed a sad breakup and harsh words being exchanged—he felt . . . better. It was cathartic to see his unfinished emotional ties from the past being closed one after another, the wisdom of his current self helping to heal the damage caused by his younger self.

The shift to the years just before his twenties was harrowing. The scenarios became more dynamic and vicious. He might have an Awakened mind, but that didn't mean he constantly considered his past and had time to look through every memory. Girls and fights. Old friends betraying him for one reason or another. His first degree and the eventual uselessness of it. He began to really pay attention to what was happening thematically with the holes.

None of the memories were happy. None were filled with joy and smiles, only heartache and precarious situations. He remembered something he used to say to his students in class when asked about what being an adult meant.

"Being an adult is based on growth. So, how do we grow? That's simple. There are three ways in which human beings become more than they currently are.

"The first way is through traveling and experiencing new places and new ideas about what we call life. It takes an open mind and a heavy wallet, but it can certainly be done.

"The second is to read and experience the first way through a different modality. Smart people read, and you can read to become smarter. The more books you read, the

more lives you live through vicariously. It's part of the reason I read fantasy. Nothing quite like reading the story of a hero slaying an all-powerful villain when you can place yourself in their shoes. Each location, each culture, and each person is a new addition to your brain. A new way of seeing the world.

"The third way is the worst. Trauma. In trauma, you see bits and pieces of who you are as your decisions set the tone for your own life. Trauma leaves a mark on you, something that sticks with you no matter what you do. It often forces you to grow, like an itchy scab that won't go away.

"People don't necessarily change unless they're either forced to or they want to. And even then, it takes time, pain, and knowledge."

It was always good advice to give to them, and in his experience, it happened to be all too true.

His twenties reared up and Valerie came in. But there weren't as many holes as he expected, not after the first stage. The beginning and mid part of his thirties barely had any at all, in fact.

In one final stretch, he dealt with some issues from his parents, and it was complete. When the last one filled in, he felt cleaner . . . better. Like he'd had a long shower after a hard day's work. Rather than a pulse in his chest, he felt a warm glow pushing into the rest of his body.

Morgan cocked her head to the side when he finished. "All done? I don't hear any more memories leaking out of you."

Walker nodded as he stood up and stretched. "Yep. I've completely filled in every hole," he said as he turned off the music box.

"Hole?" She started laughing. "Man, you're too much. Soul-holes!"

Walker patiently waited for over a minute as she got a hold of herself. "Anyway," he said when she started to calm down, "what's next?"

She straightened up, saying, "Sorry, sorry." Her grin slipped away, and she looked at him with a severe expression. "Next, you find the resonance of your soul. You've completed the first stage and the second stage. You've found and eliminated every bit of uncertainty about who you are. You know yourself. You know what you've done in the past, and you have a good foundation for who you are now. It's time to bring all of that together so you may know yourself in the future as well. Who do you want to be? Who do you need to be, Walker?" She scratched the side of her neck. "And we need to do it fast because we're running out of time." He snorted before being able to stop himself, causing her eyebrows to draw down. "I'm serious, kid. This is taking a lot of juice to hold you in here with me. This place is a resource specifically designed to hold things in while charging itself; it's not designed to allow visitors. The longer you're here, the more energy I expend to keep you. Now, sit down, dive deep, and get your shit done so I can boot you out."

"Why do I need to do that here? Plus"—he realized he'd never asked—"why are you helping me?"

Morgan rolled her eyes. "Because you need an elevated soul to help you reach the third stage, just like the first, and you need to do it here because this area is filled with diluted Alma. It's in the air of the construct and the walls as well, which is what maintains this glorious prison." She pointed at just below his chest. "Closing those holes on the outside would be like setting off bombs on Sonata with how powerful your soul has become. Here, it's such a minor blip you didn't even notice me cover it up. By placing you within the Tree of the Gods construct, I've protected your little moonlet and all those lesser idiots as well. You'd have been fine, but it would have been a near thing for those close to you. If you want to leave, be my guest," she finished, waving a hand and showing him a door in the air. "Step through that door and you'll be back in your body and mind, just like you'd never left."

He looked at the door floating a few inches off the ground before shaking his head.

"No."

"Good." The door disappeared with a snap. "As for why I'm helping you, I've already explained that. I need you to get close to the Council. I need you alive. Now"—she pointed at the floor—"let's do this." He nodded and sat down, then felt Morgan put her hand on his back. "This is going to hurt. Brace."

He placed his palms on the floor for balance, then felt rather than saw as a foreign energy stabbed into his back. Initially, he felt his soul rebuff the efforts, but Morgan asked him to open up to her, to let her in so he could help her, and after thinking about it a little longer than he likely should have, he asked his soul to let her in. It acceded, though not without roughing up the energy trying to expand in his body, including closing off any extra access points.

"Your soul is an asshole," she said in a strained voice while he gasped. It felt like a cold rush of water was pushing throughout his entire body when she took root near the middle of his soul. "Focus on your center!" she yelled out, and he did just that. As he strained his senses on the spot just below his chest, a metaphysical reality expanded and covered his mind, providing new sights for him to behold.

He was in an ample dark space with a star-filled sky. Only, unlike actual stars, these constellations constantly moved and shifted, each time forming into something else—a bolt of lightning, an open eye, two hands holding each other.

"Each of those could be your resonance, but here's a warning: you can only choose one. One idea to represent you. One icon that brings forth all of who you are. Make the right choice and gain immense power. Make the wrong one and find limits upon who you can become. Choose, Creator. Choose, Originator!"

Walker looked into the sky and expected to find a resonance with just one, but instead, he found resonances with each of them. A small piece of him felt a different meaning bounding from the starry sky. He felt the soft spots in his soul, the recently closed holes, pressing on him, demanding he make a choice that appealed to their individual needs. As the stars shifted and formed different constellations, a different part of his soul would spread warmth throughout his body telling him to pick it.

When a doll appeared in the air, Walker felt a kinship related to the seamless image of life. Who he wanted to be, who he could be, perfection in every way. As he looked at it, it turned golden and stopped moving.

"Yes! That one!" Morgan yelled out behind him, but he didn't listen. The soft spots, even the center of his soul, agreed with him. But something about it felt wrong. His instinct said that this was wrong. All of it. This wasn't who he was.

Looking next to the doll, he found a group of stars, and unlike before when they had formed on their own, he did something different. He commanded them.

Become what I need! You know me! I know me! Do what I ask of you, please!

The stars swirled and swam against each other, a celestial river flowing across space. Great bursts of light sliced across a canopy of night, mixing and blurring, making connections before breaking away. Always moving and searching for their place. Some began to settle as golden lines appeared and connected them into several ideas. Over time, leaves and branches formed, and a single image was created.

A grand tree.

Of course, he thought to himself.

He commanded his image to spread by reaching his metaphysical arms out and having the tree do the same. It spread its branches and leaves and connected not only its own constellation but multiple others as well. A large mural of ideas and suppositions found within the boughs of a tree, representing one great truth over all others, a kaleidoscope of icons under one banner.

"No, not that!"

He ignored her again.

"Stop!"

Walker mentally shut her out of his mind with a vengeance, picturing a window shutting with a bang.

A doll? Why would a doll ever represent his soul? He knew himself far better than that. Perfection was an illusion. Reaching for it was what mattered, not becoming it. It was the chase and attempts at perfection that defined someone. Progress shouldn't ever be stopped.

No, she'd been trying to do something. Something that would greatly harm him. Something that would likely let her out of this place.

He knew a trap when he saw one.

The energy in the soft spots of his soul had felt wrong. They had tried too hard to make him feel better. To feel whole. But that's not exactly who he was. He was a broken man. A conundrum. A savior and a killer. A teacher and a monster. There were no feelings of completeness for him. No ideas of a road with an end. Only the drive to do better, be better. To expand. To grow.

Like Symphony itself, its Creator didn't want limits. Didn't want the idea of perfection at all.

He commanded his soul to reach back and latch on to the energy that Morgan was providing for him. He began to pull, taking it into himself and removing her control in the process. In the outside world, he could feel as she shoved against him, trying to remove her hand from his body, but it was already too late. She'd entered his soul, and that was enough for him. It had to be. Because he needed the extra power. He wasn't enough on his own, original or not, for what he planned to do next.

But he was a Godeater.

In the metaphysical reality of his soul, Walker leaped high into the air. Looking down toward what he had been standing on, he found the face of Morgan, eyes bloodshot and a snarl on her lips as she looked up at him.

He winked and then turned to the golden lines in the sky.

As he reached the peak of where his current strength could take him, he found that his estimation was correct. He was only a small percent of the distance to the grand tree and its many connections. Pushing his hands toward Morgan's face below, he called on his soul to gather all the energy she'd been trying to control him with. It gathered, a great purple mass, and he pressed it over his body, creating a shell to protect himself with.

Walker placed a single thought in his mind as he commanded his soul, "Go!"

The Creator. The bringer of his own calamity. The late-thirties man who had cried for his losses only several months ago flew toward the golden constellation of a grand tree. Its branches reached further than his eye could behold, far into space and a never-ending night sky filled with potential.

When he arrived, rather than joining with the golden lines as he instinctively understood most of the Awakened had done in the past, he spread his hands out and clasped the sides of the expansive space in front of him.

"I will be better," he said quietly to himself. "Better than myself and better than all of you."

Walker squeezed his hands together and pressed all of the golden lines together. His hands strained, and purple haze broke away from his body, then faded into the darkness around him. A scream erupted from below him in the metaphysical world, and from behind him in the physical as well, as Morgan was drained of every ounce of Alma she had. The last of the borrowed power began to burn away from his hands; his own black was streaked with blue, green, and now purple as he continued to press and squeeze the golden lines into a single image. One thing that would represent everything else. One image. One icon. One representation of who he was and who he wanted to be.

With a *boom*, Walker's hands collapsed into each other and were immediately pressed outward again as his image took shape.

It was a book.

"I will always be better," he said quietly as he looked at the black cover. "And I won't be tricked by people like you again. I learn from my mistakes. Let me out." And just like that, he was free.

There was nothing left of Morgan when he came out, just some dust on the floor. The white room seemed hazy, like a dream fading away, and he knew his time was short.

He looked over and focused on the Tree of the Gods. It still stood the same as ever, each Primigenial unaware of the events that had just occurred with many in a heated argument, yelling across the branches.

Walker smiled as he looked down at the book again. "You and I are going to have some fun." The book warmed in his hands.

"Let's go."

As Walker's body faded from the constructed room, his overlay lit up.

Message from the System:
[. . . Scanning . . .]
The System Administrator role has been assigned to Dante!
Congratulations!

CHAPTER TWENTY-EIGHT

In the Council Chamber and Across the Protocols

In a dark room at the Center of the multiverse, a range of former Creators and legacy nobles excitedly moved around an ostentatious room. Supreme assistants moved with them, as each council member had two helping them with anything they might need. One council member stood near a golden chair showing off a plain brown leather bag.

"It's wondrous! I can't believe how many different items this beauty can hold."

"How much did it cost you, Councillor?" a supreme assistant in the shape of a small green ring asked from beside him.

"Only enough to create a mid-sized planet. Truly, a frugal purchase," he said with a smile. "When we next hold the inter-council retreat, I will be the center of all attention. The Bravo Protocol is going to eat themselves alive."

"Well done," a supreme assistant added, standing on his other side.

"Three!" a sizeable nebulous being yelled out. Where the sound projected from nobody but the speaker knew. "You need to stay on top of your assigned strands! We're losing resources every minute you're not commanding your assistants."

"Shove it up your ass, Seven! You're just jealous! And stop calling me Three!"

"You just called me Seven!"

"Language," a Sentinel on a platform near the wall said as he looked over the room. The rebuked man's face scrunched up momentarily before it settled down. He placed the bag in his pocket and walked over to his station.

"That damned genius really put a lot of work on our heads!" Council Member Four yelled out from his station. "I'm having a hell of a time making sure that the Life strands are collected properly. They're constantly trying to break away from their vessels and have already infected hundreds of storage vats."

"Just do your best," the longest-standing council member said. "Where's Five, anyway?"

The nebulous council member snorted. "Who knows, One? He's probably still trying to get that supreme assistant to countermand his new primary directive. How we lost control of an assistant, let alone the assistant connected to that genius, is beyond me. You'd never betray me, right LAD20?" he asked the gray jelly assistant near him.

"Never, Council Member Seven."

"We wouldn't dream of it," his other assistant echoed.

"See! It must have something to do with that Creator, Dante—no, Walker. Something in his genetic material, perhaps. Either way, we may have to quarantine the whole ren—"

He was interrupted by a message hitting every overlay at the same time.

The System Administrator has fallen!
[. . .]
A new System Administrator has been found.
Please stand by for any future changes to the Protocol System as
the new Administrator begins their work.

If a person were to enter the room at that moment, they wouldn't have been able to hear a sound—not a breath, not even a silent shudder coursing through their bodies. Just the utter stillness of this exact moment being recorded mentally by everyone involved.

A second later, one of the Sentinels on the wall bowed and said, "It has been a privilege," before disappearing.

"What?" Council Member Three said in confusion. "They've never left a post empty before."

"It has been a privilege," another said with a bow before they, too, disappeared.

One by one, each Sentinel bowed, said the same line, and then disappeared. Nobody in the room knew where they had gone, which the ensuing pandemonium all too clearly showed.

"What's happening!"

"Is this some kind of attack? Have the Awakened come for us?"

"The Origin! We must escape to the Origin!"

"They'll never take us back, you moron! Contact our embassies! The other Council chambers!"

While all the council members panicked, one stayed relatively calm as he turned his eyes to the last remaining Sentinel.

"It has been a privilege."

"Wai—" Council Member One said as he reached a claw out, but it was already too late. The last Sentinel disappeared from the Council chambers of the Alpha

Protocol, and all that was left were those in the room and their assistants. Council Member One looked around at everyone and saw nothing but fear and confusion trapped behind their eyes.

Well, the eyes he could see.

"We will not panic. We will continue on with our work for the Evolver Faction. We're going to move forward like we always have," he said, attempting to lock each member firmly on his side.

Council Member Three shook as he looked at his elder. "But the Sentinels. They—wait, are . . ." He looked at his two assistants, who looked at each other and shook their heads.

"We are with you, Council Member Three."

"Indeed," the other said.

"Oh, thank goodness."

As his shoulders slumped, his worst fears almost realized, Five stepped into the room. He looked left and right and noticed the Sentinels' absence right away.

"I see."

Council Member Three sneered at him. "You see what, exactly, you damned fool! The System Administrator, who has hidden from us for thousands of years, is dead. We don't know who the next one is, what they're planning, *or what's going to happen to us!*" he yelled out, sharp breaths quickly following. "We don't even know what's still working and what isn't! We're doomed! We relied so much on this damned system, and now it may be our downfall!"

"Well, then, let's take a page from Walker's book." Seven smiled. "Let's be better."

Each Council across the Evolver multiverse had similar reactions as the messages came in. There was a great delay in time, split amongst them, as some were accelerating within their temporal zones, and others weren't. In the Psi and Omega Councils, who always remained within an accelerated zone, the Sentinels were staying put for the time being but wouldn't answer any questions no matter how they were asked.

The Councils not within a zone were blissfully unaware, still moving about with their plots and intrigues. And where there hadn't been one since first splitting away from the Origin, a strain of worry threaded its way through the previously confident group of former Creators and nobles. Messages flew across the renditions, harsh words were exchanged, and small political battles were waged on a seemingly endless scale.

For the first time in a long time, the Evolvers were split on what should happen next.

The Slicer, having just completed its training within the Psi Protocol, watched as its mentor approached with a deep sigh.

The Universal Terror tilted its head at the slow approach, and asked, "What?"

CHAPTER TWENTY-NINE

In Another Rendition: The Slicer

Next!" a ringing voice called out.

The Slicer weaved its way across multiple unremarkable platforms, a line of creatures of various sizes and descriptions in front of it. Skyscrapers littered the landscape, each having no purpose for the Psi Protocol except one thing: holding the bloated masses who had become comfortable in their small and unimportant lives. Attacking them was useless, something it knew well from experience.

One of its abilities informed it that something humorous was about to happen. A thick, heavy-muscled arthropod was charging one of the skyscrapers seemingly on a whim. The creature's feet picked up speed, a blur of motion only those with unique abilities could see, as it targeted a single red tower shooting high into the sky.

Moron.

The Slicer committed to watching this first attempt by the destroyer; it was always a comical moment. It noticed several other destroyers doing the same, while many of the terrors were immune to the action occurring so near them, having seen it too many times.

The blue chitinous creature wound back a claw as it approached the edge of the skyscraper, then threw it forward with violent intent as a blaze of fire ignited around its arm, the atmosphere partially ignited by friction. As every terror and most destroyers knew would happen, its arm hit the bubble, and unlike the bubbles the Slicer had worked against in the 4AA rendition, this one held the creature completely still rather than rebounding it with force.

The newbie destroyer screeched, the sound not unlike air passing quickly through a tunnel, before it realized it was truly stuck. It stood there waiting for something else to happen.

Only, nothing did.

Many of those in line looked around in confusion at the lack of policing, and the Slicer even spied some of the terrors doing the same now. It found apprehension and confusion on some of their faces. Something was wrong. Something was different.

The Sentinels were gone.

The Slicer had learned this from its mentor only moments before receiving the call that it would be leaving soon. The Psi Protocol had decided that it was time the Slicer was field-tested for promotion to a higher tier. Its current rank—the low, low value of 1,005—wasn't an accurate reflection of the majesty of its strength and cunning. Thus far, all of its assignments had been minor. Destroy a city on an asteroid in this location. Wipe out a moon and make it uninhabitable. Burn the fields. To the Universal Terror, it was too simple and simply dull.

Of course, it'd lost quite a few rank levels with the Youmal incident. It didn't like to think about that failure unless it had to.

Looking at the blue chitinous creature still stuck in the wall, it realized what was going to happen.

Not a damn thing.

The creature would be stuck there until it wised up and tore off its own claw, or it would die of something else, something expectedly unexpected. Likely a terror or another destroyer deciding it was a delicious-looking snack. In their defense, it was quite a delicious-looking snack, with supple plating and a good amount of meat beneath it. The Slicer shook its head. There was only one reason this was happening.

Something had changed.

The Slicer had asked its mentor, who had lived far longer, why the Sentinels had left. The toothy creature had informed its junior that the Sentinel's disappearance was an event that had never occurred before in the long history of the protocols. Since the time the multiverse was first created, Sentinels had stood watch over the different planets within the Center.

Each was a powerhouse that few could match up against, and when they worked together, even terrors wouldn't last long against them. It would take something far greater to defeat their coordination and experienced strength. Yet now they could no longer be found. It was decidedly new.

They weren't all gone. That is to say, the Psi Council was still protected, but in the standard areas that had always held the silent guardians before, the Sentinels were missing.

The ringing voice called out from up ahead. "Wait your turn, wait your turn. If you don't, you won't have a chance at destruction and mayhem," a man looking vaguely like the Slicer's Creator said near the front. "I said hold your turn!" he yelled out as a whip of red and black particles appeared in his hand. He cracked it down against an insectoid creature, leaving a deep laceration on its previously pristine exoskeleton. The pitiful destroyer fell to the ground, several of its dozen or so mandibles twitching. "See what you made me do!" the man said, stretching in his power suit, a sense of inherent superiority unconsciously built into his every movement. "You want to kill, I get it. It's who you are. But there has to be order here! Order, I say," he finished as he raised the whip in the air again, preparing to strike the destroyer just before it could regain its feet.

"Hold!" a man called out as he quickly walked forward with long strides.

Unlike the man holding the whip, this one had black streaks on his armor from shoulder to shoulder. He pulled the whip-carrying man aside and whispered something. The Slicer's ability-enhanced hearing picked up the whip-carrying man saying, "I understand, I'll be careful." Then the man with black-streaked armor gave another conciliatory gesture before heading back to the front of the line at his superior's nod.

Just as quickly as it had appeared, the whip disappeared, and the man yelled out as if nothing had happened, "Step through the portal now!" to the insectoid creature. It stood on shaky legs and entered, the scar on its body already beginning to heal. As it disappeared, he yelled out, "Next!"

A twenty-foot-tall creature of ooze moved forward at a sloth-like speed, stopping just in front of the man. He looked at his screens before saying, "You're off to rendition 2EJ. Total destruction of the planet Septirius. No survivors are required. Please enter the portal," he said with a wave. A blue portal appeared beside him on an overly large platform. The ooze creature slithered in, and without any pomp, the terror and portal disappeared.

"Next!"

Two more destroyers followed, ones the Slicer had seen multiple times in the past. Its mentor had told it about them, using their lives as a reminder of the consequences of failure, like Youmal. Neither had passed the qualifications needed for the Omega Protocol and were forever reduced to the small auspices of the lower-ranked Psi. The portal master told them both that they would be sent to destroy cities rather than planets or even a moonlet. A delicious grass-covered moonlet. It shook the thought away, as it was now at the front of the line.

"Next!"

The Slicer undulated forward.

"Ah, you're up for your promotion, I see," the man said, looking in the air at his screens. "Are you trying to break past the one thousand mark, little one?" he asked the glorious terror.

"Yes," the Slicer hissed at him, not enjoying the name-calling.

"At least you're doing better. The first time you came through here, you tried to attack everyone and everything you could see. It's nice to see you gain some self-control."

"Self-control is a limitation placed upon you by those who believe themselves your better," the Slicer rasped at him. "I want freedom."

"I see," he said with no change in expression. The Slicer had been trained in recognizing shifts in humanoid facial expressions by its mentor, so it noticed when the portal master shifted from neutral to antagonistic by a minute change in his posture. "Perhaps you're not ready for—"

"I'm ready!" the Slicer hissed, its barbed tail having a fit before it could regain control.

"Well," he said, considering the heavily plated six-foot-long worm in front of him, "the world you're going to can't get much worse." He nodded his head. "You're heading to Capilama 3, a mining world. You're to leave the mines alone and only kill the workers. It's a rare deal the Capilama Creator made with the Charlie Council in exchange for future—"

That was more information than the Slicer needed. "I don't care!"

He sighed. "I figured as much." He waved a hand at the platform next to him and a portal appeared. "Please step through when you're ready. It'll deposit you *directly* in front of the mine. We've also expended the extra Temporal resources to allow you to stay in accelerated time throughout the mine. You shouldn't notice a difference when you finish," he said.

The Slicer undulated forward without a care in the world, only half listening. It stopped a foot away from where it knew the portal would grab it and looked back. The blue chitinous terror was now a blubbering mess. Sad wheezing sounds came from its chest as it slumped against the bubble inch by inch. The moron had tried to use its other hand to free the first one, with the obvious result of having both arms now stuck.

Looking around, the Slicer found no Sentinels coming to the rescue, and a small fight was breaking out near the rear of the line without the standard immediate action. Things were changing. It looked at the portal master, then back out to the wider world housing the Psi Protocol. It almost slithered off of the portal's platform to cause the death and destruction so near and dear to its heart. Almost. But its mentor had been training it to control instincts like this. It needed more evolutions to continue its way forward, to truly grow as a terror and evolve into something more. Something purer. An omen.

The Slicer entered the portal to Capilama 3 and the difficult trial ahead.

Each time it entered a portal, it would be standing in one place one moment and another the next. Simple. Translocation was supposed to be fast. Its vision of the Psi Protocol's home planet disappeared fast enough, but its body was fading into Capilama 3 one slow moment at a time. It was unusual, but the Slicer didn't panic. It gave it a rare moment to reflect on the turns its life had taken since first accepting its mentor's offer.

When Twenty convinced the Slicer to join the Psi Protocol, the translocation had been nearly instantaneous. One moment they were floating in space, and the next, they had been in a large facility. Not only in a large facility, of course, but in a metal room with barred windows. After an initial expenditure of built-up rage, Twenty, or Ra'jin as they gave their name, had stood outside the Slicer's cage, hands in pockets.

"They do this with every destroyer and terror," they said with no contrition in their voice. "Can you blame them?" They nodded to the cages around them. Their inhabitants all seemed mad with rage, like the Slicer had been only moments before. Even though it always had the same results when attacking the protocol bubbles, it never stopped to consider what this action showed to its captors: a disturbing lack of control.

The Slicer only had to wait two days before they would release it to its mentor, who informed it of some general rules that all destroyers and the ranks above them were forced to live by.

1. Attacking the cities and citizens of the Psi Protocol will not be tolerated.
2. Violations, or not following the directions you are given, will result in a demotion of rank.
3. Following the directions you are given to an upstanding degree will result in a promotion of rank.
4. Any entity within the Psi Protocol that falls under the rank of 5,000 will immediately be placed back within the rendition and location of their original recruitment.
5. Any entity that moves up in rank will receive unique benefits befitting their station.

The benefits, of course, were not unique. Sure, they told all of the destroyers that, but it just wasn't true.

When the Slicer first arrived, the unique benefit given to anyone between the ranks of four and six thousand was the reward of a mentor. Every new terror and destroyer was ranked between the five and six thousand mark, with a two-month opportunity to move past the cutoff for displacement.

Some did, many didn't.

The Slicer was lucky enough to have a very high-ranking mentor, who had survived experiences similar to its own. Thus, for the first time in the Slicer's life, it had what a normal person would call a friend. The impulse to attack and destroy was there, it was always there, but that clawing and grasping creature in the back of its mind seemed to be quieter anytime Ra'jin was around.

Of course, the memory of the sheer size and power of the creature had nothing to do with it.

After the Slicer's release, its mentor immediately started its training, explaining that their personal rank could increase if their pupil did well in the Psi Protocol. For every thousand ranks the Slicer moved, its mentor would move one, and if the Slicer reached the top one hundred, its mentor would gain a bonus rank for each point after that. Thus, its success was its mentor's success, and Ra'jin did not enjoy failure.

The first bit of training had to do with self-control and the delay of gratification. Ra'jin had placed a dummy in a small arena. The dummy looked just like the Slicer's former Creator. His stupid face, stupid useless hair, and horribly ugly clothing. It had torn him to pieces. And again. And again. Over fifty dummies had come and gone in that small arena. On the fifty-first, the Slicer had enough control to stop itself for a moment. Although the action seemed infinitesimal to it, its mentor had clapped and applauded.

"Took me over a month to learn that kind of control. You're doing fine," Ra'jin said reassuringly. On the 121st round, it was able to stand there and yell obscenities about those who had procreated this massive waste of space. On the two-hundredth, it was able to merely glare.

The second bit had to do with expanding its vocabulary, as Ra'jin said the Universal Translator left much to be desired.

The Slicer slowly learned to read within a specially designed Temporal Chamber, which doubled the standard speed of time that everyone else used, thereby allowing the Slicer to absorb the knowledge and wisdom of those who had come before without further delaying its impending deployments. It was not a pleasant time for the Slicer—naturally, it was not a calm and silent being. The torn-up pages of many books had littered the chamber by the time the Slicer finally exited. Ra'jin had taken one look inside before snorting, and they had continued on.

The Slicer was trained in evolutionary pathways, learning how to push the system to grant the specific evolutions it would need once it unlocked a higher limit. It also learned about how to deal with non-sapients, humanoid and non-humanoid sapients, and was given a smattering of foundational scientific and technological knowledge.

Its first deployment was easy: destroy a village. As if that would have been any trouble for the Slicer before the Psi Protocol had picked it up.

Its initial success was enough to finally reach the three-thousands in rank and obtain the next reward. Its "unique" gift had been a training yard of its own, which was quite the blessing, as the common training areas were all incredibly loud and chaotic. Evolutionary abilities and the rare use of magic littered the training yard and forced the Slicer to work on upgrading the dodging skill it had once picked up when traveling through a moving asteroid field.

It also slept there, as it didn't have an evolution that disallowed this need. This constantly vexed the Slicer because it lost a lot of time; instead of sleeping, it could be training or volunteering for early deployments so it could move up in rank.

The Slicer's second and third deployments were easy, but moving up the ranks became more difficult the higher it climbed. By the sixth mission, it was destroying planets again, and its rank increases were coming in sporadic numerical gains. Sometimes the Slicer would even move down in rank as another terror or destroyer passed it on their own missions.

After the tenth mission, it came to a point where the Slicer was only getting a fifty-rank increase for each. They were also growing more difficult, as the system constantly added new parameters that tested its knowledge and understanding of what was required. Multiple times the system asked it to set up a planet to fail at speed rather than have it destroy it outright, as was its prerogative. Ra'jin explained when the terror asked about it.

"It's about the Temporal resources," they said while chewing some kind of dry meat with their large white teeth. "They have to spend quite a few each time you're deployed. If they didn't, the Psi Protocol would move on in accelerated time, and you'd still be on your first deployment." They swallowed the meat and took another out of a sealed bag. The Slicer noticed its mentor didn't offer it any. "They're asking each terror who shows promise to set up the planet for failure quickly so that they can cut off the time acceleration the moment you leave. It's simply economical."

"Economical?" the Slicer asked.

"Efficient and careful when using resources."

"Ah."

"So, it makes a certain sense."

The Slicer nodded while still not entirely understanding.

The two-thousand mark in rank finally gave something actually unique. An evolution that, once given, couldn't be taken away and handily bypassed the system's cap on the Slicer's current number of allowed evolutions.

The ability to shapeshift.

It was enormously painful, as it conferred the shapeshifting ability without the full knowledge of how it worked. With most abilities, there was an inherent understanding to them. To activate its dodging ability, the Slicer instinctively knew what to do and pushed on something in its mind. The feeling was reminiscent of the first time it ever pulled a lever. Abilities were simple. A pull and a catch, then it was dodging. It worked the same way with all of them. Meteoric Fall, Acid Splash, each a lever in its mind waiting to be tugged on. However, shapeshifting was different because it was assigned rather than earned.

The Slicer had been forced back into the Temporal Chamber for some time as it experimented on its own body, retching and spitting blood and fluids. Ra'jin said the goal was to appear humanoid; that way, it could blend in with populaces for the more complicated deployments. But it was so very painful. The Slicer didn't step out of the chamber until a month had passed within. Well, the creature that stepped out didn't step at all but slithered as was usual.

"What are you doing? Didn't you work on your shapeshifting?" Ra'jin asked, after waiting for the Slicer outside.

The Slicer spat, "I am what I am. I can change into any shape I need to for the mission, but only for the mission."

And that was that.

Its mind pulled out of its recollections as its body had almost fully translocated to Capilama 3. One last thought dug into its brain.

Youmal.

When the Slicer was honest with itself, it didn't find any blame on its side. Its first promotion mission required that it only kill any blue-skinned creatures found on the planet, not any and all. Right before they'd sent the terror in, it had tried to warn the portal master, but a small push came from a distracted destroyer behind it, and it was already too late.

The first issue was that they didn't place it in the right spot upon arriving. The Slicer had translocated in quickly and found itself surrounded by creatures in every direction, bumping and jostling into it every which way while not paying any attention to its great majesty. It was annoying, and if the Slicer was honest with itself, slightly frightening.

The second issue was that the Slicer assumed they had skin and it was just colorblind. That's what it was trying to warn the portal master about. The mission was doomed to failure the moment the terror had been sent.

Instinctively understanding this, it did what came naturally. It leaped into the sky and activated Meteoric Fall, which blew the planet to pieces after only three attempts at the same location.

The subsequent translocation and dressing down didn't sit right with the Slicer. It was their fault, not the Slicer's. They just didn't know it. This mission should be much simpler.

The translocation was almost done, ending on the tips of its barbed mouth, when it stalled and stopped. That had never happened before. It began to grow worried. Always before it had been fast, and never before had it stopped. Without warning, the translocation turned off entirely, and the ends of the Slicer's mouth disappeared.

"What!" it hissed, looking around as the pain in its mouth escalated. The planet was abandoned. Everywhere it looked, nothing was there at all. It was a barren and desolate world with nothing on the surface.

To its right, a blue light began to go off. Inch by inch, a creature was translocating in beside it. The creature had large wings, a small head, and a body one would associate with a lion. Only, it was translocating as slowly as the Slicer had been. It waited several moments for the creature to finish translocating, embracing its training to remain cool and collected as Ra'jin had taught it. When the creature finally finished coming in, it looked around and found the Slicer's eyes immediately.

"What's happen—" the Slicer tried to ask, but the creature attacked immediately. The terror snipped the bastard's head off quickly, then stared at the body on the ground as blood pooled around it.

A blue light began to go off in the near distance.

"What the fuck!"

CHAPTER THIRTY

On Earth: Alexander and the End Times

The boy and his father continued to travel across the barren Earth. Constantly pursued by things they couldn't name, they'd barely been getting along. Monsters covered in and made of shadow. Strange things in the night's air, attacking anything that came close. There were also others, other creatures. People. Humans.

Alexander, or Lex, as he preferred to be called, was adrift in a sea of horror. He'd learned to navigate the current over the last three months of his life, but not without being rocked by waves almost too great to overcome.

It had all started with the freeze in time. One moment, he had been working on his homework at a whorled brown desk, sitting in a chair two years past uncomfortable. As he was mentally cursing his math teacher, something strange seemed to hit the atmosphere. The next thing he knew, he had been trapped in place. Then, slowly, his mind, then a finger, then a thumb unfroze. One by one, parts of him had unglued themselves from whatever reality they had been trapped in, and as his ears followed with the rest of his body, the sounds started to stoke an already ebullient fear in his mind. Raising it. Taking his nerves to a new level of terror.

The world wasn't ending—it already had. And in less time than it would take to watch a film.

They had hidden out in a small hotel nearby, thinking maybe it had the elusive food and water necessary for their weak bodies to survive. Then that woman, the angry one who reveled in spilling blood, came and ended most of his family in a moment. Why she had let him go, he didn't know. He just knew that the moment she'd laid her eyes on him, something had changed within him. Something primal and uncontainable. It had struck his body with a pain that could never be eclipsed by any other for the rest of his life. He was sure of that. Not emotional but physical, vomit-inducing pain.

His grandmother had died shortly after, and his father had wheeled him out on an old flimsy piece of wood, each bump cascading new torturous feelings through his body. Even with his eyes closed, the sun had still reached its angry hand through, burning him. His nerves twitched with the wind, and his sense of smell left nothing to the imagination after being holed up for so long without water.

It was his father who kept him going, who explained what had happened over the two weeks he had been slipping in and out of consciousness. He often awoke only long enough to be fed a simple broth by a man who was so terrified of their circumstances that he couldn't say more than "Drink quietly."

They had found shelter multiple times. A family here, not so overcome by the apocalypse to ignore a hand in need. Scavengers there, who they could steal from without their knowing. It wasn't until a month after escaping the woman who destroyed his life that he was able to walk on his own. And that was when he started to notice the changes that had been wrought on his body.

After he was finally able to stand on his own two feet, he found the first steps hard to take—literally. A strange skipping would occur with each push off the ground, as if everything felt . . . lighter. Each landing jarred his already sensitive body, but slowly and surely, he learned how to move again. A little less pressure when lifting his foot and a bit of a slide on his back leg kept him rooted to the ground. His father said it looked like he was dancing everywhere he went, but Lex didn't mind. Dancing through the apocalypse sounded quite nice.

Even though walking felt a little like floating, he needed to learn how to run. But there were problems. When he had recovered enough for the attempt, he found himself unable to. He hadn't adjusted to the strange new feeling of his joints and muscles. They were too tight and begged to be released the moment he applied a little pressure. He'd asked his father, but the man didn't know what to think. They'd looked him over from top to bottom but found nothing visually different. His acne had cleared up, which was a blessing in itself, but that was it.

Lex stood near a terrible scene, staring at it with dull eyes. Thinking it was time to test just how strong his changed body was, he walked over to a nearby hill and found a series of boulders alongside the road. These were not naturally formed; they had been dug up from the earth by a plane crash, its flames long spent. Bodies of different ages littered the area, and he tried not to look at the half-rotted skeletons still wearing the clothes of the living.

The dredged-up boulders were scattered but easy enough for him to find. He located one early on in his search that was no larger than a bowling ball. Before the end of the world, Lex would've had a little bit of trouble lifting the weighty object, but now, he wasn't so sure.

His father walked up behind him. "What are you doing?'

"I need to know," Lex said simply.

"Know what?"

"How strong I am now. What's different about me. There has to be more to this. A reason."

The man put a hand on his shoulder before he could start his attempt. "You're still you, Alexander. You're still your mother's son."

He nodded without looking back. "Of course I am. But there's something else going on here. I need to know my limits."

They stood quietly like this for a long moment, a father trying to comfort a distraught son, before he removed his hand and stepped back. "As you wish."

Lex bent over without wasting time and easily lifted the boulder. To test himself, he palmed it as best he could and held on with only one hand. He turned to face his father. "This isn't normal," he said as he lightly tossed the boulder up before catching it again.

His father's eyes followed the light throw. "What's normal anymore?"

Lex let the boulder fall with a loud thud before finding another, this one slightly larger than a tire. Bending forward, he still had no issues at all with the weight. It should have weighed several hundred pounds, yet to him, it felt like no more than a dozen or two. Too unwieldy to palm, he instead lifted it over his head and thrust it up with one arm. It wobbled a little but held.

"A little strain with this."

His father nodded. "So, one of your arms is a little stronger than the strongest human ever to live," he said in an unimpressed voice.

Lex smiled at him as he remembered them watching strongman competitions in the past, his father always cheering them on loudly, knowing they couldn't hear him. His father's sense of humor had changed since the events that led to their exit from London. He used to laugh openly, but now everything had a dry tinge to it, as if humor were another casualty of these times.

He put both hands underneath the boulder and shot it toward the sky as hard as he could, bending and flexing his knees quickly with a slight hop. It rocketed through the air, arcing in the direction they'd come from. He would never have done this at night when the shadow monsters could get them. But aside from some scavenging bands of humans, it was relatively safe during the day.

Lex's sharpened eyes watched the boulder fly. Its descent pushed it into a series of trees, many of which parted with *snaps* and *cracks* that could be distinctly heard miles away as the boulder finally landed with a *boom*.

He smiled again at his father, who gave a tired smile in return.

That was two months ago, just before his father had died doing his very best to keep his son going. To keep him strong. Alive. The shadow monsters had surrounded them, slowly peeling away any routes they had for escape. His father had shoved him into a dark tunnel, then continued his run. His last words were a quickly shouted "I love you," then all that could be heard were receding steps and heavy breathing. Lex had been too shocked to follow after him, then remembered his father's warnings about being a hero. He didn't want to waste his father's sacrifice. So he had sat in a small tunnel in the dark and waited until daylight.

Blessedly, he didn't hear his father's screams.

He now stood alone as he stared down at the largest active settlement he'd seen since the end of times had come. Laughter rang up from below, the chatter of those unburdened by the failure of the world to stay together. Lex watched them, focusing his eyes over a mile away on a couple sitting at two stools, the woman's hand on the man's knee while he told some kind of story.

It's not fair, Lex thought to himself. *Why do they get to be happy? Why do they have this, this place? I've been running for months!*

As he began to stand up, he heard the easily identifiable click of metal on metal. The cock of a gun's hammer.

"Don't move," a tense voice said behind him.

"Or what?" Lex couldn't help but ask.

"Or you'll find a round between your shoulder blades."

Thinking back to his father's sacrifice, he held still without speaking.

"What's your name?" the voice asked. It was the higher pitch he was used to hearing in females, and a slight tremor landed on the final word.

Lex couldn't help but laugh. "Names? As if names matter anymore! Everything's dead and gone!"

"And yet, I'll still have it."

"Lex . . . Alexander Lewis."

"Well, Alexander . . . um . . . we have a problem."

"What problem is that?"

There was a pause before she began speaking again. "We don't know you, and, um, that's the, uh, problem."

"You know my name," Lex fished, trying to get the nervous girl aiming a gun at the back of his head to calm down a little.

"Yes, but . . ."

A branch snapped behind them loudly. Lex heard the trigger pull before a loud noise snapped out, and he felt something punch into his back.

Not the head.

He stumbled forward onto all fours while the girl had a panic attack behind him.

"Oh my God, oh God, oh God. I'm sorry, I didn't mean to kill you! Oh my God!"

"Calm down. You didn't kill me," he said, standing up. He turned around to face his accidental attacker.

A girl no more than five feet tall stood there, red hair spilling down and around her shoulders in a river of scarlet. When she met his eyes, she put a hand across her mouth. "How?"

Lex shrugged. "I don't know. Something weird happened to me in London, and a lot of pain followed. I discovered my body is much tougher than it should be."

"Are you okay? Really?" she asked, not quite believing that he was perfectly healthy.

"I'll have some bruising, but nothing worse than that. What did you shoot me with anyway?"

She held up a small pistol, likely from the Second World War. "It was my nana's."

He nodded. "I see. Well, are you planning on using it again?"

She shook her head slowly.

That brightened him up a little. "Great! What's your name?"

"M-Maria."

Lex held out a hand. "Nice to meet you, Maria. What do you call that place down there?" he said, pointing down at the town filled with people.

"We call it The Last Refuge."

"That's fitting. Let's go down, shall we?"

Without turning to look at her, Alexander Lewis began to walk down the hill. A moment later, a nervous girl loosely holding a small pistol followed him.

Notes

                    Holy Scripture #3:

. . . and that is how deductive logic works. It is about taking larger theories and placing them in smaller situations or scenarios. For instance, if all men are mortals, and Joe is a man, then Joe must be mortal. Simple and yet profound at the same time.

This scripture has taught you quite a bit for the last sixty pages. From basic math to algebra and geometry. From the greatest of punctuation marks, the all-powerful comma, to how paper is created and books are bound. From governments, philosophy, architecture, and standardized sewing, to what I understand and have learned of fundamental evolution and the magical variety. I have taught you much in these writings, but I'm afraid we're already coming to the end of my writing implements. If I had known that I would write a scripture for a burgeoning religious text, I would've brought a serious amount of paper. Alas, my hindsight is still mortal after all. Do not worry: the moment the crisis of creation begins to settle down, I will expand on this.

For now, let us focus on how we, as a religion and not individuals, will operate. There is a grand story from my world, wherein a council of high-level monks ran a cross-galaxy policing force for the good of the universe. They were barred from having children and were taught from a very young age to control and often negate any form of emotion. I know it's a story and not a proper reflection of reality. How? Because the idea that multiple high-level fighters would agree on something for the common good of a massive amount of people is almost impossible. While the idea in theory is nice, they were wrong, and we are not them.

There is another story, this one of how two people represented an entire race of fighters. Throughout their history, they had indulged in their passions and fought against what they perceived as the "weak" or the "coddled" of their universe. They built grand empires, destroyed others, and ultimately fell from grace through great corruption. Building a society on the power of the few can often lead to betrayals, only allowing the strong and cunning to prevail. They were wrong, and we are not them either.

The two representatives and the council are both inventions of an imagination far more significant than mine. The writer told stories where time and again he would pit these two civilizations against each other for the entertainment of the reader. These fictions contained great moments of triumph and conflict, heartache and loss, and inspirationally moved me as a child. They represented a grand idea of what a civilized society could be and what it would take to bring one down. There's a quote from my world that applies to why I just taught you about them: "Good artists copy, great minds steal."

And thus, we will take from the greatest of stories and religions my old planet held to build a foundation for what is needed for Symphony.

Each high-level Horizon Chaser will mentor those below them. If your path has crossed a similar one of a younger member, one who has real potential that you believe in, then it is your duty to help them gain competency in their path. Be a guiding hand for their route up the Unending Summit, not the trail. Show them the signage with a pointed finger, not an unearned map. Each path is our own to walk, and only we can grow from our ordeals.

Each junior Horizon Chaser will seek a mentor for the right path to elevation. Do not attempt to force them to take you on, as that may lead to an early grave and the shrugged shoulders of all who watched it occur. Your mentor's relationship with you will not be individually scrutinized or regulated. If they decide you are no longer worth the effort and choose to move on, then that is that. Place yourself in a position of value for your mentor and see them guide you to a new level. But always remember, it is a privilege to receive another's hard-earned wisdom.

Ranks within the Unending Summit will always be earned. From tests to time and opportunity, moving toward the top is a choice for every Chaser. There will be a unique selection process for the Zenith. Those selected will likely always be the Chasers who follow the intended spirit of the Unending Summit and have a proven track record of their juniors progressing down their own paths.

It is not up to us to tell a person whether the path they are choosing is right or wrong. Leave that up to the institutions that will naturally form across the map of the world. Those two representatives, whom I mentioned just a moment ago, were just as necessary to the welfare of their galaxy as the council was with its misguided notions. It is often said that you have to destroy in order to create. If you feel morally self-righteous and begin to burn all those around you who don't hold up the values you proclaim to be the best, then you never gave them the opportunity to reach the end of their road. You never granted them the time to find their own path to help form Symphony's relatively young history.

I'm not saying not to stand in front of those who intend to do great evil. If you feel that you must, then more power to you. But I ask that you first look at the bigger picture of what is happening. My father used to say, "There are three truths in an argument. Your truth, their truth, and the real truth." Attempt to find the "real truth," and you will be much better off as a person and as a member of the Unending Summit.

Before we dive back into your academic lessons, I wanted to say something that I consider important. If you believe you've found great love but in being with them you may diverge from the path of the Summit . . . make your choice and stick to it. There is nothing wrong with no longer fighting others for the betterment of the world. If you feel you have gone long enough down the path, please put up your feet and enjoy the time you have remaining with your loved ones. Constantly fighting will wear anyone down. The horrors of war and morally gray decisions can haunt the strongest person, regardless of the size of their muscles.

Also, remember that there is such a thing as vacation. A nice beach can help to cure a worn-out soul.

Now, as I only have a limited amount of space left, the following is a series of breakdowns of basic hygiene, healthcare, and self-aid buddy care, or SABC. Cleaning yourself is paramount. Nobody wants to smell you as you walk by . . .

2   Holy Scripture #4:

. . . so please do not attempt to "bleed" people to make them feel better. Perhaps there will be unique afflictions that affect others in time, but the idea of "bleeding" people to make them feel better has been disproven multiple times in my world. You also cannot help people by putting generic environmental cleaning solutions into their circulatory systems. Cleaning solutions like that are meant for clothing and other things, not people. That is all I have to say on hygiene and health. Moving on!

This is the final page of scripture. I am out of space and out of time. Because I obviously knew this page was significant, I set aside some final items I needed to present before you complete the reading. Pay special attention to what I've written here.

Once, long ago, I was returning from a battlefield where a friend of mine had been killed. We had fought for multiple days, and I was thoroughly exhausted, both mentally and physically. As I stepped out of our return vehicle, two men of much higher rank sitting on a food chest looked at me in silence. My clothing was torn, and I had a few red-stained bandages covering parts of my body. As I limped past them, they asked if I had been injured in the fighting, and when I said that I had, they stated I must have prayed to God to stay alive at all.

That is a standard from my world. There are three great religions that somewhat dominate Earth. I won't get into much detail here, as I do not have the space, but understand that they each worship God, an omnipotent and omniscient being, in their own particular way. They are what you would call monotheistic. For the uninformed, mono means one or single, and theistic means belief in. That isn't to say there weren't polytheistic religions there, where poly means many. But there was a certain size to the single-god belief system on my homeworld.

What is commonly forgotten, or plainly ignored, is that there are many, many religions that aren't a part of the big three. Hinduism, Confucianism, Daoism, and Buddhism are another few I can name off of the top of my head. If I had to associate the Unending Summit with a single religion from my homeworld, the closest would be Buddhism. It believes that to solve *dukkha*, or suffering, one must "ride" the pain and let it run its course. I won't get into Buddhism too closely here, but just understand that they believe in the karmic value of people: that we all live many lives, and the value of the life you live, the good and the bad, is brought into your next one.

We are not them, but that isn't to say we can't learn from them. We are a way of living more than a religion. The Unending Summit is a support system that presents the truth of Symphony, enhances the world's knowledge, and provides mentorship to those in need. Our goal is to travel ever on up the road of progressive strength and insight, not simply to increase our membership's size and shame others who do not hold to our values. Please do not spend your time attempting to spread the word of the Unending Summit. It is for others to join based on their values and ideals, not because they feel pressured to do so.

It is essential that you always remember that or the travesties of my world will assuredly visit this one. More wars on Earth were started in the name of religion than anything else in our history. I will not allow that to spread across Symphony.

The home of all of our operations will begin in, of all places, a library. Other religions may have churches, synagogues, and temples, but we will have libraries. The Unending Summit will be the first faction to touch base on Symphony's soil and will have a few extra rights because of that. I do not apologize for creating this world and then placing its first faction with a leg up on others. My world, my rules. The library will host all of our knowledge and will be a place for our members and leaders to reside.

While I was given a task recently to create a library for Symphony, it was always my plan to do so, which worked well in my favor. There were libraries in my world, and we never appreciated them nearly as much as we should've. They were placed for the disenfranchised and ignored to congregate so they could build upon their knowledge and better themselves at their own speed. Now, they are viewed as superfluous locations for the poor and the unsanitary. That will not be a view we hold. If there is a single holy item this religion will see, it is the book. If there is a single holy site found throughout Symphony, it is the library. Treat all librarians with great caution and respect or face an assuredly deserved rejection of entrance.

For a final note on the almighty library, there will be one greater site and many branches. Should a great city rise, a library will rise with it. In this, you have my promise.

I wish I could write more, but that is not the fate of this, the original scripture. I promise to add more to it as I can. Thus, my last words here will be quite simple and to the point—words to live by.

Be fair. Be earnest. Be strong.

Acknowledgments

As always, thank you to my wife and family. They put up with me being exhausted all the time, including the grumpiness that comes with it. I apologize, and since it's written, I never have to do it again. Them's the rules.

This time around, honestly, I'm going to thank myself. The second book experience, thus far, has been vastly different than the first. I regularly work twelve-hour days and I still got this done.

So, yah, thanks, me. You really kicked ass this time around.

About the Author

J. D. Mullenary Sr. aka AbnormalVAverage is the author of the Symphony series, originally released on Royal Road, as well as a teacher and esports coach. He grew up on temperate California beaches and, after completing his first degree at nineteen, felt he needed to grow up, so he joined the military. He served for four years, earned a second degree, and was honorably discharged. Soon after, Mullenary married the love of his life and raised two sons. He then returned to college with a focus on English and education. He lives in Texas, where he spends his time writing, teaching his students the value of critical thinking, and fostering the strays his wife brings home.

RESPAWN YOUR CURIOSITY

follow us on our socials

podiumentertainment.com

@podiumentertainment

/podiumentertainment

@podium_ent

@podiumentertainment